CROSSING OVER

London-born Anne Cadwallader went to schools in Hertfordshire and Suffolk before graduating in 1978 from Exeter University where she was vice-president of the Guild of Students and edited the student newspaper.

A scholarship student in journalism at City University, London, she began her career with *The Bradford Telegraph and Argus* in 1979 before moving to Ireland in 1981 as a radio journalist with BBC Northern Ireland.

Since then, she has worked in both Belfast and Dublin and was employed by RTÉ, *The Irish Press, Reuters, The Irish Echo, Independent Network News, The Christian Science Monitor* and others.

She is the author of *Holy Cross: The Untold Story* (Brehon Press, 2004) and the best-selling *Lethal Allies: British Collusion in Ireland* (Mercier Press, 2013).

Anne left journalism in 2009 to work with The Pat Finucane Centre as an advocate for victims of the conflict and has testified before US Congressional, British, Australian and Irish parliamentary committees.

Anne's father, mother and the younger of her two sisters served in the British army. Her brother was a police officer. Now retired, she lives in Belfast and County Donegal.

Crossing Over

A novel

Anne Cadwallader

MERCIER PRESS

MERCIER PRESS
Cork
www.mercierpress.ie

© Anne Cadwallader, 2026

ISBN: 978-1-917453-60-8

978-1-917453-61-5 eBook

978-1-917453-62-2 Audiobook

Cover design: Chris Rychter

All characters and events in this book, except for those who are identifiably real and recognisable in the public domain, are entirely fictional. Any resemblance to any person living or dead which may occur inadvertently is completely unintentional.

This book is sold subject to the condition that it shall not, by way of trade or otherwise, be lent, resold, hired out or otherwise circulated without the publisher's prior consent in any form of binding or cover other than that in which it is published and without a similar condition including this condition being imposed on the subsequent purchaser.

No part of this publication may be reproduced or transmitted in any form or by any means, electronic or mechanical, including photocopying, recording or any information or retrieval system, without the prior permission of the publisher in writing.

Printed and bound in the EU.

Dedication

FOR
GERRY AND SUE

'Only in the agony of parting do we look into the depths of love.'
(GEORGE ELIOT)

Prologue

December 1987 – Glenbarry, County Down, Northern Ireland

The man pulled into a gateway and switched off his motorbike engine. There was just enough moonlight to see the cottage across the road. Moving silently, he crept into the front garden, lit a cigarette in the lee of some shrubs, and studied the outline of the cottage.

A red Mini, parked on the gravel drive, told him she was at home. He stubbed the smouldering cigarette stub between hardened, yellowed fingertips and tucked it carefully into a trouser pocket. Warm light spilled from the downstairs windows. With his back to the wall, he edged around the side of the building to the rear. Peering through the patio doors, he saw a dark-haired woman moving about in the kitchen. She seemed to be by herself, but he had to be sure. Now she was sitting, elbows on a wooden table, face in her hands, shoulders lifting. She's crying, he thought, as well she might. After a minute or two, when only a ginger cat padded towards her, he felt certain she was alone. The night was moving on. Snow could be on the way. He retraced his steps to the front of the cottage, the gun now held low in his right hand, and lifted the brass knocker.

1

'Violence in these so-called "war zones" is usually very localised.' Her employer's attempts at reassurance came to mind as Eleanor Dawson cast a wary eye over Belfast from the deck of the Liverpool ferry. For the queue of foot passengers on the quayside, there were no 'Welcome' signs or shelter from the rain. The city, she mused, looked rather like the corpse of a dead whale, chimney stacks like bones pointing to the clouds. Much later, she reprimanded herself for not escaping while she could. Driving down the car ramp, she contrasted the bleak tableau before her with her arrival in New York twelve months earlier, the start of a remarkable year in which she had played a starring role, flying home to Braithwaite & Beresford in London trailing clouds of glory. How would she feel after a year in Belfast? she wondered.

The road through the docks weaved through pyramids of coal and rusting cranes before it joined a six-lane motorway, fringed by derelict red-brick factories. The rain never paused. She had not expected charm, but the city failed even as gritty drama. The road signs carried names familiar from reported atrocities, 'Short Strand', 'Antrim Road', 'Crumlin'. After fifteen minutes criss-crossing bridges over a muddy-brown river, she parked in a side street to consult her map. The company she was to work for had provided a flat near 'Malone Road'. Geraldine, the chatty office manager at Gordon & Company, had phoned with the address, giving her the identical advice as David Braithwaite in London: 'Don't believe what you see on the news. You'll love Belfast.'

Eleanor had crossed the personal Rubicon leading her to Belfast on the first morning back in London from New York. She had arrived at the office early for the regular Monday meeting, hoping for a quick catch-up with her old school friend and fellow solicitor, Georgina Taylor, who, after a quick hug, had remarked approvingly on her changed appearance.

'That's one hell of a smart suit, Lena,' she had said, using the familiar diminutive.

'New Yorkers judge your appearance almost as ruthlessly as your work rate. I should have listened to your advice years ago.'

'Still, well done,' Georgina replied.

'Let's face it, if it weren't for you, Georgie, I wouldn't have been there at all. It was a great experience. I managed to pass the New York bar exam and represented clients in the lower courts.'

'My goodness. They certainly do things differently over there.'

'They do indeed, and what's more, I was good at it. No one in New York called me "Lena the Dreamer".'

'It'll be tough settling back here after all that but let's get to the boardroom before all the seats are taken.'

As they waited for the lift, David Braithwaite was in his office below, getting papers ready for the meeting he was about to chair.

'Eleanor Dawson's back at work today,' he told his partner, Andrew Beresford. 'Did you read Steve Sullivan's report? Somewhat incredibly, he seems to have allowed her to represent clients in the district courts. The report says she was "decisive, hard-working and a team player".'

'I saw that. Our "Lena the Dreamer" is unrecognisable,' said Beresford.

'Rarely have I come across anyone less suited to the cut and thrust of our profession,' said Braithwaite. 'If her father hadn't been an old army friend, and a vicar to boot, I would never have agreed to take her on.'

'I fear our Miss Dawson exemplifies the old adage, "The wheel is turning, but the hamster is missing",' said Beresford.

'And now I've got to press-gang someone to go to Belfast for a year,' complained Braithwaite. 'I can't say "volunteer" because no one will actually want to go.'

'Who in their right mind would?' said Beresford, holding the office door open.

'Belfast hardly has the same cachet as New York,' agreed Braithwaite, heading for the lift.

By the time Lena and Georgina arrived in the third-floor boardroom, the junior solicitors and paralegals were already settled in, noisily slapping files down on tables and telling competing stories about their weekend exploits before the chatter subsided and the meeting began. Braithwaite's routine was to ask the person seated on his immediate left to comment on what cases were due in the courts that week and then work clockwise around the table. Early arrivals took seats to his left while the later arrivals, on Braithwaite's right, were forced to come up with ever more inconsequential suggestions. As Lena walked in behind her friend, there were gratifying signs – a raised eyebrow, a second glance – that her colleagues were also noting her improved appearance. Braithwaite will already have seen Steve Sullivan's report from New York, she thought. Today, of all days, I will be spared coming up with anything clever.

'I am sure we would all like to welcome Lena Dawson back from New York,' began Braithwaite. 'Sullivan & Cullen say they'll miss her on Wall Street. Welcome home, Lena.' A few feeble 'hear, hears' followed.

Lena, as far as her colleagues were concerned, had arrived in the office five years earlier when there was no advertised vacancy. It had not taken them long to discover her father, George Dawson, a country parson, and Braithwaite had once soldiered together and to draw the rather obvious conclusion. The rest of them had served their time in small-town solicitors' offices before managing the big move to London. Lena, they decided, was a girl whose self-effacing modesty was amply justified and who had only got her foot in the door by hanging on tight to her father's cassock.

'At the end of the meeting,' Braithwaite continued, 'I will be calling for volunteers to cover for maternity leave at an old friend's firm in Belfast. Working with William Gordon would be a valuable opportunity for anyone wanting to develop their skills-base in human rights law.'

Everyone around the table began silently listing their reasons to decline. At first, Lena was no different, but the usual marriage break-ups, house purchases and probate work were hardly enticing after the challenges of New York. Neither was the obvious resentment of her work colleagues. Belfast was a pretty appalling prospect, but she began to toy with Braithwaite's offer. As the meeting drew to a close, he began reading from Gordon's letter. The lucky volunteer could expect to 'represent both loyalist and republican paramilitaries and engage in preparatory work for Troubles-related trials and inquests,' he said. If he had hoped this would propel hands into the air, he was sadly mistaken. Lena's antennae, however, had begun to quiver and she heard her own voice saying, 'I'll go, as it seems nobody else wants to,' her words dropping into silence.

'Are you sure, Lena?' asked Braithwaite, turning to face her. 'You're only just back from America.'

'Positive, David. I haven't taken on any new cases since I returned, so there's no need for any complicated handovers, and, as you say, it will broaden the firm's capacity.'

Braithwaite, slightly repelled by her ingratiating tone, turned to scan the table. 'Anyone else?' Lena noted their stony silence. Many had domestic or financial obligations in London and even those without did not fancy spending a year in a place known only for its meaningless violence and repugnant politicians. Around the table, a cheerful consensus grew that 'Lena the Dreamer' was setting herself up for a fall, and a bad one.

'All right, Lena, it seems you have it,' said Braithwaite, relieved not to have to phone Gordon empty-handed. It was a cue for everyone to push their chairs back and return to their desks. Georgina Taylor and Lena Dawson being the last to leave.

'What on earth came over you?' Georgina asked in the corridor.

'I'm going nowhere here,' Lena said. 'They all complain about me behind my back – including Braithwaite. He's not forgiven himself for taking me on in the first place.'

After a lifetime of complaining, Lena hoped her decision impressed Georgina. Their families had been friends and neighbours in Hampshire for decades. Charlotte Dawson and Georgina's mother, Hermione Taylor, were as close as two women with highly elevated opinions of themselves could be.

Five years older than Lena, Georgie had witnessed the petty punishments imposed by the Dawsons, chiefly Charlotte, for her friend's perceived academic inadequacies. One summer in the 1960s, as charabancs full of over-excited schoolgirls had left for the centre court at Wimbledon, Lena had been left behind – her parents' punishment for a D in Latin. The following year, while the rest of the school went to see *Doctor Zhivago* in London, Lena was not amongst them (a fail in Maths). A splinter of steel slid into Lena's soul as she paced the echoing school corridors alone. 'There should be a law against it,' Georgina had said on her return.

The novel concept of something to protect her from maternal disapproval had resonated deeply with Lena. Imagine, she thought, a rule to prevent her being the object of everyone's scorn and pity. So, she had followed Georgina and read law at university. Ten years on, during the flight from New York, she had vowed never to complain to Georgina again. She was a grown woman in her thirties. It was time for a clean break with the past.

Much of the credit for her newfound self-confidence, Lena knew, could be laid at Steve Sullivan's door. Before leaving for New York, Braithwaite had told her how they had met at a legal conference, describing him as a 'mover and shaker'. Lena had expected a brash Irish-American, throwing his weight around but Sullivan surprised her. Self-deprecating, despite his wealth and influence, it was he who had encouraged her to take the New York bar exam and who, henceforth, passed her ever-more challenging cases – even giving her informal lessons during weekends away at his beach-front home on Long Island. 'Dangle the carrot but never cry wolf,' he had once said of relations between the law and the press, prompting Lena to playfully complain about mixed metaphors. In short, he had boosted her self-confidence and helped her find her voice.

In much of her court work, she had acted for Black communities in Harlem, fighting attempts at mass evictions by landlords intent on gentrifying the area. She learned the law could challenge and even defeat powerful interests and gradually took on more significant cases, winning many small battles – and some not so small. Once, she had even noticed Sullivan sitting, incognito, at the back of a civil court where she was representing clients. At the end of the year, he did his best to persuade her to stay rather than return to London – 'that class-ridden backwater' he had called it. But Lena was intent on showing both her family and her detractors at work – even Georgie – how 'The Dreamer' was now a winner.

There was only one issue on which Lena and Sullivan had crossed swords. It had amused him – and angered her – that he easily won their skirmishes on the law in Northern Ireland, where she knew he was a regular visitor.

'I'd wager a dollar or two you know more about apartheid in South Africa than about the law in Belfast,' he had once said.

'People there surely have exactly the same rights as anyone in Britain,' she had said.

'Oh yeah?' he had replied. 'So you don't know that Hendrik Verwoerd said he would scrap all his repressive legislation for just one regulation in the Northern Ireland Special Powers Act.'

There was definitely unfinished business, Lena thought, between her and Sullivan and it might even have subliminally influenced her decision to volunteer. Now, here she was, lost in Belfast, passing a church as a Sunday morning service ended. The women, arm in arm with their husbands, wore pastel-coloured polyester suits in lilac and peach with matching hats, a throwback to the sixties, the fifties even. The church itself was a Victorian pile in grubby-pink sandstone that she immediately compared, unfavourably, to the flint and weathered-brick church over which her father held sway in Hampshire. Finally, she found herself in a quiet street off the Malone Road. The apartment was in the attic of a red-brick Edwardian house at the end of a gloomy, rhododendron-lined driveway – a poor relation, she decided, to the light-filled apartment in Kensington where a school friend was now house-sitting. The beige-painted living room smelled slightly musty, as did the rest of the flat. In the kitchenette, she found brief instructions on how to light an old-fashioned gas fire and where to find a twenty-four-hour shop. It will do for a week or two, she thought, unpacking the few clothes and books she had brought with her and deciding to phone her father to stop him fretting. George Dawson, so enthusiastic about her move to New York, had been appalled about Belfast. She shuddered remembering the moment, on their way home from Andover railway station, that she had broken the news.

'I've something interesting to tell you,' she had said at red traffic lights. 'I'm going to work in Belfast for a year, covering for a solicitor on maternity leave.'

When the expected acclamation failed to materialise, she had glanced over at him, puzzled, but he was focused on the stationary traffic. She had waited. The lights turned green and he had accelerated away, still silent. Unable to endure it any longer, she asked again. 'Exciting, isn't it?'

'Lena, I'm trying to think of an appropriate response. You must be out of your mind. It's a tribal snake pit.'

Unsympathetic words, she thought, for a man of the cloth.

'It's for less than a year and will look great on my CV.'

'You're making a huge mistake. Career suicide. It's the land that time forgot, for good reason. A hopeless, never-ending miasma.'

Remembering that he and Braithwaite were old pals, she used his name to try and turn things around.

'Braithwaite asked me particularly,' she lied.

'Braithwaite? I'll have a word with him and get it called off.'

Lena reached for a second little fib.

'He's promised me high-profile cases in Belfast.'

'Do you watch the news? Someone is murdered there twice a week. And yet no one anywhere gives a damn.'

For the third time, Lena lied. 'My new boss, William Gordon, is very well connected.'

She didn't get any further.

'William Gordon, you say?'

Lena nodded, 'Yes, he's a friend of Braithwaite's and owns the firm in Belfast, but what difference does that make?'

'All the difference in the world. Gordon and I soldiered together in Kenya in the 1950s, when you were just a baby. A most obliging fellow. I'll get on the blower to him this evening and extricate you.'

Lena was infuriated. Her father still thought he could decide where she worked.

'You will not,' she said. 'It's all settled.'

'Well, at least I'll talk to him. It's been years since I saw him.'

'For heaven's sake, leave it. I don't want him to think I'm a little girl being fussed over by her daddy.'

That evening in the rectory at Little Woldham, as she sat deep in an armchair beside Charlotte watching television, Lena heard her father's animated voice on the phone in his study and guessed to whom he was speaking. She glowered as he emerged.

'I did ask you not to ring,' she said.

'Only to reassure myself. That's the least I can do to settle poor Charlotte's nerves. William has promised to look after you.'

Charlotte Dawson, absorbed in the television programme, heard her name mentioned and developed a sudden interest. 'What has Lena done to unsettle my nerves?' she asked.

'Nothing Mummy. Dad's just joking. I'm going to work in Belfast for a bit and he doesn't approve,' she said.

'If you're stupid enough to work somewhere that ghastly, you deserve everything you get,' Charlotte had said.

On the phone now to her father from her new flat in the 'sectarian snake pit', Lena wanted to make sure he did not intervene again.

'It's very quiet over here,' she said. 'Very normal.'

'I've been talking to William Gordon,' he replied. 'He'll be in the office tomorrow to settle you in.'

She managed a calm reply.

'By now, he probably thinks I'm incapable of making a cup of tea.'

Back in the flat, she opened a bottle of wine, figured out how to work the television and began to wonder what the hell she had landed herself in. She knew next to nothing about Belfast and had managed, so far, to make a virtue out of it, telling anyone who asked that she had an 'open mind' and was 'looking forward to observing events close up'. One summer, she had taken a brief interest when an IRA bomb exploded at a telephone exchange near the Old Bailey. She was in court observing a trial when there was a dull thud and the building trembled. Alarm bells began ringing. Dust rose from the ancient tomes on the judge's bench. A moment's pause, and then people began a relatively disciplined stampede out of the building. After some hanging about in the street outside, she had gone home early like everyone else.

The newspapers had claimed the next day that Londoners were 'defiant' and showing 'the bulldog spirit'. No one had been killed or even injured, Lena thought. It did not take much to be brave in those circumstances. When soldiers' funerals were shown on TV, people sighed but it seemed to be happening far, far away, across the sea – grim, to be sure, but largely ignored. Before leaving

London, she had started reading articles about Belfast in *The Guardian* and *The Sunday Times*. Both said the IRA, ostensibly fighting for a united Ireland, was in fact a small, criminal gang funding itself by extorting protection money from builders and property developers. They leeched off working-class communities through squalid drinking clubs, gambling dens and taxi rackets. It sounded grimy and sinister. And now here she was.

On her last week in London, Georgina had invited her to dinner with her husband, Martin Porter, at their rambling home in Hampstead. Porter, a leading defence QC, had worked for a while in Northern Ireland in the early days after the violence erupted. Georgina had suggested he might be able to offer advice and Lena had quickly accepted the invitation. The more frequently you were invited to 'Porters' Parties', the higher your social and legal status. The undisputed star of the London legal firmament, he was the focus of attention in every courtroom in which he appeared. His court hallmark, when ready to issue a legal *coup de grâce*, was to lift a languid hand and tuck imaginary strands of hair into place behind his peruke. Such moments were eagerly awaited by the solicitors, barristers and even judges who flocked to his appearances. Porter could feign convincing expressions of scepticism to order – fixing a jury with a basilisk stare or a slightly raised eyebrow – before delivering a well-constructed killer line as if they were an audience. Which, in a way, they were.

That evening, Lena had managed to corner him on a sofa for advice.

'I'll be out of my depth over there,' she had begun.

'You've already negotiated the legal vipers' nest in New York, so Belfast should be a stroll in the park, but I'm happy to offer a few words.'

'Please do.'

'First of all, keep any views on the Troubles to yourself – even in private amongst friends. Never, ever discuss religion or politics with anyone.'

'It's all about Catholics against Protestants, isn't it?'

'It's a smidgeon more complex than that. You know the basics – Catholics want a united Ireland, Protestants want to maintain the status quo and so on and so forth. But it's also about power and control and history. Didn't you learn anything at that expensive school you and Georgie went to?'

'Ask me about Anne Boleyn or Napoleon Bonaparte and I'll write you an essay. Ask me about Ireland, and aside from a vague feeling that Oliver Cromwell isn't exactly a local hero, I'd be struck dumb.'

'You'll need to learn the alphabet soup pretty quickly. Just remember any acronym beginning with 'U' for Ulster is likely to be Protestant and pro-British while one beginning with 'I' is likely to be Catholic and in favour of a united Ireland,' he said.

'Well, even I know about the IRA,' Lena had said, half-whispering the three letters. Even spoken privately, they conjured up images indelibly burned into the common memory; lumps of dead horses in Park Lane, broken chairs in Birmingham pubs and sinister mug-shots of angry men staring into the camera lens.

'Ah yes,' Porter had replied, airily. 'The IRA. We all know about them. Or think we do. I'd stay well away from them and their sympathisers. "Mad, bad and dangerous to know", as Lady Caroline Lamb said of Lord Byron.'

'Stop Martin, you can't make fun of the IRA,' Lena had said, looking around to see if they were overheard but only Georgina was near and joined them.

'Don't frighten Lena, Martin,' she said. 'She's looking forward to an exciting adventure.'

'Judging from her recent triumphs in New York, it would take more than me to frighten her,' said Porter, winking knowingly at Lena who, still finding it difficult to accept a compliment, looked down modestly at the carpet.

At their goodbyes in the hallway, her taxi at the front door, Porter had some final private words of advice. 'The Irish have a saying, "Whatever you say, say nothing". You could do a lot worse. But, if you need assistance with any really interesting cases, you know where I am.'

His voice lowered.

'Another thing. I hate to sound overdramatic but, if you do phone to ask for help, be careful. They're fond of listening to other people's conversations over there. Just make a reference to something happening "upstairs" and I'll understand. "Upstairs" will be our codeword.'

Lena had thought it a bit theatrical but filed it away for possible future use.

Now, here in Belfast, on the first morning of her new life, she woke with his words echoing in her head: 'Whatever you say, say nothing.' It was freezing cold in the bedroom and she was steeling herself to throw back the covers when she heard a female newsreader on the radio say a man had been shot dead in Belfast overnight.

'The victim, who has yet to be named but is believed to

have been from Ardoyne, was found early this morning by a man walking his dog close to the Forth River near the Ballygomartin Road. A post-mortem examination is to be carried out later today. The RUC say it has all the hallmarks of another sectarian murder. No group has yet claimed responsibility.'

Lena wondered how far away Ardoyne was. The news report also said that the Ulster Defence Association – or UDA – was calling for the strengthening of the Ulster Defence Regiment. She had to remember. The UDA were loyalist paramilitaries. The UDR was a locally recruited British Army regiment. How on earth was anyone expected to make sense of it?

Hurrying now, she rushed from bedroom to bathroom and back again, hoping the few clothes she had brought were suitable. Brushing her hair, she frowned at the white face in the mirror. Why did she always look either angry or sad? Her smile never seemed to reach her eyes. Where did those deep furrows on her forehead come from? At least God might have made her a little taller. Georgie had once told her not to believe what she saw in the mirror. 'You only think your face is stern, darling, because you're scowling at yourself,' she had said. 'Other people don't see you like that at all.' Ah, well, Lena thought, better to look serious than silly. Applying her make-up with a little more care than normal, she then phoned the taxi firm recommended by Geraldine, the office manager.

'Where to love?' the cheerful driver asked after she clambered in.

'High Street, please. The offices of Gordon & Company.'

'You're not from around here, are you? What brings

you to our lovely city?' the driver asked as they drove into town.

'I'm working here for the next few months.'

'Don't believe what you see on the telly. Belfast people are the best in the world.'

It was, she realised, the third time someone had insisted on that. Either it was true or people were suspiciously keen to persuade her.

The driver chattered on as they passed red-brick residential roads until they stopped in a street of modern office buildings with a clock tower at its end, leaning slightly to the right. She paid the fare and jumped out, buzzing the intercom for 'Gordon & Co. – Third Floor'. Inside the lobby, she found an old-fashioned lift with folding metal grilles that needed a firm shove to open. The lift scraped the concrete sides of the shaft as it rose, setting her teeth on edge. At the first floor, she yanked the grille open again and found herself in another tiny hallway with a sign asking visitors to 'Press Buzzer and Wait'. The door was opened by a middle-aged woman wearing letterbox-red lipstick, over-large spectacles and a wide smile.

'You must be Eleanor Dawson. I'm Mr Gordon's office manager, Geraldine,' the woman said. 'Welcome to Belfast. Sorry about the lift. It's not been the same since the IRA bombed British Home Stores next door but the insurers say it's quite safe.'

Lena tried not to look startled and noted that the first encounter Gordon & Company's clients had with their legal representatives was a tiny reception area with no framed certificates on the wall, and no houseplants. It had a vinyl-tiled floor that could do with a deep clean and a basic reception desk. Public relations is clearly not a priority here, she thought.

'Do you like the apartment, Miss Dawson?' Geraldine asked. 'Mr Gordon knows the owner. The Malone Road is lovely, isn't it?'

Choosing to keep her opinion on 'The Beige Box' (as she had begun to think of it) to herself, Lena nodded and said, 'Please just call me Lena. The apartment is very nice.'

'I'll show you into Mr Gordon's office,' Geraldine said, leading her around the back of the lift and opening a door. 'We have a great view of the Albert Clock. It's our own leaning tower, just like Pisa. Mr Gordon will be here shortly. I'll get you a coffee while you wait.'

Pisa? thought Lena, looking out through the driving rain at the clock face across the road. This place has an inflated opinion of itself. There was no word processor in her new employer's carpet-tiled office, just a large desk, a couple of button-down, fake-leather chairs, a wooden sideboard carrying a wide array of drinks and some filing cabinets. She walked to the window and gazed out into the wet, grey morning and the heavy traffic on the junction below. When Geraldine returned, the coffee was just as awful as she had expected, quite in a league of its own. She had barely deposited it on top of a filing cabinet when the office door opened and her new boss strolled in, dumped his briefcase on the desk and held out a slightly moist hand for her to shake. Her first impression was that he seemed well past retirement age.

'Hello, my dear, welcome to Belfast. What a pleasure to meet George Dawson's wee girl. Hope you'll enjoy working here,' he boomed.

Gordon had grey hair, a florid complexion and carried too much weight. Lena was disappointed. She couldn't imagine Steve Sullivan-style sparring matches with him.

'You found the flat? Excellent. You must have your father's sense of direction. He was always very keen on maps. It belongs to a friend. There's a parking space set aside for you across the road, behind *The Belfast Independent* building. It's an old bomb site. A lot of them around here, but at least we have plenty of parking space, not like London, eh?'

'No, sir. Not like London at all. You are all very welcoming. Your letter to David Braithwaite spoke of preparing for inquests. It sounds so interesting. Can you tell me a bit more?'

'Plenty of time for that later. Let me show you around.'

Gordon hauled himself to his feet again and turned left into a large open-plan office. There, she realised with some dismay, the mainly male junior solicitors (to whom she was introduced) and the female typists (to whom she was not) worked side-by-side, their desks piled high with folders and box files. Dickensian, Lena thought, nodding politely as they all looked up from their work for a few seconds and gave her wan smiles. Gordon finished his tour by showing her into a small, glass-partitioned office off the main reception area.

'And this is Heather Collins' office,' he said, 'and yours while you are here. She does most of my personal legal work. She's left notes and a diary, and you can open that pile of mail on the desk. I'll say goodbye now if I may. I've calls to make and friends to meet for lunch. You just settle in.'

Back in his own office, Gordon phoned Trevor Gibson, assistant chief constable of the Royal Ulster Constabulary, to arrange lunch.

'I dislike having any stranger in the office,' he said over steak pie and a bottle of Merlot in the Reform Club, 'but Heather is on maternity leave for who knows how long.'

'The new girl will settle down,' said Gibson.

'I thought mentioning terrorism cases in the letter to Braithwaite would deter volunteers but here she is and already asking about inquest work. It's all very well, Miss Eleanor Dawson from Hampshire wanting to get involved but setting her loose in the courts is fraught with danger,' he fretted.

'Can't you speak to her father?' asked Gibson. 'Weren't you both in the same regiment in Kenya?'

'We were indeed. He left the army and became a military chaplain, but not before he caused no end of trouble, making claims about a patrol allegedly killing Mau Mau. The soldiers were acquitted, of course, but their careers were ruined. I hope that, on this occasion, the apple will fall far away from the tree.'

'You have friends in the courts who'll keep a close eye on her. The moment she puts a foot wrong, rein the filly in.'

Back in High Street, Lena was flicking through the case files on her desk and examining Heather's 1987 appointment diary, quickly deducing that she carried out very pedestrian work – mostly conveyancing and probate. There was nothing criminal or corporate in Heather's case list and certainly nothing related to the violence which was, apparently, raging outside. For the moment, however, she would heed Martin Porter's advice, listen and learn. As her father said, 'Better be silent and thought a fool than speak and remove all doubt.'

For the next few days, she kept a low profile, learning her route from 'The Beige Box' to the bomb-site car park, reading the case files and buttering up Geraldine, who – like all solicitors' office managers – was a mine of information. William Gordon, it seemed, had decided to take the rest of the week off, either in what Geraldine described as his 'big place out west in County Fermanagh' or his second home in nearby Hillsborough, a 'sweet little village outside Belfast'. To impress the visitor from London, she claimed that politicians and leading QCs were frequent visitors to the office but, by the end of Lena's first week, she was rock-solid certain that Gordon's was no match for Sullivan & Cullen in New York. She would lobby William for more interesting work and find a home a great deal more satisfactory than the Malone Road apartment.

The only gratifying moment in that first month was putting in a call to Steve Sullivan in New York informing him she was working in Belfast. He immediately approved, but it wasn't long before they clashed again. The news of the day was an IRA mortar-bomb blast at a County Tyrone RUC station during which a local pensioner, a member of the unionist community, had died of a shock-induced heart attack. Intent on showing off her recently acquired local knowledge, Lena had ventured the opinion that unionists were justified in asking London to extend the role of the Ulster Defence Regiment to include intelligence-gathering.

'At the moment,' she said, 'they're not allowed to do much, apart from patrolling and checking cars.'

'Aren't there enough UDR men already spying on their neighbours?' Sullivan had replied.

Lena was not for backing down. She was now, after all, living and working in Belfast – Sullivan was over 3,000 miles away.

'The British government has to use what resources it has at its disposal. The IRA must be put out of business. Your government would do the same, faced with the same problem.'

'I do hope not. Giving the UDR an intelligence role would alienate the nationalist community even further. London makes the same mistakes over and over again, particularly in the courts as you will soon find out.'

'The same laws apply in the courts here as anywhere else in the UK.'

'Oh Lena, please. Have you already forgotten our discussion about the Special Powers Act? The law is being stretched to breaking point. They've abolished trial by jury and even the BBC is accusing the RUC of beating people during interrogation. Now you've got these "supergrass" cases where they're trying to send dozens of people to jail on the word of self-confessed murderers. It's just one stupid mistake after another.'

Lena felt right back where she had been in New York.

'Well, at least I'm over here now and learning,' she said, rather lamely.

'Yes, I'll give you that,' he said.

'Don't think,' she added hurriedly, 'that my arrival here had anything to do with you. It's purely coincidental.'

'I don't imagine you could have engineered it, even if you'd wanted. Full marks for leaving London though,' Sullivan had said, trying to sound conciliatory. 'I'm on the end of a phone if you ever want to talk anything over.'

As the days passed, Lena decided it was time to intervene. First, though, she would find out more about her employer by taking Geraldine out to lunch. Tucked into a café around the corner from the office, over a bowl of grey fluid that advertised itself as 'vegetable soup', she began fishing for information.

'I'm a bit out of my depth,' she began. 'Tell me about the others in the office.'

Geraldine was not used to being asked for her opinion and unleashed a stream of useful indiscretions. 'Mr Gordon doesn't do much legal work these days, just drops in once or twice a week. He still brings in lots of business by networking and so on. He often lunches with Trevor Gibson – he's an assistant chief constable – as well as up-and-coming barristers like Geoffrey Hamilton.'

'He sounds interesting,' said Lena.

'Mr Hamilton is a leading QC and writes about politics in *The Ulster Monitor*. People say he'll give up the law to stand for parliament before long.'

Perhaps her father was right, Lena thought. Gordon did seem to be well-connected.

'But,' Geraldine said, 'I've saved the best 'til last. You haven't met Edward. He runs the family hotel business and drops by to see his dad most Friday afternoons.'

'Mr Gordon has a hotel business? Bit of a joke, isn't it? Unless there's a market for tours around bomb sites and cemeteries.'

Geraldine was taken aback. Running a chain of hotels was high-status work.

'They seem to be doing very well,' she said tartly. 'The Gordons own the biggest hotel in Belfast and there's one in the Glens of Antrim – you'll not have been there yet. Then there are two more along on the north coast, four in all.'

'I wonder why Edward didn't go into the law like his father,' said Lena.

'He travels a lot,' said Geraldine. 'He's in the US and Canada right now on a tourist board visit. There are photos of him every month in the *Ulster Tatler*. They call him "Ulster's most eligible bachelor". He's super-tall and,' she finished with a flourish, 'he's a part-time officer in the UDR.'

'Impressive,' said Lena, trying to sound sincere and imagining the kind of man Edward Gordon must be, bossing chambermaids about and checking bar receipts, the inheritor of family wealth and authority and not shy about wielding it.

'The UDR,' she said. 'Don't they patrol around the countryside checking cars?'

'It's dangerous work,' said Geraldine. 'The IRA are always trying to kill them.'

Lena listened politely for the rest of the hour to stories of under-car booby traps and farmers getting shot on tractors in the countryside. Her father had fought the Mau Mau in the mountains of Kenya. The IRA might be able to bomb bars and shoot unarmed civilians, but it was hardly hand-to-hand combat. Halfway through that Friday afternoon, hearing Geraldine going into her boss' office, she followed her in and asked him politely if they might discuss her workload.

'As you already know, I regularly represented clients in the New York civil courts.'

'Yes, yes,' said Gordon vaguely, abandoning his tea and walking over to his drinks trolley, packed with rows of whiskey bottles and heavy cut-glass tumblers.

'A wee dram?' he suggested, lifting a bottle. 'This whiskey comes from the oldest distillery in the world.'

'I think the Scots might have something to say about that.'

'Oh no, my dear, but it is. It's from the village of Bushmills on our north coast,' he said, uncorking the bottle and tipping it towards her with a raised eyebrow.

'Thank you, sir, but it's a little too early for me.'

'Well, I'm officially retired, you know, my dear. I just drop in here from time to time.'

He downed his whiskey in two large gulps before lifting his briefcase and announcing his departure for home.

'Can we agree on a date to discuss a work plan?' she asked.

'It'll have to wait until Monday, m'dear,' he said, picking up papers randomly from his desk and pushing them into a briefcase.

'I suppose so, sir, but I do want to make the most of my stay here.'

'Of course, of course. We'll talk it over on Monday. I'll see you then.'

On Monday, Lena discovered Gordon was not expected at work again until Friday. It would soon be March, and she had made no real progress. Her frustration coloured her view of Belfast which was, she decided, a mixture of the banal and the sinister. City Hall seemed overblown with its huge, green dome and a forest of domineering pillars. The familiar shopfronts of 'British Home Stores' and 'Marks & Spencer' were almost comforting when placed next to the paraphernalia of urban warfare. Grey, corrugated-iron sheds, draped in barbed wire, squatted at the entrance and exit routes from the main shopping centre. Inside the sheds, a silent ritual of bag-searching continued from dawn 'til dusk under dim strip lighting. Shoppers queued silently while ill-tempered 'civilian searchers' in dark grey uniforms poked and prodded coats and handbags. All year round, damp poppy wreaths swayed in the wind, hanging from metal cages and look-out sangars, marking places where the IRA had blown UDR and RUC men to pieces. Square, pink 'security zone' signs, attached to lamp-posts and bollards, warned drivers not to leave their cars unattended. There were black-humoured stories of out-of-towners returning from shopping trips to find the British Army had blown up their vehicles. The city streets had gaping holes. Bomb sites were either used as car parks or filled with ugly cement bollards to prevent bombers from abandoning cars to cause yet more dereliction. There were no supermarkets, no shopping malls, no cafés or restaurants, just two moth-eaten department stores.

Asked by Georgie at around that time to describe life in Belfast, Lena had said, 'The gloom creeps into your brain like fog and you can't imagine anywhere in the world where people laugh and meet up after work to socialise and live without crippling fear.'

The next time she heard William Gordon's voice in his office, she knocked firmly on his door, reminding herself she wasn't the mouse that had flown out to New York.

'Mr Gordon,' she began, 'I would be of much more use if I took on more challenging cases.'

'My dear, you are a valuable addition to our staff but we can't throw you to the wolves.'

'I volunteered,' she said, 'because you promised in your letter to Braithwaite that my work would include representing paramilitaries at court hearings.'

Lena stood her ground as Gordon shifted in his seat and finally caved.

'I suppose that's fair enough,' he conceded. 'You're on probation, but I'll get Geraldine to ease you into some court work.'

'Persistence pays,' she told her father that evening.

'Be careful, Lena. Keep your views to yourself, I don't want you embarrassing William.'

Ignoring the insult which, being unintended, was even more offensive, she told him not to worry. 'No one here even hints at an opinion, Dad. What's happening out on the streets seems to be taboo.'

In a phone call to Georgina in London, Lena had already mused over this bizarre contradiction – that people living in the middle of Europe's longest-running violent conflict never spoke about it to each other.

'Maybe it's because the staff don't want to get into arguments,' Georgina had suggested.

'And there's no social life after work, no book launches, no legal get-togethers. If things don't look up, I'm bailing out early.'

'Patience, Lena. You've only just arrived. Something will turn up,' said Georgina.

The following day, something did turn up in the form of a stiff, white envelope, the kind that can only mean an official invitation. Geraldine dropped it onto Lena's desk as if it was scalding, then stood waiting for her to open it, shamelessly curious. Inside the envelope was a gilt-edged invitation from the Law Department at Queen's University to a social event marking the conclusion of an international symposium on 'The Law and Counter-Terrorism'. Lena held it up for Geraldine's inspection, but she just said 'Boring' and returned to her desk. Left alone, Lena analysed her own feelings. Other than clients, taxi drivers and shop assistants, she had yet to meet anyone in Belfast outside the offices of Gordon & Company. She would be exposing herself to a possibly perilous environment, but her thoughts were interrupted by the phone ringing. When she lifted it, she heard a familiar American drawl.

'That you Lena? Steve Sullivan here. Guess what? I'm in Belfast next week.'

'Steve. How wonderful to hear from you,' Lena tried not to sound too eager.

'Someone dropped out and I'm coming to a two-day symposium at Queen's University. There's cocktails on Wednesday to wind it up. You interested?'

'That very invitation has just dropped onto my desk. Your symposium sounds grim.'

'The law and counter-insurgency? Right up my street. Looks like the top brass of the RUC will be there as well as every lawyer in town. You should be there too.'

'I'm just an *ingénue* fresh out of London, Steve. I know nothing about counter-insurgency, as you well know. The farewell drinks are more my level.'

'C'mon kid, I'm sure you're learning fast. We'll have dinner afterwards, okay?'

'I'll book somewhere, but I'm warning you now, Belfast is not Madison Avenue.'

The following week, as flocks of squealing starlings circled above the mud of the River Lagan, a suitably booted and suited Lena stepped into a taxi for Queen's University. Belfast taxi drivers, she had discovered, were either silent or chatty. Nothing in between. At first, she preferred the friendly ones until she realised, on hearing her accent, they were just fishing for information and began playing with them, dropping morsels into the conversation and then clamming up. But tonight, she was nervous and declined to respond to the usual banter. You never knew when Belfast people were being genuinely friendly or when they were, in effect, spying. Nothing was impersonal. No menial service could be performed in a respectful silence. Every move you made – paying in a shop, buying a newspaper, asking directions – inevitably became a conversation. Always the same inquiring tone, occasionally tinged with the merest hint of menace. Tonight's taxi driver got the message and stayed silent until they reached the mock Tudor-Gothic brick façade of Queen's, where she disembarked and walked towards the main entrance, heels clicking on the stone steps. She was resolved to be cautious and keep her mouth shut. Belfast's legal fraternity might be London's country cousin, but it would be easy to misstep. When you go home this evening, she told herself, you don't want to feel damaged goods.

Squaring her shoulders, she plunged into the echoing Great Hall and the hum of conversation. Steve Sullivan shouldn't be too hard to find, she thought. He was taller than most and his well-groomed white hair would make him stand out. But she could not see him. Adopting what she hoped was a nonchalant air, she wove her way through the throngs of strangers. After one circuit of the floor, she decided to join one of the chattering groups and noticed a face she recognised from the local TV news – Gordon's buddy, Trevor Gibson, the dour-looking RUC assistant chief constable. He was listening to a rotund man in his forties, who she also vaguely recognised from somewhere, his face flushed pink with exertion as he spoke, strands of fair hair working themselves loose over his forehead. Lena subtly inserted herself into a gap in the circle. The red-faced man speaking to Gibson had spotted her, however, and turned towards her.

Then she recognised him – Geoffrey Hamilton, the QC Geraldine had told her was another of Gordon's regular lunch companions and a writer for the unionist-leaning *Monitor*. It was unusual, she had once remarked to William, for a barrister in the Belfast courts to feel able to express strong political opinions in such a public arena.

'Geoff Hamilton? He's a rising star and rarely loses a case,' Gordon had replied. 'We've known his family for years. He's a regular guest at Gordon Hall and the DPP's go-to man in the courts although he's being tipped as next-in-line on the unionist ticket in Fermanagh/South Tyrone.'

Hamilton was now staring at Lena which meant the entire circle also turned its gaze towards her. 'Well, well – a new face,' he said. 'She seems to be interested in our conversation, yet she wasn't at the symposium. Who do we have the pleasure of meeting?' Lena was mortified, finding herself just where she had determined not to be – the centre of attention.

'My name is Eleanor Dawson. I'm working with Gordon & Company for a while.'

'Of course, William's latest recruit. Let me introduce you to our little group. Ladies and gentlemen, here we have, fresh from London, Miss Eleanor Dawson, working with one of our great legal firms.'

'Now you have the advantage,' Lena said, trying to shift the focus of attention. 'Who do I have the pleasure of meeting?'

'I'm Hamilton. Geoffrey Hamilton. QC.'

Lena smiled and held out a hand. 'Please just call me Lena.'

'May we continue our conversation?' he asked.

'Oh, of course, please do,' said Lena.

As his columns in *The Monitor* revealed, while Hamilton was not a politician, yet, he had strong opinions which he believed others would benefit from hearing. That evening at Queen's, he was in full flight, delighted to have an international audience for once. The conversation centred on the legal hot potato of the day – what the local press were calling the 'supergrass system' – wherein the police were asking the courts to convict defendants on what defence barristers were calling 'the uncorroborated word of former associates'. Lena had been reading arguments both for and against. The Director of Public Prosecutions and the RUC were jointly propelling arrest statistics off the scale and the prisons were filling up nicely with both loyalist and republican defendants on remand awaiting trial. Questions were already being raised, however, about the quality of evidence admissible before no-jury courts.

'The police,' Hamilton told his listeners, 'cannot hope to defeat terrorism while juries are intimidated and terrorists destroy forensic evidence. In normal times, such a process might be said to have drawbacks. But do we live in normal times?' No one in the circle replied, fully aware Hamilton was about to answer his own question. 'Most assuredly we do not,' he went on. 'If the critics in London had to search under their cars for bombs every morning and attend their friends' funerals every week, they'd soon change their minds.'

Hamilton turned to Lena. 'And here we have just such a Londoner. Are you one of the critics, Miss Dawson?'

Lena hesitated, trying to think of an anodyne response, but a man to her right spoke up first.

'Not to interrupt Hamilton, but if the courts accept a lower standard of evidence, it can only lead to trouble. The judiciary is beginning to question the validity of these "supergrass" trials. It's hardly a comfortable position for a judge to be in – to advise himself from the bench on the credibility of witnesses and then switch identity to bring in an unbiased verdict.'

Everyone turned to look at the new speaker. Lena could have hugged him. 'Apologies for the interruption, Miss Dawson, I had better introduce myself. Brendan Casey.'

It had not taken Lena long to deduce from the local newspapers that, in Northern Ireland's shallow legal pond, Casey was almost as prominent as Hamilton who, she saw, was most displeased at him entering the fray.

'But, my dear Casey, the outcome speaks for itself,'

Hamilton responded. 'The terrorist murder statistics this year are significantly reduced.'

Casey was undeterred. Like Hamilton, he did not often get the ear of an international audience.

'Perhaps I should explain for those of you from outside Belfast,' he said. 'Our assistant chief constable, Mr Gibson here, has what's officially called an "assisting offender" in protective custody who is shortly due to appear as Queen's evidence against no fewer than sixteen defendants which raises some potentially interesting legal points.'

Gibson, who had not anticipated controversy at what was meant to be a social event, frowned and examined the bottom of his wine glass. Casey still had the floor.

'This particular supergrass, a Mr Leonard White, rejoices in the nickname "Snowy" – perhaps because of his name, perhaps because he sports an unlikely shade of blonde hair, but more probably because of the chemicals he habitually stuffs up his nose.'

Smiles replaced the glum expressions on the faces around the circle.

'Picture the scene last week, my friends, when Snowy appeared in the witness box, screened off by a red velvet curtain. In the dock were the sixteen defendants whose friends and relatives graced the public gallery, all eagerly awaiting Snowy's arrival,' said Casey.

The circle of listeners was now more relaxed, enjoying Casey's story.

'When he made his appearance,' Casey went on, 'the defendants' female relatives pulled bags of ice cubes from beneath their nether garments which they proceeded to throw at the red curtain. Deprived of a clear target, however, they began throwing missiles at the bench, several landing dangerously near His Lordship. Those in the public gallery may not have trained at Surrey Cricket Club, but their bowling would not have disgraced The Oval. The Lord Chief Justice was not at all amused.'

Casey's audience, on the other hand, was.

'In a further scandalous act of defiance, the defendants then began ripping up their witness statements, tossing them at the press gallery. More like bath night in the ape house in Bangkok Zoo than one of Her Majesty's courts.'

Restrained laughter was now rippling around the circle.

Another voice, attracted by the increasingly obvious mirth, joined in the conversation. 'It was quite a spectacle,' said the newcomer, 'yet nothing of these entertaining events makes the London newspapers. I had better introduce myself, David Murray, agency court reporter.'

Hamilton, seeing a way to recapture control of the conversation, pounced on Lena again. 'Is Mr Murray, correct, Miss Dawson? How are the press in London reporting our "assisting offenders"?'

Lena was once again on the spot but, after weeks of boredom at Gordon's, was ready for the challenge of a live legal debate.

'I fear Mr Murray has a point,' she began cautiously, still anxious about saying something terribly wrong. 'Few in London take much interest in events in Belfast.'

'Clearly you are an exception though, Miss Dawson,' replied Hamilton. 'You chose to come and work here. What do you think of the "supergrass system"? In confidence, of course. Chatham House Rules, you can give your honest opinion.'

Lena knew everyone's eyes were on her. At least one of those listening was a senior police officer. Others were probably living in fortified homes with twenty-four-hour bodyguards. The outcome of the present debate was, for them, a matter of literal life or death. But the gauntlet was down. She drew on her new-found resilience.

'The law is a servant of the society it is designed to protect,' she began formally. 'If the law fails to hold those responsible for illegal violence to account, it is incumbent on those who make the law to adapt it. Through parliament, of course.'

Heads, including Gibson's and Hamilton's, nodded sagely but Lena had not finished. For the first time since leaving New York she was in command of an audience. Words swirled up into her head.

'Having said that, bending existing laws, even with the best of intentions, is acutely dangerous.'

It was almost like being in court again, she thought, intoxicated at realising they were all hanging on to her every word.

'The use of uncorroborated accomplice evidence to convict multiple defendants in no-jury courts stretches the law to breaking point, perhaps even beyond breaking point.'

Most of the listening circle then began examining their footwear with unusual intensity. Not Hamilton, though.

'As I imagined,' he sighed. 'Why would I expect anything else? Are we to be sitting ducks indefinitely, watching low-lives like Luke Maguire spout propaganda on the TV news even as his minions prepare to slaughter us?'

The group of listeners now realised they were caught

up in 'a situation'. The naming of Maguire, a notorious IRA 'godfather', was chilling. They had only come to drink a glass of wine and say their goodbyes, not become embroiled in a public row.

Lena, while shocked at Hamilton's words, was in too far to back down. 'I certainly don't regard anyone here as a duck, sitting or otherwise,' she began. 'I believe I gave a nuanced view, but my main point stands. The political context here makes it even more, not less, important to uphold the strict letter of the law.'

As she spoke, she realised she was making a point perilously close to Sullivan's in New York and then, miraculously, there he was, tall and suave as ever, the cavalry to her rescue.

'Here you are, Lena, hiding away,' he said.

Sullivan's intervention rescued them all from a tight spot. There was an almost audible sigh of relief from everyone, bar Hamilton.

'You must excuse me,' Sullivan said, calmly absorbing the strained atmosphere. 'I've been searching for this young lady all evening.'

His urbane smile, his twinkling eyes, how glad she was to see him.

'Please excuse us,' he said, before putting a hand firmly in the small of Lena's back, guiding her away. Just as the circle closed again behind them, however, a man even taller than Sullivan stepped into their path.

'Why run away when you are doing so well?' the man asked Lena.

'This is my last night in Belfast,' said Sullivan. 'Miss Dawson and I have a dinner date.'

Lena then intervened, determined to show Sullivan she could stand her own ground.

'How can you possibly say I'm running away?' she asked the tall man angrily. 'Doesn't everyone support the impartial application of the rule of law?'

'The law isn't much protection against an Armalite rifle,' he said.

'Interesting,' Lena replied, 'that your counter-argument immediately relies on the threat of extreme violence.'

The two of them, Lena and the tall man, faced each other – one poised and assured, the other pugnacious, defensive.

Sullivan stepped in to end it, his twinkle gone. 'This discussion is over,' he said firmly. 'I'm taking this lady for dinner. Right now.'

'If you must,' said the tall man, turning away.

'What the hell was going on?' asked Sullivan as they left the room. 'I was only in the bathroom a minute and I returned to find you in the middle of a blazing row.'

'That man Hamilton knows I'm new in Belfast and thought he could bully me,' she said. 'I wasn't for rolling over. Let's get out of here.'

Over dinner, Lena told Sullivan of how she had faced down Gordon and would soon be working on Troubles-related cases.

'I hope he doesn't hear about the skirmish tonight though,' she said. 'Both Hamilton and Gibson are Gordon's buddies and I annoyed them in public.'

'From what you've told me, you stuck to universally accepted legal principles, but Belfast can be a dangerous and unpredictable place. I've been around the block a few times but even I am taken aback by how fast arguments can escalate around here.'

After dinner, they walked the short distance to his hotel, hugging briefly on the footpath before Sullivan reminded her to phone if she needed support or advice. On the short taxi ride home, Lena heard sirens in the distance and wondered if someone else had just been killed. No doubt she would find out on the morning radio news. News of death was becoming almost routine.

2

Even before she turned the radio on in the morning, Lena groaned and cursed her disregard for Martin Porter's rule of *omertà*. Sullivan had rescued her but not before she had crossed two of her boss' chums. When she turned on the news, the lead story was of a Catholic bus driver shot dead as he left his depot in East Belfast. It explained the sirens as she left Sullivan's hotel.

At the office, she focused on work and, by the afternoon, was diligently finishing a summary of her casework when Geraldine brought in a cup of tea along with a request from Gordon to join him in his office. Lena's stomach fluttered. Belfast was a small place. Maybe he had already heard about the row at Queen's? There were two men in the office as she opened the door. William was sitting behind his desk but standing and looking out towards the Albert Clock was another man in a brown tweed jacket. When he turned around, Lena was stunned. It was the tall man who had challenged her leaving Queen's.

'May I introduce my son, Edward,' said Gordon, rising slightly from his seat before sinking down again. 'He says he met you at the university last night.'

As Lena stared at Edward, her teacup began rattling on its saucer. She had planned to be polite but distant when she met her employer's hotel-manager son. Instead, she was caught flat-footed and flustered. How much had he told his father about the supergrass row?

'Hello again,' said Edward and, seeing her surprise, added, 'I didn't plan to ambush you like this.'

Gordon, watching closely, could not fail to notice the tension between them.

'But it seems you have "ambushed me",' Lena replied. 'You might have introduced yourself last night.'

'I didn't get a chance. Your American friend – Stephen Sullivan isn't it – spirited you away.'

He's enjoying this, Lena thought. Seeing her flash of anger, Edward turned to his father.

'Perhaps I should take Lena round to The Evening Star to get better acquainted. Can she have an early night?' he asked his father.

'Must she, dear boy?' William replied, smiling.

'Oh, I think so,' Edward said.

'Very well, then,' said William.

Lena, growing angrier by the second, saw the amused look passing between father and son. How dare they discuss her as if she wasn't there? Without a word, she placed her teacup on Gordon's desk and walked back to her own office to fetch her coat and scarf. Edward was already at the lift, holding the door open, but she stamped past him down the stairs. Outside, it was already getting dark. The city was emptying, shops closing, office workers scurrying home to the safety of the suburbs, lines of people queuing at bus stops.

'We seem to have got off on the wrong foot,' he said, catching up with her on the footpath.

'That's hardly surprising,' she said, deciding to give no quarter. 'What surprises me is that you were at Queen's at all last night. The invitation was for lawyers and academics.

You're neither. I believe you're a hotel manager.'

'Four hotels, actually, and what's wrong with that? I'm sure you've stayed in a few,' he said. 'I was standing in for my father.'

Lena, trying to think of another put-down, quickened her pace, feeling dwarfed beside him.

'Where did you and Sullivan have dinner last night?' he asked. 'You should have taken him to one of our places.'

'I really don't remember. Some Italian place, near Queen's.'

'Next time he's over, you'll have to invite him to the Gordon Central Hotel.'

Does this man know any other way of speaking to people other than patronising them? she wondered.

Arriving at a near-empty Evening Star, Lena sat down at a table and asked for a gin-and-tonic. As Edward walked to the bar, she had a moment for closer scrutiny. Leaning casually against the counter, he was even taller than she remembered, one foot resting on the brass shoe rail. He ordered their drinks with the easy authority familiar from a hundred London 'somethings in the city'. She hadn't expected to find that in Belfast. He turned, caught her watching him and smiled. How inappropriate his jacket was, she thought. Did he not know of the 'no brown in town' rule? As he sat down beside her, she remained resolutely silent to convey her continuing annoyance.

'Now,' he said, 'why were you so determined to escape last night?'

'I was not "escaping",' she said. 'I had won the argument and was trapped in an awkward situation.'

'You strike me as someone quite capable of getting out of awkward situations.'

Lena recognised the olive branch but was not ready to reciprocate.

'I was sure of my ground but it was not the time or place for such a confrontation,' she said.

'I wouldn't say it was a confrontation, just a robust exchange of views. It isn't often that Geoffrey Hamilton meets his match.'

He seemed determined to compliment her, so she let him carry on.

'For what it's worth, I think you're right. The police think they're on the winning side, for once, but I suspect this supergrass thing has a limited life expectancy. But let's talk about something more pleasant. Why don't you visit us in Fermanagh one weekend this spring? Have you ever travelled out west?'

'No. As you are very well aware, I've only just arrived in Belfast.'

'Being a stranger in this place can't be easy.'

'As you have already conceded, I'm managing fairly well.'

'Managing is not the same as enjoying.'

He's not going to win me over that easily, she thought.

'I don't mean to sound ungracious, but I don't take off for weekends with men I hardly know, even if they are my employer's son.'

He was calm despite the provocation.

'Our fathers were friends,' he said, gently. 'We should be too. You'd like Enniskillen. It's a quaint old town.'

Lena thought of the alternative – more boring weekends on her own.

'I'll give it thought,' she said.

Their drinks finished, Lena quickly stood up to avoid the offer of a second and made for the door.

'I promised you a lift,' he said.

'You actually didn't, and I don't need one anyway,' she replied. 'My car's parked around the corner. I can hardly leave it there overnight. Your UDR friends would probably blow it up.'

It was the perfect exit line. Outside the bar, she held out her hand, formally, before striding purposefully away, feeling his eyes on her back and congratulating herself on a dignified departure. Back in the dingy little apartment, though, she tried and failed to finish the case notes she had started that morning. Reliving the exchange with Edward was far more appealing. None of Lena's previous relationships had turned into anything serious and she had decided long ago she was not the kind of woman men either lusted after or settled down with. She supposed they saw her as blunt and disputatious. Georgie had often advised her to relax more in male company and accept compliments when they came her way. Edward, Lena thought, as the good-looking heir to a wealthy father was the nearest thing Belfast had to an eligible bachelor and therefore way out of her league.

Just before midnight, she turned on the BBC Radio Ulster news. The police were appealing for information after the discovery of the body of a taxi driver, a Catholic father of six, in North Belfast. That was a killing on two consecutive nights. The first victim was not even buried before the second was murdered. She wondered if she had ever been in the poor man's taxi. It was the last item on the news, just before the sport and weather. Two men shot dead. Two families broken into pieces. One line on the news in London. It was more than depressing. It was shocking.

At work on Friday morning, she found a note on her desk asking her to see William in his office at midday. He began by asking how she and Edward had got on.

'Very well, sir. He has invited me to Fermanagh.'

'As have I,' said Gordon but before he could continue, she jumped in.

'With your permission, I'm going to pop up to the Crumlin Road courthouse later today. If I'll soon be representing clients there, I would like to get a feel for the place.'

'Go ahead, my dear,' he said sighing.

Lena had long looked forward to getting inside Her Majesty's Crown Court on the Crumlin Road but rang Brendan Casey first to invite him for lunch and dig for information, determined to avoid making a show of herself in court.

'I've sat in on dozens of civil actions in London and New York,' Lena said over their meal, 'and I've helped out at coroners' courts but I have never prepared for a full-on criminal trial, let alone one involving terrorist charges.'

As she had anticipated, Casey's views on how the law was administered in Northern Ireland were less than glowing, his air of restrained amusement a response to the many idiosyncrasies of the Belfast legal system.

'I'm afraid you'll be underwhelmed,' he began. 'The majority of cases in Crumlin Road involve defendants, of either the pro-British or pro-Irish persuasion, but don't expect fireworks. It's all very low-key.'

'How is that possible?' she asked.

'You'll find the normal cut and thrust between prosecution and defence is less – well – less obvious here,' said Casey. 'There are certain, what shall I say, understandings between lawyers and judges. I'm afraid the atmosphere is more often collaborative than adversarial.'

Lena had been looking forward to the usual verbal fencing, lawyers taunting each other, exchanging offensive insults as if they were flowery compliments, that sort of thing. Court hearings in London and New York reminded her of a zoo, the apes picking out each other's fleas or snarling and baring their teeth.

'But being combative is so fundamental,' she said.

'You'll also be disappointed by the acoustics,' Casey went on. 'Whoever designed our courts had no thought for defendants hearing what is being said about them.'

'Surely, they can hear witnesses being cross-examined?' she asked.

'Nope,' said Casey, 'and neither can their families. Even the court reporters complain – as that press agency man, David Murray, the one you met at Queen's, will doubtless tell you.'

'But that's appalling,' Lena said. 'People shouldn't be tried and convicted without hearing the evidence against them. What about "Justice being seen to be done?"'

'More honoured in the breach than the observance in Belfast I'm afraid,' said Casey ruefully. 'I overheard a convicted felon on his way to the cells last week ask a prison warder how long the judge had sent him down for.'

'That's intolerable,' she said.

'This place will never change,' he said. 'You either put up with it or leave.'

When Lena arrived to observe events for the first time at Crumlin Road, she parked her red Mini behind the courthouse, on yet another potholed bomb site, and took a hard look at the building. It had been built around 1850 but had long ago lost whatever neo-classical appeal it might have once possessed. Someone had thought it appropriate to paint its pillared frontage in various shades of orange and peach. Like all public buildings, it was garlanded in barbed wire and surrounded by rusted corrugated iron sheeting. Across the road, the even less attractive Crumlin Road Gaol, or 'Her Majesty's Prison, Belfast' to give it its proper title, squatted like a fat, brown toad.

She was searched, allowed inside and approached court staff who gave her permission to sit on the legal benches so she had at least a remote chance of hearing what was going on. Before long, she was agreeing with Casey. Superficially, there was the same hierarchy as in London – judges first, lawyers in the middle and defendants bringing up the rear – but the relationship between defence and prosecution lawyers was subtly different despite the high stakes. The absence of hostilities, she thought, was worrying. It changed the dynamic. Defendants were regularly being sent to prison for decades – yet it was done almost casually. If the prosecution won, prisoners were dispatched downstairs to a tunnel linking the decrepit courthouse to the even more decrepit jail from where they were eventually taken to Her Majesty's Prison Maze and the notorious H-Blocks, site of the 1981 hunger strikes, south-west of Belfast. If the defence won, a rare occurrence, the defendants were also taken downstairs but then escorted to meet their families outside.

The big winners in this game, she decided, were the police, lawyers, judges and court staff who had cushy jobs for life, so long as they maintained an indefinite supply of defendants – and always providing the associates of said defendants did not blow them to kingdom come.

The first day that Lena took her allotted seat as a working solicitor in the well of the court, she noticed a subtle change, a wariness. She was an outsider and, therefore, suspect. David Murray turned up in court from time to time but he seemed to be just another part of the legal furniture – chatting to lawyers and the court clerks who helped him by handing over daily charge sheets. There was no sense that he was the eyes and ears of the public, exposing dodgy verdicts and police practices. Despite Porter's advice, Lena was finally unable to resist giving him the benefit of this opinion. The two of them had ambled off for lunch after a case adjourned early. Over a glutinous, grey gruel that seemed to be the only soup available anywhere in Belfast, she tackled him.

'I don't mean to criticise, but did you get into journalism to churn out stories by the yard?' she asked. 'Those seven kids from Turf Lodge were in court again this morning but you were nowhere to be seen.'

'Nothing about them has the remotest chance of making it into the papers,' Murray said bluntly.

'But they're innocent. Everybody knows it. The only evidence against them is their own confessions that they say were beaten out of them. Three of them were sixteen when first arrested but were released and re-arrested after their seventeenth birthdays, so they were charged as adults. That's hardly a coincidence.'

'None of the editors I work for could give a damn.'

'But it's a blatant ploy. They wouldn't get away with it in London,' she said.

'I don't make the rules,' he said.

In the meantime, Lena thought on her way back to the office, seven teenagers who should be in school are about to be shunted into jail. Along with what Casey had already told her, she was beginning to wonder about the quality of justice dispensed in Belfast.

Later that week, halfway through the afternoon, she was in the middle of a complex phone call when there was a knock on her door and Edward walked in. Unbidden, her stomach did cartwheels. She had firmly written off any repetition of his polite invitation to Fermanagh but, as she continued her phone call, he scrawled something into a notebook on her desk and left. When she turned the notebook around, it read tersely, 'Dinner. Friday 8 p.m. Gordon Central?'

At least there was a question mark, she thought and phoned Georgina to pass on news of this unexpected development. 'I was rude to the point of insolence last time we met but now he's asked me to dinner. Commanded is more accurate.'

Georgie, who had once overheard Charlotte Dawson describe her daughter as 'a snub-nosed, flat-chested, quarrelsome little brat', decided this was a moment to give Lena's self-image a boost.

'He must be fed up with girls fluttering their eyelashes at him,' she said. 'You held your ground and must seem a bit of a challenge, darling. What's more important is if you're interested in him?'

'He's the type you and I usually despise – alpha-male, over-fond of the golf course and rugby match. His hair's too short and he orders people about.'

'So, a terminal case of Napoleon complex.'

'In his favour, he's not bad-looking and filthy rich.'

They both laughed.

'Seriously Lena, you've upped your game at work – it's time to do the same socially. Go out and enjoy the evening. You're more than capable of giving as good as you get.'

After Lena put the phone down, she returned Edward's serve by leaving an equally terse note on his desk: 'OK. Lena.'

As she waited for his arrival, in the hotel restaurant his family owned, she tried – and failed – to avoid comparing the contrast in their status. She was a mere office junior, a know-nothing from London, while he was her wealthy employer's son. As he sat down beside her, however, she vowed she would make no concessions.

Edward threw the ball in by asking politely if her father ever talked about his days in Kenya.

'My father rarely speaks about his experiences in the army. I suspect it's confidential,' said Lena.

'What's it like, having a clergyman as a father?'

'Dad hardly talks about God or the Bible – at least not to me.'

'So, what do you talk about?'

'I suppose, like most adults, we discuss the merits and demerits of the British Empire; Mrs Thatcher; privatisation of the railways. Now that I'm a lawyer, we talk about judicial reviews and so on.'

Lena had hoped to gauge his character on how, and which, of these topics he picked up, but he ignored them all.

'You haven't told me about your mother – Charlotte, isn't it?'

Of all the subjects he might have chosen, she thought, her mother was certainly the least appealing.

'Well, Mother loves gardening, but her arthritis makes it difficult. She can't cook which annoys Dad. He says there are two things a woman should do by instinct and one of them is cook.'

As Lena had hoped, this caused Edward's fork to pause midway between plate and mouth.

'So, enough about me. What about your family?' she followed up sweetly.

'You already know about the hotels,' he said, making a quick recovery. 'I manage them in theory but not hands-on. It's mostly marketing, telling people abroad about Northern Ireland. I go to a lot of conferences, meeting travel agents and so on.'

'Sounds fascinating,' she said, half hoping he noted the sarcasm.

'As you know, I spent most of last month in North America,' he ploughed on regardless, 'but my weekends are different. Has my father told you about the UDR?'

So he wants to boast about playing soldiers, Lena thought. I'll see about that.

'The UDR's a bit like the part-time army reserve, isn't it?' she said. 'You hide in ditches, poke around haystacks and check the cows aren't booby-trapped.'

As intended, her levity touched a nerve.

'Yes, we do spend nights in ditches – cold, wet ones – otherwise the IRA would have succeeded in starting a civil war long ago.'

Lena knew she was skating on thin ice but something urged her on.

'You're not after loyalists then?' she said. 'Just the IRA? What is it Sinn Féin says? That the UDR are soldiers by day and the UVF by night? Any truth in that?'

'For heaven's sake, Lena. If one of my men were a paramilitary, he'd be out on his ear. Maybe Geoff Hamilton was right that day at Queen's. You people don't have the faintest idea what we are dealing with.'

Slightly alarmed, Lena changed tack and began a charm offensive with amusing accounts of her army childhood; how, as a toddler each morning, she had stood to attention at the end of her bed for her father's daily inspection, how she'd taken pride in polishing the brass buttons on his dress uniform and helping to shine his shoes. Edward began to relax again, even neglecting his food and grinning at her stories.

He reciprocated with tales of UDR life at the barracks in Enniskillen, named – he said – after the Grosvenor family who 'own thousands of acres in Fermanagh as well as most of Mayfair'. He and his men patrolled, he said, mostly by boat or, in the air, by helicopter.

'People say that half the year, Lough Erne is in Fermanagh and the other half Fermanagh is in Lough Erne. The county is surrounded on three sides by the Irish Republic, so the IRA attack and run back across the border if we don't catch them first.'

Dinner over, he asked to be excused to speak to the head waiter and, left alone, Lena decided honour had been satisfied after the office ambush. All that patrolling, she thought, evidently kept him fit. His wiry black hair, firmly divided in a dead-straight parting, was so short it left an inch of stubbly sun-tanned neck above his shirt collar. Anyone could tell, even out of uniform, he was a soldier. But, she reminded herself, he was just his father's son, just a small-town hotel manager with a high opinion of himself. Returning, he suggested a nightcap in the hotel bar where someone was playing a shiny grand piano. They settled into easy chairs and, to make conversation, she asked him about the tune.

'It's called "The Black Velvet Band" – about a Belfast man whose life is ruined by a dark-haired young lady.'

'Well, you're from Fermanagh, so you're quite safe,' she replied.

'What kind of music do you like?' he asked.

'I've been singing in church choirs since I was small. Dad gave me Britten's "The Young Person's Guide to the Orchestra" when I was about ten and that was me into Beethoven and so on.'

'What about Irish music?'

'I know "Danny Boy" but that's about it.'

'We will have to change that,' he said, standing up and walking over to the pianist who stopped playing mid-tune and rose from his seat. Edward took off his jacket, sat down and began playing a mournful, unmistakably Irish tune. It was not an easy piece, yet he played it effortlessly. She watched as Edward's long fingers moved deftly over the keys. This was unexpected. The buzz of conversation in the hotel bar fell silent as people turned to watch the imposing man at the piano. There was something immensely attractive, Lena was forced to admit, about a man who played with such focus and intensity. What, she wondered guiltily before quickly banishing the thought, would it feel like to have those long arms wrapped around her? As he finished, Edward leaned back and sat, seemingly lost in thought, for a moment. Then he looked over towards her, his serious expression melting into a smile and he began playing again, a jaunty tune this time. A small group in the lounge began quietly singing along. By the time he walked back to sit beside her, people were looking over at them curiously.

'Well, you kept that a secret,' she said.

'I had a good music teacher at school in Enniskillen. I'm competent enough.'

Competent? she thought. There's a lot more to it than that.

'What was the first tune?' she asked.

'It's "My Lagan Love". You know, after the River Lagan that runs through Belfast.'

'Ah yes, the murky brown river beside the office.'

'The Lagan actually is lovely, further upstream.'

'And the second?'

'A song from south of here, "The Star of County Down". I had to liven it up because people had stopped drinking and the hotel has to turn a shilling.'

His self-deprecating tone seemed to acknowledge and gently mock her earlier barbs about the hotel business. She had to smile. When he asked again about a weekend in Fermanagh, she agreed and they arranged to meet in the office, after his next Friday afternoon meeting with his father, and drive down together. They shook hands saying their goodbyes and, sitting in the back of a taxi on the way home, Lena acknowledged to herself that, although she had started the evening not caring a jot if he liked her or not, now she did care. Quite a lot.

Over the next few days, she took her time packing, anticipating a close examination, not only by Edward but also by his mother. It would hardly be a casual break. When she joined William in his office for the regular end-of-week Bushmills, Edward was already overdue for their Friday meeting. Outside, the Albert Clock struck three.

'Edward's invited me to Fermanagh this weekend,' she said.

'Good,' said Gordon. 'Margaret and I will pick you up at the Malone flat.'

'My bag is here in the office. Edward and I are travelling down together,' she said.

Gordon's eyebrows raised.

'Very well, my dear. You young ones enjoy yourselves. See you at dinner.'

After work, Edward carried her bag to a dark green Range Rover parked behind High Street and Lena hauled herself in, welcoming an aroma familiar from her father's car back home of mud and diesel. As he jumped in beside her, she realised that they were going to be together, confined in this small space, inches away from each other over the handbrake, for over an hour. How should she handle it – chatty and amusing or cool and silent? She quietly watched Edward's driving. There was no laddish showing-off. He kept to speed limits and was courteous at roundabouts. As they left the city, she decided to open conversation.

'I've been here nearly three months,' she said, 'but the only places I've seen are Belfast city centre and the Malone and Crumlin Roads. I've never seen the Mourne Mountains that Geraldine goes on about or the Giant's Causeway.'

'Wait until we pass Lisnaskea,' he said. 'Some say it's the land that time forgot.'

Lena began chattering on about what she had observed so far in the courts but she got no response from the man at the wheel.

'You're very quiet,' she said.

'Well, maybe we humble hotel managers can't match your sparkling repartee,' he said.

Touché.

'Tell me more about your piano teacher in Enniskillen.'

'Not much to say. He was an unusually patient man. I never really thanked him. I'm grateful now, of course, but he died years back so it's too late.'

'Did you ever think about going on to study music?'

'Thanks, but I'm not that good.'

'I think you are,' she said and then forced herself to shut up for a while, looking out over the bleak landscape that was just beginning to show signs of spring, willows sprouting, yellow catkins waving in the roadside hazels.

As they left the motorway, the thought suddenly occurred to her that she was about to meet a group of people about whom she knew precisely nothing.

'You'll have to tell me who'll be there this weekend,' she said.

'Apart from Dad, there's my mother, Margaret. You'll also meet Mr and Mrs Wilson, they're a couple who look after the house while we're in Belfast.'

That clears up who irons his shirts, Lena thought.

'Then there's one of my closest friends,' he said, 'Paul Donaldson. He's an RUC man, based locally, who generally stays overnight. We also have the Grahams coming for dinner. John Graham has a furniture shop in Enniskillen. Your sparring partner at Queen's, Geoff Hamilton, is also joining us, although he'll be leaving early to get home to Dungannon.'

Lena was not looking forward to meeting Hamilton again, quickly calculating there would be seven for dinner, all doubtless watching her like hawks. The further west they drove, she thought, the more reflective Edward seemed. What had stopped her, she wondered, from noticing how attractive he was? Not that it mattered. He was just being polite to the daughter of his father's old army chum. As they turned into a long, tree-lined driveway, Gordon Hall came into view.

'We're lucky. It wasn't large enough for the IRA to bother burning,' Edward said gruffly as they bumped over a cattle grid.

The house was a large, grey, cut-stone building surrounded by parkland – lonely-looking in the sweeping green landscape. A small lake glittered in the valley beyond. Edward parked on the gravel driveway near the front door which was opened by an elderly man with a suitably subservient air, introduced as Wilson, who took her bag as she entered the cavernous black-and-white tiled entrance hall.

'If you don't mind, I'll go and say hello to Mother,' Edward said. 'Wilson, would you show Miss Dawson to the Blue Room? Lena, why don't you change for dinner? I'll see you in the library.'

Although he was giving orders again, Lena – obedient for now – passed her case to Wilson, who led her up a wide staircase to the right of the hallway, their steps muted by a deep-pile maroon carpet fastened by gleaming brass stair-rods. More of Mrs Wilson's work, Lena thought. She took her time changing into a long black skirt and cream ruffled blouse before pinning half her hair up and adjusting her make-up in preparation for the scrutiny that doubtless awaited. As she returned downstairs, there was a loud knock at the front door, the sound booming through the entrance hall. Lena paused on a landing and watched as Edward strode across to open it.

'Hello Paul,' he said. 'Come in, come in. Dinner's nearly ready.'

Paul Donaldson was tall, broad shouldered, auburn haired and – she guessed – slightly younger than Edward. As he came through the door, he clapped Edward on the back and they turned together to cross the hallway. Paul was carrying a large, battered hold-all which, he said, he would 'dump in the usual place and be down for a large Bush'.

'Sorry friend, you've been evicted. I've brought someone down from Belfast and she's in your room for the weekend. Here, I'll take your bag and show you where you'll be residing tonight.'

'Evicted, is it? There's loyalty for you. I will have to inspect this lady, especially if she looks anything like the last one.'

'No need to wait,' said Lena, mildly irritated that, even sight unseen, she was being judged. 'Here I am, all ready for inspection,' she said, gliding down towards them, telling herself she looked her best and aware she was making quite an entrance. A more confident man would have laughed it off, but Paul blushed deeply as he held out a hand.

'This is Eleanor Dawson,' Edward said. 'She's over here from London to work for a while in Dad's office.'

'You weren't meant to hear that, Miss Dawson,' said Paul. 'He's been keeping you well under wraps.'

'You can call me Lena,' she said. 'I hope I pass muster. Let's be sure to sit together at dinner so you get a chance to investigate forensically.'

'That can be arranged,' said Edward quietly, taking Paul's case. 'Lena, if you go to the library down the corridor, they're having drinks in there. We'll be down in a minute.'

The two men walked upstairs together as Lena, her heels clicking, first on the tiles and then the parquet flooring, walked into the library. Heads turned as she opened the door and she thanked heaven she had dressed up. William introduced her to the Grahams, who asked her politely how she was settling in. Geoffrey Hamilton, standing by the fireplace, said, unconvincingly, that he was glad to see her again. Edward's mother hung back a little, but William finally remembered to introduce her. Margaret Gordon, in her late sixties Lena guessed, still had the serene beauty that must have attracted William when they were both younger. You hardly noticed the wrinkles beneath her gracefully swept-up grey hair.

As the conversation resumed, Lena was unsurprised as Hamilton tried to control its direction, although everyone else seemed more interested in hearing about her family in England. At dinner, Edward ensured she sat next to Paul, who, she established, was from the county and had gone to school in Lisnaskea, unlike Edward, who had been a weekly boarder in Enniskillen. Lena enquired about Paul's work. That generally did the trick.

'I trained at the RUC college in Enniskillen,' he said. 'Then did a few specialist courses in Belfast but I'm now based here, working along the border.'

'What sort of specialist courses – or shouldn't I ask?' she asked demurely.

'Community policing mainly.'

'So, you're not in Special Branch or anything exciting?' Paul didn't react.

'I'm just a very ordinary country policeman.'

'But being a country policeman so close to the border is far from ordinary, I would imagine,' she said. 'It's certainly a stunning landscape.'

Lena had, by chance, found a subject Paul could talk about endlessly. Over the next half-hour, she learned more than enough about trout fishing in nearby Lough MacNean and hiking the Cuilcagh Mountains. Several glasses of wine later, she asked Paul how he and Edward had met.

'He arrived at the barracks in Lisnaskea one night after we sent for UDR and ATO support.'

'More acronyms. I'm drowning in them,' she said. 'I know what the UDR is but what the heck is an "ATO"?'

'It stands for "ammunition technical officer". You'd

call them the bomb squad. We'd found a command wire stretching towards the border attached to an unexploded culvert bomb.'

'You had better explain about command wires and culvert bombs too,' she said. 'Remember, I've just arrived from London.'

'A culvert is just a ditch under a road. The IRA hide bombs in them attached to command wires. They watch until security forces are passing, then detonate the bombs using the wire, sometimes from across the border. They've done it so often in South Armagh that the army only patrols by helicopter.'

'I see,' said Lena, deciding that Paul was probably not 'just an ordinary country policeman'.

'We found this one and staked it out. At least one of the gang had to be hiding out nearby. Edward and his patrol were called in. He and I spent the night in an extremely cold ditch and talked to keep our spirits up although the IRA never returned to their bloody command wire. Every time we get close to arresting one of them, they skip across the border where the gardaí can't, or won't, lay a finger on them. We know the names of virtually every active IRA man along the border between Fermanagh and Monaghan – but getting sufficient evidence to bring them to court is virtually impossible.'

Lena imagined Edward and Paul on patrol, talking about the stupidity of their superior officers or the ineffective politicians who ran the place. Paul's family, she guessed, would have been small farmers for generations back, or maybe shopkeepers, whereas Edward's were the local gentry. It spoke well of him that they were friends.

Towards the end of dinner, talk around the table turned to the economy and politics. Lena hoped they would not ramble on too long. Northern Ireland politics, she had decided, were impenetrable while its spokesmen, on both sides, were clumsy and short-sighted. But Hamilton was in full flow.

'In the South, they've managed to exploit every grant available from Brussels,' he said to nods of approval around the table. 'But who in their right mind would invest in this place while the IRA is bombing all round us?'

Lena suspected his audience had heard all this before. Edward then gave a short account of his latest trip to the USA and Canada, agreeing with Hamilton that tourism would never take off until the IRA campaign was over.

'Why don't you go into politics yourself, Edward?' Lena asked.

William's ears pricked up. He had asked his son this question many times before. Edward then surprised them.

'Actually, I rang old Armstrong in the Ulster Unionist office in Lisnaskea last week and signed up.'

William, delighted, lifted his glass. 'Well done, my boy.' Around the table, they all dutifully lifted their glasses. Lena was both amused and irritated at how seriously they were treating it – as though they were initiating Edward into some cult. At London dinner parties, people had lively disagreements over politics and the law. Here, there seemed an unspoken consensus.

'I know I'm new to this,' she ventured, 'but politics here seems very black-and-white. There's no nuance. If you all stay in your silos, refusing to talk to each other, how will the violence ever end?'

The hush that followed was embarrassing. It was Hamilton who broke it.

'Well, Lena, it's not we, here, who are dividing people. There can be no dialogue until the legally constituted forces of the state defeat terrorism. When you've been here a bit longer, you'll understand.'

His condescension was annoying but Lena heeded Martin Porter's advice not to be provoked and merely commented, archly – but not too archly, she hoped – that he 'knew so much more than her'.

The party then gathered around the library fireplace for brandies and cigars, their talk focusing on local characters and the price of land. Hamilton was the first to leave for his home in Dungannon. After the Grahams departed, William and Margaret went upstairs and Lena followed soon after, leaving Edward and Paul deep in a fireside conversation about border roads and customs posts.

She was grateful for the warm nightdress she had packed, lying in her cold bed, watching as the moon, through tall windows, threw shadows on the quilt. As the old house settled for the night, its floorboards creaking, she began thinking how she might escape her Belfast flat. Edward's friends might be eminently forgettable but he had contacts. Maybe he could find her somewhere?

In the morning, everyone was up early for breakfast. William had recently purchased a small herd of deer who were doing their best to escape. Edward and Paul were noisily wolfing down their breakfasts before leaving to spend the day mending fences. Given this *fait accompli*, Lena decided to spend time with Margaret, hoping to learn more about her son. They took their coffees to a quiet pool of sunshine in a cosy room next to the kitchen and Margaret began talking about Edward.

'He was always near the top of his class at school. He's never given us a moment's bother, except for that discussion over university. You know he plays the piano?'

'Yes, exceptionally well. Why didn't he study music at university?'

'How could he with this house, the law firm and the hotels to mind? William wanted him to take law but they compromised and Edward took business studies instead so at least he could manage the hotels,' she said.

This did not sound like much of a compromise to Lena.

'But,' said Margaret, 'you and I know what Edward loves doing best, don't we?'

Do we? thought Lena, leaning forward.

'It's his commitment to the UDR that really motivates him,' said Margaret. 'The IRA killed a UDR man not far from here just three months ago. And look at Edward now – out with Paul miles from anywhere. It scares me half to death.'

Lena realised with a jolt that Margaret was talking about the possibility of Edward being murdered. Today. But no one knew where he was, other than the family. It seemed a bit dramatic.

'Edward won't speak about it so I can only guess the danger he faces every time he puts on his uniform. The IRA lie in wait for patrols or sneak up on farmers on tractors in the fields. Tradesmen would be a problem for us if it wasn't for the Wilsons. They know every family from here to Enniskillen. At least I have no worries about who's doing the plumbing or electrics.'

Margaret, Lena realised, felt marooned in a sea of hostile enemies, despite her family's obvious wealth and influence. Whether or not she was exaggerating, it was sincerely felt.

'But, my dear, I'm sure you understand,' she ended. 'Your father and my husband are friends from their days in Kenya. It was like that there too, farmers worrying about being picked off in their fields.'

How could you compare the two? Lena wondered. After lunch, she borrowed Margaret's car and drove into Enniskillen. Staring across the dark grey expanses of Lough Erne, it was difficult to believe Margaret's account of danger lurking behind every hedge. It was so peaceful and, frankly, deserted. In the town, she bought a cream towelling dressing-gown from an old-fashioned department store. Before dinner back at Gordon Hall, Edward suggested they view a newly built stable block. In the courtyard outside, they were alone for the first time since the drive from Belfast.

'So you considered studying music at university,' she said.

'I suppose Mother told you. Does it matter?'

'It matters that you have no real interest in the hotel business.'

'It takes money to keep this place going. You can't make a living playing the piano. I'm an only child. I have to take my parents' views into account.'

'What about your own views? It's not easy – but possible – to make a living from music. It's certainly a lot more difficult to spend your life doing something you don't really care about.'

'Well, maybe, but I didn't know that at eighteen.'

'Your mother seems to be living in fear of an imminent IRA attack.'

'She never talks to me about it but I'm not surprised. You probably think she's exaggerating. She might be, but not by much. Fermanagh has always been contested territory.'

'But this place has been in your family for generations.'

'Sometimes we still feel we don't belong,' he said. 'I'm glad you're learning more about the family, they all seem to like you.'

With that, he reached out and put a hand on her shoulder. To her huge surprise, he then roughly pulled her towards him and kissed her forehead. During the brief embrace, she was grateful the darkness hid her astonishment.

'We should join my parents and Paul in the library,' he said softly, his arms still around her shoulders. Nervous about his parents' reaction, Lena stepped quickly ahead of him through the kitchen door and walked into the library first. She badly needed a diversion to give her time to analyse this astonishing, but welcome, development. Noticing a baby grand piano tucked into a corner, she asked Edward to play.

'Play what you played for me before,' she asked. 'Play "My Lagan Love".'

Edward frowned but walked to the piano while Lena sat down beside his father, telling herself sternly that what had just happened was a friendly hug that meant little or nothing. The lovely tune rose from the piano, permeating every corner of the room. They all stopped talking, although William, she noted, stared into the fire, unsmiling. When Edward finished, she turned to him saying quietly, 'Your son is a very talented player.'

'There's no living in it,' Gordon replied gruffly, keeping his eyes on the fire.

'I wouldn't be so sure,' she said. 'Few people play with as much controlled intensity as Edward. He's practically concert standard.'

Gordon's frown deepened. It was clearly unfinished business between father and son. She changed the subject, asking Paul about the deer fencing. Later, in bed, she relived Edward's touch on her shoulder, the brief kiss on her forehead. It was probably just a brief gesture between two people whose fathers had once been friends. She would not be idiotic and make anything of it. Then her mind moved to Margaret's disturbing fears. If there was that depth of hostility between neighbours, a hate that crossed the line into actual violence, what caused and sustained it?

On Sunday morning, they all went to church. The inside of the small, white-washed building was decorated only with a few ragged union flags and wall plaques commemorating long-dead soldiers. The Church of Ireland congregation of about forty souls included Paul's family, who sat halfway down the aisle. The Gordons, naturally, had their own pew at the front, immediately below the pulpit.

'Oh God, our help in ages past,' they lustily sang, 'Our hope for years to come, Our shelter from the stormy blast, And our eternal home.'

It was one of Lena's favourite hymns, but the congregation almost shouted the words – not so much a hymn of praise as a defiant declaration. An elderly minister then gave a short and almost unintelligible sermon. How different, she thought, from Little Woldham where the blue-robed choir sang like angels, the light poured in through stained-glass windows and people openly admired her father's erudite little speeches from the pulpit – more of a social event than a religious sacrament.

After lunch, it was time for the homeward drive to Belfast. William had decided to stay an extra night in Fermanagh with Margaret and, after farewells, Lena and Edward drove the eighty miles back to Belfast in companionable silence, arriving at Malone Road as darkness fell. He parked up, dropped her suitcase at the front door and returned to where she stood beside the car, waiting to say goodbye. Without hesitation, however, he put his hands firmly on her shoulders and pulled her towards him. Lena was more prepared this time and lifted a reciprocating arm. They kissed deeply. As they came up for air, he held her tight against his chest for a few seconds before letting go. She waited to see what he would say next.

'I'm on UDR duty in Fermanagh on Wednesday, but I'll be in the office as usual to see Dad on Friday. Will you be there?'

'I think there's every possibility,' she said and then, fearing she sounded negative, 'I'll look forward to it. That was a lovely weekend.'

She was floating on air as she reached the upstairs apartment.

3

Lena woke smiling that Monday morning before noticing an urgency in the radio presenter's usual placid intonation. Something was up.

'BBC Radio Ulster news at seven o'clock. The RUC has just confirmed that two British soldiers and a member of the UDR were killed in an overnight explosion in County Fermanagh. There are unconfirmed reports that police found a command line crossing the border between Swanlinbar in the Republic and Lisnaskea. The two British soldiers were based at Grosvenor Barracks in Enniskillen while the UDR man is believed to be from Irvinestown.'

Lena froze – she and Edward had driven that road just the previous afternoon. 'The attack,' the newsreader went on, 'has been strongly condemned by the Prime Minister, Margaret Thatcher, while the Ulster Unionist MP for Fermanagh/South Tyrone, Ken Maginnis, says he will be demanding an expansion of the UDR's role when he meets her later today. The DUP's Willie McCrea says he wants what he calls "the gloves" taken off the UDR.'

A short clip followed of the DUP leader, Ian Paisley, calling for 'IRA nesting places' to be 'cleaned out' in towns Lena had never heard of – 'Buncrana, Bundoran, Clones, and Drogheda'. If Ulster were ruled by the Israelis, Paisley said, there would have already been retaliatory air raids 'as far south as Cork'.

Lena lay in bed as the bulletin continued, imagining

the shock waves in Colchester or Catterick or wherever the British soldiers had been based. There would be public funerals followed by decades of private grief for the widows and children.

This was why Edward was out in the dark patrolling in the evenings and weekends. She had seen him checking under his car, dropping to one knee like an automaton, presumably looking for bombs. How could she and Martin Porter possibly have joked about the IRA? Suddenly the Troubles were no longer theoretical, confined to radio bulletins and newspapers. Sure, the daily diet of bombings and shootings was depressing, but now, for the first time, she felt real, personal fear. Barely was one victim buried than another was killed. The deadpan voices of the local newsreaders made the appalling attacks seem even more futile, as did the heartbreaking TV reports showing sobbing widows clutching the hands of bemused toddlers at their fathers' funerals. None of the single murders made headlines in Britain. Only if there were multiple killings did they feature on the television news. Hamilton, she thought, was right to say the IRA must be defeated. As for the loyalists, they were nothing short of barbaric with their alphabet soup of acronyms, UDA, UVF. Who gave tuppence for their pretentious, stupid names?

On the phone to Georgie later in the day, she talked over her weekend in Fermanagh. 'You heard about those three soldiers killed last night? Edward lives very close. It's lovely countryside and everything seems normal at first. Then you start noticing little differences – not so little, really. Do we wonder if our neighbours in Hampshire harbour murderous intentions?'

'Of course we don't.'

'Do we wonder if the electrician fixing the lights is looking for a safe exit after shooting us? Or that the gardener is scouting an escape route while he's pruning the roses?'

Georgina muttered an obligatory 'How awful', just as Lena herself would have done a couple of months ago. Now she was so angry she pressed on.

'Do we know exactly, I mean to the nearest foot, where the border lies between Hampshire and Wiltshire? Not only do these people know exactly where what they call "the frontier" is, they honestly believe murderers are lurking across it planning to kill them.'

'Never mind Lena, you'll be home in six months,' said Georgina. 'How are you and Edward getting on?'

'Heavens, Georgie, the soldiers being killed put it out of my mind but I actually think he might be interested.'

'Then it's just as I predicted. You're an intelligent, attractive young woman who's unafraid of him. Of course, he's interested, darling.'

The following day, sitting on her desk, she found a pile of unfamiliar box files. The promised new case had come at last. She ran to find out more from Geraldine.

'What's it about?'

'He's a loyalist, a UDA man. Even you may have heard of him. Darren Barrett. A clown with a mouth as big as Lough Neagh. He's on remand, so you'll have to visit Crumlin Road Gaol to get the full story.'

'Nobody in Belfast ever gives me the full story, Geraldine. But thanks.'

Her new client was one of the sixteen defendants

facing trial on the supergrass evidence of Leonard 'Snowy' White – the case that she, Brendan Casey and Geoffrey Hamilton had debated at Queen's. Barrett had a string of previous drug convictions as well as a nasty reputation for street fighting. The medical reports said he 'showed psychopathic traits'. He was now charged with killing a Catholic 'bread-server' in North Belfast ten years ago. Bread-server? Lena wondered. Must be like milkmen at home. She devoured the case files all morning until Gordon arrived back from Fermanagh.

'I'm dreadfully sorry about the news,' she told him, not knowing what else to say. 'It's truly shocking.'

Gordon's face was as grey as his hair.

'I stayed on to visit the barracks in Enniskillen, to pass on the deepest regrets of the community. Edward is most distressed. He knew the Irvinestown man.'

'It's just awful,' Lena said helplessly.

'I despise that windbag Willie McCrea,' said Gordon, 'but we're going to have to do something to protect ourselves. The RUC haven't got the capacity on their own to stop the murdering vermin.'

Lena wondered what he meant by 'protecting ourselves' but, after a suitably respectful moment, changed the subject.

'I hate to mention it at a moment like this, but Geraldine has passed me the new case. Can I have a word with you about it?'

'Ah, yes,' said Gordon, his slumped head jerking up. 'Darren Barrett, one of Gavin Buchanan's cases. He normally handles the loyalist ones, but he's about to retire and it's going to drag on a while yet. You should have a word with him. Barrett is a rather unpleasant man, I'm afraid, but you did ask for a Troubles-related case.'

In the afternoon, Lena ran across to Belfast Central Library to read every newspaper report she could find featuring her new client. Barrett was sniffing glue by the time he was fourteen and had enlisted in a flute band rejoicing in the name 'The Shankill Young Conquerors', which – so the newspapers said – was, in effect, the youth wing of the UDA. Surprisingly, he had then nearly turned his life around by becoming a body-builder, attracting an agent under whose influence he had sculpted himself into a tattooed caricature. For the next five years, Barrett had taken part in lucrative wrestling contests across Scotland and England, becoming known as 'The Shankill Stinger', even appearing on Saturday night television. A broken leg, resulting from a fight outside a bar on the Shankill Road, had kept him off the wrestling circuit, however, and he had fallen back into his old ways before reaching his current nadir, a twelve-by-seven-foot cell in Crumlin Road Gaol.

Buchanan, when she spoke to him the following morning, added little other than Barrett's convictions were mostly for small-time drug dealing in cannabis and amphetamines. Barrett was an impossible optimist, he said, always believing he would escape legal retribution despite clear evidence to the contrary. Unless Leonard White, the loyalist-turned-Queen's evidence, withdrew his testimony, said Buchanan, 'and there's no sign of that,' the RUC could comfortably keep him and his fifteen co-defendants off the streets on remand in jail for months. Lena listened in deferential silence before returning to study the files. She knew she had to move carefully. If she fouled this case up, it could be her last. The only strategy she could think of was the obvious: challenge the sole evidence against him – the uncorroborated word of Leonard 'Snowy' White. She would dig into his past to find out more.

Political opposition to the new supergrass tactic, she already knew, had been tried and failed. The 'moderate, constitutional' SDLP was calling it 'internment by another name', but their objections fell on stony ground in London where the only priority seemed to be reducing the weekly kill rate. Sinn Féin's objections, needless to say, were similarly ignored as mere propaganda on behalf of the IRA, its 'armed wing'. To date, the judges appeared content to wait until the first full trial when they could properly assess the supergrass evidence. Snowy was not the only informer. There were other cases in the pipeline, mainly where the defendants and their accusers were from the republican side. Features in the Belfast newspapers were already speculating that, if the RUC and the Director of Public Prosecutions succeeded in using Snowy as a credible witness, it could be a turning point. Many of the leading paramilitary players were already in jail awaiting trial and there was a significant downturn in the number of both loyalist and republican paramilitary attacks. There was clearly a lot more at stake here than Barrett's liberty. Lena decided to meet him.

Buttoning her coat tight against a wind whistling down from Divis Mountain, she drove the following afternoon to Crumlin Road Gaol. In the cramped legal block, there were already several other solicitors holding *sotto voce* meetings with their clients. Lena waited, as calmly as possible, for Barrett to arrive. She caught herself wondering what someone might look like whose heart was so pitch-black he would sneak up on a defenceless fellow human and shoot him dead. But, she quickly reminded herself, Barrett's guilt or innocence was for the courts to establish, not her. The door opened and in came a bull-necked warder followed by the equally tough-looking Barrett. He was limping slightly but it didn't stop him swinging a leg dramatically over the bench on his side of the table, giving her an unwanted eyeful of his crotch. Lena cast a quick eye over her new client. He was, as she had anticipated, a shaven-headed, heavily-tattooed, muscular man straight out of central casting.

'Hello, doll. So, you're Buchanan's replacement,' he opened.

'How do you do Mr Barrett. My name is Eleanor Dawson. Pleased to meet you. As you can hear, I am English, but I am fully apprised of your case. Perhaps you can begin by telling me your understanding of how it stands?'

'Miss Dawson – it is Miss isn't it? – we have an hour together but you'll be gone in five minutes if we talk about my case and that would be a shame. For me, anyhow. I don't have many visitors.'

'This is not a social call, Mr Barrett. I am here to discuss your legal situation. I have other work waiting for me back in the office. If you choose not to give me your thoughts, I can leave. On the other hand, we might discuss how to get you acquitted.'

'For all I know, you could be one of those lefty English

do-gooders who think the poor Catholics are downtrodden and the IRA are the good guys.'

'My views on the IRA and the organisation with which you are allegedly connected have no bearing on you as my client.'

'What do you think of Ian Paisley then?'

'My views on him are also irrelevant. You're facing a murder charge, Mr Barrett. That's what I am here to discuss.'

'There's no one over in your bloody parliament can hold a candle to Paisley, but you all think you're bloody superior, so you do.'

Lena, simultaneously shocked and amused, tried to hide a smile by leaning under the table to lift documents out of her briefcase. Barrett, however, had noticed her reaction and his mood darkened. He had a short fuse.

'Don't you dare laugh. You lot haven't got a fucking clue. You think you know what's going on over here but what do you care about the IRA blowing up women and children?'

Lena decided the only sensible response was to become more distant, professional.

'Mr Barrett, I share your outrage at violence – and these are clearly difficult and important matters – but we are not here to discuss them. I'm here to talk to you about the charges you face – very serious charges. Your statement in the file says you're innocent and the evidence against you is untrue. Tell me about that instead. I am here to listen and to help.'

Barrett grunted and settled down.

'The charge against you,' Lena continued, 'is that you

attacked, in fact you shot dead, a Catholic bread-delivery man in September 1979.'

'I'm no angel, so I'm not, but I didn't kill him. I'm not sorry he's dead, mind. He deserved to be shot. But I didn't kill him. The UDA will back me up – go and ask them.'

'I don't think a UDA denial will have much credibility with the judges or the Director of Public Prosecutions.'

'The only evidence against me is from Snowy White who broke my bloody leg three years ago. He's a lying bastard and the police know it. He'll say anything they want to make sure I rot in here. He knows what's coming to him if I ever get out.'

Trying to ingratiate himself, Barrett leaned in and lowered his voice.

'You're English. We're on the same side. I bet you have brains to burn. Beauty *and* brains. I'd court you myself, so I would.'

Lena managed to keep a straight face.

'Let's discuss bail,' she said. 'We can try to convince a judge that the evidence against you is so weak that you have every incentive to turn up and challenge it at your trial. White is, as you say, already safely tucked away somewhere so the Crown cannot claim you could interfere with his evidence. How does bail sound to you?'

Suddenly, Barrett was pathetically grateful, pumping her hand and leaning over the desk so close she could smell the mint from his chewing gum.

'Buchanan never told me anything like that.'

'When it comes to the committal, we can argue Snowy's evidence is false,' she said.

'What's a committal?' he asked.

'That's when a judge decides if there's sufficient evidence against you to justify a trial in the higher court.'

Lena reached for her briefcase under the table to end the meeting, but Barrett hadn't finished.

'Would you ask my mother to visit? Her name's Sharon. She lives just behind the courthouse. She's sending my letters back unopened. I can't stand that she won't come and see me.'

Oh heavens, thought Lena, they all love their sainted mothers. Delivering messages was certainly not her job, but it was a chance to find out more about Snowy so she agreed and left. Belfast's rush-hour fumes seemed fragrant compared to the dank air inside the jail as she walked the two minutes to Sharon Barrett's house in the Lower Shankill estate where crude depictions of various paramilitary leaders snarled down from the gable walls. Mrs Barrett's front garden was at least tidy with primulas in pots on the doorstep. Lena walked up to the front door, knocked and turned round to take a closer look at the neighbourhood. As she waited, two tough-looking young men walked past – giving her hostile stares. Lena waited a second or two and then shouted through the letterbox.

'Mrs Barrett? My name is Lena Dawson. I'm your son's solicitor. Darren says he had nothing to do with the shooting. Can I give you a message?'

'Not a mission. Away on,' came the riposte through the closed door.

Lena waited a few moments and turned to walk away but, as she closed the squeaking garden gate, she heard a woman's voice behind her.

'You've got five minutes.'

Inside, the tiny house was clean, warm and tidy. After settling Lena on a sofa in the over-furnished living room, Sharon went into the kitchen to make tea.

'I'm going to try and get him released on bail pending his trial,' said Lena, balancing tea and scones on her knees.

'I'm sorry the way Darren turned out. The schools around here are useless. We get everyone else's leavings and those marching bands are a bad influence. I thought he was going to make something of the wrestling but the broken leg didn't help and the UDA had their claws in too deep by then. He's not a bad boy at heart.'

Lena made encouraging noises. Then she brought up the business in hand.

'Mrs Barrett, what do you know about Leonard White, the man who's turned Queen's evidence, the informer? You might have known him as Lenny when he was a kid. The name he has on the street is Snowy.

'Everyone round here says there's wiser eating grass, love.'

It took Lena a second or two to figure out what she meant and she hid a smile before carrying on.

'If we can challenge Snowy's credibility, we might have a chance of getting Darren acquitted.'

'All the men around here rabbit on about "defending the area" but it's more a gang war than anything else,' said Sharon.

'Oh?' said Lena, encouragingly.

'Mind you, Lenny White didn't have it easy. Maureen, his mother, died when he was about twelve and, from what I hear, his father, Graham, wasn't much use. Lenny was bullied rotten at school and I'm afraid my Darren joined in.'

'Your Darren has made quite a name for himself as a fighter.'

'He certainly did, until Snowy White broke his leg.'

'How did that happen?'

'A fight outside some bar. Lenny's mob were from up near Ardoyne and my Darren is from here, the Lower Shankill. It doesn't take much to get them fighting. They were fighting even before they left school.'

'How did Darren and Snowy get on – that is between the fight and Darren being charged and jailed on remand?'

'Darren vowed, even before he left hospital, to get Snowy back. It was the old school vendetta between the two of them, just a lot worse.'

So, Lena thought, Barrett had openly threatened revenge on Snowy for wrecking his wrestling career. A piece of potentially useful information.

'What about your own husband? Billy, isn't it? I know you're separated but does he know the White family?'

'I think Billy played in the same flute band as Lenny's father back in the day.'

'Where might I find Billy?'

'I'm glad to say I don't know. He used to spend Saturday afternoons in "The Jubilee Bar" at the bottom of the Shankill. Probably still does. He watches Man United there with his mates.'

'That's very helpful. There is just one more thing. It would help Darren if I told the court he could live here, supposing he was bailed pending his trial.'

'You can give the court my address, but Darren won't stay here for long. And to tell you the truth, I don't think I could put up with him for more than a few days.'

'Thanks Sharon. That will do. Also, will you read Darren's letters? He wanted me to ask.'

'I might. I'll not be visiting him in that place, mind. Filthy dump.'

'I don't much like the jail myself, Sharon,' she said.

As Lena walked back to her car away from the tidy little house on the Lower Shankill, her stomach full of tea and buttered soda bread, she realised she had warmed to Barrett's mother. A possible defence was also slowly forming in her head. If Snowy wanted Barrett out of circulation, it would have made him more susceptible to RUC suggestions. The defence might suggest to the court that Snowy's evidence was compromised by a desire to put Barrett behind bars to avoid retribution for the broken leg. Surely, though, Gavin Buchanan would have already looked into all that?

As Lena drove back to the High Street office that Wednesday afternoon, Edward and Paul were eighty miles away, walking behind the coffin of the Irvinestown UDR man the IRA had killed on the border. Unable to contain his curiosity, Paul began fishing for information.

'Lena seems to like Fermanagh,' he said. 'She says she'd like to take a boat out on Lough Erne this summer.'

'We'll have to arrange that,' said Edward, reluctant to discuss personal matters at a funeral. During the service, however, his mind wandered. Lena was the first person who had ever suggested he might have defied his father and studied music, something that still preyed on his mind. She seemed very self-reliant. Maybe she thought him weak-willed? He felt as if he was on the top platform of a diving tower, looking down at a small square of blue water far below. But he would definitely be jumping.

Lena, meanwhile, was preoccupied with winning Barrett bail. On Friday, before heading to court, she remembered Sullivan's advice about publicity and phoned David Murray to tip him off. The Shankill Stinger, she reckoned, made for good news copy, even without the supergrass angle.

As she took her place in the courtroom, Hamilton, who was Crown prosecuting counsel in the case, was already sitting at the other end of the legal bench, acknowledging her presence with the slightest nod.

'Your worship,' Lena began, making full use of the *de facto* advantage her English accent gave her, 'I appear for Mr Barrett. The sole evidence against my client comes from a man who the police have in protective custody. That man's whereabouts are unknown to the defence, so there is no possibility that my client could interfere with his evidence.'

She saw Hamilton's head lifting. He had not anticipated any need for further argument on the Crown's behalf that Barrett should remain behind bars awaiting trial.

'On the defence side,' Lena carried on, 'we are eagerly awaiting the committal when we hope to produce evidence to challenge the credibility of the prosecution's chief witness. Given that there is no incentive or opportunity for my client to either abscond or interfere with witnesses, we respectfully ask that he be granted bail.'

The judge seemed uncomfortable, shifting in his seat and asking supplementary questions of the Crown side – but Hamilton had nothing substantial to add. After a decent interval, he had no alternative but to reluctantly announce he was granting bail, under the strictest of conditions. Barrett would be curfewed dusk to dawn, live at his mother's address, check in daily at Tennent Street RUC station and avoid his usual UDA drinking haunts. Lena avoided Hamilton's glare as she left to meet an ecstatic Barrett downstairs in the holding cells.

'There are two things I have to tell you, Darren, and if you don't listen, we will both be in deep trouble. Firstly, you are not to speak to anybody connected to this case – anyone at all. Are we on the same page here?'

'Yes, sure.' Barrett was itching to get out. He would have said yes to anything.

'That particularly includes Snowy's father, Graham White. If you see him by chance in the street or anywhere else, turn around and go home immediately. Secondly, there may be a photographer and a reporter outside here when we leave but you are to say absolutely nothing that might influence your trial.'

The two of them then walked together out of Crumlin Road Courthouse where David Murray, some photographers and a couple of local TV crews were waiting for The Shankill Stinger. Barrett stuck his chest out and gave his best impression of a UDA hard man for the photographers but waved questions away with a chubby fist. Lena restricted herself to saying that she and her client were looking forward to challenging the prosecution evidence when it came to trial. When the evening edition of *The Belfast Independent* was delivered to William Gordon's office later that afternoon, a slow smile spread across his face. Maybe he had been wrong about George Dawson's daughter. Lena's face now adorned the front page behind Barrett's bulk under the banner headline 'Stinger in Bail Shock'. He called Geraldine into his office.

'Look,' he said, pointing to the front page. 'Do we have a scrapbook?'

'I don't think we do, sir.'

'Then go out and buy one.'

When Edward arrived in the office, Lena was basking in William's praise. Life was definitely looking up.

Unbeknownst to her, however, someone other than William Gordon was drawn to the late edition of that Friday's *Belfast Independent*. In the West Belfast 'Felons' Club' – so named because only former prisoners can join – Luke Maguire, once dubbed 'Britain's Most Wanted', was staring at the same front page. He even put his mug of tea down and put on his glasses for a closer look. Barrett's massive shoulders and bald head dominated, but Maguire was more interested in the dark-haired woman in the background. He glanced at the caption: 'Darren Barrett and his solicitor, Eleanor Dawson, of Gordon & Company, speaking to the press outside Crumlin Road Courthouse'.

'Who the hell is Eleanor Dawson, Peadar?' Maguire asked his companion. 'I know the name of every solicitor in this town, and she's not one of Gordon's usual underlings.'

He passed the newspaper across the table.

'So, they bailed that murdering ape. To be expected, I suppose,' said Peadar.

'No, not expected, Peadar. That wasn't in their plan at all. Who's this woman here, in the picture, behind Barrett?'

'I saw her on the news. English. Voice you could slice roast beef with.'

'English? So she's new to our legal eccentricities and still managed to get Barrett out of jail.'

'The Crown generally gets what it wants.'

'Well, they didn't want Barrett out on bail. If she's prepared to take on the courts and the judges for a neanderthal like him, she could do the same for us.'

'Are you still on about your brother's inquest? It's the road to no-town.'

'That's because our lawyers cave too easily, Peadar. That woman – Dawson – maybe she won't.'

'Wise up. You'll never get justice in a British court.'

'Maybe not, but I'm damn well going to try, even just for Sinéad's sake. She fought like a tiger for Danny when I was in jail. That's what probably caused her heart to pack up. Now it's my turn. I'll phone this Miss Dawson straight after the bank holiday.'

Unaware of the Felons' Club's existence, let alone that her future was being debated there, Lena was meeting Edward at the Gordon Central, diplomatically expressing her sympathy for the death of the Irvinestown UDR man.

'He had three kids under ten,' said Edward. 'It's about time the government listened to people on the ground in Fermanagh rather than the idiots they ship in from London.'

After a suitably respectful pause, Lena tentatively broached the subject of her living arrangements.

'I'm grateful, of course, for the flat on the Malone Road but it's hardly ideal.'

'What's wrong with it?' he asked, surprised.

'It's tiny, even compared to my apartment in London. You'd be trying to find somewhere else too, if you'd spent a night there.'

'Well, surely,' he grinned, 'but then I've never been asked.'

'I'll ignore that remark,' she replied, her heart missing a beat.

'What are you looking for?' he asked.

'Somewhere with character, reliable central heating, a spare room for an office, maybe a garden, preferably in the country, within an hour's drive of Belfast.'

'Not much then. I'll do a ring round. Are you free to drive to Fermanagh tomorrow? It's a bank holiday weekend.'

A second invitation to Fermanagh, so soon after the first, was effectively an official announcement. Her heart sang. On Saturday morning, however, he rang with news that a friend working in Canada was thinking of renting out his home in County Down.

'We'll cancel Fermanagh and view this place later today if you want,' he said. 'You could move in tomorrow. Monday's a bank holiday so plenty of time to settle in.'

Half-an-hour later, they were driving south through the undulating hills of County Down before Edward turned into a gateway where stood a small, two-storey cottage with a tall brick chimney, surrounded by bushes. Lena took a deep breath of cool air as she got out of the car. This can't be far from the sea, she thought, hoping the building wasn't damp. The front door opened into a quarry-tiled hallway. One door led into a cosy, furnished living room with a wood-burner and French windows onto a back garden. A second door in the hallway led into a small kitchen, while upstairs there were two bedrooms, one larger than the other, and a shower room. There were views through the back windows of fields and hedges. Strangford Lough glinted on the horizon to the east and in the distant south stood the Mourne Mountains.

'I suppose I should ask where we are,' she said as they both stood in the kitchen looking out towards the lough.

'Glenbarry,' he said. 'Just a townland – not even a village. There's only a small shop. It's two miles to the lough and about five to the nearest village, Killyleagh. I was at school with the guy who owns it – quantity surveyor, name of Niall Harrison.'

'I'm not even going to ask what the rent is. I'll take it.'

'I'll call Niall later,' he said. 'It's too early for Toronto. Let's drive to Newcastle and get something to eat.'

After lunch, they drove to the Mourne Mountains and walked around the Silent Valley Reservoir. Geraldine was right, she decided, it was a magical place. Edward knew the names of the individual peaks and spoke of them as if they were old friends – Shimna, Binnian, Slieve Donard, Ben Crom. In England, she thought, a place like the Silent Valley would be full of hikers and tourists. There would be pubs and burger vans. Here, there was just the strong east wind, wide-open spaces and the hugest boulders she had ever seen, piled up into walls dividing the fields. Back at the apartment in Belfast, still unsure of how Edward felt and anxious not to put him on the spot, she leapt from the car, saying she'd see him in the morning.

On Sunday, it didn't take them long to carry her few boxes into his Range Rover.

'I got you a house-warming present,' he said, opening a door to reveal a large television set on the back seat. 'Even we hotel managers have our occasional uses.'

'Will I ever be forgiven for that jibe?' Lena asked, before getting into her Mini and following him away from the Malone Road. Once her belongings were inside the Glenbarry cottage, he plugged in the TV and sprawled on the sofa watching a rugby match as she unpacked. Coming downstairs, she noticed a ginger cat rubbing itself against the French windows.

'I forgot to say,' Edward called to her from the sofa. 'Niall Harrison says the cat comes with the cottage. The next-door farm has been feeding it. He hopes that's okay.'

'It'll have to be. What's its name?'

'Haven't a clue. Do cats have names?'

'I'll call it Peanut. It's the colour of peanuts.'

She opened a tin of tuna, put it down for the hungry animal and they stood together watching it eat. By the time she finished unpacking, the cat had made itself at home, lying on the back of the sofa, nuzzling Edward's neck.

In the evening, they found a pub in Killyleagh that served food. As the meal progressed over a bottle of wine, it struck Lena that it was extremely unlikely that Edward would be dropping her off at the cottage and driving back to Belfast. He had said nothing, asked for nothing, but she had to assume he intended staying the night. She began to wonder what to expect. Her previous encounters had mostly been with English lawyers who made love elegantly but self-consciously – almost distantly. She rather hoped Edward would be different. Back at the cottage, they watched the ten o'clock news, sitting beside each other on the sofa, his arm reaching behind her shoulders, gently edging out the cat who settled in an armchair. As the programme switched to local news, she felt his fingertips moving very slowly under her collar and brushing against her right shoulder. Then he leaned towards her and his mouth glanced the nape of her neck. She shifted slightly to look at him and he gently lifted her chin. Here we go, she thought, I wasn't imagining it. As his arms tightened further, she gently broke away, saying softly, 'Not here.'

Standing up, she drew him towards the staircase and, once upstairs, began unbuttoning his shirt before they fell onto the bed, half-clothed.

'Close your eyes,' he whispered, authoritatively. Lena leaned back onto the pillows as he kissed, first, her forehead and cheeks with a control that he abandoned as she responded. Typical of first couplings, she decided later, what it lacked in elegance it made up for in enthusiasm, but that was okay. It had been a long time since she had been enfolded in strong, male arms. Afterwards, he held her close and murmured endearments before falling asleep and she gently disentangled herself. When he turned, she stretched herself against his broad, warm back, perfectly content. In the morning, she crept out of bed to shower, returning to the bedroom wrapped in a towel which he playfully tugged.

'You can find your own towel in the bathroom and some of your friend Niall's clothes in a box in the other bedroom,' she said. 'You're about the same size. I'm going out to get the makings of breakfast.'

By the time she returned, he was dressed. After breakfast, they read the papers and she set up a study in the smaller bedroom. In the afternoon, they walked along the shores of Strangford Lough, both trying to get used to their sudden intimacy. At dinner in Killyleagh, the atmosphere was relaxed enough for Edward to ask why she had chosen to come to Belfast. He didn't imagine it was a popular posting.

'I had an overwhelming desire to get out of London.'

'Why on earth was that?'

'I'll try and make this short. Did your father ever tell you about the Nakuru affair during the Mau Mau uprising when they were both in Kenya?'

'No. Do explain.'

'In the 1950s, my father was climbing the ranks, until a junior soldier told him he'd witnessed the unprovoked killing of four unarmed local people at a place called Nakuru. Dad raised concerns and it sparked a full-scale inquiry.'

'How to throw a career away,' Edward said drily.

'The soldiers involved left the service but, although there were no convictions, Dad's name was toxic. He left too so my mother was stuck with a blackballed outcast. Dad re-trained as a military chaplain which meant, from her viewpoint, being dragged from Kenya back to Britain and then on to Malaya, Cyprus and Germany.'

'Moving every three years between military billets,' Edward said.

'Dad came good in the end, sort of. He retired into a country vicar's position in Hampshire, which came with a cosy rectory.'

'And this made you want to leave London?'

'I'm getting there. Dad had high ambitions for me. He wanted me to be a barrister, standing up for the truth as he'd done at Nakuru – but for that you need a brass neck and I'm afraid mine is made of marshmallow.'

'But I heard you were head-hunted by David Braithwaite, another of my father's old army pals.'

'Untrue. That was the "Dad's Mafia". I was treading water at a solicitors' near home when Braithwaite called, offering me work in London. I was thrilled, flattered. I only found out later that Dad had twisted his arm, still wanting me to follow in his footsteps. At least it explained why everyone in the office resented me. So now you know my dirty little secret.'

Edward leaned over and squeezed her hand.

'Listen, Lena, if you weren't any good, you wouldn't have kept that job in London. Dad says you got a brilliant report from the US and you're already making waves here.'

'You were right that evening in Queen's,' Lena said mournfully. 'I run away from everything. I ran to New York to get away from London and now I've run away again.'

'Don't be so hard on yourself. You're not the only one to disappoint their father, Lena,' he said softly. 'I point-blank refused to take over the law firm to do this awful job with the hotels. Cheer up and let's go home and be imposters together.'

In the morning, Lena woke in bed, alone. She heard the front door closing and ran to the window. His car was at the gate, turning right for Belfast. He had left without a word. What the hell happens now, she wondered. Had her confession scared him off? He had been kind, of course, but he was probably used to high-flyers and over-achievers.

Downstairs, she began angrily shoving laundry into the washing machine and found his weekend clothes already lying there. Then she spotted a note on the kitchen table: 'Good morning, Bonnie. See you during the week. Love, Clyde.' She was still smiling when she arrived at High Street but one glance at Geraldine wiped that off her face.

'You look as if you've seen a ghost, Geraldine,' she said.

'Worse,' she said. 'Let's go into your office, Lena. I've something to tell you in private.'

Lena opened her office door, dumped her handbag on the desk and waited for Geraldine to start.

'I just had a phone call. Someone asking for you,' Geraldine began, then swallowed and continued. 'Have you heard of a man called Luke Maguire?'

Lena had indeed heard of Luke Maguire, most recently during the scene at Queen's. A police mugshot featuring his bearded face, arched eyebrows and defiant glare was familiar from newspapers and TV. She had heard his slow, ponderous voice hundreds of times on radio and television, the usual clichés tumbling out.

'What about Luke Maguire?'

'He rang here half an hour ago.'

Geraldine swallowed hard and carried on.

'I told him you weren't in yet. He said you should ring the Sinn Féin office on the Falls.'

'Did he indeed?'

Lena inclined her head towards Gordon's office and asked, 'Did you tell the boss?'

Geraldine shook her head. 'I thought it best not to,'

she said. 'You don't have to call him back. Maybe that would be best.'

'I suspect he's the sort of person who doesn't take "No" for an answer,' said Lena. 'He'll just keep ringing until I do. I'll get back to him tomorrow.'

'If he asks, please don't agree to meet him. It's not safe.'

'This isn't a banana republic, Geraldine. No one in Belfast attacks solicitors,' Lena said.

Geraldine placed a slip of paper on her desk with a phone number written on it.

'Please don't agree to anything until you've spoken to Mr Gordon. You could get into a pile of trouble.'

'Geraldine, please don't worry. Thanks for the advice but I had better get on with some work.'

Lena made no real attempt at work that morning. Instead, she returned to the Central Library at the top of Royal Avenue. Using the date of Maguire's most recent conviction, she sent for the relevant microfiche files, figuring that there would be post-trial profiles and backgrounders in the main newspapers. Barrett's file had not been pretty reading, but Maguire's was positively gruesome. The Sunday newspapers, in particular, were full of stories peppered with words like 'brutal', 'barbaric' and 'savage', referring to him as a 'godfather of terrorism', a 'ruthless, sectarian killer'. In 1974, she read, Maguire was convicted of 'possessing information likely to be of use to terrorists' and of arms offences. Sentenced to fifteen years in jail, he had survived fifty-five days on the 1981 hunger strike. He was still in jail in 1984 when his twin brother, Danny, was shot dead after crashing through a RUC roadblock but was released two years later, just before Christmas 1986. The newspapers said that Maguire was now transformed from an 'active paramilitary' to a 'Sinn Féin spokesman', cutting his hair and abandoning jeans and sweaters for trousers and jackets. According to the more recent reports he had also become 'cynically adept at fielding reporters' questions'. He was living, not in his hometown of Lurgan, North County Armagh, but in West Belfast.

Armed with this basic information, she returned to the office and, making sure the door was closed, rang the number Geraldine had given her. A gruff, male voice with a Belfast drawl answered the phone.

'*Dia duit.* Sinn Féin.'

'May I speak to Luke Maguire?'

'Who's asking?'

'Mr Maguire called me earlier, but I was out of the office, and he asked me to call back. Which I am doing.'

'And your name?'

'Eleanor Dawson.'

No response.

'If you prefer,' she said, 'we can end this conversation right now.'

'Wind your neck in, I'm trying to find him,' said the voice on the other end of the line.

She was on the point of putting the phone down when she heard a click and a new voice.

'Is that you Miss Dawson?'

The slow, deep voice was familiar from the TV. Lena steeled herself to continue.

'I believe you rang me earlier Mr Maguire.'

'I'd like to discuss a case with you.'

'When can you come to our office?'

'I won't be coming to your office. You'll have to come here.'

'I'm afraid that is not how it works, Mr Maguire. We hold initial consultations in our offices, unless the client is ill or in jail.'

'You're new to Belfast, aren't you? Do you have any idea how impossible it is for me, and how dangerous for you incidentally, if I came to see you?'

Oh, here we go, she thought, another drama queen.

'Really, Mr Maguire?'

'Really.'

A pause. She suspected William Gordon would not appreciate Luke Maguire turning up in his office so she said she was prepared to make an exception, 'just this once'.

'Three o'clock tomorrow then. You know our office. The one with the Bobby Sands mural.'

The following afternoon, Lena drove up the Falls Road, telling Geraldine she had a meeting at Crumlin Road Gaol. Aside from the political murals, it could be anywhere working class in England with the usual convenience stores on street corners. The only large building was the Royal Victoria Hospital, or RVH as everyone in Belfast called it. Stopped at traffic lights, she glanced up a side street of red-brick, one-up/one-down terraced houses. Women were sitting on their front doorsteps in the early summer sunshine. Lines of parallel white legs stretched out over the footpath as they shouted cheerfully across the roadway to each other. Kids played with balls and bicycles in scenes straight out of *Coronation Street*. The area was, she decided, marginally preferable to the modern white pebbledashes of the Lower Shankill. Before long, however, the influence of endemic violence became evident. Gigantic, white-painted rocks, almost the size of her red Mini, dotted the footpath outside the Sinn Féin office. She knew their purpose – to prevent car bombs from being parked too close to the building which was covered from footpath to roof in a protective wire cage. She rang the bell on the mesh gate. A man's voice crackled through an intercom system.

'Yes?'

'This is Eleanor Dawson to see Luke Maguire.'

A buzzing noise and then a loud click. The door in the cage opened smoothly and she stepped over a metal threshold before pushing on a heavy door in the brick gable wall. An elderly man was sitting at a small table in the dimly lit hallway, reading a newspaper. He stood up unsteadily and asked her to follow him down a narrow corridor. She passed an open door into what must once have been the front room of the house. It was packed with women and children. She had heard about Sinn Féin's daily bus runs to the Maze prison. This was the other Belfast – a world Lena had long suspected existed but had never before encountered, a world where prison, poverty and politics collided and people suffered.

Following the taciturn man into the front hallway, she nervously climbed up the stairs behind him with some difficulty, her heels occasionally sinking through the sticky carpet into rotten wood. The empty room she was shown into was papered in ragged posters with a threadbare carpet and a single-bar electric fire, despite the warm spring day.

'He'll be with you shortly,' the elderly man said before turning and closing the door behind him.

After what seemed a long wait, during which she tried self-consciously to focus on a crossword, the door opened again. Two men walked in, one introducing himself as Luke Maguire. Lena stood up and shook the bony hand he held out. The second man, introduced only by Maguire as 'Peadar', stood silently just inside the door. Maguire's unkempt dark hair and beard made his skin seem almost translucent.

'Thanks for coming,' Maguire said without sounding like he meant it.

'No thanks needed. I haven't done anything. To be clear, my presence implies no commitment and prospective clients don't usually keep me waiting.'

'Please sit down', he said, ignoring her complaint and placing a battered cardboard concertina file on the desk between them.

'I'm not even looking at that,' Lena said, 'until you tell me what this is about.'

Maguire sighed. 'My family is taking legal action on behalf of my twin brother, Danny, who was ambushed and shot dead, executed, by RUC Special Branch in 1984 near Drumfad in County Derry. We want you to help us. You'll find all the available background in that file.'

'Why me? You must have more experienced solicitors already acting for you.'

'You've just arrived from London and you'll doubtless be returning there before long. We reckon you've nothing to lose if you stir things up a bit. That's it for now. I'll leave the file with you. When you've decided what we should do next, ring me and we'll talk it over.'

'Don't be so precipitate Mr Maguire. I haven't decided yet if I will take on your case.'

'Well, you read the file and let us know. You have the office number if you need to contact me, but the phones here are bugged, so be careful what you say. Thanks again for coming in.'

This is going much too fast, Lena thought as Maguire stood up and headed for the door.

'I'll have to check with my head office,' she said. 'I presume you are not in a position to pay me. We'll have to check your legal aid status.'

Maguire said nothing but Peadar spoke over his shoulder as they left the room.

'Wait here for twenty minutes before going back to your car. If you try to leave any earlier, they'll stop you downstairs.'

And that was it. They were gone. Despite what she had just said, Lena found a curious hand straying towards the battered file. It seemed to be a jumble of newspaper cuttings along with statements sent to the coroner. The first cutting was the front page of *The Belfast Independent* dated 14 November 1984, headlined: 'Police Kill Two IRA Men'. It reported that two heavily armed IRA men had been shot and killed on a road outside Drumfad in south County Londonderry late the previous evening. Police said they had been forced to open fire in self-defence after a bronze Ford Fiesta car, laden with homemade explosives, had crashed through a roadblock. Both of the men's families had immediately claimed the RUC were involved in a 'shoot-to-kill' operation. A second article, also front page, this time from the nationalist-leaning *Irish Tribune*, dated the following day, 15 November, carried more detail about the two dead men who had not, after all, been transporting explosives. One was Danny

Maguire. The other was a younger man, Seán Reid. Both, it said, were known IRA men. Other articles, written in the days after the shooting, reported that the men had not, after all, been armed either. There were gloves in the car, but no trace of explosives. Both Sinn Féin and the SDLP were asking questions about the RUC opening fire. From inside jail, Luke Maguire had sent out a message backing his family's claim.

Ten days before the shooting, two young RUC men had been blown to pieces in an IRA culvert bomb on a laneway in Portglenone nearby, a mixed area not known for republican activity. They were both married with children, serving as community officers, answering a supposed emergency call from a woman being attacked by her partner. There was understandable political outrage. The Maguire family must have linked the two incidents as the file included accounts of their funerals, two white-faced widows, small children clutching their skirts, union flags draped over the coffins, against a backdrop of dark uniforms and grim-faced senior officers pledging to hunt down the killers. Within two weeks, Danny Maguire and Seán Reid were shot dead. As she finished reading the cuttings, the elderly man from downstairs returned to say she could leave, and Lena walked to her car.

As soon as she was back in the office, she began reading statements provided to the coroner's preliminary hearings. The police version of events seemed straightforward. The operation had been carried out by members of the RUC Headquarters Mobile Support Unit (or HMSU) which came under the aegis of Special Branch. It consisted of 48 men, half of whom had been trained by the SAS in Hereford in 'speed, firepower and aggression'. Its members were armed with rapid-firing automatic weapons. Six members of the unit had set up a joint RUC/UDR roadblock around 11.30 p.m. on Tuesday night, 13 November 1984, acting on intelligence that explosives were being moved in the area. The UDR patrol leader said the police had asked for military backup as Drumfad was known to be an area where the IRA operated. His soldiers had placed large metal warning signs saying 'STOP' prominently in the roadway, illuminated with red lighting. Once the hardware was in position, the UDR patrol had stood back, allowing uniformed RUC officers to assume primacy by stopping cars and questioning drivers.

In total, three RUC and three UDR jeeps had been involved, parked up on either side of the road. The police vehicles used their blue flashing lights to alert approaching cars to the roadblock, while the UDR patrol's headlights remained on. Two armed RUC men had taken up defensive positions, one on either side of the road, lying on the grass verges, their night sights focused on the roadway. The officer on the west side of the road was focused on cars coming north from the Randalstown direction – the one on the east focusing on cars travelling south from Drumfad.

Shortly before midnight, a car had come on the scene, driving north from Randalstown towards Drumfad. It had initially slowed but had then suddenly increased speed, said the statements, veering towards the officers on the left-hand side of the road. The police and the UDR men had shouted 'halt' repeatedly and had fired warning shots into the air but were forced to leap to safety. As the car slewed towards the grass verge on the left, the armed policeman lying there had opened fire in self-defence, intending to stop the car. The police officer lying on the right had not opened fire as to do so would have risked hitting his colleagues on the opposite side of the roadway.

Crown lawyers, in their opening statements to the pre-inquest hearings, stated the driver, Danny Maguire, a long-suspected IRA man, had ample warning to slow down and stop. He must have seen the blue and red lights, they said, even if he missed the warning shouts. Instead, he had deliberately steered the speeding car straight towards the police officers and soldiers on the left. The police officer who had opened fire made a split-second decision to shoot, probably saving the lives of his colleagues.

Seán Reid died at the scene, Maguire later in hospital. An RUC scenes-of-crime report produced for the inquest noted Seán Reid was found dead, slumped in the front passenger seat. Maguire, who was found half-in and half-out of the car, had been taken from the scene to hospital in an ambulance. A photo in the file showed the car, massively pock-marked with over 100 bullet holes on the passenger side of the vehicle.

As the news agenda moved on, the bereaved families had persisted in asking why the men had not been arrested. Why would an unarmed man drive straight at the police who, he must have known, were heavily armed and prepared to fire? They claimed that the roadblock was an ambush and that the 'execution' of the two men had been planned in revenge for the bomb that had killed the two young police officers in Portglenone. There was no evidence for this theory. Questions, certainly, Lena thought, but no answers.

A row had begun as soon as the inquest opened with the Crown side deciding to use a legal device called a public interest immunity (or PII) certificate that Lena had never encountered in the London courts, although she seemed to be reading about it repeatedly in the Belfast newspapers. Nationalist politicians were routinely referring to the PII certificates as 'gagging orders'.

She had asked William Gordon about their use and he had explained the orders had their origin in English common law, dating back centuries to 'Crown privilege' which conferred immunity on the sovereign. As amended more recently, he said, they allowed the state, in the form of a cabinet minister (such as the secretary of state for Northern Ireland) to withhold evidence in any legal proceedings if its disclosure would, arguably, compromise 'the public interest'. Although there were frequent tussles in the courts over whether the system was being extended to deliberately restrict public access to the names of state employees, such as police officers, Gordon was all for it.

'Can you imagine,' he had asked Lena, 'if court hearings led to the IRA finding out the names of every police officer who they claim had over-played their hand at protests and riots? Or of firing plastic bullet guns inappropriately? Their lives would immediately be at risk. No, no, no. That can't be allowed.'

'Some lawyers are calling them "gagging orders",' Lena had said.

'Absolute nonsense,' said Gordon. 'There are safeguards against abuse. A court first has to decide whether the public's demand for justice trumps the national interest in keeping the identities of some witnesses confidential.

There's an appeal process. It's all above board.'

A niggling voice had nevertheless prompted Lena to ask if it was appropriate in the twentieth century to use some ancient bit of common law (originally intended to confer immunity on a British monarch) to allow police officers to hide their identities and exonerate them from explaining why they had killed unarmed men. She had decided, however, on this occasion, to defer to 'Porter's Law' and say nothing.

The families' lawyers had also protested that, of the thirty-nine security force personnel on the official witness list, they had sight of only four statements by the time the case went to the Appeal Court to rule on the anonymity and exoneration issues.

Lena was immediately absorbed – fascinated by what she was reading. Why had the RUC press office told journalists the men were armed and dangerous when it was highly probable that, in time, the truth would emerge? Could the men in the car not have been arrested? Was the shooting legitimate self-defence?

An Amnesty International report, dating back to 1972, was attached to the file stating soldiers and police could open fire only 'if there is no other way to protect yourself, or those whom it is your duty to protect, from the danger of being killed or seriously injured' – but this was no blanket exemption from civil law. The families' lawyers, of course, had rejected the use of PIIs but the coroner had sided with the Crown, as did the High Court in a subsequent legal challenge, whereupon the families' lawyers had appealed. Media interest in the case had waned as the inquest remained log-jammed, waiting for an Appeal Court hearing, with every possibility it would eventually land before the European Court of Human Rights at Strasbourg.

She could see obvious reasons to decline taking the case, both personal and professional, but the Barrett and Maguire cases were precisely what she had hoped for in Belfast. Maybe Gordon would be thrilled if she brought such a high-profile case to the firm but she somehow doubted it. She would need to work out a strategy. She didn't have to tell Gordon now. Not just yet. Nor Geraldine. She typed up a letter herself, informing Maguire he would have to wait a few weeks for her answer, and then switched her attention back to Barrett and how she might mount his defence. Looking up the football fixtures, she saw Manchester United were playing Arsenal that Saturday afternoon, almost guaranteeing Billy Barrett would be in The Jubilee. If she found him, she could ask him to arrange a meeting with Graham White, Snowy's father.

Interrupting Edward and William's Friday meeting, she made excuses for absenting herself from Fermanagh that weekend. She and Edward had mutually agreed not to discuss their relationship with his father so she limited herself to saying the Barrett case was keeping her busy. In front of his father, Edward was a study in indifference. He had a UDR shift on Friday, he said, and he might catch a rugby match on Saturday with Paul Donaldson. Lena then headed home with the case papers of two of the highest profile legal cases in Northern Ireland in her briefcase and the delicious, albeit slightly scary, realisation they would make or break her time in Ireland.

4

On Saturday, Lena drove into Belfast to catch Billy Barrett at The Jubilee. Securing Darren's acquittal depended on evidence – evidence not even a Northern Ireland judge could ignore – that Snowy White was a compromised witness. If she could persuade White senior to swear, on oath, that his son feared Barrett and had good reasons to want him behind bars for a very long time, she had a chance of persuading a judge that he had a motive for manufacturing evidence. If Billy Barrett backed him up, stating on oath that Snowy was responsible for The Shankill Stinger's broken leg and premature retirement from the wrestling circuit, an acquittal would be entirely possible.

Half an hour before kick-off at Old Trafford, Lena walked into the bar where a mix of cigarette smoke, mouldy carpet and stale beer assailed her nostrils. A dozen pairs of suspicious eyes looked up from their pints as she entered. She was wearing jeans and an old anorak she kept in the car, hoping they made her inconspicuous, but it clearly convinced no one. Leopard-print leggings and pink hair extensions would have been a better bet. When she asked the barman if Billy Barrett was present, he jerked his head in the direction of the television and she approached a group of men absorbed in the pre-match punditry.

'Sorry to interrupt but is Mr Billy Barrett here?' she ventured, prompting a chorus of whistles and a mocking voice suggesting 'they've finally found you, Billy'.

Barrett, a stoutly-built, grey-haired man, stood up and hurriedly moved away from his companions towards an empty corner of the saloon. 'Who the hell are you and what do you want?' he asked.

'There's nothing to worry about. I'm your son's solicitor,' she began. 'You know I got him bail – I'm now working to secure his acquittal. He's facing very serious charges.'

'Oh, I know that all right, the wee bastard,' said Barrett senior.

'Then you must also know that the only evidence against him comes from Leonard White, the man the newspapers are calling Snowy. If I'm going to help Darren, I've got to find someone who knows this Mr White.'

The seconds were ticking by until kick-off. Billy needed to get back to the TV.

'I suppose it was bloody Sharon told you how to find me. For all I know you could be some kind of agent. Special Branch has spies everywhere.'

'Mr Barrett, why would I be asking about Snowy if I was a police agent? He's in their witness protection programme. Darren is in serious trouble and I'm trying to help him.'

Billy glanced over to his friends to see if anyone was watching.

'Me and Graham White, Snowy's father, were in the Ballysillan Conquerors' Flute Band together for years,' said Barrett.

'I need to speak to Graham. What are the chances he'd meet me? Will you ask him? If he agrees, will you ring me? Can I have your number?'

'You're asking an awful lot of questions.'

'It's urgent that I speak to Graham White.'

'I haven't seen White in years. He may be in some sort of police protection himself.'

Lena had done her homework. 'I've been reading the newspapers and he was away from home when Snowy disappeared. I don't think the police have got to him yet.'

Billy relented.

'Darren's a bad 'un but he's no murderer. I'll give it a try.'

'We haven't got much time. Your son is due in court very soon.'

'Okay, okay, but get out of here, will you? The match is about to start.'

'Your phone number, could you write it down for me?'

As he wrote his number down, she began to worry if he would keep his word.

'I'm leaving now,' she said, retrieving her notebook. 'But I'll ring you in a few days and, if I have no answer, I'll be back next Saturday – and the Saturday after if needs be.' She hoped she sounded convincing.

Billy was already turning back to the group around the TV where a roar was greeting kick-off. Back in the safety of her car, Lena felt a certain grim satisfaction that, before long, she should be in possession of an affidavit from Graham White acknowledging that Snowy had caused 'The Stinger's' incapacitating knee injury and had been living in fear of a revenge attack. She would also, if things went as planned, have a backup statement from Billy Barrett acknowledging that his son, Darren did indeed harbour ill feeling, to say the least, against Snowy White for ending his wrestling career.

On Sunday morning, she stowed the Barrett file in her briefcase and turned again to the Maguire papers. Before Danny was buried, the family had won the right for an independent post-mortem examination, which was carried out by a Professor Jean Leglu of the University of Grenoble. Leglu was delightfully described in one newspaper report as 'specialising in the damage caused by bullet trajectories through the human body'. There was no full copy of his report in the file but newspaper accounts said it concluded that all the bullets recovered from the left side of Reid's body were damaged, having passed through some part of the car before hitting him. Maguire had been hit four times, also all on his left-hand side.

Ballistic reports given to the inquest recorded that three of these bullets were also badly damaged by their trajectory through either metal or glass. The fourth and fatal bullet, however, had hit Maguire on the left side of his head, without passing through any part of the car first. The state pathologist had recovered it from his body at an autopsy in Antrim Area Hospital, intact. In a statement to the first day of the inquest, a police scenes-of-crime officer had given evidence that an injured Maguire had fallen through the car door and the fourth bullet had passed under the chassis and hit his head as he lay, semi-prostrate, on the ground. Nothing in Leglu's report contradicted either the state pathologist's conclusions or the police statements. Nevertheless, Lena made a mental note to find Leglu, who had now retired.

On Sunday night, she phoned Georgie in London.

'Things are hotting up at last,' she conceded, 'although

it's hardly a glamorous life – meeting loyalists in sleazy bars and reviewing gruesome forensic reports.'

'You complained when it was boring so you can hardly complain when it's not,' came the honest reply.

Having given Billy Barrett a few days' grace, Lena rang him and he agreed to a second meeting.

'Graham White wants his son away from them bastards in Special Branch,' he said. 'I told him that's what you wanted too. He'll see you in Della's Café on Cambrai Street at four next Monday afternoon.'

With this in her back pocket, Lena went to see Gordon with a strategy ready.

'I'd like to discuss how we might get Darren Barrett acquitted.'

'Knowing you, as I now do Lena, I imagine you have a plan.'

'I've drawn up an affidavit for Billy Barrett to sign stating that his son, our client, holds Snowy White personally responsible for prematurely ending his wrestling career by breaking his leg. Then I have another statement for Graham White to sign stating that his son fears for his life should Barrett be released back onto the Shankill. That should be sufficient for us to argue in court that White's evidence is fatally contaminated and inadmissible.'

Gordon was leaning forward in his chair, listening closely.

'At the committal hearing, even before the trial,' Lena went on, 'we could summon the RUC detective handling White and ask him some awkward questions, in public and under oath, about what he knows of his star witness' extreme prejudice against Barrett.'

Lena stopped for a moment, waiting for Gordon's reaction.

'You don't let the grass grow under your feet, do you lassie? You're only here, what, three months?'

'There's something else.'

'More?'

'Although I have huge respect for Brendan Casey, who is currently lead defence counsel for all sixteen accused, I would like to ask Martin Porter QC over to defend Barrett, initially at the committal.'

If Lena had suggested inviting Jesus of Galilee to walk over the Irish Sea and appear at Crumlin Road Courthouse, it would have caused less astonishment.

'Why on earth would a man like Porter travel to Belfast and defend a nonentity like Barrett?' Gordon spluttered.

'Undermining the supergrass policy would be quite the feather in Porter's cap. His involvement will also ensure press coverage in London but I require your approval now,' she said. 'Porter will need time to read the papers.'

'Ring him by all means,' Gordon said, 'but I doubt he will agree.'

Gordon thought he was marking time – but it was game, set and match for Lena. She closed her office door behind her, took a deep breath and rang Porter.

'Hi Martin. Could you fly over and help me clear a repulsive loyalist thug of a murder charge?'

'Sounds irresistible. Tell me more if you don't mind, but be quick, I have the builders in upstairs and they're making a shocking racket.'

Lena froze. She had forgotten their agreed code and certainly didn't want the RUC knowing her plans. She chose her next words carefully.

'The police say the killing took place *upstairs* in a house on the Shankill Road but we can challenge that as our client's leg was broken at the time. He could not possibly have walked *upstairs*.'

'In that case, you're in luck,' Porter replied. 'I'd welcome a break from all this noise but please find me somewhere quiet to stay.'

'No problem,' Lena said. 'Are we settled?'

'It seems we are.'

'I'll courier the papers to you on Monday.'

As she put the phone down, Lena smiled. She had just drawn up an ambitious plan and implemented it against stiff opposition. An appropriate reward, she decided, would be to buy herself the sharpest suit that the fine city of Belfast could provide – one befitting a solicitor who was about to give the chief constable of the Royal Ulster Constabulary a kick up the arse.

Within an hour, she was at the city's only department store, signing a large cheque. Wafting through the fragrances of Lancôme and Givenchy on the ground floor, she had just exited the revolving doors when the world began to collapse around her. There was a thundering noise and the glass from dozens of windows began shattering down, thin shards smashing onto the footpath inches in front of her. She heard a faint 'puff' as something flew past her ear. She looked down at her hands and legs. They were fine. For a millisecond, she stood stunned at the evolving tableau of glass, blood, dust and screaming. People were running out of the shop behind her, banging against her back. She was caught in the tide and carried further out into the street, struggling to keep upright. An elderly woman lay in front of her, navy pleated skirt blown up, exposing her legs. She was clutching a bleeding thigh and struggling to lift her head off the footpath. Blood was seeping through her fingers. Lena, looking for a tourniquet, quickly realised her own coat belt would do. Untying it, she knelt and wrapped it tight around the woman's thigh, watching as blood soaked into the soft material, before easing the shopping bag containing her new suit under the woman's head.

'You're going to be all right,' she told the old lady. 'Don't move. The ambulance will be here soon.'

The whimpering stopped, and the wrinkled eyes, which had been screwed up in pain and fear, suddenly opened wide, their expression changing to anger.

'Leave me alone and fuck off back to England.'

Lena was stunned and rocked backwards.

'I'm trying to help you.'

'I don't need your help.'

The old lady's face was bruised and grubby from the footpath where she had fallen – but still defiant. Lena began to hear groans from others lying nearby.

An old man was clutching his forehead and leaning against the pole of a traffic light. Blood from a cut over his eyebrow was streaming down his face and wrist. Lena did her best to stem the flow with a tissue from her handbag, holding it hard against his forehead.

'Thank you, love. Thank you, miss,' he kept on repeating.

People in uniforms carrying stretchers were now arriving. The angry old lady was carefully lifted into an ambulance and taken away. There goes my good belt, Lena thought, retrieving her shopping bag from the footpath.

The old man was helped into another ambulance. RUC men were guiding the walking wounded away. The street was littered with abandoned bandages, wrappers, broken glass and bloodied clothing. Lena steadied herself by leaning onto a concrete pillar between two shattered shop windows. She had seen no bodies, but ambulance sirens were still wailing around the corner in Donegall Square. Tears of relief and shock began to sting her eyes.

'Are you okay?' asked a young police officer, wandering by.

'I'm fine,' she said, recovering her composure. 'I think a piece of shrapnel skimmed past my left ear, but I'm not hurt, although a woman I was helping had the nerve to swear at me.'

A grim smile crossed the cop's face. 'That's Belfast for you but I have to ask you to move away now. You'd better walk home, there'll be no buses for the rest of the day.'

Lena began picking her way through the wreckage, decided against going back to the office, instead walking to her car and driving shakily home from where she phoned the office to say she was okay. Turning on the six o'clock news, she heard that three people were dead. Others were seriously injured – suffering what a police spokesman euphemistically called 'life-changing injuries' which, she suspected, meant either blinded or losing limbs. She felt shaky for hours afterwards but lucky to be alive, wondering again if she should take on the Maguire case.

After a good night's sleep, and determined not to be knocked off course, she prepared Graham White's affidavit in the High Street office. When Geraldine brought in the lunchtime post, there were letters from both the

Education Board and the Health Trust asking that Snowy's next-of-kin authorise the release of his records so she drafted up replies for White to sign.

She then had time for a guilty dive into the Maguire file, drawing diagrams of the roadway and the grass verges where the two police officers lay when opening fire. She marked the precise location where the car had come to a halt, assessing whether the trajectories of the bullets matched the police account. Reid had been hit in the left chest by two bullets that had passed through the windscreen. He also had multiple wounds in the abdomen and head from bullets passing either through the passenger door and window or the upholstery of his car seat. He must have died almost instantly. As for Maguire, the first two bullets had hit the front of his left shoulder, continuing into his chest, having first smashed through either the passenger door or windscreen. They could have rendered him unconscious, but had not killed him instantly. The third bullet had passed through the windscreen and had hit him in the chest.

The police account was that after being hit three times, Maguire had lost control of the car which had continued to veer towards the left-hand verge. The grass and mud had slowed it down and, by the time it came to a halt, he was unconscious. He had then slumped to his right, falling onto the driver's door which had swung open, allowing his upper body to fall to the ground outside. The fourth and final bullet had then passed underneath the chassis and hit him in the left-hand side of his head. He was taken to hospital, where the bullet had been recovered, undamaged, from just under his skull, but he had died in the early hours of the following day. There was no apparent discrepancy in any of the police forensic and ballistic evidence. The car itself had been measured, photographed and preserved for the standard period of two years and then destroyed – although two years seemed a trifle perfunctory. By the afternoon, her early enthusiasm was waning, although she was curious to know if Leglu, the French pathologist, had ever heard of another case where a bullet had passed underneath a car and killed a man after he had half-fallen out. With the weekend ahead and Edward expected in the office, she put it out of her mind. Fermanagh was a much more appealing prospect.

She was now a regular at Gordon Hall. Before dinner, provided neither Paul Donaldson nor Geoffrey Hamilton were present – neither of whom, she felt, trusted her – Lena would entertain Edward, William and Margaret in the library with well-embellished tales from either the courthouse or the jail at Crumlin Road. The 'Chronicles of Crumlin' she called them. When she returned to London, she thought she would be able to match Martin Porter, story for story.

At the appointed hour, she sallied back to the upper Crumlin Road and Della's Café on the corner of two narrow streets of red-brick terraces, its windows streaming with condensation. Darren Barrett's father, Billy, and Leonard White's father, Graham, were both inside, tucking into large plates of bacon, eggs and soda bread. As diplomatically as possible, she began to ask White about his son's dispute with Darren Barrett. In typically infuriating Belfast fashion, he answered her first question with one of his own.

'What has you so interested in my Lenny?'

'As you know, Billy's son, Darren, is my client. I need to persuade a court he is innocent of murder. Your son's honest fear for his life, should Darren be released, calls your son's evidence into question,' she began. 'By helping your son I also help Darren.'

Following on quickly, to prevent another query, she asked, 'How much did you know about the bullying Leonard endured at school?'

'Lenny used to come home every day covered in muck. The kids tore his uniform to pieces. It cost us a fortune. My wife, Maureen, before she passed, went to meetings at the school but it made no difference. Leonard was just one of those kids who got picked on.'

'And after Leonard left school? What do you know about his fight with Darren Barrett?'

'The two of them were in rival gangs at school and nothing changed after they left. As far as I know the fight you're on about was between the UDA in the upper Crumlin Road, where we lived, and the Lower Shankill brigade. There was a whole mob involved. Nothing extraordinary.'

'But Darren ended up in hospital.'

'Nothing was the same after that. Lenny hardly left the house. He was talking of leaving for Scotland. The whole Shankill was watching and waiting. Leonard knew it was only a question of time before the UDA called him out for a six-pack.'

'What's a "six-pack"?' asked Lena.

'That's when they shoot you in both ankles, knees and elbows.'

Lena was thrown for a second but recovered and noticed how closely Billy Barrett was listening. For the plan to work, she needed the two fathers singing from the same hymn sheet, a chorus of agreement that Snowy's evidence was motivated by sheer terror.

'I'm sorry you're hearing all this, Billy,' she said, 'but it should help Darren in the long run.'

Billy nodded but said nothing.

'I don't blame Darren for being pissed-off that his wrestling days were over,' conceded White. 'I'm just sorry my Lenny was in the frame.'

With every word spoken, Lena became more confident her defence strategy would work. Snowy was clearly terrified of her client and would say anything, true or false, to keep him off the streets. It must have been easy for the RUC to turn him.

'Mr White, I know you haven't any idea where the police are keeping your son but are you allowed to speak to him?'

'He's allowed one phone call a week. He calls me on Sunday evenings at a public phone box on Agnes Street.'

'How are the police treating him?'

'He says they're talking about setting him up in a witness protection programme, so long as he gives evidence against Barrett and the others, but he doesn't trust them. He doesn't want to live in Scotland the rest of his life. He knows he'll have to come home someday.'

Billy Barrett then broke in. 'If your Leonard withdraws his evidence,' he said, 'I'll make sure Darren and the others leave him alone and call the UDA off. I may be a veteran but they'll listen to me.'

Graham White was stunned, as was Lena.

'Would you do that?' White asked. 'Do you think Darren would agree?'

'Yeah, I'm damn sure he would,' said Barrett. 'He's had plenty of time to think it over in the Crum.'

Things could hardly be going better, Lena thought.

'That could be just the breakthrough we need Billy,' she said. 'Graham, when you speak to Lenny next Sunday, you be sure to tell him what Billy just said.'

'If he's still worried,' said Barrett, 'I'll make sure the brigade staff issue a public statement saying the feud is over.'

It was time to end the meeting before anyone had time for second thoughts. Lena put Graham White's affidavit on the table in front of him.

'This explains the dispute between your son and Billy's. If you agree, sign it. These other two documents are letters allowing me to apply for your son's school and medical records which will also greatly assist the defence.'

White got his glasses out of a pocket, cleaned them, read all three documents and signed each without objection.

Having paid for their breakfasts, she dropped them both off further up the Crumlin Road. Alone in the Mini again, she gave herself a metaphoric pat on the back. When Graham White's affidavit was disclosed to the prosecution, they might even abandon plans to put Snowy on the stand.

Her thoughts then went deeper. The longer she spent in Belfast, the more questions she had about how the place was run. From top to bottom, things were not as they appeared. Although she had heard British ministers on TV praising the education system in Northern Ireland as a 'model of excellence', it seemed it had a serious bullying problem. For the police to exploit White's fear of the UDA ... well, it was not pretty. The way Barrett and White had casually mentioned 'a six-pack' was shocking, the law of the jungle. Some of the assumptions that guests voiced around the table at Gordon Hall about their Catholic neighbours were also disturbing. Hamilton had once made a decidedly off-colour joke about rabbits and the Catholic birth rate. There was a lot going on, she was beginning to think, that would never happen in London – whatever about Mrs Thatcher claiming Belfast was as British as Finchley.

On her way back to the office, she hit gridlock on the mainly nationalist Lower Ormeau Road and noticed a crowd surrounding four British Army vehicles. With the traffic going nowhere, she parked on a side street and walked back to take a look. Soldiers were crouched on the footpath, swivelling their rifle sights directly into the faces of passers-by. Uniformed policemen were marching in and out of a tiny terraced house. A woman, bent over double in fury at the front door, was screaming at the police officers. Several kids bawled in the street, one a baby in a pram. Two soldiers, upstairs in a bedroom, were throwing blankets and pillows through a window onto the muddy patch of garden below and she could hear the sound of a pneumatic drill inside.

Despite the woman's attempts to block the door, a man, dressed only in a vest with blood on his face, was frogmarched from the house, writhing like a snake against the four pairs of hands that gripped him and shoved him into a police jeep. The woman's screams grew even louder as the jeep drove away. This had no effect on the soldiers and RUC who continued their work, systematically ransacking the house.

More women gathered, shrieking abuse until a soldier lost his temper and smashed one of them in the face with his rifle butt. The decibel level rose even higher. The injured woman fell to the ground, blood pouring from her nose. Repelled yet fascinated, Lena stood watching, feeling a voyeur at witnessing such violence. Borrowing a phrase from Geraldine, she told herself to 'Catch herself on'. The RUC and soldiers had a job to do and – for all she knew – the man bundled away was a murderer. Nevertheless, the level of sheer physical violence was unsettling. She had just seen a soldier bashing an unarmed woman in the face who had not laid a finger on him. This was happening within an hour of London. Would it be covered on the radio that evening, even locally in Belfast? She suspected not. Who was to blame? The arrested man? The soldiers for their enthusiastic wrecking of a family home? As she continued watching, a police officer walked slowly towards her across the road.

'What are you doing, miss?' he said.

'Just looking on.'

'You'll have to move along.'

'I'm not interfering.'

'That's your opinion. I think you're risking a breach of the peace and that's an arrestable offence.'

'I'm sorry, but I have to respectfully disagree. I'm a solicitor and I know my rights. I'll leave when I want to, not on your orders.'

'If I say you're causing a breach of the peace, you are. So, move along now please.'

Their exchange had been noticed and a child walked over to watch.

Hearing Lena's accent, and possibly mistaking her for a journalist, he held out a grubby hand in which was a pale-brown object, roughly the size of a packet of Smarties.

'Plastic bullet, miss? Only a fiver.'

'You see,' said the policeman, 'now we have a child crossing the street in heavy traffic trying to sell you a baton round.'

'Baton round or plastic bullet, I'm not paying £5 for it,' she told the child who stuck his tongue out at her.

The policeman began speaking into his walkie-talkie. Two of his colleagues looked across from the other side of the road and began walking over towards her.

The older of the two, who seemed to be in charge, asked for her name and address. She gave them.

'And what do you know about recent terrorist activity?'

'I know nothing about terrorist activity recent or otherwise,' she replied. 'I was merely watching you go about your work.'

'A few minutes ago, you saw what happens to people who cause a breach of the peace around here. There's a spare jeep over there with your name on it if you don't do as this officer has politely asked you.'

Lena was not eager to put this to the test and decided discretion was the better part of valour.

'I'm due back in the office anyhow,' she conceded, 'so you can take your jeep and use it however you like.'

As she got into her Mini and began driving away, she noticed in her rear-view mirror that one of the cops was noting its registration number. She had, in effect, been intimidated into leaving. At the office, she began telling Geraldine.

'There's a house being torn apart on the Ormeau Road, really wrecked, women screaming in the street, blood, kids bellowing.'

Geraldine shrugged. 'Happens every day, all the year round. You'll soon get used to it.'

Chastened, Lena retreated into her office to prepare briefing notes on The Shankill Stinger for Martin Porter. Two weeks later, on the first day of Barrett's committal hearing, her stomach churning, she drove to meet him at the former RAF base that was now the main airport serving Belfast. It was a half-hour drive to the flat eastern shores of Lough Neagh – a huge body of relatively shallow water which the tourist board touted as 'the largest lake in the British Isles' (or 'just a very, very large puddle' as Lena called it once, making Edward laugh). She was surprised at the comforting feeling that Martin Porter sweeping towards her in arrivals gave her – someone from familiar territory in this ocean of strangeness. Her nerves settled as they chatted in a quiet corner of the airport café.

'So, what am I meant to be doing over here?' Porter began.

'This will tell you,' she said, handing him a bullet-point summary of the vendetta between Darren Barrett and Leonard White that had ended in a vicious fight on the Shankill Road. As Porter read, he began chuckling.

'The prosecution aren't going to know what hit them when this comes to trial,' he said, looking at Lena with respect.

'We'll keep most of it in reserve,' she said. 'I haven't disclosed what you're reading to the Crown side yet. Today is all about how a judge can handle cautioning himself, on the one hand, to consider the witness' veracity and, on the other, attempting to independently assess his testimony with no jury. It borders on the insane, but that just about sums it up.'

'When the time comes, we'll hold their feet to the fire. How are your relations with the local press? It would help if the judge knew he was being observed.'

'The main court reporter here is a friend. I've tipped him off. He'll be there.'

Lena drove Porter into the city through the Belfast hills, pointing out the now-familiar landmarks – the green dome of City Hall, the yellow cranes at Harland & Wolff, the blue sea of Belfast Lough. When they arrived at Crumlin Road Courthouse, a surprisingly large group of camera crews and reporters was already bunched on the footpath. Porter recognised some of the faces and whispered to Lena that the London papers had sent people over.

'A knockabout TV wrestler facing murder charges?' he said. 'Absolute bloody gift for the colour writers.'

The moment Lena took her seat in the well of the court, she knew enlisting Porter was the right call. Gone was the relaxed camaraderie between the police, lawyers and tipstaffs. The air crackled with tension. People bustled about – busy looking busy. Journalists were checking the names of the sixteen defendants while, on the legal benches, solicitors and QCs muttered to each other and the court clerk shuffled his papers. One of the London papers had even dispatched a court artist who had joined the press benches, adding to the sense of occasion. In the steeply tiered public gallery, separated from the rest of the courtroom by a slatted wooden screen, the families, friends and neighbours of the defendants squeezed into place, waiting for their men to enter the dock from the cells below.

Lena doubted that the family of the dead murder victim was in court. The public benches, crammed with loyalists, would be an intimidating place.

She spotted Sharon Barrett, hair neatly coiffed under a headscarf, sitting quietly at the end of the back row. Heavily armed police officers stood with their backs to the panelled wall beside every row of seats in the public gallery, ready to pounce should anyone misbehave. As Lena settled down, Hamilton entered the courtroom and bared his teeth at her in a grotesque attempt at a smile. There's going to be a few tricky moments around the dining table at Gordon Hall, she thought, if we win this case. Barrett and his co-defendants then swaggered into the dock, grinning and giving thumbs-ups to their supporters in the public gallery. Lena's client, an oily grin on his face, winked knowingly at her where she sat on the solicitors' bench. Then – lights down, curtain up. The hubbub ceased. Showtime. Lena loved this moment. The last few seconds of adjustment, then a pregnant silence, like a concert hall when the orchestra finishes tuning and anticipates the conductor making his appearance. The door behind the judge's bench opened.

'All rise,' said the court clerk.

With varying degrees of respect, the defendants, their

supporters and the lawyers rose to their feet whereupon the judge, His Lordship Edmund Campbell, took his place on the bench under the royal insignia.

'Before we begin,' he said in his high-pitched, slightly nasal voice, 'may I welcome Martin Porter QC to our humble courtroom. We don't often have the pleasure in Belfast of hearing from such a distinguished jurist.'

The flattery was over the top, obsequious. Lena was sure she was not imagining it. Porter inclined his head very slightly for a second in Campbell's direction, appearing to graciously accept the compliment. The court clerk then began reading the long list of charges faced by each of the sixteen defendants. It took nearly half an hour. He looked relieved as he sat down, red-faced, his part in the drama over. Hamilton opened for the Crown, giving his skeleton argument against the accused – Leonard White's name in virtually every sentence. The defendants ceased whispering and strained through the dreadful acoustics to hear details of the crimes they had allegedly committed. Hamilton's droning speech, barely audible surely – even to the judge – was a mere *amuse bouche* to the main course which came when Porter rose, cleared his throat and began speaking, clear as a bell, in a voice that everyone could hear. The courtroom took on an entirely different atmosphere. People stopped fidgeting and instead focused on the elegant figure whose wavy grey locks threatened to burst out from beneath his barrister's wig and who made no recourse to notes.

'I appear, my Lord,' he began magisterially, 'for the defendant Darren Barrett instructed by Gordon & Company. My learned friend, Brendan Casey here, appears for the fifteen other defendants, instructed by Keane & Moran. I do not propose to take up much of the court's valuable time at this juncture except to say that, although there will be dozens of witnesses called to give evidence at the trial – should Your Lordship decide a trial is justified – only one will claim to identify my client as a perpetrator. The reliability of this witness – who is, I understand, in police protective custody – will then, of course, be critical. I must inform the court that I anticipate bringing testimony at the trial proper, questioning the motivation and reliability of the evidence given by this prosecution witness. The court will, even today, also hear something of its incredible nature and its inconsistencies and dubious claims.'

Barely stopping for breath, he continued. 'The main concern I wish to raise at this early stage is a matter of some comment, both in Northern Ireland and increasingly in London. A no-jury court is asked to hear uncorroborated accomplice evidence. My Lord, at the trial you will hear yourself directly from the main Crown witness. You will hear a challenge to his credibility. In normal circumstances, that credibility would be adjudicated by a jury. Here in Northern Ireland, however, there will be no jury – yet upon that chief witness' credibility rests the fate of the sixteen men before you in this courtroom. Not only will you, My Lord, have to decide whether the chief prosecution witness is perhaps a liar or a fantasist, you will also have to decide the weight you should accord his evidence. On that, the guilt or innocence of the defendants will entirely depend.'

Hamilton was on his feet at that. 'These are matters, surely, for the trial. These pleadings are premature.'

'I'm minded to allow them, nevertheless,' said Campbell, who was enjoying the flattering tone of London's pre-eminent QC.

'The Crown will not, as I understand it, claim that its witness is a converted terrorist,' said Porter. 'Far from it. He is a man who might otherwise face a very long prison sentence. Inevitably, in those circumstances, a witness considers the possibility of striking a deal with the police, knowing he may benefit by being set up in another country with a new identity. Once that is in prospect, there will be only one thing uppermost in his mind: self-preservation.

'He will want to make the most convincing case possible to get immunity, even to the extent of telling falsehoods. He may try to incriminate as many former associates as he can. He may play down, in as far as he can, his own part in the crimes in which he was involved. He may seize the chance to work off grudges. He is highly likely to pretend that he knows, as a matter of fact, things which are only gossip, rumour or hearsay and – above all – he will want to give the police and the courts the evidence that he thinks they want to hear.

'The police, in such circumstances, will be tempted to suggest names, given that they often publicly state they "know that certain people are terrorists". People will be implicated, not because the witness has first-hand evidence, but because he believes he knows what the police want to hear. I do not think that anyone, irrespective of his legal training, would like to be responsible for listening to such a man giving evidence about incident after incident and then having to decide, with no corroboration, whether that person is telling the truth or telling lies.

'The judge, however good a judge he is, cannot hope to sift the truth from the lies. When that kind of evidence is given in a court of law, justice becomes a gamble; innocent people are convicted; guilty men escape and the system of justice as a whole is discredited. These are my general opening remarks. When it comes to my own client's personal criminal record, it consists of minor drug offences. For the moment, I am pleased to hand over to my learned friend Mr Casey.'

Casey then took up the argument, using copious past examples from both British and international law, focusing again on the normally critical division between the role of a judge and that of a jury which, in 1980s Belfast, had been rolled into one. It was something of an anticlimax after Porter's performance – a steady progress with multiple references to previous case law against the use of 'assisting offender' evidence. The afternoon was taken up by clarifying various maps and diagrams lodged by the police and prosecution. At the end of business, people were already looking forward to the appearance of the chief witness, Snowy White, the following morning.

Lena drove Porter to his hotel. 'You have no idea the difference you are already making,' she said, battling rush-hour traffic. 'Although it must be just another day in court for you.'

'Delighted to be of assistance,' Porter replied. 'I can't wait to meet The Shankill Stinger in the flesh and then eviscerate White's evidence at the trial. A refreshing change from my standard run-of-fare at the Old Bailey.'

He excused himself from Lena's dinner invitation, saying he had work to do so she checked him into the

Presidential Suite at the Gordon Central and drove home to Glenbarry. The following day, she took him to meet their client in a consulting room at the courthouse. Separated from his swaggering mates, Barrett was in a state of high anxiety at the thought of finally hearing his tormentor in the witness box, even though it would be curtained off from sight of all but the judge and lawyers. Porter's ineffable confidence lowered the tension slightly, but Barrett was still sweating profusely as they left him.

'Well, he didn't disappoint,' Porter whispered as they walked into court. 'If the future of the union relies upon people like Barrett, Dublin had better start preparing.'

The high drama of the opening day of a major court hearing normally settles down on the second but, with the chief witness due to give evidence, the atmosphere was even more tense as actors and audience settled down for the drama to recommence. Even the usually impassive police and prison warders were jumpy. Kick-off was due at 10.30 a.m. but, at the allotted time, there was no sign of the judge. By eleven o'clock the defendants were restless – as were the hoi-polloi in the public gallery. The press, crammed into a narrow bench, chatted nervously amongst themselves while solicitors and barristers consulted their notes. After a further half-hour, with still no sign of the judge, the atmosphere changed from consternation to alarm. Sensing trouble ahead, the court clerk surveyed the scene, left his desk and stepped through the door behind the bench that led to the judge's chambers. When he returned five minutes later, everyone's eyes were glued to him as he whispered a few words to Hamilton on the Crown lawyers' bench. Hamilton then also left the courtroom, following the clerk towards the judge's chambers. Porter frowned and raised an eyebrow. Chatter in the public gallery and the dock grew louder, but order was immediately restored when Hamilton returned and Campbell appeared at long last.

'Silence in court,' said the clerk. 'All rise.'

Everyone rose up – and sat down. There was a slight pause. Then Campbell coughed and began speaking. 'Due to circumstances beyond the court's control,' he said, 'we have to adjourn today's proceedings. Mr Hamilton informs me we will be able to resume when we have an update from the RUC …'

Quick as a whip, Porter was on his feet, interrupting the judge.

'But my client's committal has already begun. He has every right to hear the evidence against him. Should the prosecution have no evidence to present, then I suggest the court make this clear and the prosecution withdraw its case.'

The word 'withdraw' prompted hysterical whispers to run through the public gallery while, in the dock, the sixteen defendants' heads were swinging from side to side like spectators at a Wimbledon final. Campbell hammered a clenched fist on the bench.

'Silence in court or I'll clear the galleries.'

Porter, adopting an air of pained impatience, waited until calm was restored.

'My Lord, my point remains unanswered. If there is no evidence to be offered, then this committal should be halted and my client released along with the other fifteen defendants.'

As the word 'release' joined 'withdraw', unrest grew in the dock. Campbell gestured towards Hamilton to approach the bench, but he was already deep in conversation with a dark-suited man who had, seconds previously, strode into court. Porter's frown deepened – any air of indifference had vanished.

'Who's that talking to Hamilton?' he mouthed behind his hand to Lena sitting opposite him. She could only shrug, but the ever-alert Casey passed her a note reading 'McGinley – top Special Branch'. Lena passed the note to Porter whose brow furrowed even deeper. The attention of the entire courtroom – judges, lawyers, defendants and the public gallery – was now focused on Hamilton and his whispered conversation with the newly arrived man in the dark suit. White-faced with fury, Campbell asked Hamilton to 'please advise me of the position. Immediately counsel!'

The hum from the public gallery grew louder as Hamilton cleared his throat.

'I am afraid, My Lord,' he said, 'I have no explanation available to me at this moment other than we are not ready to proceed.'

Porter was on his feet immediately to push home his advantage.

'I have to insist, then, that the prosecution now accept there is no evidence to offer and the case be dismissed.'

Hamilton looked entreatingly at Campbell. 'May I beg the court for the indulgence of a few moments to make further inquiries?'

'We understand you need to take advice,' Campbell replied, regaining his composure. 'This court will rise early for lunch. We will resume at two precisely. Mr Hamilton, please join us in chambers.'

Campbell rose and quickly left the court to avoid the ensuing din from both the public gallery and the dock.

'What the hell is going on?' Lena asked Porter who appeared seriously displeased.

'There's only one thing that can be going on,' he said. 'Their star witness is missing. And Campbell shouldn't be seeing Hamilton alone without defence counsel present. It's against all the rules even in courts where there is a jury.'

'Typical of this place,' said Lena. 'They make up the rules as they go along and no one ever challenges them.'

'Well, not on my watch,' said Porter. 'I'll be making an issue of it when they return.'

Prison warders were already herding the defendants down to the cells while their families scrambled to get out of the courtroom. Reporters hurried off to find public phone boxes and confer with news desks. It was barely midday, but Lena, Casey and Porter walked to a small café around the corner on the lower Antrim Road for lunch.

'So, you think Snowy has melted?' Lena asked as they settled down at their table.

'A thaw certainly seems to have settled in,' Brendan Casey replied with typical Belfast *sang froid*.

Porter was still seething at being omitted from the meeting between the judge and prosecuting counsel and was making vague threats about a written complaint. After an hour of discussing the Barrett case and anything else they could think of to pass the time, the three lawyers returned to the courthouse. At 2 p.m. on the dot, Campbell resumed his seat. The court held its breath. Geoffrey Hamilton, unused to such indignities, rose, cleared his throat and spoke, doing his very best to sound as if he was in control of events.

'I am afraid, My Lord, that I cannot say at this precise moment when the Crown's chief witness will be available to appear in court. Accordingly, we are not in a position to proceed and therefore, I regret to say, the prosecution can offer no evidence against the defendants.'

Campbell was impassive and stoic. 'On that basis, then, I have no alternative but to dismiss the indictment, with leave to re-present should the Crown's chief witness become available.'

With the defendants staring at him, wondering what he meant, Campbell continued. 'I direct all of the accused to be released with a stern caution to do nothing that might be construed as an attempt to interfere with the course of justice.'

He then rose and marched out to avoid the indignity of seeing his court erupting.

The word 'released' had told those in the dock all they needed to know.

Yelling triumphantly, they rose from their benches and turned towards their relatives in the public gallery until a dozen prison officers re-imposed order by hustling them back down to the cells. The families in the gallery clambered chaotically down the tiered benches towards the public exits while a knot of stunned-looking plain-clothes RUC officers filed out of the lower half of the court.

Left behind, Hamilton busied himself collecting his papers and, without a word being exchanged, Lena, Porter and Casey similarly collected their papers and began climbing towards the exits. Outside in the main lobby, Casey announced he was leaving to speak to his clients in the cells below the courthouse, prompting Lena to suggest to Porter that they do the same. A prison warder brought them down the dimly lit, narrow corridors into an underground holding cell where a highly excited Barrett was waiting for them.

'Where's Snowy? Why didn't he turn up?' he asked frantically as soon as they entered the room.

'I don't know, but quieten down and hold your horses, Darren,' said Lena. 'This might not be as straightforward as it seems. Tell him, Martin.'

'Miss Dawson is correct, Mr Barrett. There's nothing to prevent the police from arresting you and bringing you back to court again if they persuade Mr White to take the stand – or if they discover any new evidence. The RUC can be quite persuasive, as you know already.'

Barrett's face fell.

'So, it's not over?'

'It is for now, Darren,' said Lena. 'Remember my advice about the press. Let someone else do the talking. For once in your life, keep schtum. Do you hear me?'

'How did you manage it?' he asked her.

'I'm not sure, Darren. Remember, stay well away from any member of the White family, keep your mouth shut and go home to Sharon. Revive your wrestling career.'

'Sure, sure,' he said, unconvincingly.

Lena and Porter re-joined Casey in the main lobby and

all three followed Barrett and his co-defendants as they left the building. Casey, who wanted to avoid publicity, whispered to Lena he would meet her later in the car park behind the courthouse, but she and Porter remained to watch the ensuing impromptu press conference in the street. Sweating, red-faced, one after another, the men shouted into the cameras.

'I am an innocent man,' said one. 'The Branch framed us. White is a fucking Walter Mitty. They must be paying him a fortune. We've spent the last six months in jail for nothing.'

'Why don't they go after the IRA instead of loyal citizens?' asked another. 'Snowy White's nothing but a scumbag trying to save his own skin.'

Some followed up with a medley of loyalist slogans, 'No surrender' and, even worse, 'Up the UDA', undermining their earlier expressions of outraged innocence.

Several journalists spotted Barrett in the huddle of loyalists at the microphones and directed questions directly at him, but he was uncharacteristically taciturn. Eventually, the sixteen defendants and their relatives got fed up with yelling at the cameras and surged around the back of the courthouse and into the Lower Shankill estate, where the off-licences were about to do a roaring trade. A couple of enterprising cameramen ran after Barrett as the press conference ended, but he departed, at some speed, towards the Shankill.

After the chaos subsided, several reporters hung back and waited to see if the defence lawyers would say anything. An important test case had backfired spectacularly. Their viewers needed an explanation. For his part, Porter had not flown to Belfast to hide his light under a bushel and walked confidently towards the microphones.

'Our clients are gravely disappointed at being unable to confront the evidence of the chief prosecution witness,' he declared, his voice redolent of disappointment. 'Mr White's failure to appear in court today has cheated them of challenging his credibility. But today has delivered an unambiguous message to the prosecution service and to the RUC. The disputed word of a former alleged associate, uncorroborated by any other evidence, should never be sufficient to level charges, let alone murder charges. Bribing or intimidating witnesses to get people before the courts, charged with the most serious of offences, including conspiracy to murder and murder itself, is and always will be, unacceptable – even more so before a court with no jury.'

Bravura performance delivered, Porter stopped and looked across at Lena who realised with dismay that he expected her to say something. Her heart pounding, she managed to get a few words out.

'Our clients are considering their next move,' she said. 'We will be seeking compensation for wrongful arrest and false imprisonment. The public might ask themselves the true cost of these events.'

Porter ended with a flourish. 'The Director of Public Prosecutions for Northern Ireland should be considering his position.'

As the cameramen and reporters ran to their cars and vans, Lena and Porter began walking in the opposite direction, meeting Casey in the car park.

'There's literally no one,' Lena said once she could no

longer be overheard, 'who believes either that the defendants are innocent or that the police played a clean game.'

'I can't see the RUC giving up yet,' said Casey. 'They've invested far too much in Snowy White. I've advised my clients to keep a very low profile.'

'Same here,' said Lena, 'but wait until you see the six o'clock news. You were casting your pearls before swine, Brendan. It was hilarious.'

Across the rudimentary car park, Hamilton was picking his way through the potholes towards them.

'You've won this round Lena but I know how you managed it and so do the RUC,' he said as he reached them. 'As a result of the deal you negotiated with the UDA, a gang of psychopaths are now walking the streets. Well done indeed.'

'We played by the rules,' said Lena, shocked at Hamilton's vehemence.

'What's not in the rules, Lena my dear, is for a servant of the court to broker a deal between a prosecution witness and the Ulster Defence Association.'

'I've never even spoken to the UDA. I wouldn't know how to.'

'Lena was well within her rights,' intervened Porter. 'All she did was investigate White's motives for giving evidence.'

'Be that as it may, I'll be having a wee chat to the Law Society. I'm not sure they'll share that view,' said Hamilton.

Neither Lena, Porter nor Casey had ever witnessed such open hostility between lawyers. It silenced them as

Hamilton stamped away, coat flapping in the wind.

Lena's elation had been short-lived. 'What is he on about?' she asked.

'There's only one thing he could mean,' said Casey. 'Didn't you meet White and Barrett senior at Della's Café?'

'Yes ... so?' Lena's voice trailed off.

'And didn't White say he spoke to his son once a week?'

'Yes.'

'And did Billy Barrett suggest anything Graham White might tell his son?'

'Barrett said he'd call off the UDA if Snowy White withdrew his evidence.'

'It's entirely possible then,' said Casey, 'that White failed to make an appearance today because he'd rather take his chances with the UDA than with RUC Special Branch.'

'Oh God,' said Lena.

'He's bluffing,' said Casey. 'All you did was bring the two fathers together but Hamilton was humiliated today. I'd steer clear of him for a while.'

'What about Snowy?' Lena asked Casey.

'The RUC won't turn him loose for just yet,' said Casey. 'They'll work on him for a week or so. And he won't budge until he hears from his father that the Barretts have called the UDA off.'

'You people live fascinating lives,' said Porter, who had been listening to this discussion with barely concealed amusement. 'I am not at all sure my colleagues in London would believe the goings-on – but, if you don't mind, I'd like to escape while I can.'

'I'll drive you to the airport,' said Lena.

She found the TV report that night of yelling loyalists outside the courthouse highly diverting until the phone rang and she heard her father's voice.

'We just saw you on the news. Why didn't you let us know?'

'I had no idea the trial would collapse so early.'

'Your mother says you need a haircut. When are you coming to see us?'

Lena had no plans to return to England. She promised her father it would be soon with no intentions of interrupting this new, fascinating life for a while yet – even for a weekend.

5

The days following Barrett's committal were an anticlimax. Having expected to be planning his defence, his unexpected release left a hole in Lena's diary. At least there was no mention of Hamilton's threatened complaint to the Law Society. From the moment they crossed swords at Queen's, she sensed animosity. Over dinner in Fermanagh one Saturday night, he began protesting about the recent arrival of immigrant workers near his home in Dungannon.

'Half the shops in the town are run by Poles or Portuguese these days,' he complained. 'I'm told they're grafters – but I draw the line at granting them citizenship rights.'

As so often around the Gordon table, there was muted agreement with Hamilton's observations.

'You live near Dungannon, Geoffrey,' Lena piped up, irritated. 'But didn't the Hamiltons originally arrive over here from Scotland?'

'Yes, Lanarkshire as it happens. What relevance does that have?' Hamilton asked.

'Well, as I understand it, your family was not alone. Have you ever thought,' she turned to ask the table in general, 'that many of you are descended from immigrants who came here for economic reasons? One might ask where's the difference between your families migrating here 400 years ago and the Poles and Portuguese in Northern Ireland today?'

This novel thought had evidently never occurred to Hamilton but his barrister's training came to the rescue.

'To be precise,' he said, 'most of the Protestant community here in Fermanagh came over from England but the Scottish Presbyterians, my own ancestors, came to Dungannon to escape religious discrimination. They weren't migrant workers.'

'So, they were asylum seekers,' said Lena.

At that point, Edward stepped in to end the discussion.

'We will all be seeking asylum from you before long Lena,' he said to relieve the embarrassed looks around the table. She suspected that, had she made the same observation privately to Edward, he would have laughed and agreed, but he felt unable to do so in public. His public image and his private personality sometimes seemed divided, although their two lives seemed to be inexorably intertwining. A camouflage jacket now hung in the small bedroom at Glenbarry while a UDR beret, with its harp and crown, could be found on the hallway table. Conversely a pair of her walking boots now resided under the bed in the Blue Room in Fermanagh and her toothbrush in the second bathroom. Edward had arranged the arrival of an upright piano at Glenbarry and, at weekends or in the evening, he would play for hours as she read case papers ('almost like an old married couple,' she told Georgie). Some evenings, the phone would ring and an English voice would ask for him (usually an officer about a change in UDR shifts). As he answered, he would adopt his 'phone voice'. In a public setting, talking over dinner at the Hall perhaps, or to his father at the office, he seemed austere, aloof, so different from the man who lost himself playing Chopin or Bach in Glenbarry. She wondered if she would ever find out which was the real man. Some nights, he would arrive at the cottage before dawn and creep silently into bed beside her, his body chilled from Fermanagh's lakes and ditches. She would turn sleepily over, curl her arms around his neck and let him make love to her. In the morning, she would gaze at him sleeping beside her, strong, brown arms tucked neatly under a pillow, like a young boy, bits of grass and leaves in the duvet.

'I used to find him scary,' she told Georgina on one of their regular phone calls. 'If I'm honest, I still do, slightly.'

'You're quite his equal, darling,' Georgie replied.

'It's just he's so obviously eligible.'

'And you're not Lena?'

'Every day seems vacant until I see him. When I hear his car arriving at the cottage, my heart skips a beat.'

'I'm almost jealous.'

Lena had decided, for the time being, against discussing her gnawing anxiety over the Maguire case with Georgie, especially over the phone. The fewer people who knew, for as long as possible, the better. The file was locked in a small suitcase (and then a larger one) and stored under the bed in the second bedroom at the cottage, the keys inside an empty can in a kitchen cupboard. Sooner or later, Edward would have to be told. His mother would feel betrayed. There were times at Gordon Hall when you could almost smell Margaret's fear. It was men like Maguire who gave the orders to stalk and kill her neighbours – and place bombs at City Hall. The more she thought about it, the less sure she was of taking the case. Everything was going so well. Why risk it all for a seemingly futile case? After several days agonising, she came to a decision. She had other cases in the pipeline and was on a hiding to nothing with Maguire. He was delusional, chasing a chimera. She made an appointment to give him the bad news.

'I'm just popping out to tell Luke Maguire I can't take his case,' she told Geraldine as she waited for the lift in reception.

'I'm sorry, Lena, but if you're off to meet Maguire, I'm going to have to tell Mr Gordon. I could lose my job.'

That was the kind of man Maguire was, Lena thought. Trouble wherever he went. As she arrived at the Sinn Féin office, she lifted the tattered concertina file from the boot of her Mini. I'll be glad to get rid of you, she thought as she rang the bell in the security fence and was shown into the same room by the same dour old man. Maguire duly arrived half an hour later, unshaven, his black hair unkempt.

'I suppose congratulations are in order,' he said cheerlessly. 'You seem to have defeated Special Branch's plans to put us all in jail.'

'Not just you, Mr Maguire. They were intent on the same for the UDA. My client, Darren Barrett is a loyalist, as you very well know.'

'He's also a brainless ape. The only reason they wanted him put away was to give themselves cover for arresting dozens of us.'

Positively paranoid, Lena thought.

'Be that as it may, Mr Maguire, we are not here to discuss your opinion on my clients. I'm afraid I have decided you cannot be one of them.'

He sat up straight at that and began barking at her.

'You can't say that. You were all for it at our last meeting.'

'Not true, Mr Maguire. I remember very clearly saying I would have to consider the file first. I'm sorry if you misunderstood me.'

'Well, you're not the only one who's come to a decision. I'll get a better chance with you. The Barrett case just proved that.'

'I'm sorry, but I'm not taking your case. Here's your file back.'

Lena stood up, leaving the file on a table, ready to close the meeting but Maguire remained seated.

'Why are you refusing to help us?'

'Because there's no evidence of a breach in the RUC rules of engagement or the remotest chance of ever finding one.'

'Do you believe in the rule of law?'

'Of course. What a ridiculous question.'

'If you do, you'll take this case. My brother was executed by an RUC death squad. He would never have tried to break through a roadblock.'

Lena hid a smile at the histrionic description 'death squad' which was clearly absurd.

'Look, Eleanor, that's your name, isn't it? You listen up. My brother and his friend were simply driving home that night after meeting friends. They were unarmed. Someone decided to take revenge for the RUC men killed at Portglenone. They couldn't get to me as I was in jail, so they picked on my brother. It was an ambush. Danny drove straight into it.'

'That's pure speculation.'

'Why would anyone drive a car straight at a posse of heavily armed RUC men with military backup? Danny was no idiot. Even if he had been armed, he knew better than that.'

'He might have panicked. We don't know what was going through his mind.'

'You're grasping at straws, Miss Dawson.'

Having got nowhere by being tough, Maguire began softening his tone. Lena sat down again.

'If it makes any difference, Danny left behind twin teenage sons and a widow, Sinéad. She's just had two heart valves replaced and isn't able to work. What about their rights?'

'I have no experience of this kind of case.'

'I don't believe in British justice. But you do. If you refuse to take this case, you'll be denying everything you stand for.'

Recognising the moral blackmail, Lena's temper got the better of her.

'I'm doing no such thing,' she said. 'It shouldn't make any difference but I might as well tell you that my father was in the British Army and I'm dating a UDR man. I am certainly not the person you need.'

'I don't care if your father is a general and you're screwing the secretary of state. I'm hiring you because I think you're honest, intelligent and prepared to dig for evidence.'

Lena, recognising this was, by Maguire's standards, a dazzling compliment, looked for a compromise.

'You're waiting for a ruling from the Appeal Court over the Crown immunity order. Assuming it doesn't go your way, I'll start drafting another appeal, just while I'm in Belfast for the next few months. That's all though. I'll not be able to act for you at the inquest.'

'That's fine. I'm sorry if I sounded harsh. It's just that I was in jail, frustrated and powerless, for years after Danny died. By the way, did you find anything of interest in the file?'

'It's mostly just publicly available material. I'll make an application through the coroner's office today for the full police file and let you know.'

Leaving the Falls Road, Lena realised anything Maguire did was news – even a technical fight in the Appeal Court over Crown immunity. It was bound to make the newspapers. She would have to tell Edward. First, though, she had to face his father. Creeping past his office door back at High Street, she heard him making phone calls, but almost immediately, Geraldine put her head around Lena's office door.

'The boss wants a quick word.'

Lena guessed what was coming and steeled herself. Even before she sat opposite him, he launched his attack.

'I presume you have an excellent reason for visiting the Sinn Féin office today,' he said icily.

'I went because Luke Maguire wishes to engage us in his family's challenge to the Crown immunity order protecting the identities of those who killed his brother,' she replied.

'Over my dead body does this firm represent Luke Maguire,' almost shouted Gordon. 'He's a malignant tumour in this society that needs to be cut out.'

'But we are already acting for Darren Barrett who stands accused of a disgraceful sectarian murder. You're surely not suggesting that because one is a loyalist and the other a republican, that representing one is acceptable and the other is not?'

'Of course not. What a suggestion,' he said.

'Equal representation is a cornerstone of British justice.'

'Is that the justice Maguire gives his victims?'

'We don't descend to their level though, sir, do we?'

Out-manoeuvred, Gordon played dirty.

'How will Edward see it?'

Lena was ready for that.

'You can remind him I have professional standards.'

'I doubt very much he will see it that way. If this firm takes Maguire on, it will go to a senior and more experienced member of my staff.'

Lena had planned for this eventuality and went for broke.

'I will conclude, then, that you have no confidence in me. Under those circumstances, I could hardly continue working here.'

Gordon sat silently in his chair for a few moments. He suspected Edward was staying in Glenbarry with increasing frequency. He had not forgotten the unpleasantness over his university course. He wanted no repeat. Let Lena take the flak.

'I will allow you then to work on the immunity issue. Nothing else. Just for a week or two. No court appearances,' he said. 'But I absolutely forbid you to visit Maguire. Any discussions will be by phone. The idea of you, the daughter of my old friend, sashaying up the Falls Road to meet a man like that doesn't just chill my blood, it freezes my very bones.'

'Thank you, Mr Gordon,' she said demurely.

'And if you find anything startling in the Maguire file,

anything at all – as you did in the Barrett case, you will come to me immediately. Is that clearly understood?'

'Of course.'

Lena returned, trembling but relieved, to her office and drew up a letter to the coroner, asking him to apply to the RUC for the case file. She then spent the rest of the afternoon wondering how to break the news to Edward. She reckoned she had two weeks' grace before a court hearing when the newspapers would inevitably publish something. Later that week, a freezing body crawled into her bed after midnight, pressing itself against her back, a cold hand feeling for her breast.

'Edward, you're going to have to stop this. You might at least phone. I thought you were on duty in Fermanagh.'

'I drove eighty miles through the night to be here. How does that make you feel?'

She turned over and wrapped her arms around him.

'Wonderful,' she said.

'Show me how wonderful,' he replied.

When the alarm rang at 7.30 a.m., she gently extricated herself from his sleeping body and took a shower. As the warm water ran through her hair and gurgled in the drain, she had time to think. She had to let him know before the newspapers did. Towelling herself dry, she heard him downstairs in the kitchen. By the time she joined him in the living room, he was at the piano playing Grieg's 'Morning Mood', his brown forearms poking out of the dressing gown she had bought on her first trip to Enniskillen. Sunshine poured through the open patio doors. What a heavenly day, she thought, and I'm about to ruin it.

As she put his coffee on the piano she asked him to keep playing but he stood up, wrapped his arms around her and sank his face into her neck.

'Edward,' she began, gently breaking out of the embrace, 'I think I should tell you about a new case I'm working on. I've been asked to represent the Maguire family.'

Edward turned from her, lifted his coffee and sat down on the piano stool.

'No, you are not Lena,' he said coldly. 'What on earth is Dad playing at?'

'I'm perfectly capable of handling it.'

'I don't doubt it but that man is toxic and his brother got nothing more than he deserved.'

'If I'm asked to work on a case, I cannot ethically refuse.'

'Of course you can. I'll have a word with Dad.'

'Don't you dare,' said Lena, trying to laugh it off.

It had the opposite effect.

'There's nothing remotely funny about it, Lena. Men like Maguire are trying to kill our friends and neighbours. And us, incidentally.'

'A key principle of the law and democracy is that everyone, no matter who they are, is entitled to legal representation.'

'Give over. Where does it say you have to be Maguire's solicitor? This town is coming down with lawyers. I sometimes think it's the only growth industry we have.'

'You want Protestant solicitors for loyalists and Catholic ones for republicans? Sectarianism in the legal profession as well as everywhere else? I can't turn him down just because my boyfriend doesn't approve.'

'I can't support you on this, Lena. You're on your own.'

It was not going well. She decided to play for time.

'I'll talk to William,' she said. 'Maybe he'll decide the firm shouldn't take it on.'

'That would certainly make sense.'

The peaceful morning was shattered. Edward hurriedly dressed and drove off, leaving a dejected Lena to make her way into work. Towards the end of the day, her phone rang. Steve Sullivan – the first time they had spoken since the evening at Queen's.

'Hi kiddo, how's it going there in balmy Belfast? Haven't heard from you in a while. You must be busy.'

'There's a lot happening, Steve. I managed to get charges against a loyalist dropped on supergrass evidence and I'm now acting for a republican, you may have heard of him, Luke Maguire.'

A whistle came down the line from New York.

'I've met Maguire,' he said. 'He's impressive, one of the young Northerners taking over Sinn Féin.'

'He's also short-tempered and obstinate. But there's good news too. You remember the tall man who tried to stop us as we left the reception at Queen's?'

'I certainly do.'

'Well, he turned out to be my boss' son, and we're dating.'

'He seemed an arrogant type. You discovered different?'

'Let's just say he's got hidden depths. As you can imagine, he isn't keen on me being involved in the Maguire case.'

'Why not? It's mighty high profile.'

'He's a part-timer with the Ulster Defence Regiment.'

'A UDR soldier Lena? You're acting for Maguire and dating a UDR man? Christ almighty.'

'They know about each other but, yes, it's not ideal. Wish me luck.'

Lena sighed as she put the phone down. Until she had spelled it out to Sullivan, she had not realised quite how much she was taking on. Maybe it was time for a break – go home to England for the weekend and think it through. When she phoned Edward to explain, he was glacial.

'Maybe your father will talk some sense into you.'

That hurt but, she told herself, he would come round. The thought of a weekend at home, away from all this drama, sounded suddenly very enticing. She rang and booked a flight.

The world seemed a very different place after eight hours of unbroken sleep in the rectory at Little Woldham. Nestling deeper into her bed, she revelled in the unalloyed pleasure of knowing she was completely, utterly safe. Nothing could possibly have prepared her for the sense of impending catastrophe that permeated life in Belfast. Only on this sunny morning in Hampshire did she fully appreciate that. For the next forty-eight hours, there would be no ethical choices to defend, no looming disasters. Sunlight flooded through her bedroom window onto the faded pink roses on the wallpaper and her oldest possessions – an ancient wicker sewing basket, a pale green dressing table and a cracked pottery rabbit. She could safely turn on the radio without fearing news of another murder. She would hear no sirens wailing today nor the sound of gunfire or a muffled explosion. But she had decisions to make and, driving home from the airport, she had asked her father for time to discuss 'a particularly challenging case'. They had agreed on Sunday afternoon and she had then chattered on to him about Edward and the cottage.

'William's son, eh? And he plays the piano. Classical of course?'

Lena decided this was not the moment to tell him of her growing enchantment with traditional Irish music. He would probably denigrate it as 'diddly-eye'. She merely answered, 'a bit of everything.'

'You'll have to invite him over for a weekend this summer,' her father had said.

Now, in the deep softness of her childhood bed, she leaned back against the pillows and looked up at the ceiling, delightfully planning her day before heading to the kitchen to join her mother, who was grumbling about arthritis and making a half-hearted attempt at cooking breakfast.

'It's lovely to be home, Mummy. Belfast can be a bit depressing,' she said.

'Well, you've only yourself to blame. All those terrible people killing each other. Ghastly. You must meet the most frightful types. Murderers and terrorists.'

Lena knew not to expect maternal sympathy, but her mother's *schadenfreude* was galling.

'Some of the "frightful types" are intelligent, even the ones we call terrorists,' she said.

Charlotte was not listening. 'Just thinking of you in the same room as them makes me shiver.'

What would her mother make of Barrett and Maguire? Lena wondered. Not much. And what would they make of her? Even less. As her mother's disdain for anything connected to Belfast seemed immutable, she took her coffee upstairs, showered and left the rectory for a walk in the churchyard opposite. Everything was reassuringly just as before: the mossy graves, the wooden lych-gate, the flinty church, the hand-embroidered kneelers inside.

She had arranged to meet an old school friend in Salisbury and, driving there, she stopped for petrol at Matt's garage. Since her childhood, Matt had helpfully checked the oil levels and tyre pressures on the Dawson cars without ever being asked.

'Hello Miss Lena, it's four months now, isn't it? They still fighting each other over there?'

'Yes, Matt, I am afraid they are.'

'Well, nothing changes much here either,' Matt replied as he dried her car windscreen.

Mercifully, Lena thought. Never had the cliché 'no news is good news' seemed more apposite.

As the car made its way west and the spire of the great cathedral came into sight, Lena felt a sudden desire to gambol through the fields in her bare feet, to sink her face into the wildflowers and throw her arms around the soft purple lupins and pink roses. Beautiful England – lovely, peaceful and uncomplicated. There was no need to wonder if the people who owned that farm, over there, were Protestant or Catholic. There were no tell-tale painted kerbs or ragged flags hanging from lamp-posts. In Ireland, every house and village seemed to have a back story. Who lives here? And who wants to drive them out? On the weekends she and Edward didn't travel to Fermanagh, they would sometimes drive through his favourite places, the dramatic, wild landscapes he tried so hard to sell to tour operators in the US and Europe. Early on, he had taken her on the high road across the basalt plateau of County Antrim, explaining how history had shaped the division of land.

'Most of the good farming land is in the valleys,' he said. 'Up here, the mountains are only good for grazing sheep or growing conifers.'

Lena by now knew the significance of this comment and had gazed out of the car window at the modern farmhouses and bungalows dotting the Antrim countryside. Where were the sectarian boundary lines? she wondered. Which contour on the map divided the land? The houses along the road to Salisbury were built of flint and ancient red-brick. Clematis-draped gateways revealed tantalising glimpses of manicured lawns and perennial borders of waving hollyhocks and delphiniums. She caught herself comparing them to the pebble-dash bungalows in Ireland but quickly reprimanded herself. If your main priority was shelter from the rain and cold, she thought, you mightn't be inclined to waste money on mere decoration.

Lena arrived early at the Cathedral Close café in Salisbury and began thinking how she might persuade her friend, Olivia, that her move to Belfast was not the disaster everyone had confidently predicted. Bang on cue, once they'd ordered sandwiches, her friend echoed Charlotte Dawson's assumptions.

'It must be absolutely frightful living amongst all that hatred and violence.'

Lena started off by saying that, while the violence was deeply depressing, there were compensations. 'The countryside is lovely – quite unspoilt and empty. The cottage I'm renting is 200 years old and only five minutes from the sea.'

'You're very brave,' said Olivia. 'Still, four months gone already and not long until you return to civilisation.'

'Strangely,' Lena persisted, 'leaving won't be easy.'

'Okay,' Olivia said. 'Persuade me.'

Lena quickly ran through in her head the stories she could tell, and those she could not. Maguire was definitely off-limits. Even Olivia would have heard of him.

'The work is far more interesting than in London. One of my clients, for example, is a Protestant paramilitary. He was charged with murdering a Catholic delivery man, but we got him acquitted.'

Olivia's eyes widened. It seemed encouraging so Lena continued. 'You'll find this hard to believe, but he's really quite entertaining.'

Olivia broke cover at that. 'How can you possibly call a terrorist, who may have killed someone just for his religion, "entertaining"?'

'I'm not sure he was guilty. He says the police intimidated an informer into giving false evidence against him.'

'The police did what? Got an informer to lie about him? Listen to yourself, Lena. Police officers have more than enough to do without locking up innocent people.'

The conversation had turned far sparkier than either intended. Lena changed the subject, discussing her plans for the cottage garden – and then, inevitably, Edward merited a mention.

'He's a straight-talker and quite handsome, if you like them a bit over-supplied on the testosterone side.'

Olivia was quick to translate.

'And what does he do, this gorgeous man?'

'His father runs the legal firm I work for, but Edward manages the family hotel business.'

Olivia's face fell. Lena could see her conjuring up visions of unappealing dumps on dreary seafronts. Clacton or Skegness with added pointless violence. A month or two earlier, she would have thought the same. A man who managed hotels in places most sensible people avoided was hardly a catch.

'There's a lot more to him than that,' Lena jumped in. 'He wanted to do music at uni, but his father insisted on business studies.'

Olivia looked even more downcast. Wondering how she might rescue the conversation, Lena hit upon the only virile-sounding description she could think of at short notice.

'He's also in the army, part-time. You won't have heard of the UDR, the Ulster Defence Regiment,' said Lena, doing her best to sound nonchalant. 'I'd never heard of them myself before I went over. They support the police, looking out for IRA suspects, mounting checkpoints, patrolling the border – that sort of thing.'

'Lena, you're dating a squaddie?'

'You'll just have to suspend judgement until you meet him,' Lena said limply.

Coffee and sandwiches consumed, photos of the cottage admired, it was time to go their separate ways – awkwardly, but promising to keep in touch.

On her drive home, Lena reproached herself for failing to explain her growing affection for Northern Ireland. The biggest decision Olivia seemed to have taken since they last met was what colour to paint the new extension – the sort of thing that might once have exercised Lena's own idler moments. It must have been quite a shock to hear one of her oldest friends talking quite calmly about murderers and the IRA. She wondered how Olivia would describe the meeting to her husband. 'Lena Dawson is a mess. She's going out with a squaddie but seems to believe the police in Northern Ireland are corrupt as hell.' Would that have been it?

She turned on the car radio to rid herself of a sense of inadequacy and caught the two o'clock news.

'Six heavily-armed IRA men were shot dead earlier today in an SAS operation in County Tyrone. An RUC spokesman says a passing member of the public was also fatally injured during the incident in the village of Loughside.'

Lena pulled straight into the next lay-by to assimilate the news. For a second or two, she wondered if Maguire was one of the dead, then told herself he was now Sinn Féin so it was highly unlikely, although he probably knew some, or all, of the IRA men. There's no real escape from Belfast, is there? she thought as she pulled out of the lay-by.

On Sunday, it was time for the catch-up with her father. He was in his study, reading a newspaper through his trademark half-moon spectacles. As usual, it felt like an encounter with the headmistress at school – never an altogether cheerful experience. Father and daughter had made most of the key decisions of her life sitting beside each other like this, before reaching a consensus that strangely resembled his opening position. This little chat, however, was going to have a harder edge. She was no longer a child.

'I've been asked to represent the family of Danny Maguire, an IRA man who was shot dead three years ago, along with a friend. The dead man's twin brother, Luke, and his widow, Sinéad, are my clients. They say it was a police ambush – a so-called "shoot-to-kill" case.'

'There was a shooting yesterday,' he said. 'Six IRA men dead, isn't it?'

'Yes, Dad. That's right. This other one – this alleged other one – was three years ago, in November 1984.'

'Luke Maguire,' he said. 'I've seen that name in the newspapers. Sounds a decidedly sinister character.'

'He's not someone you instantly warm to,' she conceded. 'But everyone, whoever they are, has the right to legal representation.'

Lena then outlined the case, her father listening closely.

'Get your boundaries very clear, Lena. You're a solicitor, not an investigator. You're not the police. You can't answer this man's questions. Your role is only to take whatever evidence the police can provide and ensure your client gets a fair hearing.'

'As a lawyer, I can introduce new evidence to the coroner, Dad. It's my job to see if there are any gaps or contradictions in the police evidence, to turn over stones, to see what's underneath.'

'Surely, that's a role for the press? And what about Edward? How does he feel about you taking the side of this IRA man? He could be forgiven for thinking you're trying to undermine the state he's protecting.'

'I am not taking sides or trying to undermine the state. Edward might not like it but he knows I have a professional duty, just as he has.'

'Fine words, Lena. But that's all they are. Be honest, if you go ahead, what's the real reason?'

Lena decided to be completely open. 'Because I'm bloody curious. I want to know the truth and, being selfish, it's a huge challenge. If I turn the case down, I will always wonder, for the rest of my life.'

'How does William Gordon feel about it?'

'He's not keen, but he won't stop me.'

'Well, I'm with William. I can't stop you either. But don't put your career at risk.'

'Didn't you make a similar decision in Kenya, Dad? The Nakuru affair? Your conscience told you to speak the truth, that soldiers had killed the four men in cold blood, that the law should take its course, despite it embarrassing the army. Isn't this the same?'

'I never intended for the soldiers to be dragged before a court, Lena. All I did was express my concerns to a junior diplomat at a social event. What happened afterwards was out of my hands.'

Lena was speechless. This was not what she had always understood.

'I thought you deliberately tipped off someone, hoping to hold the soldiers to account. They had, after all, killed four unarmed civilians.'

'Not at all, Lena. You misunderstand my role in the affair.'

She knew this was nonsense. He had always told her that he had wrestled with his conscience before deciding to break a confidence.

'But Dad, you told me you never regretted speaking up.'

'You're imagining it,' he said dismissively. 'Now let's go and have tea with your mother.'

Lena felt chastened as she followed him into the kitchen. When he drove her to the airport that evening, he could not meet her eyes as he lifted her suitcase out of the car and gave her a brief hug. Throughout her life, before any big decision, she had sought his endorsement. Now, for the first time, he was silently withholding support. The peace she had earlier felt was shattered. It was time to face the music in Belfast.

On Monday morning, she decided to share her involvement in the Maguire case with Georgina Porter.

'It's one of those "shoot-to-kill" cases, isn't it?' said Georgie. 'A massive challenge, Lena, well done.'

'Just one problem, Edward thoroughly opposes it.'

'Well, you can't refuse a client just because your boyfriend doesn't like it.'

'He's become much more than a "boyfriend", Georgie. I'm living in his world and I feel valued for the first time in my life, well since New York anyway.'

'You're not falling into the "Mr Darcy" trap, are you Lena? The only reason he was interested in Lizzy Bennet was because she was independent.'

Don't most women, Lena thought as she put the phone down, secretly want a 'Darcy'? Someone to admire, who makes them feel loved and secure? Re-evaluating her involvement in the Maguire case produced only one result but, counter-intuitively, it confirmed her decision. It would be far easier to walk away but, in the mix of reasons for studying law had been a desire 'to afflict the comfortable and comfort the afflicted' although that had somehow got lost along the way. She sighed and decided to locate Leglu, the French pathologist who had carried out the second autopsy. Ignoring Gordon's orders, she drove up the Falls Road to get Maguire's signature on the letter switching solicitors.

'Did you know any of the men killed at the weekend?' she asked as he signed.

'Of course,' he said impassively. 'I'm going to spend most of this week at their funerals. I've no doubt they were set up and executed, just like Danny was.'

'The circumstances are entirely different,' she answered. 'They were all armed to the teeth and were trying to blow up a police station. Lives were saved.'

'You're easily conned,' he said bitterly. 'The station wasn't manned. The IRA knew that. The Brits knew the IRA knew. There were no lives at risk. It was an ambush.'

It could hardly be that simple, she thought, but didn't want an argument. Handing back her pen, Maguire asked if she would like to meet Danny's widow.

'Sinéad's a strong woman, I think you'd like her.'

Lena was suspicious at this half-compliment. Maguire said nothing by accident.

'Do I really need to? She's just had open-heart surgery and hardly wants a stranger on her doorstep asking a load of questions.'

'I've already talked to her and she's up for it. She enjoys talking about Danny. Ask her for a few stories about his exploits.'

Lena would have preferred not to hear about a dead

IRA man's 'exploits' but Sinéad was her client and they had not yet met.

'This is where she's staying,' said Maguire, scribbling on a scrap of paper. 'Memorise these directions and hand it back. Sinéad is in a secure location to ensure the RUC doesn't harass her. No one visits except family. And you.'

Lena read the short note and handed back the scrap of paper. Maguire put a match to it in the empty fireplace. How ridiculous, she thought, repressing a smile. He saw and his face clouded.

'The RUC have raided this office about once a month for the last five years. Every scrap of paper is taken away for forensic examination. Sinéad will expect you at 2 p.m. this day next week. Go on your own.'

Lena put in some calls to people with links to the forensic science community, trying to track down Leglu. Many had heard of him, but none were sure where he was based after leaving Grenoble. Edward had not phoned after their row, so she spent a quiet weekend alone in Glenbarry, urging herself not to worry and failing dismally.

On Monday, she studied a map and set off for her meeting with Sinéad, taking the motorway west into County Tyrone and branching south towards the border. What would she be like, Lena wondered, the widow of an IRA man? She would doubtless try to persuade her that Danny Maguire was a man of impeccable character, cruelly maligned by the press. Following directions, she ended up driving down a muddy track to a modern, white bungalow surrounded by tall conifers. Lena's first thought when Sinéad Maguire opened the door was that she had once been a good-looking woman until widowhood and heart failure had done their worst. Her fair hair was scraped back off her face and there were deep lines between the corners of her mouth and chin. Sinéad first glanced over Lena's shoulder to check she was on her own, then returned a steady gaze to her visitor.

'Thank you for seeing me,' she said, holding Lena's hand and drawing her into the house. 'This must all seem so strange to you, coming from London.'

Lena withdrew her hand as soon as she decently could.

'Please sit down. You'll have tea?' Sinéad asked. 'The armchair is more comfortable than the sofa.'

Lena settled beside the fireplace where some logs were burning. The room was fragrant with wood smoke, but the fire did not give out much heat. As Sinéad made tea, she explained that Luke was over-concerned about her heart.

'Provided I don't overdo things, I'm expected to make a decent recovery,' she said, before showing Lena a photo of Danny, a carbon copy of Luke except for smiling eyes and moustache. As Lena made approving noises, Sinéad was encouraged enough to show her photos of her identical twin sons, Brendán and Ciarán, both studying at an Irish language teacher-training college in Belfast.

'Their father would have been so proud of them,' she said. 'They visit me at weekends and I see them when I go for cardiology check-ups in Belfast.'

Lena, thinking the conversation was becoming too personal, changed her tone from encouraging to professional.

'There's something we need to discuss,' she began crisply, pulling out a clipboard. 'I'm sorry to be blunt but why is your family so sure Danny didn't break through the roadblock and on what evidence are you accusing the RUC of murder? Because I can't find any.'

Even as she spoke, Lena knew she had gone too far but it was out there. Sinéad was silent for a moment, then looked at Lena through narrowed eyes.

'You are well aware I was at my husband's bedside when he died, and that I've just undergone open-heart surgery. Yet you say something like that. Luke warned me you're a straight-talker, which is fine, but I think what you just said was intentionally cruel.'

It was Lena's turn to be silent.

'I will do my best for you but I won't raise expectations. There is no hard evidence at all to show your husband was murdered. Now, tell me a bit more about him.'

Sinéad took a sip of her tea, wrapped her shawl around her shoulders even tighter and began.

'I'm assuming you know little about County Armagh, where Danny and I lived. Am I right?'

Lena's heart sank. She did not want a history lesson.

'Correct,' she said, 'but what has that to do with the case?'

'The countryside around here has been a battleground for over 400 years.'

'So, over four centuries ago,' said Lena. 'I'm more interested in what happened three years ago.'

Sinéad ignored her and ploughed on.

'It's where unionist-dominated councils refused to allocate houses to large Catholic families while single Protestant men got new-built, four-bedroom homes. This land is disputed; every village, every bridge, every field.'

'Very good. Could you tell me a bit more about Danny?' she asked.

Sinéad's face crumpled and Lena realised, her heart sinking even further, that she was going to start crying. Turning her face away, Sinéad patted her eyes then blew her nose before throwing the damp tissue into the fire and reaching for another.

'I'm sorry,' she said. 'I can't control it. It's exhausting.'

'From what Luke said, I gather Danny was quite a character,' Lena said, hoping to sound more encouraging.

'Oh, he was a man in a million. Everyone cheered up when he walked into a room. Even the ordinary police in Lurgan liked him. I wouldn't know where to start.'

'Start at the beginning then. Where was he from? How did you meet him?'

'He was born in Lurgan; you must have passed it on the motorway. He and Luke were the youngest of the Maguires. Lurgan and its neighbour, Portadown, were always segregated. Tensions were bubbling just under the surface. None of us Catholics could get work in the big engineering and pharmaceutical firms but there was no killing until July 1972 when the Orange Order marched through a Catholic part of Portadown. The police and British Army stood by, saluted them even, and the evil genie was out of the bottle. Everything changed overnight. Parts of town emptied, the ones that were mixed. Both sides, mind. I'm not saying it was just one side.'

'This is all interesting, Sinéad, but Danny, I want to know about him.'

'When I first met him, he was just a schoolboy, not at all like Luke, happy-go-lucky. But then Mikey was shot and everything changed.'

'Mikey?'

'Mikey Byrne was Danny's best friend. They grew up together, went to dances together, played Gaelic together, cycled down through Banbridge to the Mourne Mountains together, camping and staying in hostels. Then, one night, Mikey didn't come home. Four days later, they found his body tied to a mattress in the Bann. He'd been tortured. Word on the street was that a UDR part-timer was involved.'

Lena shuddered. The motorway she had driven down earlier had crossed the River Bann.

'Danny disappeared after Mikey's funeral. Took off for weeks. He was found eventually in a byre on the edge of town. He'd been living rough in Sligo. Nobody could help him, not his parents, not other friends, not me even, although everyone tried. Danny was a lost soul, killing himself with grief and drink. I don't know how he did it but Luke gradually brought him back to us again. They went to meetings together. It was around then that we got married.'

'Okay, got it. Now tell me what he was like.'

'He wasn't good-looking in the usual way. He just made people love him. He was always in trouble but usually managed to talk his way out of it, like the day he and Luke robbed the tickman in Portadown.'

Lena sat up in her chair. 'Now Sinéad, please don't tell me anything compromising. At least not about anyone who's still alive. About Danny, you can say what you like. What's a "tickman"?'

For a second time, Sinéad's eyes narrowed, but she carried on.

'The tickman would go around the estate every Friday collecting each family's weekly dues on their televisions and washing machines to put in his brown leather satchel.

Danny had a great idea one week. He told everyone to beg, borrow, empty their piggy banks, anything, and pay off their debts. When the poor fella did his rounds, he must have thought all his Christmases had come at once. Each family was paying up, and he was crossing them off his list. The IRA robbed him just as he was leaving the area. It was drinks all round in the GAA club that night.'

'Didn't the police investigate?'

'You're kidding. The RUC didn't dare come into the estate. Then there was the day Danny and Luke ambushed a meat lorry at the petrol station just off the motorway. Held up the driver at gunpoint and sent the container around Craigavon, handing out steaks and roast beef. We ate like kings for weeks.'

'So, no reason at all for the RUC to shoot him then?' said Lena, bringing Sinéad back to earth with a bump.

'I don't know where you come from, but around here, we don't think it's right to kill someone who provides food for people living on the breadline – or for getting loan sharks off their backs. You want to know why I'm certain Danny was assassinated? Because he was street-wise, he knew how to stay alive. No one, and I mean no one, would break through a police roadblock. Even if you were desperate, hiding something – or someone – in a car, you wouldn't do it. No IRA man, or anyone with any sense, who saw a roadblock ahead, would speed up or drive at it. He was just coming home to me and the boys. It could not have happened the way they say. It's a lie, and everyone knows it: the police, the judges, the ordinary people. Even Fearghal McNally knows it's a lie.'

'Who's Fearghal McNally?' Lena asked.

'The MP for Newry/Armagh. SDLP. He hates republicans like poison. Even he's been asking questions at Westminster.' Sinéad looked straight at Lena. 'It's only you, Miss Dawson, it seems, and the newspapers, who believe the police.'

'Call me Lena, please, and what I believe is irrelevant,' she said. 'But thanks for giving me a clearer idea of who Danny was. He sounds memorable, indeed. Can we discuss now what I am planning to do?'

'Of course, talk away.' Sinéad was getting tired of explaining her life to this stranger.

Lena said her priority was finding new evidence.

'I'm going to study whatever forensic papers and photographs I can get my hands on and try to track down Leglu, the forensic pathologist. Very unfortunately, the RUC have already destroyed the car Danny was driving. Your previous solicitors wanted to see the full police file and I'll be pressing for that too.'

'You're our only hope,' Sinéad said to Lena's discomfort.

'I believe you were called to the hospital after Danny was shot. Did he say anything at all of any evidential value?'

'We had to threaten legal action to get me and the boys in – but Danny was beyond speaking coherently by the time I arrived in the ward, drifting in and out of consciousness. I held his hand until he stopped breathing.'

Gazing into the fire, Sinéad seemed to go into a trance.

'He looked so beautiful lying there,' she said softly. 'The sound of his breathing seemed lovelier than any music I have ever heard. We had been on such a long journey together, my Danny and I, and we were alone together when his journey ended.'

Lena found, to her great consternation, that her eyes were filling. She dropped her clipboard to allow her to conceal her face as she picked it up, only managing a weak 'how awful'.

Her words snapped Sinéad out of her day-dream.

'Sorry, I've embarrassed you,' she said.

'Not at all,' said Lena, more annoyed by her own over-emotional response than embarrassed.

She had heard more than enough. It was time to go.

'I have to get back to the office. You've been very helpful,' she said, closing her briefcase.

As they both stood up, Sinéad said she would be coming to Belfast for a cardiology appointment soon if they needed to talk again. At the front door, Lena went through the usual end-of-meeting routine, handing over her card. Driving down the lane leading from the cottage, she told herself that Sinéad's stories of Danny's 'exploits' had been restricted to Robin Hood-style tales of wealth redistribution rather than placing no-warning car bombs in busy city centres or attaching under-car booby traps.

But the overall account of her life and Danny's was disturbing. There was more going on here, much more, than just a sectarian tit-for-tat battle between Catholics and Protestants. Agriculture, housing, the courts, education, policing – every aspect of life was affected. Back at the cottage, she treated herself to a large gin-and-tonic before bed. It had been nearly two weeks since their row, and she was aching to see Edward again. She woke at four o'clock from a nightmare. A mattress floating in the River Bann, swirling and turning over in the foamy, brown current, Edward's body tied to it, his face swollen and white.

6

'Did you hear on the news about a man being arrested in Larne off the ferry from Scotland with a pile of drugs?'

Lena wondered if there was anything Geraldine enjoyed more than breaking bad news.

'No, but I guess you're going to tell me,' she replied.

'It's Darren Barrett. The desk-sergeant at Castlereagh is just off the phone. He wants a legal visit pronto. You'll have to go right away.'

Lena sighed. As if she did not have enough to worry about, she now had to drive to the RUC's main interrogation centre at Castlereagh, deep in dreary East Belfast.

What an idiot, she thought as she headed for the lift. Only out of jail a month or so and already he's back in trouble. As she drove through East Belfast, she thought it could be Ealing or Harpenden – somewhere nothing ever happened – unless you knew that the kerbs on the footpaths, just out of sight down the side streets, were painted red-white-and-blue and that wooden pallets and other rubbish littered every patch of urban green space in preparation for Eleventh Night bonfires. Checked through security at Castlereagh, she was handed Barrett's charge sheet and perused it in a tiny consulting room waiting for her client to be brought in. The police had thrown the book at him, she thought, and who could blame them?

'Darren, have you any explanation for this?' she asked as he arrived, noting he had at least the grace to look a little bashful.

'I was on the ferry coming home from a Rangers match in Glasgow,' he said. 'They stopped me coming down the ramp.'

'Don't play around. I haven't got time,' she said.

'I was just bringing back a wee bit for myself and a bit more for a party.'

'A party? Fifty kilos of top-strength cannabis and 20,000 tabs of ecstasy? Some party.'

'We all carry a wee bit of stuff over with us or a wee bit back, depending on how the market sits.'

'So, there wasn't any party. You were planning to sell your "wee bit of stuff" to make money. I despair. Whatever happened to the rebirth of The Shankill Stinger?'

Barrett's blushes then gave way to whingeing. 'You don't expect me to pay for the gym and supplements with my dole money, do you? Someone on the Shankill must have tipped the Peelers off. They've been watching me like hawks, so they have.'

'If you knew that, why didn't you keep your nose clean? Don't blame the police, they're just doing their job. It's always someone else's fault with you, Darren. According to the custody record, the drugs were found inside the door panels of your own car, registered in your own name. At least if it was borrowed or hired, we might have had a defence.'

'It was just bad luck, I'd got away with it before. You're smarter than a barrel of monkeys, Lena. You'll think of something.'

Which, she wondered, was more irritating? The usual phoney bravado or this new wheedling? The door opened. Two detectives came in, introduced themselves, and began questioning him. After half a dozen 'no comments' from Barrett, they left saying they would be back with photographic evidence of what had been found in his car, leaving Lena and Barrett alone again.

'Say nothing when they come back in and I'll try and get you bailed,' she said. 'Although, it won't be easy. This is hardly your first drug bust.'

The two detectives came back in with photographs. Darren shrugged his shoulders and looked sheepish but said nothing. When they left, his confidence in her was undimmed. 'You'll get me off, I know you will,' he said.

'I'll try, but you're going back to jail for a while. Behave yourself and I'll come and see you in a week or two.'

There seemed no escape for her from Crumlin Road and its stink of rotten food and sweaty men.

Later in the week, Steve Sullivan phoned. She filled him in on Barrett's arrest before he asked if she was still seeing Edward.

'He's not speaking to me after I agreed to represent the Maguire family.'

'And how is that going?'

'I've not seen the full police file yet – forensic reports, eyewitness statements, the autopsy, photographs, et cetera.'

'That's basic stuff.'

'It should be, but it's far from easy to access. I write to the coroner, he passes it to the police. They write back to the coroner and he writes back to me. You know the "dog ate my homework" excuse? It's nothing compared to what the RUC come up with. Either it's "we're short-staffed" or "it's the marching season", "someone has been promoted", or "the files have been moved". They're inventive, I'll give them that. They get one more chance or I'm taking a judicial review.'

'Why not cut to the chase and go for one now?'

'I don't believe in taking judicial reviews every two minutes and, to be honest, I also want to keep it out of the newspapers. Once I appear in court as Maguire's solicitor, I can't see how Edward and I can ever patch things up.'

'Is he really that important to you? You've only known him a couple of months.'

'Yes, Steve, he is. It doesn't take long.'

'Point taken. Isn't there any other avenue you can follow?'

'Well, yes. After his death, the Maguires kept Danny's body in the freezer for a month while they won the right to an independent autopsy. It was carried out by a French pathologist, a Professor Jean Leglu. His report did not contradict the official one, but it's probably worth speaking to him.'

'It sure is. He mightn't have held back some suspicions in his report.'

'He's retired and is proving hard to find. I've not told Maguire because it may be a complete waste of time.'

'It's still worth pursuing,' said Sullivan.

After Lena put the phone down, a darkness crept over her. It was weeks since she and Edward had spoken. She had heard him talking to his father in the office two consecutive Friday afternoons and had hoped for a knock on her door but, each week, the whine of the lift descending told her he was leaving the building. How was it possible to turn against her so quickly?

Then, one night, a cold body climbed into bed beside her. After a moment's panic, she remembered the many nights the same welcome, cold body had arrived unannounced. Half asleep but smiling, she turned and entwined her arms around his neck. The smell of stale alcohol hit her. His stubble rasped against her cheeks and neck. Repelled, she prised herself away from him before grabbing a dressing gown and standing over the bed.

'Who on earth do you think you are? Arriving here drunk in the middle of the night?' she said.

'Aren't you glad to see me?' he slurred. 'Maybe you prefer sleeping with that terrorist you work for.'

'How dare you,' she said, slamming the bedroom door behind her and running downstairs.

What on earth should she do? She could hardly throw him out into the night. He was lying upstairs, naked, in her bed. Edward, the controlled, the disciplined, behaving like a drunken thug. She would have to deal with it in the morning. Making herself a cup of hot milk, she bedded down in the spare room. Early next morning, she crept into her own room and fetched clothes. Edward was asleep on his back, sprawled diagonally across the bed. How sweet he looked, she thought, how innocent. She longed to lie down beside him and rest her head on his chest but closed the door and left for work. On the road, she began planning how to respond when he rang to apologise.

Around 11 a.m., with no call from Edward, she took a taxi to the library at Queen's University, continuing her search for Leglu. The criminology section kept journals on forensic science. Lena began searching the index in each one and, after an hour or so, hit the jackpot. Leglu had written a piece on the effects of dum-dum bullets on the human body for a Swiss publication, the *International Journal of Ballistic and Forensic Science*. Having photocopied details, she headed back to the office, deciding not to endure another Friday afternoon listening to Edward's voice talking to his father, knowing he would make no effort to speak to her. At home, she opened the spare room cupboard. His clothes still hung there. He might have taken them when he left – but he hadn't. It seemed a hopeful sign. She changed into pyjamas, opened a bottle of wine, and sat watching TV with Peanut.

As Lena sat in Glenbarry, praying for the phone to ring, Edward Gordon and Paul Donaldson were at a meeting with other mid-ranking RUC and UDR men at the barracks in Enniskillen. They rarely discussed personal matters but Paul could not stop himself raising the rumours he'd heard of Lena working on the Maguire case.

'It's probably just barrack-room gossip,' he said. 'Likely nothing to it but I thought you should know.'

'Unfortunately it's true,' Edward said.

'Surely your father could stop it,' said Paul, trying to hide his surprise.

'He's already tried. She dug her heels in.'

'You could do without the aggravation.'

'There's no aggravation, we've split up.'

'Then the women of Ulster had better form an orderly queue.'

Paul's feeble attempt at humour passed Edward by. He was thinking of how he'd adopted a stray kitten when he was little. His mother, finding it on his bed, had exiled it to the stables where it grew up catching mice, hardly recognising its former saviour and scratching him if he tried to pet it. His piano tutor had remarked on the lines of little scabs up his arms. But the kitten had always been forgiven.

The exchange with Paul meant the situation was public, or soon would be. He had to make a decision. A few days later, Lena found a note on the hallway floor.

'We need to talk. I'll ring later. Edward.'

Before she had time to think, the phone rang.

'I'm in Killyleagh, I'll be there in five minutes,' he said.

'What makes you think you're welcome?' she replied but the line was already dead.

When his car drew up, she was waiting for him at the front door, arms folded.

'Whatever you've come to say, you can say it here.'

He stood awkwardly, looking round.

'I'm not going until we've sorted things out. Please, Lena, be reasonable.'

She waited, glaring at him in the driveway, before turning and walking through the front door. He followed and sat at the kitchen table, unable to meet her eye.

'Firstly, I apologise for the last time we saw each other,' he said, looking out of the window towards the lough.

'I don't think you saw me at all,' she said.

'Ah Lena, don't make this any harder than it already is. I don't know what else I can say.'

'You're not the victim here, Edward.'

He sank his head into his hands, covering his eyes.

'Okay, here's the explanation. I was training at Ballykinler UDR base that week, about twenty miles from here, with some of the lads from Enniskillen. We were out celebrating our last night and one of them started going on about "Provo lawyers". I had too much to drink and nearly smashed his face in. I shouldn't have been driving at all, let alone come here.'

'But you did.'

'Yes, I did. All I wanted was to talk it over.'

'Can't you think of a more convincing excuse? You didn't do any talking. I had to fight you off.'

'Lena, please. I feel bad enough already.'

'For God's sake, Edward. My work for Maguire will be over in a few weeks,' she said. 'It's work, a professional commitment.'

He silenced her then with one line.

'I met up with an ex-girlfriend last week. Someone I was seeing before you arrived.'

Lena's stomach hit the floor.

'It was a mistake,' he said. 'I had nothing to say to her.'

'Is that supposed to be a compliment?'

'Look, Lena, we can try to make this work, or we can let it go. It's up to you.'

It was a tricky moment. She had to think quickly. The way her stomach sunk had given her an answer, of sorts. She honestly could not bear the thought of living without him.

'If you ever turn up here drunk again, or abuse me,' she said, 'you and I are finished. Now, let's get out of here. I need to eat.'

Neither of them knew what to do after that except get in the car and drive.

'Where are we going?' she asked, hoping to break the tension.

'Somewhere special, just ten minutes away,' he said.

They drove deeper into the drumlin country between Glenbarry and Ballynahinch and Edward began, rather formally, telling her how, during his teenage years, he would spend his summers on a friend's farm nearby. He had ordered his first pint of Guinness, he said, in the place they were driving to. He had met his first girlfriend there. They had written throughout the year but the magic was gone by the following summer.

'Before the Troubles, none of us had any idea what was around the corner. Everyone in the bar we're going to was local, mainly small farmers or farm labourers – and the occasional over-privileged kid like me. Most of the clientele now are teachers and civil servants – commuters from Belfast. But it still feels like a place that time has passed by. And there's sometimes music.'

When they drew up to The Halfway House it looked nondescript enough to Lena, just a two-storey white-washed building with a black front door. Inside though it was warm and welcoming, with deep armchairs and an open fire. They ordered bar food and settled down in a corner of the lounge. From a room close by, Lena heard someone tuning a violin, followed by the sound of fiddles and a tin whistle.

'Where's that coming from?' she asked, looking around but seeing no musicians.

'In there,' Edward replied, pointing at a side door.

'What's in there?'

'It's a small room where the local Catholics used to sit. They sat in there – and we sat out here.'

'You were segregated here, even before the Troubles?'

'I suppose it suited both sides. I hadn't heard Irish traditional music until I came here for the first time. That's another reason why this place is special. For me anyway.'

The two of them fell silent, unspoken words still hanging between them, eating their food and listening to the music that was drifting towards them over the gentle murmur of conversation. Lena leaned back in her chair. As each tune ended there was gentle applause.

'That was "On Raglan Road",' Edward said. 'Patrick Kavanagh wrote the words, a poet from County Monaghan, just across the border.'

After a pause, the music started again.

Edward began talking about plans for the weekend. A visit to Fermanagh was probably not a good idea, he said, until the Maguire case was over. Understatement of the year, thought Lena. Then the sound of an unaccompanied male tenor voice started flowing through the bar like cool, fresh water. Lena reached over and touched Edward's knee, holding a finger to her lips. He stopped talking and listened, like everyone else. Even the barmen stopped serving. The singer's voice was perfectly controlled, the words crystal clear:

> I hope the day will surely come,
> When we'll join hands together-oh
> 'Tis then I'll take my darlin' home,
> In spite of wind and weather-oh.
>
> And let them all say what they will,
> And let them reel and rally-oh,
> For I shall wed the girl I love,
> The Flower of Magherally-oh.'

A moment's silence, then muted applause.

'You know something,' said Lena, 'I'm beginning to

think I might not go back to London at the end of the year.'

'I had rather taken that for granted,' Edward said softly. 'Why would you go?'

Looking back much later, she realised it was at that precise moment – listening to 'The Flower of Magherally' – that she decided to stay in Ireland, with all its dangerous ambiguities, its stinging hatreds and its aching beauty. And she knew she loved Edward, who loved her back, even as she used all her wit and wisdom to defend the rights of someone he believed to be his deadly enemy. England, Hampshire, London – all that undoubted loveliness and prosperity now seemed trivial, shallow. Back at the cottage, she took Edward by surprise, shutting the door on the outside world and marching him straight to the stairs. During the night, words came to both of them that neither had ever thought to use.

'I love you so much,' he whispered, his arms encircling her. 'You're my "Star of the County Down".'

'You're my sun, moon and stars,' she whispered back. 'There's nothing left for County Down.'

In the morning, Lena woke first and crept out of bed, tiptoeing downstairs in her dressing gown. As she moved about the kitchen, he arrived beside her, wearing a towel around his waist and last night's shirt – both of them self-conscious.

'What happens now?' he finally said in a low voice.

'You wash and get dressed,' she said briskly, pretending not to understand the question. 'We both have work to get to.'

He meekly went upstairs. She heard water running.

Then he was downstairs again, dressed and ready to leave.

'Despite how it began, we had a lovely evening,' Lena said.

He stepped towards her and held her so tight she could barely breathe, then left to go to work. Lena stood at the kitchen window for some minutes, in a state of euphoria that only ended when she thought of the calamity that lay ahead – unless she managed to extricate herself from the Maguire case as cleanly as possible.

When she called the forensics journal in Geneva, its editor said he would pass on the message to Leglu. That would be the final piece of the jigsaw in the exit strategy she was planning. She would speak to Leglu and, if he had nothing further to add, present Maguire with a summary of her findings allowing her to wriggle her way out of anything other than the work she had already prepared for the immunity hearing.

The best way of implementing the strategy, she thought, was to trap Maguire into an advance agreement so she rang and arranged a visit in what she had come to regard as his 'lair' on the Falls Road. After the usual annoying wait for his arrival, Lena tried once more to convince him how impossible it was to prove the RUC had ambushed and killed his brother.

'Suppose they did ambush his car and cobbled together an agreed account. How are we going to prove they're all lying? If evidence exists, the police have it – the same people you say are the perpetrators. Unless one of them incriminates the others, you're banging your head off a brick wall. What's more, you're banging Sinéad's head off the same wall when she's extremely ill.'

Maguire remained calm but his words were as sharp as needles.

'You believe what you like Lena but you are completely out of order for even mentioning Sinéad's illness. The last thing she wants is anyone using that as an excuse to abandon inquiries into her husband's murder.'

Lena felt humiliated. Worse, she knew she deserved it.

'Is there any mileage, do you think, in finding Leglu?' she asked innocently. 'He retired last year, so he'll be hard to locate.'

'You'll find him, Lena. I know you will.'

'If I do, he may refuse to meet me. Even if he agrees, he may have nothing further to add.'

'We'll face that one if we have to,' Maguire said.

'I want you to understand something very clearly, Luke. If I locate Leglu and he agrees to meet me and has nothing further to add, I will regard that as ending any further commitment to you – other than preparing for the immunity hearing.'

'If you say so.'

Lena now had her escape route.

Three days later there was a telephone number on her desk in Geraldine's writing. Leglu, now living in Strasbourg, had agreed to speak to her. She immediately rang and introduced herself.

'Professor Leglu, I am calling you on behalf of the Maguire family. You wrote an independent report in 1985 into the shooting of Danny Maguire and Seán Reid. I wonder if you remember the case?' she asked.

'*Naturellement*, I remember. I only wish I had been able to do more for the family.'

Lena wondered if pathologists remembered all the grim results of their work, all the tear-stained faces.

'Is it possible you still have the notes on which you based your report, the ones you wrote at the time?'

'Yes, I have them stored securely.'

'I am acting for Danny Maguire's family. Could you retrieve the notes if I fax you a signed consent form? I'd like to come and speak to you.'

'If you wish, although I do not think I have anything to add,' said Leglu.

'Danny's twin brother, Luke, was in jail when you worked on the case. You never met him. He is anxious that I speak to you myself.'

'Very well, if it helps. I will be at home in Strasbourg for the rest of this week, but on Monday, I leave for a symposium in Australia.'

Leglu gave her his address and they agreed to meet at lunchtime on Sunday in Strasbourg. There were no direct flights, even from Dublin, so she booked an early flight on Sunday morning to Heathrow and a connection to Frankfurt where there was a bus service across the border into France. Then she drove to get Maguire's signature on the consent form. She was aghast when he immediately demanded to go with her.

'I want to see his face so I can tell if there's the slightest doubt in his mind,' he insisted.

Lena had a brainwave. 'But that's impossible,' she said. 'The only flight is through Heathrow and you're banned from England under the Prevention of Terrorism Act.'

'You fly through Heathrow,' he said. 'I'll find another way.'

She reluctantly agreed to meet him at the gothic cathedral in Strasbourg at midday on Sunday. The next hurdle was explaining her absence for the weekend. Telling Edward she was flying to France to discuss an old pathology report with Maguire in tow did not seem expedient, so she phoned him with what she hoped was a credible story about her mother having a private medical appointment with an arthritis specialist in London.

'Driving to London and back in a day is too much for Dad and he can't miss Sunday morning services in Little Woldham so I've offered to drive Mum up. We'll stay with her sister in Putney and I'll be back in Glenbarry by Sunday evening.'

'Of course you have to go,' Edward said. 'I'll travel with Dad to Fermanagh. Give your parents my regards.'

'I'll start planning for your visit in the summer while I'm there.'

'Thought you'd never ask. Safe trip. Love you.'

And that was it. Done. On Sunday morning, she parked the Mini at Belfast's second airport, nearer the city centre, and made a smooth connection through Heathrow, catching the Strasbourg bus in Frankfurt and reaching the cathedral before midday, hoping Maguire had changed his mind. But he was already there, waiting underneath the astronomical clock, looking unusually smart in a jacket and trousers. He had caught the ferry from Rosslare to Le Havre, he said, and a supporter had driven him overnight across France from there.

They took a cab to Leglu's modern apartment. He was slight, bespectacled and wore jeans, a black polo-neck and a sad smile. Lena and Maguire sat at a glass-topped table in his immaculate kitchen while he made strong coffee. Maguire's leg began a nervous jiggle against a table leg, causing the glass to shake and making ripples in his mug. Leglu noticed and got straight to the point.

'Mr Maguire, please ask me any questions that trouble you but I am unable to add anything to my report on how your brother and his friend died. I remember well the case. It was a pleasure to visit your lovely country – although in sad times.'

Maguire jumped straight in.

'Sir, I would like to know if you had any doubts that you did not include in the report. How did the last bullet hit Danny without first penetrating the car?'

'I have re-read the papers from my secure depository,' said the pathologist. 'The police account is clear, that your brother, already seriously wounded, fell through the car door and onto the ground. The fatal bullet then passed under the car and hit poor Danny's head. I found this part of the police account difficult, though not impossible, to believe – that a bullet would fly unimpeded through the narrow gap of about eighteen centimetres between the chassis and the ground …'

'If you had doubts, why didn't you put them in your report?' interrupted Maguire.

'My doubts were only my opinion – not based on evidence. It would not have been right to disturb your family with them. Danny being hit under the car – it's what you say in English "an unlikely story" but there is nothing to contradict the police account.'

'Did you examine the car?' asked Lena.

'I specialise in bodies, you understand. The effect on

bone and flesh of traumatic force. In that, I am an expert – not of what happens when bullets hit metal, glass and plastic. From the photographs, the car was – you say "riddled", yes? – with bullet holes. The police, they were making very sure no one got out alive.'

'Can I see your notes?' Maguire asked Leglu.

'Yes, of course, I retrieved them from my store. Here they are.' Leglu had a box-file ready and pushed it across the table at Maguire.

'I have not included photos of your brother. I do not think you need to see them,' he said.

Inside were hand-written notes, diagrams and police photos of the car, canes pushed through the bullet holes to show the angles from where bullets had been fired.

'Do you wish to study them?' asked Leglu.

'Please,' said Luke.

Leglu turned to Lena. 'Mademoiselle, shall we leave Mr Maguire here for a few minutes?'

'Yes of course. Luke, take your time.'

Lena and Leglu walked into his *salon* where they talked about some of his old cases and the upcoming symposium in Melbourne. After thirty minutes, they both agreed to return to the kitchen.

'Mr Maguire, I wish with all my heart I could help you more,' said Leglu.

Maguire stared at the floor and pushed the papers away. Lena thought no man she had ever met lost his temper so quickly – except perhaps Barrett. Maguire stood up and went to the window before asking Leglu if he could have a copy of the notes.

'That will not be possible, I am afraid. They are my

personal property. You have my official report,' he replied. 'Everything is in that, based on the evidence.'

With Maguire staring out of the window, Leglu looked at Lena, raised his shoulders in the Gallic way and placed a finger over his lips. 'He is hurting,' he mouthed to her before standing up and joining Maguire, putting an arm around his shoulder.

'My dear man, you are torturing yourself,' he said softly. 'Your twin brother was a young man, a loving husband and father – but he is gone. You have done enough.'

Maguire was silent. Leglu turned towards Lena.

'It's always the same,' he said quietly. 'The police have all the evidence. The family has no power.'

They phoned a taxi, said their goodbyes and left the apartment, Maguire sullen and silent. On the footpath outside, Lena asked him how he was getting home.

'I'm going home with you,' he said.

'But you can't. You're barred from England,' she said.

'Yes,' he said, speaking as though she was a child. 'But what can they do to me in Heathrow? Deport me to Belfast? I couldn't risk being stopped on the outward journey, but going home – no problem.'

Lena could only sigh and ask the taxi to drop them at the bus station. From there, the coach left for Frankfurt, two-and-a-half hours east across the flat German countryside. As soon as she was settled in her seat, she plugged in earphones to avoid conversation with Maguire. After half an hour, as she turned the tape cassette, he asked what she was listening to.

'Elgar. The "Cello Concerto",' said Lena, hoping it would shut him up.

'Bit of a dirge. Shame about his politics.'

'What?'

'Edward Elgar signed the Ulster Covenant in 1914.'

'He did what?'

'The Covenant, pledging to fight against Irish Home Rule "by any means necessary". They signed it in blood. If you knew some Irish history, Lena, uncouth people like me wouldn't catch you out.'

'You haven't caught me out. What do I care about Elgar's politics?'

'You're surprised I've even heard of Elgar, aren't you? We had culture in Ireland, you know, before you lot had agriculture.'

She supposed that was his idea of humour and let it sit. Maguire shrugged and they carried on in silence. On the plane, she had time to think. Although she had no intention of informing Maguire, Leglu had revealed a potential line of inquiry during their discussion. He had never examined the car before it was destroyed. It might now be crushed, with very limited – if any – evidential value, but it was still worth a look. She'd not let Maguire know, however, unless something emerged.

Between connecting flights at Heathrow, Maguire phoned ahead and told his driver to double-park at the terminal in Belfast for a speedy departure back to the Falls. He then advised Lena, as if it were necessary, that they should walk separately through the terminal and stop for nothing, even if the police arrested him. It was dark by the time they landed. The airport was busy with passengers returning from weekends away. Without checked luggage, Lena and Maguire walked separately towards the main exit, Maguire leading. Standing behind him on a down escalator, Lena heard someone above calling her name. She turned round, looked up and froze. About a dozen steps behind her were Edward and Paul Donaldson. She waved cheerfully at them, then pointed downwards, signalling she'd meet them leaving the escalator. Then she nudged Maguire's back with her knee and whispered, 'Get out quick. I've been spotted.' He did not turn, just walked briskly away and was gone. One advantage of being a habitual criminal, she thought, was being quick on the uptake. At ground level, Lena turned and waited for Edward with a welcoming smile. He gave her a quick hug.

'This is lucky. The London flight landed just before ours. Here, give me your case,' he said.

'I thought you were off to Fermanagh for the weekend,' she said.

'Paul and I decided to escape to the Algarve for some golf.'

Paul was already looking for the exit through the maze of glass partitions when his police training kicked in.

'That's a sight I never thought I'd see,' he said. 'Luke Maguire in an airport. Isn't he barred from England under the PTA?'

'What?' Edward said.

'It's him, over there, getting into that black cab,' said Paul, pointing at Maguire's back.

Edward stared through the glass wall and then back at Lena. 'What's Maguire doing here?'

'How would I know?' said Lena. 'He can go wherever he likes, I guess. Did you have a good weekend?'

'He certainly wasn't on the Faro flight,' said Paul. 'He must have been on your flight, Lena, from Heathrow.'

'Possibly,' Lena said airily, beginning to walk towards the exit but Edward held tight onto her arm, turning her to face him.

'You and Maguire were on the same plane? That's some coincidence and I don't believe in coincidences.'

Lena realised she was caught. Paul had discreetly moved away.

'Okay, Edward. Cards on the table. I had to see a witness in Strasbourg. Maguire insisted on coming with me.'

'My God. I don't believe it,' Edward said before walking through the exit towards the car park, Lena behind him and Paul following. At his car, he threw her briefcase into the boot and jerked his head to indicate she should get into the passenger seat before saying goodbye to Paul. Lena's Mini was parked nearby but she decided not to point this out. When she and Edward were on the motorway into Belfast, she began explaining.

'There's no need for a huge row, Edward. I was in Strasbourg speaking to the pathologist who gave the Maguires their second opinion. It had to be done. If you don't believe me, you can ring him yourself. His name is Professor Jean Leglu.'

'I don't care who he is. I care that you lied to me and put my friend anywhere near the vermin you're working for. I advise you not to say another word.'

After a silent drive to Glenbarry, he lifted her case out of the car and dropped it onto the gravel driveway before leaving. She stood and listened to the last sound of his engine fading, walked forlornly into the back garden and sat on a cold, concrete bench in the dark, the scene at the airport replaying in her head, before dragging herself indoors.

In the morning, there was no alternative but to call a taxi back to the airport, pick up her car and drive into work. On the way, she turned on the car radio and immediately wished she hadn't. The bloody IRA had blown up some poor policeman in Armagh city the previous evening.

'An RUC spokesman said the terrorists planted an under-car booby trap device that detonated as the officer reversed his car out of his driveway,' said the newsreader as if she was reading a laundry list. Ian Paisley was demanding the re-introduction of internment. Willie McCrea wanted to bomb County Louth from the air. James Molyneaux wanted full integration with the UK. She was sick of it all, sick of Edward's temper and sick of Barrett and Maguire. But worse lay ahead. When she arrived at work, Geraldine had a message for her.

'Luke Maguire has been arrested for that bombing in Armagh, Lena. He's in Castlereagh and wants you to come straight away.'

What else could go possibly wrong? she wondered, making her weary way back to her car before driving to Castlereagh and the inevitable hostility of the duty desk sergeant. Maguire could not have reached home on the Falls Road when the Armagh policeman was killed, forty miles away. On the custody notes, she saw Maguire's home address in Kashmir Road written down – the address he had told her was so secret she should never think of visiting. What a farce. In a holding cell, Maguire was running his hands through his hair.

'You know I couldn't have been involved, Lena. We were in Strasbourg. Tell them and get me out of here.'

'I'll see what I can do. I've still got our boarding cards in my handbag.'

She asked at the counter to see whoever was in charge. After a long wait, two detectives arrived.

'The bombing last night, what time was it?' she asked one.

'About ten-thirty.'

'Mr Maguire and I were out of the country, together, until after ten last night when we landed back in Belfast. Here are our boarding cards. He couldn't possibly have been involved in planning or carrying out the attack in Armagh.'

'Where were you?' he asked.

'We were in Strasbourg, seeing an expert witness.'

'And who might that be?'

'A forensic pathologist. Professor Jean Leglu.'

'We'll be checking with the airline – and your pathologist.'

'Check away, but he was due to leave for Australia this morning.'

She handed over the boarding cards and went back in to see Maguire.

'They're talking to the airline. You should be out shortly.'

'Who were you with at the airport?' he asked.

'So you noticed. Not that it's any of your business, but it was my boyfriend, my lover. As you can imagine, he wasn't too thrilled to see us together.'

'I'm sorry, Lena. That was unlucky.'

'As you Irish say, I "don't have my sorrows to seek",' she

said. 'Let me know when you're out and I'll be in touch during the week.'

Back in the office, Geraldine stopped her again, looking pleased this time. Her harassment of the Courts Office had worked, she said. The Appeal Court had set a day aside at the beginning of the autumn legal term to hear arguments on the disputed immunity certificates. The news helped Lena come to a decision. Heather Collins had visited the office the previous week, showing off her new baby. The original arrangement was for Lena to return to London in December but she could leave two months early. As the Albert Clock struck five, she walked into William's office.

'I've been here over six months now,' she said. 'Heather will be returning to work soon. I think it's time I went home. Edward and I don't see eye to eye over Maguire so perhaps we should call it a day.'

'I hope you can see his point of view.'

'Of course, although I can't share it. The Appeal Court hearing is listed for two days in early September. Someone else can take over after that.'

In the privacy of her own office, she sank into a chair with her head in her hands. She hadn't told him about the fiasco at the airport. Edward was humiliated enough. Mr Gordon had made no effort to persuade her to stay. He was probably glad she was leaving with her highfalutin opinions about what Edward should have studied at university.

She left the office early and drove to the Silent Valley Reservoir in the heart of the Mournes, hoping the water and mountains would help clear her mind. New York and Belfast had toughened her, she told herself. There was still time to make partnership at Braithwaite's before she turned forty. In London she would be untroubled by dilemmas over shoot-to-kill, loyalists and republicans, the UDR and the IRA. Her father had been right. Coming to Northern Ireland had been a bad career move, a waste of time. She was sick of it all.

On the way home to the cottage, she noticed posters outside the Glenbarry village newsagents: 'Armagh RUC bombing – Lurgan Man Held' read one. 'RUC Arrest Maguire for Armagh Explosion' a second. Maguire would be demanding she take a defamation case next but she would not be around to listen to this insanity. She would pull herself together and stop feeling so bloody sorry for herself.

The following day, there was a message on her desk asking her to call Sinéad Maguire. It was a timely reminder that the least she could do was let Sinéad know she was leaving. Her own troubles had helped to moderate her opinion of Sinéad. She no longer thought of her as a cynical IRA apologist but as someone who had fought, while Luke was in jail, not only against her heart failure but to persuade a hostile world that her husband had been murdered.

Sinéad had a cardiology appointment the following afternoon but was free in the morning. When they met in a small café opposite a side entrance to the RVH, Lena told her of the looming High Court date on immunity and then of the visit to Leglu.

'I'm afraid he had nothing to add except his personal doubts about the final bullet that killed Danny. He thought the police story about it passing underneath the car was unlikely, but not impossible. I should also let you know,' Lena went on, 'that I've started judicial review proceedings to get full disclosure of the police file. Hopefully, they'll produce it before September. Would you let Luke know when you see him? He doesn't like me discussing such matters on the phone.'

'You've been busy,' said Sinéad.

'There's something else I need to say, Sinéad. When we first met, I was harsh with you. I've had time to reflect since and I'd like to apologise.'

'Don't worry, Lena. We're notoriously hard to love.'

'I don't disagree but that's not why I'm leaving Belfast, once the immunity hearing is over.'

'You're leaving?'

'It's personal, I'm afraid. I've had an acrimonious break-up with a man I've been seeing.'

'Has it anything to do with the case?'

'Yes, but it's my personal responsibility.'

'I won't try to change your mind. With or without you, we'll continue to fight. That hateful woman, Thatcher, once said "there is no alternative". She's wrong, of course, there's always an alternative. But this isn't your fight.'

'I'm a solicitor, Sinéad. I should be well used to death and deceit by now.'

'Not this kind of pain, not these kind of lies. No one gets close to us without being damaged.'

'But you soldier on, despite your illness and losing Danny.'

'People feel sorry for me because of the heart failure – but nothing will ever be worse than watching Danny die,' she said. 'You know in *Wuthering Heights*, when Heathcliff implores Cathy's ghost to return to him through the window? I never understood that at school but now I often pray Danny would come back, even if only to haunt me.'

As Sinéad gazed out of the steamed-up window at the traffic on the Falls Road, Lena realised this might be their last meeting, her last chance to ask the question that had been nagging her.

'Sinéad, I hope you're not offended but do you ever wonder if your Danny might have caused another woman the same misery that his death is causing you?'

'I'm pretty sure Danny never killed anyone himself, personally,' she said, 'but that's not the point. He was part of an organisation that did kill people. We're all collectively responsible. Nothing can justify the misery and loss, but our history maybe explains it. If people are not treated fairly, it always ends in tears. You can only stretch people so far. In the end, they break.'

'But not everyone joined the IRA. Everyone has free will, a choice.'

'Of course, but it was inevitable some would take up arms after the civil rights movement stalled and the whitewash after the Paras shot thirteen dead on Bloody Sunday. But it has to end. In a way, all three of us – Luke, you and I – are working to end the violence in our different ways.'

Lena had never considered herself part of any such joint enterprise, but she said nothing.

At home, she thought back to the evening with Edward in The Halfway House when she had first heard 'The Flower of Magherally' and believed the jigsaw of her chaotic life was falling into place at last. She desperately needed to regain that certainty, that sense of journey's end. What if she approached it as a lawyer would? Slowly, almost imperceptibly, the germ of an idea began to grow. Maybe she could figure out a way after all.

7

Lena phoned her father the next day letting him know, without discussion, that she was bringing Edward to visit. They would spend Friday evening and Saturday at the rectory, she said, and on Sunday drive to stay overnight in London. George Dawson was too surprised to argue. Not for the first time, he decided, Braithwaite was right: for better or worse, Lena's time in New York had transformed his daughter.

'And if you could fix concert tickets for Sunday night in London, some piano music, that would be lovely,' she said.

The second stage of Lena's plan was trickier. When Edward arrived in High Street on Friday as usual, she did not wait for him to ignore her. Instead, she confronted him in reception. Mercifully, Geraldine wasn't there but Edward blanked her as she barred his way to the stairs.

'Do have some self-respect and get out of my way,' he said.

'If you don't listen, you'll not understand.'

'Oh, I understand all right. Remind me. Your mother's arthritis? An aunt in Putney?'

'We have to talk it over.'

'I've said everything I have to say to you.'

'Your spare uniform is still at Glenbarry.'

'I don't have time to think about that now.'

'Let's meet later then. At the very least you need to pick your stuff up from the cottage. I'll be in The Evening Star at six.'

'Be wherever you want – nothing to do with me.'

The half-hour Lena spent nursing a gin-and-tonic waiting to see if he would arrive was painful in the extreme, but arrive he did, sour-faced. She had a Bushmills on the table waiting and, as soon as he sat down, she began apologising.

'Edward, I am so, so sorry I was not straight with you.'

'You lied and then humiliated me in front of Paul.'

'I know and I'm sorry. But I wanted to avoid an argument. It will never happen again.'

'You're damn right it won't.'

'Maguire insisted on going to Strasbourg with me. Can't you try and understand?'

'Why on earth should I?'

'You came to me with an apology a few weeks ago, which I accepted. Have I acted worse?'

He hesitated and Lena, who had the natural instincts of a moderately good poker player, decided this was the moment to play her strongest card.

'Before all of this blew up, I had already made plans for you to meet my parents. Look, here are our flight tickets and Dad's booked us into a London concert.'

Reaching into her handbag, she brought out two airline tickets. She knew how intrigued he was about her family. He had often asked about the rectory, the church, her father – but he now sat feigning disinterest as she outlined her plans. After a moment's silence, she made the move she hoped would clinch it.

'There's no need for you to make your mind up right away. Think about it for a day or two. It would be a shame to waste the tickets.'

'I'll give it some thought.' It was a hopeful sign.

'May I get you another drink?' she asked.

'Okay,' he said.

Lena knew then that she had won. If he had already decided to reject the invitation, he would not have stayed a second longer. She repeated her apology when she returned with their drinks and, by the time they parted, he had grudgingly agreed to meet her at the airport on Friday evening.

On the flight to London, however, they barely exchanged a word. At Gatwick, her father gave her only a peremptory hug before becoming engrossed in conversation with Edward. The two men sat in the front of the car chatting about rugby and regiments. As they arrived home, she waited for the magic she was relying on to work. It was a stunning sunset and the rectory's old Georgian brick radiated a warm glow, the peachy-pink sky reflected in its tall sash windows. In the silence, as George Dawson pulled on the handbrake, the sound of Evensong bells at St Michael's and All Angels, slightly muffled in the humid summer air, began floating over the fields and hedges. All three of them sat in the car, listening. Not until the very last echo had completely faded, did George break the spell by lifting their suitcases out.

'It's not exactly Belfast, is it?' Lena whispered to Edward in the driveway. 'No checking under the car.'

As her father opened the rectory door, Lena and Edward remained outside, listening to the deep, peaceful stillness. There was absolutely no chance whatsoever of hearing the thud of a bomb, only the plaintive, faraway sound of cattle bells in the fields. They would have stood even longer if her father had not called to them.

'Come on in you two. Edward, I have some old photographs of your father to show you.'

The two men led the way indoors to the living room where Charlotte held up a languid arm from the depths of her sofa. Edward bowed deeply and kissed the back of her hand, asking after her arthritis. The old-fashioned gesture had the desired effect and he was invited to join her in a pre-dinner drink.

'In a minute, darling. He's coming to see some photos first,' said George Dawson, drawing Edward into the study with an arm around his shoulders, leaving Lena to haul their bags upstairs to their separate rooms.

'Can I freshen up before dinner?' Edward asked when he emerged from the study.

'It's upstairs on the right,' Lena said.

As they heard his feet creaking on the staircase, her parents both spoke at once.

'Well, I can see he's besotted with you,' said George.

'He seems a real gentleman,' said Charlotte but she was hardly noticed as George gushed on.

'Of all the men you've brought home, and you've brought home some crackers as well as some stinkers, he's streets ahead. You'd be a fool to lose him by fighting a hopeless case on behalf of some terrorist or other.'

Charlotte's face fell. 'What *are* you talking about George?'

Lena got up from her chair without a word and walked smartly across the room to make sure the door to the hallway and staircase was firmly shut.

'Nothing to worry about, Mum, it's just a case I'm working on in Belfast. Dad, we're hoping to get away from all that while we're here. And, both of you, before Edward gets back, when we arrive at Greenwich on Sunday, I want a few minutes with him, on my own, before we join you in the apartment. Is that understood?'

Charlotte sniffed and said nothing but a chastened George agreed, 'fair enough old girl.'

Over dinner, the men talked military history, leaving Lena and her mother to chat about Georgina's parents and the rectory garden. When it was time for bed, Lena and Edward said goodnight rather formally at the top of the stairs. He was still distant but the outright hostility seemed to be diminishing.

After breakfast on Saturday morning, Lena and Edward left to meet Olivia in Salisbury. On the way they stopped on a bridge and watched the waving green weeds in the crystal-clear waters of the River Avon before arriving for a picnic at the archaeological site at Old Sarum, chosen by Lena because it was quintessentially English, a place of ancient myth and magic.

'Some people say this is the true heart of England,' she said, unfolding a tartan rug in the sunshine and laying it on the warm grass. 'The ruins are over 2,000 years old. They allegedly handed the Domesday Book to William the Conqueror here – and over there in the distance is Salisbury Plain. Stonehenge is only ten miles away.'

As they left, she remarked that Isaac Watts, the author of 'Oh God, Our Help in Ages Past' had been born nearby. Then it was on to Salisbury, the road passing well-tended thatched cottages, old pubs, streams running through village greens – chocolate-box England. Olivia was waiting for them at a table outside the café in Cathedral

Close. Lena was slightly worried that a twee coffee shop would not show Edward off at his best. His bulky frame might seem clumsy, his large hands ungainly holding a bone-china teacup. But Olivia was so consumed by curiosity she did not notice such mere details. They shook hands politely and sat down around the small table, Lena taking a back seat and watching as her friend and Edward weighed each other up.

'So, Lena tells me you spend your weekends on duty with the army. My husband used to be in the Territorials when he was younger, yomping off on training weekends,' Olivia began.

Lena did not know whether to be amused or appalled. Playing soldiers on Salisbury Plain hardly compared to Edward's bitter-cold nights along the border, where an IRA sniper could kill him without so much as a by-your-leave.

'Only some weekends,' Edward replied.

'And your family, I believe they run hotels?' said Olivia, rather less enthusiastically.

'Yes, we have four. One in Belfast, one in the Glens of Antrim and two further around the coast at Portrush. Have you ever considered visiting?' he asked.

Olivia's eyebrows lifted but Edward did not notice.

'I know people think they'll be shot the moment they arrive, but that's all just press nonsense.'

Lena knew her friend would rather eat cat food than spend a weekend in Northern Ireland.

'Terrorism is limited to a few urban areas,' Edward barrelled on. 'Everywhere else is fine.'

The word 'terrorism' – casually dropped into otherwise

polite conversation – shocked Olivia. Lena felt, rather than saw, her friend stiffen. Edward, completely unaware of the dismay he had prompted, blithely continued.

'Maybe you'll bring your family over some time, as my guest, at one of our hotels.'

Olivia nodded and said that would be wonderful, next year, perhaps. Edward was satisfied, but Lena knew there was no chance. Northern Ireland was a grim and ghastly news story – not a place for Olivia to bring her family, even for a weekend. She intervened to say they had just visited Old Sarum and the conversation passed to less contentious issues, the beauty of the Hampshire countryside and fishing in the River Avon before they politely embraced their goodbyes. Back at the rectory, the evening was warm enough for a walk in the garden with a glass of wine before dinner. Lena lay in a hammock slung between two wizened apple trees, Edward beside her in an old deck chair. The coolness between them still hung in the air like a dense patch of fog. She made no attempt to break the tension, content to wait for the next phase in her plan to unfold.

The following morning, Lena woke to hear a faint creaking as Edward padded downstairs. She delayed for a few minutes and then followed him down, arriving in the kitchen to find him leaning on the sink, drinking in the morning air through an open window. Creeping up behind him, she gave him a hug. His back muscles stiffened but at least he did not pull away.

George joined them from his study while Charlotte, the last to appear, complained about her knees and Edward made suitably sympathetic noises. Lena fried bacon and scrambled eggs and laid the table while Edward went upstairs to shower and change. Over breakfast, George engaged Edward in a discussion about the water table under Salisbury Cathedral until the Sunday newspapers arrived and the conversation moved on to whether Margaret Thatcher's third government would go full term. Shortly before 11 a.m., Lena and Charlotte, now in their Sunday best, walked Edward through the wooden lych-gate and up the gravel path to St Michael's before settling into the family pew.

Across the nave, Lena noticed two elderly ladies from the village staring at Edward and whispering. They were very probably not alone in wondering which of the disagreeable 'warring tribes' in Northern Ireland he was from. She hoped Edward would not notice.

'Today's sermon,' George Dawson began from his pulpit, 'is taken from Luke, chapter ten, verses twenty-five to thirty-seven. "And, behold, a certain lawyer stood up, and tempted Him, saying, 'Master, what shall I do to inherit eternal life?' And He answering said, 'Thou shalt love the Lord thy God with all thy heart, and thy neighbour as thyself'".'

Dawson paused and leaned over the top of his lectern, peering at his flock through the half-moon spectacles.

'My dear friends, look around this church. Every last person here is your neighbour, whoever they are and wherever they are from.' A wry smile flickered across Lena's face. Her father was gently chastising his curious flock. People queued up to shake Edward's hand leaving church, as if he were a VIP.

After lunch, they set off for London, the car finally

drawing up at the main gates into Greenwich Palace, dazzling in the afternoon sun, its pilasters shining purest white against a backdrop of closely mowed, almost electric-green lawns. Edward was puzzled. 'Isn't this the Old Royal Naval College?' he asked. 'Are we visiting?'

'Didn't Lena tell you? Naughty girl,' said George from behind the steering wheel. 'We're staying here overnight. We retired military chaplains have a small "grace and favour" apartment in the lower palace.'

After a uniformed batman came with a trolley to take their luggage, George took firm hold of Charlotte's elbow and steered her towards the nearest door, calling over his shoulder to Lena and Edward, 'we'll see you in a few minutes.' Lena then linked her arm in Edward's and led him across the lawns towards the slow-flowing Thames.

'Why didn't you tell me?' he asked, once they were out of earshot.

'I knew you'd love the palace history. Both Henry VIII and Elizabeth I were born here. Let's sit down for a moment beside the river.'

They sat on a bench, just inside the perimeter security fence. Then Lena began the speech she had been refining for days.

'Edward, I think you'll agree that both of us have been a bit overwhelmed by recent events. So much has happened so quickly. Visiting Fermanagh has helped me understand how much you love your home. Now, you are visiting mine. We both respect and love where we come from. No more than you, I could never bring dishonour on my family or my home and what they stand for. Families who have suffered grievous loss, like the Maguires, and who fear the state was involved, have an inviolable and absolute right to the truth. If law and order means anything, it means that. If there's nothing sinister to be found, it will end there. It will then just be you and me, our heads held high. Neither of us with anything to regret or apologise for.'

Lena curled her right arm around Edward's shoulders, coaxing him to turn towards her, but Edward continued staring sullenly out across the brown waters of the Thames.

'Does any of that make sense?' she asked eventually.

'You've certainly gone to a lot of trouble to persuade me,' he said, 'but it doesn't justify you lying.'

'I made a mistake, and it was a bad one, but it was made with the best of intentions, to protect our relationship. I've apologised and it will never happen again,' she said.

'I need time to take all that in.'

'Take all the time you want. When you've decided, I'll be waiting.'

They sat another five minutes in silence before walking slowly, hand-in-hand, to a door in a corner of the palace and climbing two flights to the apartment. Sandwiches and teacakes for four were laid out in the small kitchen. Lena carried them in to her parents in the drawing room, leaving Edward alone with his thoughts in the kitchen, gazing out over the palace grounds and the river. The four of them then changed into evening clothes and took a taxi to the Royal Festival Hall. During the concert, Lena noticed Edward sat bolt upright, only relaxing during the finale, the first movement of Beethoven's 'Moonlight'. As the beloved notes flowed over them, he squeezed Lena's hand several times and she fought back tears, suspecting he was close to the same.

There was the usual rush in the morning, the early alarm waking them for the airport. Back at Aldergrove, on the otherwise featureless green plain beside Lough Neagh, Edward seemed to have reverted to type, Lena thought – the stern businessman who demanded universal respect by virtue of merely existing. As they stood beside her Mini in the airport car park, it took all her fortitude to ask him the as yet unresolved question.

'Are we back on track?'

'You can't disappear off again with Maguire,' said Edward. 'He's a dangerous man, more dangerous than you know. Death follows him around like a dog.'

'Is there anything I can do or say to make it up to you?'

'I need time to think it over,' he replied.

It sounded ominous. They said their goodbyes and drove out of the airport, she into Belfast, Edward to the north coast.

All week she waited then, returning home on Friday, his Range Rover was parked in the driveway. She could hear the hypnotic notes of the 'Moonlight' coming from indoors and crept in as quietly as she could, according Beethoven his full six minutes before placing a large Bushmills on the piano and waiting for an answer.

'I know you want me to say something,' he said. 'I'm finding it extremely difficult, but I'll try.'

He took a large gulp of whiskey.

'On Sunday morning at the rectory,' he said, 'I woke up early, went down to the kitchen, opened the window and listened to the countryside outside waking up. It felt like a different world entirely from Fermanagh and I was a different person living in it with no thoughts in my head at all of patrols and checkpoints. I've spent far too many nights in wet ditches and too many afternoons looking at hotel balance sheets. I'm sick to death of them. Then I imagined you and I returning to Little Woldham for weekends and holidays, Christmas and Easter, and – supposing things work out – that we might bring our children there to see their grandparents. And it really shocked me how much I wanted that.'

Lena was shaken. He was making huge assumptions, but they were not unwelcome. She had had the same thoughts herself and could think of no adequate response.

'There, Lena. That's your answer and I won't be saying anything more. In fact, can we please avoid any deep discussions over the weekend? There's been too much drama.'

Lena nodded and for the next two days they hardly spoke. They walked in the Mourne Mountains, they read books and newspapers, he played Mozart and Bach. On Monday morning, Edward was away early, shouting upstairs that he had a meeting in Portrush. On the kitchen table was a note. Her heart thumped as she lifted it, but all it said was that he was skipping his usual Friday afternoon meeting with his father to travel to Fermanagh for a twelve-hour overnight UDR shift. He'd catch up on sleep at home on Saturday and meet her in the cottage for dinner in the evening. Once in the office, she rang Georgina.

'I think Edward and I have settled our differences.'

'Good – so long as you haven't backed down.'

'I haven't. He's actually more open to reason than I thought.'

'So, what happens next?'

'I took him to Little Woldham last weekend. As I expected, he loved it. When we got home, he told me he's looking forward to more visits, perhaps with our children.'

'My God. He's a bit ahead of himself, isn't he?'

'I think he was testing the water.'

'Oh, Lena. Is this really what you want?'

'I think so. We've negotiated a minefield of professional and personal obstacles. This could be it.'

'In that case, I'm delighted for you.'

Geraldine ran into Lena's office later the same day with news that a courier had arrived carrying a large consignment of official documents – the threatened judicial review had worked its magic. Lena watched the boxes of folders being unloaded. If she was ever to find the truth, it might be here – somewhere. They were a daunting sight, piled up high in her office. One of the files was labelled 'Autopsy Reports'. Lena opened it. Except for the moustache, Danny Maguire's dead face looked so like his twin's. It could have been Luke instead, peacefully sleeping on the shiny, silver metal – except for the small, black circle on his left temple. She began selecting the most important files to take home, telling Geraldine as she left that she would be gone for a couple of days. At home, she read until her eyes stung and her head ached, focusing on what the ballistics experts and scenes-of-crime officers had said in detail about the trajectory of each bullet that hit either Reid or Maguire.

The shooting had taken place on a straight road, a causeway raised over boggy land. On the eastern side, the land sloped down to a stand of poplars and, beyond that, the shores of Lough Mór. Elsewhere, the land was flat. All the bullets had been fired from the west, the car approaching from the south. Once she had read it all, she went for a long walk along the shores of Strangford Lough before drawing up a summary of concerns.

Why, she wondered firstly, had the police fired over 100 times? Their statements explained they had 'misinterpreted' the flashes caused by their bullets hitting the car, incorrectly assuming those inside were firing back at them. They had also 'misinterpreted' the metallic creaking of a car door opening as Seán or Danny reloading a weapon, causing them to fire even more bullets. That was an awful lot of misinterpretation.

Her next concern were the jumbled files, with no consistent index and no documented chain of ownership to preserve the integrity of the evidence, should it ever be required in court. Thirdly, criminal investigation detectives had been denied access to the shooters for over three hours and had initially been given the wrong location as the firing point. Fourthly, Seán Reid's body had been moved before the state pathologist could examine it *in situ*. Fifthly, there was no comprehensive photographic record of the entirety of the vehicle's interior. Photos appeared to have been taken, at some distance and at awkward angles through the broken car windows, although there was one of the driver's side door handle. It was flat, silver-coloured and paddle-shaped, about six inches long. A diagram in the file explained that Maguire's body had fallen onto the door, the weight of his forearm bearing down on the door handle, forcing the mechanism to open.

Sixthly, police evidence notes were written using casual terms, such as 'wanted', with no further details in relation to the two victims. Seventhly, two years after the shootings 'in accordance with standard RUC procedures', the bronze Ford Fiesta was crushed. What precisely is 'standard procedure', she wondered, for destroying a vehicle barely twenty-four months after you have fired over a hundred bullets into it, killing two unarmed people? Maguire's previous solicitors had lodged an official complaint but the car could hardly be uncrushed.

An eighth concern was that some bullets were unavailable for ballistic examination – the official explanation being that the heavy rain that night had washed them into nearby drains (highly unlikely, Lena thought). By contrast, in some ways the police investigation was commendable. They had re-enacted the scene, using officers whose height and weight matched Reid's and Maguire's, and had conducted house-to-house inquiries. Although there were certainly questions, there were no real contradictions. It was all circumstantial, with no forensic or ballistic inconsistencies. With some relief, she concluded she had turned over every rock and found no evidence wriggling underneath. By Wednesday afternoon, she was ready to call in her deal with Maguire. First, though, she would phone Steve Sullivan. He was proving a grounded and evidence-focused sounding board.

'Hi honey. You never call so something's up.'

'You know I started judicial review proceedings. Well, it worked. I got the full file.'

'Great – any stand-outs?'

'I've isolated eight concerns about the competence of the police investigation that we could raise at an inquest but absolutely nothing to stand up Luke Maguire's claims of an ambush and execution.'

She had hoped Sullivan would agree this was the end of the line. But he hesitated.

'I just can't get my head around why an unarmed IRA man would try to run down a heavily-armed RUC patrol.'

'Both of us know that's not enough, Steve,' Lena replied. 'Anything more from Leglu?'

'I tracked him down to Strasbourg but he had nothing other than what was in his report.'

'You say the police crushed the car the men were travelling in. Have you double-checked?'

'I've applied to see it. At least we have a date for the hearing on Crown immunity, it's in early September at the beginning of the new legal term.'

'That might be a good time to keep my promise to come over and support you.'

'It's a long way to come for what's likely to be an extremely boring day.'

'I also want to size-up the boyfriend – see if he deserves you. And I'd like to meet Maguire too. I've gone to meetings over here where he spoke and he's damn impressive.'

'He's a pain in the ass as a client, Steve, whatever his talents as a public speaker.'

As she put the phone down, Lena decided to focus on her main priority: the exit strategy to ensure the September immunity hearing was her full and final commitment to the Maguires. She began by preparing a bullet-point summary of her eight concerns, along with a summary of Leglu's report, leaving out her decision to inspect the crushed car. The time had come to provide her client with all the available facts and tell him she had run out of road. By early afternoon she was in the Falls Road office, avoiding the missing floorboards so her heels did not go straight through the sticky carpet. She was becoming a regular. Even the security man gave her a gentler grunt than usual. Before Maguire had a chance to say a word, Lena seized the initiative.

'Before we visited Leglu, you and I agreed it would be my final commitment, other than working on Crown immunity for the Appeal Court hearing. As it turns out, I have also negotiated full disclosure of the RUC file and analysed its contents. Unfortunately, neither Leglu nor the file have provided any new leads.'

She then produced his original jumbled concertina file along with a new buff folder containing her eight-point summary of concerns and put them both firmly on the table in front of him.

'This is my full and final analysis. It's yours, with my compliments. There's nowhere else for me to go. September's Appeal Court hearing is the end of the road, at least for me. Over and out.'

She had expected a fight but he ignored both the folders and her announcement.

'I've found a first-hand eyewitness to the shooting. We're seeing him this afternoon.'

Lena was stunned. 'Not me, Luke,' she said hurriedly. 'I already have meetings planned.'

It was a lie, but she wanted a quick exit.

'It's today or not at all.'

'Then it's not at all. There are rules. A solicitor can't

just disappear, especially with a client like you.'

'You'll be back by this evening. If you need to phone your office, you can call from across the border.'

'The border?'

'Just over into Donegal, no more than two hours away. I need you to take notes and draw up an affidavit. It has to be today, though. The witness took some persuading. He might bottle out.'

Lena made a quick assessment. Gordon was already at home in Fermanagh. Edward was due to leave Belfast at Friday lunchtime, around now, for his UDR overnight shift before catching some sleep at the Hall on Saturday morning and driving to Glenbarry in the evening. The chances of him phoning while on patrol were remote, to say the least. He had never once rung her while on duty and there was no reason for him to do so now. There was really nothing to prevent her going with Maguire, especially if the outcome could be significant new evidence.

'All right, Luke. I'll go, but I absolutely have to be back in Belfast tonight.'

'You will, you will. Don't worry.'

'What's this new witness got to say?'

'I'd rather you heard him first-hand. I'm not entirely clear myself.'

They descended the rickety stairs to the street outside, where a driver was waiting. Lena sat in the back of the car as they climbed the Belfast Hills into County Derry. It had rained all week and the fields were flooded. Gazing out of the window, Lena spotted a road sign to Drumfad where this nightmare had begun before they climbed the Glenshane Pass, passed through the city of Derry and crossed the border to Letterkenny. In a hotel car park, they stopped beside a man in a battered anorak standing next to an old Ford transit van.

'This is John,' Maguire told her. 'He's taking us the rest of the way.'

John had a timid smile for Lena as she climbed into the back of his van. Ten miles further on, passing through the village of Ramelton, Maguire turned to Lena, an unfamiliar apologetic look on his face.

'You're going to have to put this over your head,' he said, producing a grubby blanket.

'What on earth do you mean?'

'You're also going to have to duck down between the seats. It's for your own sake. If you're arrested, you can truthfully say you don't know where you are.'

'Luke, this isn't on. Who's going to arrest me?'

'The gardaí might. I'm on their watch list.'

Furious, she draped the blanket, smelling of mud and slurry, loosely over her shoulders and lowered herself down. They continued driving for another twenty minutes, the van bumping over potholes until they parked and John turned the engine off. Lena removed the blanket and looked around. The van was parked beside a two-storey white farmhouse, the sea sparkling blue nearby and the hills yellow with gorse. She, Luke and John walked inside. An old lady with a deeply wrinkled face sat in a rocking chair beside a black range in the kitchen, smiling at them before continuing her knitting. John put a large kettle on the range before taking Lena and Maguire down a narrow corridor hung with religious pictures into a room with a large round table. Maguire, Lena noted, was beginning to look nervous. Sitting down at the table, she glowered at him.

'This had better be bloody good,' she said, getting a clipboard out of her briefcase.

'You're about to meet someone called Séamus. If you ask questions, be gentle. This is going to be difficult for him,' Maguire said before leaving the room.

After a few minutes, the door opened again. Behind Maguire, a stocky man shuffled in. He seemed confused, his face flushed, his eyes darting that way and this, his body trembling as he pulled off a woolly hat and sat down across the table from her. Maguire put an arm around Séamus' shoulders, squatting down so their two heads were close.

'Séamus, this is Lena – the lady John told you about,' he said gently into the man's face, pointing at Lena who leaned forward, shook a calloused hand and put on what she hoped was a friendly smile.

'Glad to meet you, Séamus,' she said.

The man hardly looked at her, his eyes on the floor. He seemed to have a mental disability.

'Séamus,' Maguire said softly. 'Remember, we are all friends here. Would you like some tea?'

The man nodded and John, who had been standing in the doorway, disappeared into the kitchen.

'Lena is helping us back in the North. It's important you tell her everything that happened on the night of the shooting.'

'Johnny told me. I'll do my best.'

Lena had slipped her clipboard under the table until it was resting, inconspicuously she hoped, on her lap.

Séamus placed his hands heavily on his knees and began speaking slowly.

'I was playing cards with the lads, as I always do on a Sunday night. It was too late for buses so I started walking home. I needed to splash my boots so I walked down the slope to the big trees.'

From the maps in the RUC file, Lena knew exactly where he meant – the sloping eastern side of the causeway, the Lough Mór side, where the line of poplars stood.

'Then I started back up again, towards the road. The grass was wet. I kept slipping. Then I heard them coming.'

'Them? Who's "them"?' asked Lena. Maguire scowled at her for the abrupt intervention.

'The RUC. I could hear their boots on the road and them talking to each other. The moon was up and I didn't want them to see me, so I lay on my belly.'

John came in with a mug of tea for Séamus and put it on the table. Having taken a sip, Seamus began speaking again.

'I could see the jeeps and the Peelers on the road in the moonlight. Some of them were lying on the grass. Then I heard a car and the shooting started, then brakes squealing, then lots more shooting.'

'Séamus,' Lena spoke again, this time far more gently. 'May I ask, did you hear anyone shout anything like "Halt" or "Stop"?'

'No. There was no shouting. It was quiet, then the shots. Lots of them. The shouting only came later.'

Lena continued.

'Did you see any lights – red lights or blue lights?'

'No – I just saw the grey jeeps, they turned their headlamps off.'

'Their headlamps were off? Are you sure?' Lena asked again.

'Yes,' Séamus said, relieved that he had told his story, but Lena was far from finished.

'Séamus, it's important we are clear about exactly what happened.'

'I told you. The police were there. Then the other car came. I heard the shooting, then the shouting. Then a final shot.'

Lena scribbled notes as he spoke.

'What did you do then, Séamus?' Maguire asked.

'I was feared so I slid on the wet grass back down the slope on my belly. I was all wet. I walked into the trees beside the lough and took the long road home.'

'What happened then?' asked Maguire.

'I told my mother and brothers and they drove me to Castlederg, to Uncle Michael's house and they brought me here to Johnny's.'

'Thank you, Séamus. Well done. Good man. Lena, you got more questions?'

'Séamus, what time did this happen?'

'I don't know. The card game finished after eleven. I got home at midnight.'

'How do you know they were the RUC?'

'They arrived in grey police jeeps. I heard their boots on the road.'

'Have you spoken to the RUC since?' asked Lena.

'I've not done anything wrong, have I, Luke?' asked Séamus.

'No, Séamus, of course you haven't,' said Maguire, giving Lena another angry look.

Lena was hardly able to believe what she was hearing. This man had critical evidence but his family had not taken him to the RUC.

'Why didn't you go to the police, Séamus?' she asked.

'Bastards they are.'

Maguire turned to Lena and spoke as if she were a three-year-old child.

'Lena, the men doing the shooting, they *were* the police.'

Séamus was upset now. 'Them shooting and screaming.'

It was the first time Séamus had spoken about any screaming.

'What screaming, Séamus?' Lena asked quietly.

'There was screaming before the last shot.'

Maguire flinched and turned to Lena with raised eyebrows.

'Séamus,' Lena began again, quietly, 'I want to get this very clear. You heard no shouting from the police before the shooting began; their headlamps were off and there were no red or blue flashing lights – but after all the shooting there was screaming and a final single shot, on its own?'

'That's right. Then I slid back down the slope and into the trees again.'

'Okay, Séamus,' said Maguire. 'You've done well. Let's go into the kitchen and John will make you another cup of tea.'

Séamus shook Lena's hand and shambled out of the room with Maguire.

Left alone, Lena made more notes and began to consider how she might use Séamus' account. He had obvious learning difficulties, but he seemed clear enough about what he had seen and heard. He had not wavered over the absence of warning shots or flashing lights. If Maguire wanted to find someone to tell lies, Séamus was hardly a prime candidate, but that also held for his value as a witness. Lena knew very well that Séamus' mental capacity and memory would be a huge issue in court. The coroner would probably accept him as a witness, she thought, provided Séamus gave the impression he was capable of an intelligible account of events. But there were bound to be suggestions from the Crown side that he was misremembering. Geoffrey Hamilton would try and confuse him over the sequence of events, the shooting, screaming and shouting. Maguire returned, looked at her and raised his eyebrows.

'How long have you known about Séamus?' she asked him.

'I've known for a week or so. Even I know he's not an ideal witness.'

'Well, for once, Luke, I agree with you. He most certainly is not a good witness. There is little point in me drawing up an affidavit, as you suggested in Belfast. To use his testimony, we would have to produce him at the inquest, where he would be savaged under cross-examination. If you knew that yourself, why did you drag me up here?'

'Sinéad told me you were planning to leave. I brought you here to convince you that my family and I are right, that this was an ambush and execution.'

'So, you lied to me, Luke. This whole day has been a charade.'

Luke lost his temper. 'Is that more serious than murder? You're okay with two men shot dead at the side of the road like dogs, but not when someone tries to prove it?'

Lena fought back. 'The Chinese say, "If you want revenge, dig two graves". Your desire for revenge is going to destroy you, Luke.'

They squared up to each other in mutual antipathy.

'I'm looking for the truth, not revenge,' he hissed.

'Shut up and take me home,' she said.

Luke's anger turned to embarrassment. 'I'm afraid that won't be possible until the morning,' he said. 'John won't drive into Letterkenny after dark. He's going to take us where we can eat and then to a safe house overnight and, before you ask, no, there's no phone.'

Lena's fury grew. She was stuck.

'You got me here under false pretences and promised me I'd be home by tonight. And here I am, God knows where, on my own without even a telephone. This is too much, Luke. I'm finished with this case. Your little plan has backfired.'

Maguire said nothing, just walked out and got into John's van where she joined him. At least, in the dusk, he didn't insist she use the stinking blanket again. As they set off, Lena thought of Edward, stuck in some cold ditch somewhere in Fermanagh while she gallivanted around the country on a wild goose chase with people who wanted to kill him.

'Here you are,' John said, drawing to a halt and pointing downhill to a whitewashed bar above a small pier. 'I'll be back to pick you up again in an hour.'

As they walked downhill to the bar, Maguire irritatingly asked her not 'to draw attention to herself'. What did he think she was going to do? Dance a bloody samba? The bar was almost empty. They sat in a corner, ordered soup and sandwiches and ate in an awkward silence. Once they had finished, and feeling better for eating, Lena looked out of the bar window. There was a long, sandy bay and mountains beyond. In England, there would be guesthouses and a prom along the beach, perhaps even a funfair. Here the beach – smoothed perfectly flat by the retreating tide – was lit silver by the moonlight. With twenty minutes left until John returned, Maguire ordered drinks – wine for Lena and whiskey for himself. Three musicians arrived, sitting in the far corner, and began playing.

'I've a feeling I've heard that before,' said Lena. 'What's it called?'

'"An Chúileann". You'd call it "The Coolin" in English.'

'What's it about?'

'No one really knows. Stop being such a Brit. You're not meant to analyse it, just feel it.'

Lena had had enough. 'Feel it? You know what I feel?' she said. 'I feel for Edward Gordon who's on duty in Fermanagh while your friends try to kill him. Some idiot once said about you lot in Ireland that "all your wars are merry and all your songs are sad". Well, it's nonsense. There's nothing merry about this bloody war. It forces people to take sides and it should never have started.'

'Watch it, Lena, you're starting to have opinions.'

'I always had, but you won't like them. My opinion is that what you people do is despicable, appalling, threatening families on the border, killing police officers as they leave home. It's a stupid, squalid fight that's spiralled out of control.'

'And the English? Your people? They've done nothing to deserve it, I suppose? Have you read any Irish history?'

'I don't need a history book to know what's right and wrong. And blowing up people doing their shopping is wrong. Intimidating Protestant farmers along the border is wrong.'

'You really do get your opinions from the tabloids, don't you?'

'Don't be absurd.'

'Your father, Lena, wasn't he in the British Army? In Kenya and Malaya? What do you think he was doing there? Drinking tea?'

A few weeks ago she might have told him about Nakuru but her father had taken even that argument away. She had no answer.

They were both tired and irritable and it was a relief when John arrived to take them to their overnight billet. The man who opened the door of the nondescript modern bungalow did not speak. Neither did his wife as she showed them upstairs. The house was, at least, clean and warm. Lena fell onto a bed, fully clothed, and tried to sleep. Maguire's loud knocking on the door woke her in the morning. She panicked fearing that she had overslept but there was still plenty of time to get home before Edward arrived for dinner. Splashing water on her face, she went downstairs to find a lugubrious Maguire eating bread and cereal laid out on the kitchen table with no sign of the couple who owned the house. John left them in Letterkenny, where they met Maguire's man, who drove them back into Belfast. During the journey, Lena mulled over the increasingly serious doubts she had, about how Danny Maguire and Seán Reid had been killed. Séamus might be of no use as a witness, but she believed he was telling the truth. But it was too late, she chastised herself. Maguire and his family were no longer her problem while finding hard evidence would be, in any case, impossible. By lunchtime, they were back at the Sinn Féin office. On the footpath outside, Maguire tried one final time to persuade her to renew investigations.

'Have you thought of carrying out house-to-house interviews at Drumfad to see if anyone saw or heard anything?'

'Forget it, Luke. I told you in Donegal I was finished and I meant it. I've been indulging your obsessions for too long. I'll do as I promised and act for you over public immunity, that's all.'

'At least come inside to talk it over.'

'You have your own papers back along with my final summary. That's me finished, as we agreed. I'll phone you to confirm the court date in due course.'

Business concluded, she drove through County Down, stopping for groceries and arriving at the cottage around lunchtime where the sight of Edward's Range Rover in the driveway made her instantly forget Maguire. As she opened the front door, she heard him playing 'An Chúileann' on the piano, the same sad air as in the Donegal bar. Two men, she thought, two sworn blood enemies, who both loved the same music. Dismissing such high-minded thoughts, she dropped her shopping in the kitchen and walked into the living room whereupon he stood up and folded her in his arms.

'Where have you been?' he asked.

'Getting us something nice for dinner,' she said.

'At eight-thirty in the morning?'

'You were here that early?' she asked, her stomach sinking.

'I hate to admit it,' he said, 'but I couldn't sleep at the Hall, even after a long night in the wind and rain, so I drove straight here to see you.'

Lena had to think fast. How on earth to explain her absence?

'Your father phoned from Fermanagh and asked me to fly to Scotland late yesterday,' she said, her face resting on his chest. 'We needed an affidavit signed in Glasgow for Barrett's bail hearing. It was very last minute.'

'What a slave-driver he is,' he said, holding her away from him so he could look into her face.

'It was no bother,' she said. 'You were on duty in Fermanagh and what else would I be doing on a Friday night?' They were now facing each other.

'And on the subject of work,' she continued, 'the Appeal Court hearing on immunity in the Maguire case is listed for Tuesday week, the second day of the autumn legal term.'

Edward's smile was replaced with a frown.

'Ten days from now,' she quickly continued, 'it will all be over, done, finished. It will just be you and me and no Maguire ever again. He will be out of our lives forever.'

Edward said nothing, but his frown had vanished. He took a deep breath.

'Here's to us then,' he said, 'And the future.'

'So, we have a future, do we?' she said.

'You know we do, Lena, you know we do,' he said, folding her again into his arms. 'Forget about cooking – let's go to the bar in Killyleagh, like we did before this bloody nightmare began.'

At dinner, he ordered champagne. When she asked

why, he said every day with her was a celebration. Back at the cottage, he walked her firmly to the staircase. She felt as if he was consuming her that night, devouring her. Afterwards, they slept soundly, Lena thanking heaven as she drifted to sleep that she had steered a distinctly leaky boat through the storm and into safe harbour. Despite everything the Maguire case had thrown at her, she had somehow emerged unscathed.

On Monday morning, Edward was unusually attentive. He stood behind her in the kitchen as she made breakfast, his arms around her.

'You should finish work early this Friday,' he said. 'You deserve it after the trip to Glasgow. We'll drive to Fermanagh. You haven't visited in ages. My mother misses you. I'll put Paul off and ask Dad to cancel Geoff Hamilton and the Grahams. It'll just be Dad and Mam, you and me for the weekend.'

Lena was puzzled as she poured their coffee. Edward had never before suggested booting the family friends off the guest list. He left for work first, allowing her to retrieve every scrap of paper hidden in the cottage on the Maguire case so she could take them to the office for shredding or filing away. Very soon, it would all be handed over to some other poor chump. On the road into Belfast, she told herself that her focus now must be on her other cases, including how to persuade the RUC to agree to bail for Darren Barrett. All doubts arising from Séamus' testimony must be banished. During the week that followed, Edward phoned twice, for no apparent reason, just checking she could leave work early. She wondered again what he might be planning.

On Friday afternoon, she heard him arriving for his business meeting with William and was tempted to march in and say hello. Standing in reception, however, she could see through William's open door that architect's plans for a proposed new hotel in Derry were laid out on a table. Best not to interrupt them, she decided and returned to her office.

In his father's office, meanwhile, Edward was changing the subject from the Derry hotel.

'Thanks for cancelling Geoff Hamilton and the Grahams,' he told his father. 'There's a good reason. I've invited Lena down for the weekend.'

'I thought you and her were ancient history.'

'We had a misunderstanding but it's over.'

William managed to conceal his displeasure.

'I visited her parents last week,' Edward went on. 'They live in a lovely part of the world.'

'They certainly do.'

'It made me realise what's important in life.'

William waited warily, watching his son struggling. Edward's next words came in a rush.

'Dad, Lena doesn't know it yet, but I'm planning to go down on one knee this evening.'

William fell back into a chair, distraught, but Edward was oblivious, reaching into an inside pocket of his jacket and drawing out a small, black box.

'You always said I would know when the right girl came along,' he said. 'Well, she came along at Queen's University one dark night last winter.'

William stared at the diamond glittering against the velvet.

'Well, well,' he said, playing for time, 'that's quite a turn up for the books. George Dawson's daughter marrying my son, eh?'

'I'd be grateful if she could leave work early. She certainly deserves it after her dash to Glasgow last Friday.'

William frowned. 'Glasgow?'

'Something about getting an affidavit signed there – about that idiot Barrett I think she said.'

'Anything we need from Scotland, McIvor does for us,' said his father.

'McIvor?'

'You remember, young McIvor who was at university in Edinburgh with you? His father's firm helps us out in Scotland. We always fax them when affidavits need signing. Lena knows that.'

'She said it was last minute.'

'Very strange. She didn't say anything to me.'

'Well, there must be some explanation,' Edward said, making a quick recovery. 'I'll go and remind her to leave work early.'

As he walked into her office, Lena looked up, smiled, and – seeing his anxious face – immediately realised something was wrong.

'There's doubtless an explanation,' he said, 'but Dad says he knows nothing about you having to fly to Glasgow last week.'

Lena made a lightning-quick calculation. She had promised him there would be no more lies.

'Your father's right,' she said.

'So where were you?'

Lena got up and shut the office door, returning to stand behind her desk.

'I was in Donegal speaking to an eyewitness about the Drumfad shooting, but it was a waste of time. In ten days, as I told you, I'm no longer on the case.'

After what seemed like a long silence, Edward asked, 'Were you on your own?'

'I promised I would never lie to you again so, no, I was with Maguire.'

Silence.

'But you did lie to me,' he said. 'If I hadn't mentioned Glasgow to Dad, you would be lying to me now.'

Lena had nothing to say and stood behind her desk, blushing and silenced.

'You drove to Donegal and stayed there overnight with that revolting murderer and told me you were in Scotland,' he said unsteadily but without raising his voice.

'I am sorry, Edward.'

'I can't believe a word you say. This is the second time you've lied to me about him. Are you a bloody fantasist or what?'

'Of course I'm not. I just didn't want another row.'

'I think I can say with conviction that you and I will never row again. Certainly not this weekend. I don't want you anywhere near me – or my family.'

With that, he walked out of her office, closing the door firmly behind him. Lena stood motionless before collapsing into a chair, head in hands. She heard Edward and William talking to Geraldine in reception and then the high-pitched whine of the lift taking them downstairs.

She cursed Luke Maguire for tricking her into the trip to Donegal, then herself for being stupid enough to go. Whatever Edward had been planning – and she had a fair idea what it was – was over, at least for now. She sat silently behind her desk asking herself if anyone had ever been as incompetent a liar as she was? The clock on the wall said it was three o'clock but there was no point trying to focus on work. She would drive home to the cottage and try to work out how to fix things. Carrying her briefcase and handbag, she was walking towards the lift when she heard Geraldine's voice.

'Lena, before you leave, there's a letter here for you. I'd be guessing, but it looks like it's from the RUC.'

The buff envelope Geraldine handed over was indeed from the police – a letter authorising her to view the crushed Ford Fiesta in which Maguire and Reid had died, subject to her being accompanied by a police escort. The vehicle was at Seapark, an RUC secure facility on the coast near Carrickfergus, a few miles north of Belfast. Although she had pledged to end work on the Maguire case, and the family's previous solicitors had already concluded that a crushed car was of limited, if any evidential value, viewing it would at least provide a temporary diversion from Edward's disgusted face. So she rang Seapark and arranged to be there in half an hour.

8

The starlings were performing acrobatics in the grey skies over the River Lagan as Lena left the office. After a tiresome day, it was her occasional indulgence to lean against the shopfronts in High Street to watch them. How the tiny birds co-ordinated their wheeling around was impossible to fathom. This afternoon, however, their shrieking had the opposite effect. Dirty, greasy-looking birds, she thought as she hurried to her car. The over-familiar parking attendant greeted her as the exit barrier lifted. 'Enjoy your weekend, Miss Dawson,' he said. No chance of that, she thought as she turned towards the motorway leading north. As she arrived at Seapark, a former police station where Northern Ireland's many forensic exhibits were kept under lock and key, she thought how similar it looked to Castlereagh and the Maze jail – all of them depressing and dreary. A bored-looking police officer in the security hut asked her to sign a form agreeing not to touch the exhibits while a female officer rummaged through her handbag.

'What do you think we're running here?' said the irritated searcher. 'A dog show?'

She had found the camera Lena had brought to photograph the crushed metal block so she could show Maguire. A third officer, plump, male, whistling and swinging a large bunch of keys, then took her inside the security perimeter towards lines of grey buildings and Portacabins. As they walked, she wondered if Edward would tell his father about their bust-up, but doubted it. He was usually even more reluctant than she to divulge anything about their relationship to his father. But there was no point in obsessing about it, she thought, forcing her mind back to her immediate surroundings. Here, in this bleak place, were the records of twenty years of violence – guns, explosives, bloodied clothing, the wedding rings, necklaces and watches found on corpses dumped in rivers, on border roads and alleyways – now preserved for posterity in carefully labelled plastic bags, each one hiding its own tragic story. After about 300 metres, they came to the allotted shed.

Her RUC escort unlocked bolts and padlocks, opened a rusting metal door and turned on fluorescent lights. Inside the hangar were rows of shelves housing hundreds of bulky, plastic-wrapped parcels of evidence. There were also smaller banks of sealed lockers containing, she supposed, rifles, bomb-making equipment and other forensic exhibits. Then came a larger open space where dozens of cars, all covered in green tarpaulins, lay in neat lines on top of wooden pallets. She waited as the escort put on latex gloves and threw back a tarpaulin. She had expected to see a square metal block, like the crushed car in the Bond movie *Goldfinger*, but underneath, to her astonishment, was an entire car. A buff label was tied to one bumper, carrying the date of the shooting, '13 November 1984'. As the officer went around the car, lifting off the other three corners of the tarpaulin, Lena stood startled but silent. The bronze Ford had not been crushed. The exhibit record was mistaken and no one else had thought to check, probably duped by the RUC's much-vaunted reputation for efficiency. The police escort remained blank-faced as he lifted and folded the tarpaulin. Clearly, he was not surprised. Lena blessed the incompetence of the RUC forensic records department and remained impassive. There it was, right in front of her, the car in which Danny Maguire and Seán Reid were killed. She recognised it from forensic photographs, but it was still shocking to see it. The officer handed her gloves and told her she could look 'but don't touch – we don't want you contaminating evidence.'

The violent entry caused by some of the high-velocity bullets had peeled back the paint from around the bullet holes, making them appear even larger. There were jagged holes in the beige plastic seating, tufts of wadding spilling out where bullets had struck and dark brown smears that, she presumed, were dried blood. Broken glass lay beside the vehicle in a plastic bag. Lena began by circling it and took a notebook from her briefcase.

After a minute or two, she asked the police escort, who was now leaning against a nearby metal shelving unit, if she could move in closer to get a better view. He agreed but told her not to let any part of her body or clothing touch the vehicle. Lena peered in through the front driver's window and then walked around to take a look through the passenger side, squinting to get a clearer view. She remembered the police scene-of-crime statements stating the driver's door handle had been forced down by Danny Maguire's body weight, releasing the latch, after which simple gravity caused him to slump onto the ground. The final, and fatal, bullet had then passed underneath the chassis, hitting him on the left temple – the conclusion that Leglu had queried but could not disprove.

She wondered if she could somehow evade the escort's

attention, lean in and push down on the handle to see how much force was needed to release the latch. But the cop was watching her closely. She didn't want to be thrown out. She could see the handle. It was a silver-coloured metal hook, tucked inside a moulded recess in the interior plastic door-covering. And then it struck her that it did not look as she had imagined. Both from photographs and police descriptions, the handle was shaped like a paddle, or oar from a rowboat – so that if you pushed it down, it released the latch. This handle was completely different. To open the car door, you would have to curl your fingers around the silver hook and pull it horizontally, towards you. She looked away, blinked and looked again, just to be sure. The handle was not, as carefully described in all the forensic reports, a flat metal bar six inches long. No man's weight pressing down on it could have opened that car door. She felt nauseous, a bit dizzy, but somehow carried on, shifting her gaze to another part of the car, pretending to examine it.

Is there any way, she asked herself, that a dead weight, fourteen stone say, pushing down hard against that hook, from an angle perhaps, could have opened the door? There wasn't. In order to open the door, Danny Maguire would have had to be sufficiently conscious to curl his fingers around the handle and pull it towards him. This changes everything, she thought, I'd better take some bloody good notes. As calmly as she could, she began sketching while edging around the car, pretending to take a keen interest in the headlights, the bumpers, the bonnet, the boot, but darting her eyes across to the driver's door handle every few seconds. After another ten minutes, she swallowed hard, did her best to sound calm and called out to the police escort.

'Okay officer, I've seen enough, thank you.'

'Finished, Miss? You're very thorough.'

For once, she was thankful for the sexism endemic in the Northern Irish male. As far as this man was concerned, she was just a silly, wee, English girl.

'Just confirming the forensic reports,' she said, trying to sound casual but desperate to get away and think it over. Back in the security hut, the police returned her camera and she wished them a pleasant weekend, calm as you please, before walking back to her Mini and driving slowly away. Once on the main road leading back into Belfast, however, the significance of what she had just seen hit home. Her knees began shaking and she pulled into a lay-by overlooking Belfast Lough to compose herself.

Images began popping into her head of the murder scene in Drumfad, bullets smashing through the doors and windows. Seán Reid's body jerking as the bullets hit him. Once the car stopped, had a wounded Danny opened the door and tried to give himself up? Anyone familiar with police justifications for using lethal force knew they routinely stated they 'believed' the fatality had been 'reaching for a gun' or 'making hand movements as if they were armed'. Evidence was not required – their stated 'honest belief' was sufficient. Police officers' claims of firing to preserve their own lives or the lives of others, or to prevent escapes, were invariably sufficient to persuade the Director of Public Prosecutions not to bring charges or, if they were brought, to ensure acquittals in no-jury courts.

In this case, however, the RUC had decided not to go

down this well-trodden path. Lies had been concocted and written down in multiple sworn statements for reasons she could not yet comprehend. Even photographs had been faked. As Leglu said, the 'bullet under the chassis' explanation, however unlikely, perfectly explained what had happened – but it depended entirely on the door handle account. Police officers, junior and senior, as well as the UDR soldiers on the scene, must have committed brazen perjury in their statements and during multiple court hearings. Whatever had happened that night in Drumfad was so hideous it must be hidden.

Lena put her hands up to her burning face, leaned her forehead on the steering wheel and told herself to act rationally. She had been in the lay-by for a full ten minutes. She would have to drive home to Glenbarry and decide what to do next.

In the cottage, she took the hurriedly drawn sketches from her handbag and examined them again. Considering the stress she had been under, they were decent enough. They were dated and timed. Until she knew what to do, she would hide them. She folded and wrapped the three sheets of paper tightly in cling-film, put them into a zipped plastic bag and placed the slim package carefully underneath a half-full bag of frozen peas at the back of the bottom drawer of the freezer.

What a small, insignificant thing it was, she thought. A door handle. Just an inch or two of silver-coloured metal. But, properly handled, it could be enough to send at least a dozen policemen and soldiers to jail and rattle the entire RUC establishment. Séamus' account could be challenged by any competent barrister, and Geoffrey

Hamilton was more than capable. The door handle, though, was different. Then the thought struck her that, if one of the conspirators (she was beginning to think of them as conspirators) discovered the car still existed, they could move to destroy it. That must be prevented at all costs. The car was proof of perjury and possibly evidence of murder. Who could she ask for advice? Martin Porter would have been ideal but she dare not use the telephone.

The personal implications, while secondary to the legal ones, were also potentially catastrophic. Her relationship with Edward would surely be over if she provided evidence accusing the UDR of being complicit in murder. Her stomach was churning when the telephone rang. She lifted the receiver and heard Steve Sullivan's deep American accent. Of course, it was still working hours in New York. She struggled to sound calm.

'Hi Steve, what's up? Are you still planning to be over on Tuesday for the Appeal Court hearing?'

'Sure am. Just calling you now to check it's going ahead.'

'As far as I know, yes.'

'Anything new to report?'

'I've come across a minor discrepancy in one of the forensic reports.'

'Aha. I take it you can't tell me what it is?'

'Not really. It's trivial to be honest. My boss should probably be the first to hear, although it's Friday evening and he's eighty miles away in Fermanagh.'

'Well, if I were you – and I had an Appeal Court hearing in less than four days – I would make damn sure he was in the loop. See you Tuesday.'

Sullivan was right. William Gordon must be told. What

was it he had said when he first agreed she could look at the case? 'You find out anything startling in the Maguire file, you come to me immediately.' If she left Glenbarry now, at six o'clock, she should arrive at Gordon Hall just before they sat down to dinner. Ah, but Edward would be there. If she turned up in Fermanagh, he would assume she was pursuing him. He must have given his father some made-up explanation for her absence – the real one was too humiliating. Although the thought was unbearable, she had to travel to Fermanagh and see William.

Turning right at the end of the driveway, she thought of all the times she and Edward had set out for the Hall, looking forward to the weekend. Two hours later, on the long, tree-lined driveway, she began trembling. Lifting the heavy door-knocker, she heard the faint sound of the dinner gong inside. A smiling Wilson opened the door. On this occasion, his solemn air failed to amuse.

'Miss Dawson. Just in time for dinner. May I take your case?'

'I'm not staying, Mr Wilson. May I speak with Mr Gordon?'

'Which Mr Gordon? They're both in the dining room with Mrs Gordon. Are you joining them?'

'This is not a social visit, I'm afraid. It's Mr Gordon senior, I need to see. I'll wait here in the hallway.'

'I see. Just a minute.'

She imagined William's smile – and Edward's acute discomfort – when Wilson announced that 'Miss Dawson is in the hallway, sir'.

Lena steeled herself as William glided towards her, Edward behind him, stony-faced.

'Hello, Lena. Edward told us you were in Hampshire, your mother's arthritis playing up again.'

As I predicted, she thought, he's not told his father about the row.

'She's a lot better, Mr Gordon,' Lena said. 'I didn't have to go after all.'

'Very good, so you're here for the weekend,' Gordon said. 'We're just starting dinner.'

'I'm afraid I can't stay,' she said. 'I have urgent business to discuss with you.'

Then, turning to Edward, added, 'I need to speak to your father alone, Edward. I hope I'm not ruining your evening.'

'Not at all,' said Edward. 'I'm glad you didn't have to go to London.'

William, puzzled, gestured her towards the library and followed her in.

Lena remembered all the Friday evenings she had sat there with a large gin-and-tonic, ice tinkling in a heavy cut-glass tumbler, as William, Margaret and Edward laughed indulgently at her 'Chronicles of Crumlin'. Now, she felt like a servant, without so much as a glass of water.

'Lena, do sit down,' he said. 'We were together in the office just a few hours ago, so please explain why you need to speak to me so urgently.'

They sat down at two chairs in a window alcove. Lena took a deep breath and began.

'First of all, sir, is there anyone else here for dinner, or staying overnight?'

'No, we are on our own. Edward particularly asked that no one else be invited this evening.'

'I have some information, but you must keep it to yourself until Monday.'

He bridled at that.

'Well, I certainly have no intention of ruining my weekend, or anyone else's, but you know very well I cannot give you any such prior commitment.'

'Sir, you can and you must. I have done nothing illegal and there's no danger but I cannot continue without that firm commitment. You cannot refer to what I'm about to tell you, even on the telephone, especially on the telephone, before Monday. Do I have your word?'

By now, William was so curious he would have promised anything.

'Very well. You have my word. Now, please continue.'

'I have crucial new evidence in the Danny Maguire shooting.'

Gordon let out a heavy sigh. 'I might have known. I should never have agreed to you taking that case but, in my foolishness, I did. Continue.'

'I sought authorisation some time ago from the RUC to examine the car in which Maguire and Reid were killed – and today I went to see it at the Seapark depot.'

'I don't see why. The vehicle was destroyed two years after the shooting.'

'When I saw it today, it was whole, entire. The police must have catalogued it in error.'

'Shocking incompetence but I can't see how that changes anything.'

'You know the fatal bullet that killed Maguire did not pass through any part of the car.'

'Yes. Maguire fell against the door and tipped out –

the bullet passed underneath the chassis and struck him in the head.'

Lena took a deep breath.

'It could not have happened that way. It's impossible.'

He leaned towards her, forehead furrowed in concentration.

'How can you possibly say that?'

'The handle on that model of Ford Fiesta is lodged inside a moulded niche. It's impossible to open the door by leaning on the handle. You have to curl your fingers and pull it out towards you. Maguire must have been conscious when he opened that door. They shot dead a helpless man.'

A moment's silence. 'And you noted this down, did you?'

'Yes, sir. I also drew a diagram. They're in a safe place.'

Despite his age, Gordon's mind was still sharp.

'You're jumping to conclusions,' he said. 'If the police saw Maguire moving, they may have thought he was about to fire at them.'

'But then why make up a story about the door handle?' she asked. 'And why enlist all the other witnesses to tell the same story?'

Nothing like this had ever happened before to William Gordon. He struggled for an appropriate response.

'This is quite shocking, Lena. Would you like a coffee?'

'I'd love one. I drove to see you straight from Carrickfergus.'

Gordon left the room to ask Wilson for coffee. It gave him a few moments to think. This was serious. Worst-case scenario, properly presented to the DPP, it could be enough to convict a police firearms officer of murder; an entire police unit and UDR patrol of conspiracy to pervert the course of justice, and God knows what else. Why had some idiot been stupid enough to preserve the evidence in a bloody shed? Returning to the library, though, he was composed.

'Well, Lena, you have clearly discovered something that needs to be handled extremely carefully. I will, of course, respect my promise. I presume you will do the same. Be sure to bring your original notes into the office on Monday so we can discuss them with counsel.'

'That makes perfect sense, sir. May I suggest we call in Brendan Casey?'

'We'll discuss who to call in later,' Gordon said as Wilson arrived in the library with her coffee, closely followed by Edward.

'Dad, whatever your business is with Lena,' he said, avoiding her eye, 'Mother and I are already on our main course.'

'You've had a long drive, Lena,' said William. 'You must be exhausted. Why don't you stay for the night? It's eighty miles back to Glenbarry.'

Lena dreaded the long drive home but Edward's expressionless face made staying the night impossible.

'Thank you, but no. I've a lot of work before the immunity hearing on Tuesday. You and I, we'll put our heads together on Monday and come up with a plan.'

'We will indeed. In the meantime, I'm going to have my dinner and get an early night. Our conversation has given me a shocking headache.'

Lena walked to the front door, followed by William

and Edward, who watched as she reached the Mini. She wearily turned the ignition key, somehow managed to wave cheerily through the windscreen, and began driving down the long avenue. In her rear-view mirror, she caught a glimpse of their white faces in the dusk, father and son, framed in the large doorway and wondered if she would ever see the Hall again.

As she reached the main road, Lena saw the headlights of another car turning into the avenue from the right. It looked like Paul Donaldson's dark-blue BMW. He sometimes visited Edward at the end of a shift to pass on news of suspicious activity. She tucked the Mini in to give him space to pass and waved at him through the windscreen in recognition, before turning left on the main road towards Belfast.

On the dark country roads across Fermanagh, she reviewed her conversation with Gordon. He was unlikely to speak to anyone about the new evidence until Monday. He hated being the bearer of bad news. But she was damned if she would keep it from Luke Maguire. His family were her clients, and she was not going into negotiations with Gordon without consulting them. She parked at a roadhouse outside Dungannon to make the call. Its lobby was full of happy, half-drunk people at a wedding party in new suits and tight-fitting dresses. Whitney Houston's 'I Wanna Dance with Somebody' was playing full-blast in the function room but she found a quiet spot in the bar and dug her contacts book out of her handbag, wondering how she could notify Maguire without alerting whoever was, almost certainly, bugging his number. A flash of inspiration came and she dialled.

His deep voice answered on the third ring.

'Hi Luke. Lena here. Just wondering if you'll be at home on Saturday afternoon? I've got something to show you.'

'Christ, Lena, you can't possibly come here. The UDA still believe I was behind the Armagh bombing. We're all on high alert for a revenge attack. Most of us aren't staying at home. I shouldn't even be here myself and – before you ask – I'll not be meeting you anywhere else either. It'll have to wait until the Falls Road on Monday.'

'It's just that I've found something you might be interested in.'

She had to sound nonchalant to any listening ears.

'Lena, I'm not advising you, I'm telling you. What's the big rush?'

'You know that recording of Elgar you asked me about?' she said. 'The one I recommended on the way back from Strasbourg? Well, I've found it.'

There was less than a second's delay on the line, and then, 'Well, why didn't you say so earlier?'

'I'll see you tomorrow then.'

'Okay, around six if you can.'

Good man, Luke, she thought as she put the phone down, wryly telling herself that Elgar would be spinning in his grave in the Malvern Hills. She got back to Glenbarry around midnight, checked the notes in the freezer, locked all the doors and windows and had a long, hot shower. Despite two large gins, she hardly slept, watching the hours tick by on the bedside clock. Every time she closed her eyes, she saw the glazed look on Edward's face and his refusal to meet her eye.

It was no better in the morning. She obsessively tidied the cottage but by three o'clock, she could stand it no longer and drove into Belfast to double-check the original police and forensic statements. She had to be 100 per cent sure she had not misremembered anything. High Street was busy with shoppers as she let herself into the empty building and crept into her office, wondering if she had missed some detail that would explain everything. Unlocking her filing cabinet, she read two statements from scenes-of-crime officers, each noting the paddle shape of the door handle and giving the hypothesis of Danny Maguire's body falling onto it. Several junior officers and UDR patrolmen had also noted the same. All of them, she now knew, complete fabrications.

At five o'clock, she left the building, joining shoppers making their way home. She had a rough idea of where Clonard Monastery was and knew Maguire lived in one of the terraced streets close by, bizarrely named after British Indian colonial outposts, Cawnpore, Benares, Bombay – and Kashmir Road where Maguire lived. She knocked and waited as he unlocked bolts and locks inside. The door swung heavily open, and she stepped in, past his security hardware – four brackets for securing drop bars and a metal sheet bolted into the door's interior from top to bottom. There was an intricate wrought-iron gate at the bottom of the staircase. All the windows had the green tinge of toughened glass. In the living room, she looked around, curious. The floorboards had been sanded and there were floor-to-ceiling bookcases. It was summer but a small coal fire burned in a cast-iron fireplace. Luke finished putting the door-bolts in place and joined her.

'You live in a cage, Luke. Like an animal in a zoo.'

'Ah, Lena, sweet as ever. I wish I could say I'm pleased to see you.'

'Believe it or not, this isn't my idea of an enjoyable Saturday evening either.'

Before she could start, he asked about taking a libel action against the press for naming him as a suspect for the RUC man's murder in Armagh.

'If you didn't have such a colourful past,' she said, 'we could sue for defamation. But, alas, it seems you do.'

'You're turning into an excellent liar by the way,' he said. 'Using Elgar on the phone. Very cunning. But what's so important that it couldn't wait until Monday?'

'Bring me a glass of water and I'll tell you.'

She sank into the depths of a bulky sofa, took a sip of water and began to speak, slowly and deliberately.

'I decided some time ago,' she began, 'to examine the car in which Danny and Seán were shot. It's logged as stored in the main RUC depot outside Carrickfergus.'

'But there's no point, it was crushed, which is why I never asked you,' he said.

'No it's not. The RUC forensics department screwed up. The car is still intact.'

'Bloody hell.'

'As you know, as we heard from Leglu, the police say Danny's body slumped onto the door handle and it fell open, so the final bullet passed under the chassis and hit him on the left temple. Unlikely as it seems, there's no contradicting evidence. But, when I saw the door for myself, the way the handle is configured, it can't be pushed down, it can only be pulled out sideways.'

'What do you mean?'

'The handle is a metal hook tucked into a plastic recess in the door. If your brother fell onto it, it wouldn't have budged.'

'So Danny's body weight couldn't have forced the door open?'

'It's impossible. Every police officer who stated in evidence that the door handle was shaped like a paddle is in deep trouble. Danny may even have been trying to give himself up.'

'But why wasn't this noticed earlier?'

'All the photos in the official case file are of an older Ford with a paddle-shaped handle. The police account fits perfectly unless you examine the actual vehicle, which is a newer model.'

It didn't take Maguire long to cop on.

'I knew it,' he said. 'They saw he was still alive and decided to finish him off.'

'That conclusion is premature,' Lena said, 'but, yes, it is a possibility. I made notes and a rough diagram which are now in a safe place and I'll be consulting with colleagues on Monday.'

'You know what this means, Lena? You're going to have to change sides.'

Lena turned and looked him straight in the face. 'Forget it, Luke. I'm doing no such thing,' she said.

He paused and stiffened. 'I should have asked earlier. Have you told anyone else?'

'Just William Gordon down in Fermanagh.'

'You told Gordon? For God's sake, Lena. He'll run straight to the RUC.'

'He's my boss, Luke. I had no choice. It's unlikely he'll trouble his friends in the RUC over the weekend. He hates being the bearer of bad news.'

Lena had begun to tremble again as she recounted her story, the ramifications fully sinking in.

'You're shaking,' Maguire said.

'I know. I can't stop for some reason,' she replied. She seemed to have lost control of her head and neck as if she had just emerged from cold water on a freezing night.

'You can't drive home in that state.'

He was right, she thought. She had to calm down. What was wrong with her? Slow, deep breaths, that's what she needed. Maguire's voice softened.

'I'll make tea and bring you a biscuit. You just sit there a moment.'

As she heard him switching on a kettle in the kitchen, she turned on the television, muting the sound of the sports results.

'I knew we were right to engage you,' he shouted from the kitchen. 'Who else would be mad enough to trek to Carrickfergus on a Friday evening to view a crushed car?'

'Ah, but there's method in my madness,' she replied, acknowledging the rare compliment.

'What happens now?' he asked, handing her the tea.

'Top priority is ensuring the RUC don't find out and really crush the car,' she said. 'That's what we'll be discussing on Monday.'

'Who will you call in to help?'

'My vote goes to Brendan Casey,' she said, leaning back into the sofa.

'Don't let your tea go cold,' he said.

She began sipping the sweet tea as Maguire turned up the TV volume for the evening news. Margaret Thatcher was giving a speech about the poll tax. When the bulletin ended, he stood up, turned the TV off and gave Lena a wan smile.

'You seem to have calmed down a bit. I'm sure you want to get home.'

'May I use your facilities first?' she asked. 'Tea has that effect on me.'

In the hallway, he turned a key in the gate at the bottom of the stairs which swung open.

'Upstairs,' he said, 'take a left and it's the door on the right.'

Before leaving the bathroom, Lena scooped up some tepid water in the sink and splashed it on her face. It felt cool on her forehead and cheeks. As she lifted a towel to wipe her eyes, she heard a metal dustbin falling over in the street outside. It was a bit early for drunks, she thought. The bin rolled noisily over the footpath, banging as it hit the road. Quickly came another, far louder, crashing noise. Lena lifted her head and frowned at her face in the mirror.

Everything then happened very quickly. First the splintering noise of a sledgehammer, repeatedly hitting wood. Lena, finding the noise difficult to comprehend, opened the bathroom door and stood on the landing looking down at the front door. Maguire was already there in the hallway, locking the iron gate before throwing the key up at her and shouting over the noise of splintering wood.

'Lena, whatever happens, do *not* come downstairs.'

Their eyes connected for a split second before he

turned towards the front door, pushing against it. There were bulges in the metal sheet bolted to the back of the door, then the blade of an axe split through both wood and metal. Lena could not take her eyes off it. The bolts held but it burst at the hinges and fell inwards. In a blind panic, she ran back into the bathroom and bolted the door. Christ, she thought, I'm about to die here. There was a loud popping noise from downstairs. Until then, she had imagined gunfire would sound loud and dramatic, like thunder, like the movies. This didn't, but she knew exactly what it was. Then the shouting began, rough voices, inside the house.

'Time's up Maguire, you bastard.'

Bullets began to pierce through the bathroom floorboards. They were firing wildly from downstairs. She felt something hitting her left arm and the warm flow of blood. Grabbing a towel off a rail next to the sink, she held it to her arm and quickly looked around. Where to hide? There was a large enamel bathtub against the back wall. It would at least be some shelter. She stepped into it, then kneeled, head down. A bullet hit the outside of the metal bath, a glancing blow. The tub hummed and vibrated with the shock of the impact. Her knees hurt on the cold, white enamel and she rocked backwards so she could lie flat on her back in the bath, the towel pressed against her left arm. When the shooting finally stopped, she heard heavy boots kicking the gate at the bottom of the stairs, but it held. Then she heard the sound of car doors slamming in the street outside and an engine revving. Tyres screeched against the tarmac. A woman screamed in the street.

'Seán, Seán, they've shot Luke Maguire. Call the ambulance, for God's sake call an ambulance.'

Lena stood up in the bath, picked her way through the smashed floorboards and stumbled to the top of the stairs. There was smoke in the air and a bitter smell. She looked down to the metal gate. There was blood everywhere, on the white painted walls and the bottom two or three wooden stairs. Blood also on the splintered front door. Blood on the jeans and sweater of the body lying in the hallway.

Lena ran downstairs and felt for a pulse in his neck. She could sense people gathering in the street and yelled as loud as she could, 'someone for Christ's sake, get an ambulance'. Blood was pouring through Maguire's dark blue sweater. She pressed hard on the spot near his shoulder where it seemed to be coming from. She knew not to turn him. Bending her head closer to his, she whispered into his ear, 'Luke. It's Lena. Hang on. You're going to be all right. Open your eyes.' She felt tears running down her cheeks, wiping them away with a bloodied shirt cuff.

The woman in the street shouted that the ambulance was coming. Lena kept talking to Maguire. She felt for his pulse again, listened for his breathing, aware of a growing crowd outside. Then came the blessed blue lights. Strong hands pulled her away. The paramedics in their dark-green uniforms were now kneeling around him. She backed off into the footpath to give them more room. The woman in the street put her arms around her shoulders and pulled her further away.

'Come away, love, come away,' she said gently, encouraging Lena to leave. 'There's nothing you can do.'

Male voices in the crowd became more insistent.

'Who the fuck is she? Get her out of here, the police will be arriving.'

Lena was surrounded by people, pulling her this way and that. She heard her own voice, shouting, 'don't let the police near him'.

The same woman's kind voice answered. 'It's okay, pet, it's okay. The paramedics will have him in the ambulance before the police get out of their jeeps. He'll be inside the RVH before they can get anywhere near him.'

Lena watched helplessly as the paramedics put a drip into Maguire's arm. The kind woman put a blanket around her shoulders. In the few moments she had, she thought how she had cowered in the bathroom. Maguire could have opened the door at the bottom of the stairs and run up to escape, but he had faced them alone. She began silently sobbing, a hand over her mouth, watching him being lifted into the ambulance, strapped to a stretcher. A second ambulance arrived. People insisted she get in. She gave way, reckoning she would at least be taken wherever Maguire was going. Inside the ambulance, the paramedics began checking her over. They cut her shirt sleeve, bandaged a wound on her left arm and cleaned a graze on her forehead. The ambulance stopped outside the main entrance to the RVH Accident and Emergency Department but she rejected the offered wheelchair, running into the reception area and shouting incoherently at a woman behind a glass screen.

'The wounded man who was just brought in. I'm his lawyer. You have to tell me where he is.'

'If you're not his next of kin, I can't release any information,' the woman said coldly.

'I said I'm his lawyer. I have a right to know,' she insisted before one of the ambulance crew approached and told her, not unkindly, 'Leave it miss, or there'll be a screaming match.'

Lena allowed herself to be taken to a curtained alcove where she sat, weeping and helpless, as a young male doctor anaesthetised her arm, put in three stitches and applied a dressing.

'The man who was shot,' she told the medic, 'we were together, I must find out how he is. I know they can't tell me at reception but please, please can you help me?'

The doctor looked over his shoulder to check if anyone was listening before telling her Maguire was alive and in theatre.

'There's nothing more to tell,' he said. 'I've patched you up. You should go home now and rest.'

Sinéad was Maguire's next of kin, Lena thought, she could find out. Standing up and straightening her rumpled clothes, she walked through the waiting area, only to be stopped by two policemen.

'Miss Dawson, I'm afraid you'll have to make a statement.'

'As you can see,' she said, 'I've been wounded and the doctor says I need to rest. Can't it wait?'

'I'm afraid not,' one of the officers said. 'We need to take forensic samples. It won't take long.'

Lena accepted the inevitable. At Grosvenor Road police station, the two policemen continued to be punctiliously polite, taking swabs from her hands and clothes and sealing them into evidence bags.

'Can I have your address and phone number?' one asked.

'The Old Cottage, Glenbarry, County Down,' she said, adding her phone number.

'Can you tell us why you were at Kashmir Road?'

'I am a solicitor. I was visiting my client, Luke Maguire.'

'Can you tell us what time you arrived?'

'About six.'

'On a Saturday? Strange time for a legal visit?'

Lena made no comment.

'And where were you when the shooting began?'

'Upstairs in the bathroom.'

'What time was that?'

'Around seven o'clock.'

'Did you see the gunmen?'

'No. When I heard the door crashing in, I came out of the bathroom but went back in and locked the door.'

'Not the best idea in the world, was it, to visit a terrorist at his home – even if he is your client? It might have been better to meet at your office.'

'I will meet my clients at a time and place of my choosing. I don't expect gunmen to smash down their doors and attack them.'

'But the office would have been safer, wouldn't it?'

'Wouldn't you be better off searching for the men who attacked Luke Maguire than asking me these silly questions?'

'We will need to speak to you again, Miss Dawson, but for the moment you are free to go.'

It was getting dark by the time the police drove her back to Kashmir Road, where her red Mini was still parked outside Maguire's house. It was a relief to sink into the driving seat, safe at last in a private space. She slid her arm out of its sling and took a moment to compose herself. She had answered all the police questions honestly and accurately. She was Maguire's lawyer. She had been visiting him to discuss a case. That was all.

Her wretched knees began to shake again as she pressed down gently on the accelerator and moved slowly towards the Falls Road. As far as she could tell, the police were not following. She must phone Sinéad. Outside the city, on the familiar road home, the shakes got worse, and she pulled over. She had managed to blank out the attack for a while but, alone in the dark, she leaned her head on the steering wheel and sobbed until it felt as if her brain would burst through her forehead.

How very safe she had been, just forty-eight hours ago, if only she had known it, cocooned, wrapped in cotton wool – a competent young lawyer; her father a minister in rural Hampshire; working on a strategically important case under the aegis of a wealthy and influential employer whose highly eligible son adored her. Now she was a renegade, vulnerable, in danger. Maguire had said she must change sides but she was still the same person with exactly the same intentions, the same purpose. At the cottage, she turned on the midnight radio news.

'Two people have been shot and injured this evening in West Belfast. The police say it has all the hallmarks of a loyalist attack. A man with serious injuries is being treated in the Royal Victoria Hospital. A woman with him was only slightly hurt.'

Such a report would not ordinarily have caused her a second's concern. Two people injured? So what? She rang Sinéad's number.

'Lena, are you okay? Mary Cassidy from next door to Luke's rang to tell me. They're still working on him at the RVH. I didn't have your home number. Are you hurt?'

'I'm fine. Only a scratch on my arm. I'm back at home.'

'Give me your number, I'll ring you if there's any news. A good friend works in A&E. They'll keep me in the loop.'

Lena dragged herself upstairs and put a clean dressing on her arm in the bathroom. Come daybreak, she would have to call William. Thinking of him made her think of Edward and tears began pouring down her cheeks again. She had to get some sleep. In bed, Peanut curled up and settled at her feet. Just looking at him helped to calm her. Tomorrow was Sunday. She would walk along the lough shore to clear her head and decide what next for the notes and diagrams in the deep freeze.

＃ 9

The light shining through a chink in the curtains woke her early, and she turned over, burying her head in the pillow as she remembered the noise and terror of the previous day. But she couldn't stay in bed; she had work to do. She washed and quickly pulled on jeans and a t-shirt. Sinéad hadn't rung overnight, so Maguire must still be alive. She had to phone William, but it was too early, so she would eat first to settle herself. The fridge was empty, devoid even of milk. Of course. She had expected to be at the Hall.

She reached for her car keys in their saucer in the hallway and noticed a van parked across the gateway. Squinting through the small glass window in the front door, she saw a man sitting in the van pointing a long camera lens towards the cottage. A photographer. At this hour? She drew a curtain across the front door. There could only be one explanation: the police at Grosvenor Road had given her address to the press.

Instead of leaving to buy milk, bread and the Sunday papers, she went around the cottage, drawing all the curtains and blinds. A second car arrived as she watched through a gap in the curtains upstairs. There were now two of them, chatting and pointing their long lenses at the cottage. Lena made herself a black coffee. She felt like prey. An insistent knocking began on the front door. The phone was also ringing, but she let the answering machine take messages, listening in case Sinéad rang with news of Maguire. The flap on the front door letterbox started banging. Slips of paper were being pushed through and falling onto the door mat.

One read, 'Eleanor, please ring. We would like to tell your side of the story.'

It struck her then that someone like Maguire being shot would be news, even in England. Her father knew his name. He always listened to Sunday morning religious programming. She must phone him before he heard the news on a radio bulletin.

'Hi Dad. Just ringing to say I was caught up in something last night. You might hear about it on the news, but there's nothing to worry about.'

'What on earth … Lena, tell me now.'

'I was visiting a client, Maguire, the man I've told you about, and gunmen attacked the house. He's been shot, but he's going to be okay. I have a scratch on my arm, but it's nothing. This sort of thing happens all the time over here.'

'Hell's bells, Lena. Why on earth were you at his house?'

'There was something we had to discuss. You might hear reports on the news and they may exaggerate what happened and get things wrong, so you need to believe me and not worry.'

'I'm getting the next plane over, Lena.'

'Dad, no. I have an important Appeal Court hearing in two days. If you came over, it would complicate everything. If any reporters ring, please say absolutely nothing, no matter what they tell you. Don't deny anything – just say nothing at all, not a word, and put the phone down, even though it seems rude. Is that okay?'

'Don't worry old girl. Let me get your mother to the phone.'

'Your father tells me nothing. Have you been hurt?'

'Just a superficial cut. I'm fine. But if any reporters ring or come to the house, please don't say anything at all. Is that okay, Mum? Could you put Dad back on the phone again?'

'Lena my dear, isn't it time to call a halt to this nonsense?'

'I'm sorry I was abrupt earlier. Please let's not discuss it now. I'll come home as soon as I can.'

Then she phoned William at Gordon Hall.

'Lena, what a fright you've given us. Paul Donaldson phoned early this morning to say you were caught up in the shooting last night. I've been ringing your number, but it was constantly engaged. Are you all right? Edward is terribly worried.'

Not worried enough to phone me himself, she thought.

'I'm fine, Mr Gordon. Maguire is still in hospital.'

'So, it's true then, that you were at his house?'

'I decided I had to advise him. He's our client. We owed him that.'

She heard an intake of breath and barely restrained fury in William's voice.

'We agreed to wait until Monday. I kept my word. You, however, seem to have taken the first opportunity to break yours. We'll discuss this when I get to the office to-morrow. And if any reporters ring you, you say nothing until we have agreed how to deal with it.'

'Fine, Mr Gordon.'

She phoned and left a message at Geraldine's home

saying she was okay and not to worry, then checked her answering machine, hoping there was a missed call from Edward but there was just a succession of messages from reporters, leaving numbers and asking her to call back.

David Murray's familiar voice was amongst them.

'Morning Lena. I hear you're okay. I just want to warn you that you're likely to get a few phone calls from my colleagues. It's pretty big news, I'm afraid. I've not given your phone number out to anyone, but if you could call me when you can, that would be great.'

A message then came that stopped her in her tracks. 'Lena, this is Mary Cassidy, Luke's neighbour. Sinéad gave me your number. I know you're his solicitor and I thought you should know that the police and soldiers are taking his house apart.'

She knew what that meant. The floorboards were being lifted by men in white forensic suits. They would be throwing his books on the floor and drilling through the walls, searching for hidden compartments, guns, explosives and ammunition. Samples would be taken from the blood at the bottom of the stairs. They would be pawing their way through his clothes. Her own blood would be wiped off the bath for forensic examination. She imagined the scene outside the house. Knots of people gathering, yelling obscenities at the police.

She was still sitting at the kitchen table, wondering how to get out of the house without being photographed, when Sinéad rang and left a message. Maguire was out of theatre. He was not in immediate danger, but unconscious. It galvanised Lena into action. She must get expert legal advice. She was not at all sure that whatever William Gordon decided tomorrow would be in the Maguires' best interests. Above all, she needed to ensure the evidential integrity of the car at Seapark. It must not be touched. She needed to speak to someone who understood the rules of evidence, someone like Martin Porter, someone she could entirely trust, who would understand her concerns about Gordon. There was only one person who fitted the bill, Brendan Casey. She lifted the receiver, careful to remain calm for the benefit of anyone listening.

'Brendan, I am sorry to ring you on a Sunday morning.'

'Are you okay, Lena? Shocking news about last night.'

'I'm fine but I'd like a brief chat if you can spare the time?'

'Can you drive? The radio news says you were injured.'

'I'm on my way.'

There was a winter scarf hanging in the hallway. Lena tied it around her head, put on a pair of old sunglasses and jumped into the red Mini at the front door. The photographers ran to their cars and followed her to Belfast but she ran a red light and lost them.

Brendan lived in a leafy avenue, once home to the Protestant merchant and professional classes. When Catholics started earning serious money and could afford to move in, or so Geraldine had told her, Protestants had moved out to the 'Gold Coast' in North Down. Lena drew up in Casey's driveway and knocked on his front door, crying and leaning an arm against the door jamb for support.

'I'm sorry, Brendan. I'm ruining your Sunday.'

'For heaven's sake, young woman, come inside. You look shattered.'

In the kitchen, he pulled out a chair and she slumped onto it, blowing her nose. While the kettle boiled, he kept discreetly silent until she regained her composure, blew her nose and dabbed cold water from the sink on her eyes.

'You had better tell me everything,' he said. 'We'll go into my office.'

Once settled, he began questioning her as if she were a witness. It felt strangely reassuring. Someone else was in control, at least for the moment. Lena began by telling him about meeting Leglu in Strasbourg.

'He said the police theory stretched credulity but could not be disproved.'

'Nothing new in that,' Casey said.

Then she moved on to tell him about Séamus in Donegal.

'Very intriguing,' he said, 'but Hamilton would have had a field day, and it's hardly enough anyway to convince a coroner the men were ambushed and executed.'

'I know. I was giving up,' Lena said. 'Only the Ford Fiesta left. The exhibit list stated it had been crushed, but I thought I should take a look just in case.'

'Just in case of what? You're alarmingly thorough. What could a crushed car possibly tell you?'

'You're not going to believe this Brendan but – when I got to Seapark – the Ford was still in one piece. Someone in the exhibits department made an error.'

'They're even worse bunglers than I thought. Go on,' said Casey.

Lena knew Casey had to understand, perfectly, what she had seen, in case there was any innocent explanation. She walked towards his study door, pushing down on the handle.

'This is how you open a door, yes?'

'Of course.'

'You already know the police say Danny Maguire's weight fell onto the door handle, he tumbled out and the fatal bullet passed underneath the chassis before hitting him. But they're lying.'

'And your evidence?'

Lena walked towards Casey, and curled two fingers under a brass handle on a drawer of his writing desk.

'To open the door on that newer model of Ford, you have to pull the handle towards you horizontally, like this. Maguire must have been sufficiently conscious to open the door himself, although, at that stage, he could have posed no conceivable threat. He was then shot in the head, possibly at short range. The only possible reason for concocting this elaborate set of lies is to hide their illegal use of lethal force.'

Casey drew breath.

'Who else knows?'

'No one, other than Gordon and Maguire. I drove to Fermanagh on Friday evening to tell William and was at Maguire's house when the attack took place.'

'Gordon is Maguire's solicitor, but he's also a dyed-in-the-wool unionist,' said Casey. 'He'll be in damage-limitation mode. I wouldn't put it past him to drop an accidental-on-purpose comment to one of his RUC pals – or to someone like Hamilton who thinks it's quite okay to "bend the rules" – and goodbye evidence.'

'That's what's worrying me,' said Lena. 'We're due to meet first thing in the morning with my original notes. I couldn't use a camera in Seapark, but I scribbled notes and made a diagram. They're both well-hidden at home but if the police discovered any of this, they could still stick the Ford in the crusher,' she said.

'It would then be your word against theirs,' said Casey. 'If they got a warrant to search the cottage, even your notes and diagram would be gone.'

Lena could almost hear the cogs turning in Casey's brain. He rested his chin on his fingertips and gazed up at the study ceiling. She waited.

'Forgive me while I think aloud,' he finally said. 'Legally, your diagram amounts to contemporaneous evidence and is therefore admissible in court. If you add an affidavit explaining what you saw, we could get it date-stamped in the Courts Office first thing on Monday. Then it's in the system, untouchable, securely on its way to the judges but still only hearsay. We're in court for the anonymity issue on Tuesday. If we can somehow mention your notes in open court, they then, *ipso facto*, become formal legal exhibits which the press can openly report.'

'Even if the RUC sank the car in the Irish Sea,' said Lena, 'it would then be too late.'

'There's just one minor problem,' said Casey. 'We're up in court all right but only on Crown immunity. The disclosure rules prohibit mentioning anything in open court unless the prosecution has advance notice. Crown counsel in the case is your friend and mine, Geoff Hamilton. If he finds out what we have, he may also decide to alert the police. It would then be a case of "he said/she said" and that could go either way.'

Lena was first to break the silence.

'What if we sail a little close to the wind ourselves?' she

suggested. 'I know I can't appear before the Appeal Court myself but what if I hand the evidence to Hamilton as he arrives and, minutes later, you stand up and announce its existence?'

Casey frowned. 'That would be extremely sharp practice,' he said. 'Effectively joint enterprise to flout the disclosure rules. Whoever was responsible wouldn't work in this town again. I'm on your side, Lena, but I'm not going to commit professional hara-kiri.'

There was another silence before Lena lifted her head and tentatively suggested inviting Martin Porter to do the dirty deed.

'He'd never agree,' said Casey, shaking his head. 'The judiciary will take a very dim view.'

'All he has to do is stand up in court and say a few words. I'll be the real guilty party, handing Hamilton the evidence just as he arrives. I'll be gone from this place in a few weeks and I don't give tuppence for what the Belfast judges think.'

'It would be thoroughly unethical, amounting to contempt of court.'

'Frankly, if that's the only option, I know where I stand,' said Lena.

'Are you sure, Lena? You'll be burning some bridges.'

'You got an alternative?'

'Porter would have to be quick off the mark,' Casey said. 'He'll only have seconds to refer to your evidence before the judge closes him down.'

'Not a bother to Porter. Court drama is food and drink to him.'

'What about the press? They'll not turn up for arcane legal arguments over immunity.'

'I'm on good terms with David Murray, the agency court reporter. He'll trust me if I suggest he tip the networks off.'

'Okay, so we have a plan, of sorts. What time does Gordon generally arrive in your office on Mondays?'

'Never before ten – he's a creature of habit and leaves the Hall around eight-thirty. He's asked me to bring in my original notes for tomorrow's meeting. Could he take them off me?'

'It would certainly be preferable to get them date-stamped in the Courts Office beforehand. If you meet me earlier on, we'll go together.'

At least, thought Lena, I'll not be on my own for that part of the plan.

'Which just leaves one more problem,' Casey said. 'Neither Gordon nor Hamilton will take this lying down. Gordon, in particular, will be livid if we lodge that affidavit before he's had a chance to influence events.'

Lena swallowed. Casey was right. William would be enraged.

'Maybe when he realises his firm has exposed such an appalling crime, he'll see it differently,' she said.

'Very droll, Lena. If Hamilton complains to the Law Society about late disclosure, Gordon certainly won't be leaping to your defence. You could get struck off. Are you ready for that?'

'I have to be.'

'I hesitate to say this, Lena, but – how shall I put it? There are other, more personal, implications. I'm not sure who'll come down on you hardest, father or son. I believe you and Edward have become fairly close. The course of action we're planning may burn that bridge as well.'

Lena lifted her chin and looked straight at Casey. Their plan had emboldened her, at least temporarily.

'If the Gordons don't like it, they can both go to hell.'

'Your call. Just think about it over the next few hours and make sure you're certain.'

'I'll go home now and write my affidavit,' she said. 'Can I use your phone to call Sinéad and check on Luke?'

'Sure,' said Casey. 'I'll just pop into the kitchen.'

Lena realised he was getting clear in case the news was bad. But Maguire was stable. When she joined him in the kitchen, he said he had one more duty to perform.

'I've been keeping this from you until we decided what to do but you should take a look at these,' he said, plonking the Sunday papers on a worktop in front of her.

Lena looked at the front-page headlines. 'UDA Murder Bid on IRA Man – Mystery Girl Injured' read the first. 'UDA Attack Maguire's Lair – Woman Lawyer Hurt' claimed a second while a third read 'UFF in Revenge Shooting – Maguire Woman Shot'.

Lena put her head in her hands. 'Oh my God.'

'Public attention span is short. They'll be lining the bottom of a parrot cage in Ballymena tomorrow. Go home, have something to eat, write that affidavit and get a good night's sleep. Here,' he said, opening a kitchen drawer, 'take a couple of my sleeping tablets. They're mild enough. You'll be fine in the morning.'

As they walked to her car, he had one final question.

'Lena, you also need to think about what you want, long-term, out of all this.'

She didn't hesitate.

'They'll have to order a public inquiry, won't they?'

'I doubt it very much,' said Casey. 'You had better decide on Plan B. Now get out of my sight. I have to write my opening statement for Tuesday – although in the uproar, I don't expect it will be needed.'

At home, Lena parked at the back of the cottage for a covert exit should the press pack return, then checked the diagram and notes in the freezer. Casey's words came back to her. Who would come down hardest on her? William or Edward? Steve Sullivan had left a message, so she rang him back.

'Holy moly, Lena. Maguire should have stopped you from coming anywhere near him.'

'He tried but I didn't listen. Your plans for coming over this week, have you booked a flight?'

'Sure did. I'm on the red-eye arriving in Dublin on Tuesday morning and I've a hire car booked. I hope Edward Gordon is standing by you.'

'We had a falling out before the shooting. He's not speaking to me.'

'Jeez. You got no friends at all?'

'Well, there's Brendan Casey. He's the barrister helping me.'

'That's not what I meant at all, Lena. At times like this, you need someone to tuck you into bed at night.'

'At least I know you're on your way over. That helps a lot. Call me from the airport so I know you're on your way.'

Her father had also left a message. When she called him, she got an earful.

'There were reporters crowded into the church this morning,' he said. 'They waited until the congregation left and began asking some highly inappropriate questions about you and Luke Maguire. I said nothing, just as you asked. It doesn't look good, Lena. Your mother is very worried.'

'I'm Maguire's lawyer, Dad. I was at his home for a legal meeting. I've done nothing wrong.'

'Why not see him in the office? And what does William think?'

'He got a fright, but we're meeting first thing in the morning to talk it over.'

'One of the reporters said Maguire was responsible for a bombing a few days ago when a police officer was killed.'

'That's just the papers making it up, Dad. Maguire was with me when that happened.'

'What's Edward to say about all this?'

'It's a bit awkward.'

'I expect it is. No doubt you'll tell us in your own good time.'

'Yes, I promise.'

She had yet to phone Porter. If he could not come over or refused, their plan was holed beneath the waterline.

Georgina answered the phone.

'I've been sick with worry, darling, and phoning you all day. Are you alright?'

'There's a lot going on, Georgie, but I'm fine. I'll give you the full grisly details in due course but I'm up against the clock – and please don't be offended – I have to speak to Martin.'

Georgina called her husband to the phone, where Lena assured him she was doing fine and began to use their agreed code.

'There's a lot of press interest in Tuesday's hearing,' she began, 'I thought you'd be interested to know they're moving it from one of the smaller upstairs courts to a larger one off the main lobby. Would you consider coming over, just for moral support?'

'If I did, should I go upstairs or downstairs?' Porter asked.

'The upstairs room wasn't nearly large enough,' Lena said.

'In that case,' said Porter, 'how can I resist?'

Relieved, her affidavit typed up, she checked with Sinéad about Maguire, took one of Casey's sleeping pills and went to bed. Peanut jumped onto the duvet and curled up at her feet. His sweet little face and gentle purring helped her get some sleep. In the morning, she carefully removed the dressing on her left arm and replaced it with a smaller one. The small bump on her forehead was turning purple. She managed to eat some cereal before ringing Geraldine.

'Lena, there's a gang of reporters outside the office. When are you coming in? I can't handle this on my own.'

'I'm leaving home now. When is William due?'

'He rang and said he'd be here around ten. He sounded dead worried.'

I have to get through this day, Lena told herself. The best thing I can do now is pretend everything is normal, go through my usual routine, put on make-up, put on my best shirt, blow-dry my hair. Our plan is going to work.

Retrieving the evidence bag from the deep freeze, she added her folded affidavit, placed the papers in a zipped compartment of her briefcase and got into the Mini behind the house. There were a couple of photographers at the end of the driveway, but not a posse like before. Perhaps the worst was over. She put some rousing Handel on the car cassette player and tried to remain calm on the journey into Belfast. It was a bright, sunny day. The green of the hedges and hills, Strangford Lough glinting blue in her rear-view mirror, they were all unchanged, immutable. In High Street, however, reality hit her like a twenty-tonne truck. At least ten reporters were at the office door.

At reception, Geraldine silently pushed Monday's London and Dublin newspapers across at her. They were even worse than Sunday's. 'Woman Lawyer in IRA Gun Horror' said one. 'Maguire Shot. Woman Friend Escapes' was another. 'IRA Godfather Critical – Rookie Lawyer Injured' a third.

'What are you going to do?' Geraldine asked, wide-eyed. 'Mr Gordon will go berserk.'

'I don't know,' Lena replied, taking the papers into her office, laying them on her desk and flicking through the pages. Although their main focus was Maguire, with multiple allusions to his alleged role in the recent Armagh RUC man's killing, she also played a supporting role:

'Leading republican Luke Maguire, arrested by detectives investigating the IRA murder of an RUC man in Armagh city, is battling for his life after a UDA attack,' said one. In a second, she was referred to as 'a mystery brunette'. There were photos of her leaving Glenbarry, a scarf over her face, adjacent to a police mug-shot of Maguire looking particularly menacing. The mere positioning implied some kind of illicit relationship.

On Geraldine's arrival with tea, Lena pushed the newspapers away, reached for her precious handwritten notes and asked her to make six photocopies. With the originals and three of the stapled photocopies safely in her briefcase, she ran the gauntlet of reporters in High Street to meet Casey, as agreed, outside the Royal Courts of Justice.

'Porter's coming but he needs to be filled in,' she said.

'Leave that to me,' Casey said, gripping her right elbow as they walked into the court security hut. The official searchers on the main door usually had a few friendly words for the regulars checking in. Today, they were impassive.

'Brace yourself Bridget. This could get nasty,' Casey whispered as they walked up the main steps into the echoing lobby.

Waiting for a lift to the upstairs Courts Office, Lena looked around and wondered whether it was her imagination or if more people than usual were taking the stairs. There was none of the usual crush in the lift at this hour – just her and Casey. No one stopped to express sympathy or support, although they could hardly have missed the newspaper headlines. Small knots of people stopped talking as they passed, and then began murmuring again in their wake.

'Brendan, I'm not imagining it. People are avoiding us.'

'Toughen up, kiddo.'

Outside the Courts Office, she showed Casey her original diagram and notes. He whistled through his teeth as he turned the pages. Then she and Casey submitted the original documents to the clerks, along with two more stapled copies, and solemnly watched as they were date-stamped.

'That's the die cast then,' said Casey as they descended

the stairs to the main lobby. 'I'll pick Porter up from the airport. You return to the office and give Gordon the bad news – or some of it. You can leave out Porter's arrival and our plans for Tuesday.'

With a few minutes left before tackling Gordon, Lena walked towards High Street, relieved her decision was made and mentally steeling herself for the drama ahead. Let battle commence, she thought, walking into Gordon's office where he sat in glacial silence.

'Is your arm sore?' he asked.

'It hurt a bit as I typed my affidavit.'

'What affidavit?'

'The one I signed and lodged in the Courts Office this morning about the discovery in Seapark, along with my original diagram and notes.'

'You did what? You did that without my consent, without even consulting me?'

She replied in a monotone.

'My first duty, as you well know, is to my clients, Sinéad and Luke Maguire.'

For a moment, she thought Gordon would come around the table and punch her. But he controlled himself.

'Well then, madam, you are just going to have to retrieve whatever it is you handed over. We agreed to talk this through first. You will tell the Courts Office you made a mistake.'

'I'm afraid that is impossible. The file is already labelled for the judges' attention and time-stamped. The Courts Office cannot hand it to anyone other than the judges – and that's an end to it.'

Gordon, realising threats would not work, began to plead.

'Lena, what will Edward think if you take this precipitate action without consulting me?'

Two can play at that game, she thought.

'Edward will know I am doing my duty. Just as he does when he puts on his UDR uniform. And so should you, sir, if I may say so.'

As pleading hadn't worked either, Gordon resumed being bellicose.

'You do realise you're playing into the hands of the Provisionals? They'll be laughing their heads off up the Falls Road.'

'If they are, I hardly think I am to blame. Those who summarily executed Maguire and Reid – and I use the term advisedly – should be asking themselves those questions. Not me.'

'And how do you plan to proceed madam?'

'Tomorrow's hearing, as you well know, can only deal with Crown immunity but I will seek to raise the new evidence as soon as possible.'

This was, she knew, not exactly an outright lie, but very far from the whole truth. She had watched as William's face went from outrage through entreaty and back to outrage. He now looked relieved, clearly believing he had a couple of weeks in which to have a quiet chat with Trevor Gibson and nobble a judge or two.

Despite having asked Geraldine for no interruptions, the door opened and Edward strode in.

'We need to talk,' he said.

'Fair enough. Let's do that,' she replied.

Gordon weakly wafted them out.

In her office, Lena and Edward stood facing each other.

Which side of his personality would take precedence? she wondered. Would he be concerned about her injury? Or angry that she was at Maguire's? She waited to hear.

'How's your arm?' he asked.

'It's just a scratch,' she replied.

'May I ask what you were doing at Maguire's house on Saturday evening?'

'I had to tell him about some new evidence.'

'Maybe you'd like to share it.'

She took a deep breath.

'It means the RUC and UDR lied to the Maguire and Reid families, to the public and to the courts. The first person I told was your father, and only then did I go to see Maguire. He had a right to know.'

Edward stood silent, processing her words.

'I'm going out for some fresh air' was all he said before walking out of her office.

It could have been worse, Lena thought, but a few minutes later, she heard him and his father, their voices raised, heading for the lift. She hoped they were arguing, that Edward was taking her side. A ringing phone interrupted her thoughts. It was Sinéad. Luke Maguire was still unconscious and might need more surgery.

'He saved my life, Sinéad,' Lena said. 'When they were smashing down the door, he slammed the stairway gate shut.'

'He did what he had to do.'

'Are you coming to court in the morning?'

'Do I have to? I can't hear or understand anything going on.'

'I think you should. The press will be there in force after

Saturday's attack. They might be more sympathetic than usual.'

In the afternoon, Lena phoned Casey to check that Martin Porter had arrived.

'He's safely installed in his hotel. I've briefed him. He's up for it. Don't forget to speak to your journalist friend,' Casey said.

Lena had already arranged to meet David Murray.

'You're a lucky man,' she told him over tea in the Europa Hotel. 'I'm about to give you what I think you press people call a "heads-up". Make sure you're at the High Court by nine tomorrow.'

'For more interminable wrangling over Crown immunity? Not a chance.'

'I think there'll be a bit more to it than that.'

'Tell, tell, tell.'

'I can't.'

'How can I put out an all-points alert if I don't know what you've got?'

'I don't cry wolf, David. You should know that by now. Just be there.'

Box ticked, she drove home, forced herself to eat and tried to have a quiet evening. Sullivan rang from JFK as he was about to board his plane.

'I'm due at Dublin Airport around six in the morning,' he said. 'I should be at the courts by around ten. That work for you?'

'If the army doesn't stop you at the border.'

'An American accent and a New York attitude can work miracles with British soldiers,' he replied dryly.

Lena then tried to sleep. Despite Casey's tablet, she

woke at three, her body seized-up, her joints locked. She shrank into the foetal position, turned on the electric blanket, tried to avoid watching the hours ticking by on her bedside clock and finally lost consciousness sometime after four.

The phone woke her at six o'clock. Straightaway, she peered through the bedroom curtains and saw cars at the end of the drive. They were there again. Long lenses, camera crews. David Murray must have stimulated a bit of interest, she thought. She could not run away this time. She needed the press in court. The phone rang again.

'Hello, is this Eleanor Dawson? Sorry to ring you so early but we were wondering if you could go into Broadcasting House in Belfast this morning for *The Today Programme*? It's about the attack on Luke Maguire and the immunity hearing.'

The strict rule at Gordon & Company was for all press interviews to be cleared with William first, but Lena had no time for that. He would refuse, and she would have to ignore him. She was on the road at 6.30 a.m. and on air just after 7.30 a.m.

The interviewer first enquired politely about her own injury, then switched to Maguire. 'Why do you think the UDA singled him out? Is it because the police arrested him for last week's killing of the police officer in Armagh?'

'That may indeed have been the UDA's motivation but the RUC are fully aware that Luke Maguire was returning with me from seeing an expert witness in Strasbourg when the officer was tragically killed. I was able to give the police our boarding cards as proof, although the newspapers have repeatedly named him as a suspect.'

'Was the attack connected to today's court hearing?'

'My limited knowledge of the UDA tells me they're not particularly interested in Crown immunity,' she said. 'This morning's hearing is confined to legal arguments on whether the RUC officers who killed Danny Maguire can evade being identified and questioned.'

By eight o'clock she was in her office. Sullivan had left a message on the machine that he was on his way. She spent the next hour checking and rechecking her papers. A printed copy of the all-important affidavit, folded neatly into a long, brown envelope, was ready to present to Hamilton. She quickly ran off twenty copies of her press release and the diagram of the car handle. At nine-fifteen precisely, she met Casey and Porter in a café across from the courts, close to the Albert Clock. Anyone other than Porter would have been a bundle of nerves, but he was composure personified.

'Little did we think in London all those months ago that our code word would be put to such good use,' said Lena.

'I'll never be able to say "upstairs" again without a smile,' said Porter.

'You may not be smiling if this mad plan comes off,' Casey said. 'Your name will be cited in the legal textbooks for decades to come – and not in a good way.'

'Most people talk at a rate of three words a second,' said Lena. 'If the judge closes you down, say, after ten seconds, you'll only have about thirty words to say what's needed.'

'Don't fret, Lena. I was born for this kind of thing,' Porter replied.

When it was time to go, they walked together over the four-lane highway towards the courts. Porter and Casey then turned right into the Law Library while Lena headed towards the Royal Courts of Justice, knowing she was about to blow up the last of her bridges. A huddle of reporters was already waiting.

'Miss Dawson, any news of Luke Maguire's condition?' one shouted at her.

'My client is stable, but will need further surgery,' she replied.

'Was the attack linked to the bombing in Armagh last week?'

'Mr Maguire was in Strasbourg speaking to an expert witness and could not have been involved. The press might reflect on whether their baseless claims led the UDA to target my client on Saturday.'

'We just saw Martin Porter going into the Law Library. Why is he over from London?'

'Mr Porter believes that if those with a duty to uphold the law kill unarmed men, they must explain why in open court.'

She then walked through the security lodge, booked a consulting room for a post-hearing briefing and strode across the echoing central lobby. The first person her eyes lit on was Sullivan, who rose with a smile. Lena, already tense and prepping herself for her moment with Hamilton, shook her head and held a finger up to her lips. Sullivan copped on, stopped abruptly and sat down again. She walked past him and sat on a polished wooden bench close to the heavy swing doors leading into the courtroom.

Porter and Casey strode past her into court – then the

small drama they had planned swung into action. First, she heard Hamilton's voice to her left and quickly stood up to face him.

'Lena, may I say how shocked we all are about your dreadful ordeal? Have you seen the cameras outside?'

'Just my fifteen minutes of fame, Geoffrey. They'll be gone tomorrow,' she said.

This was the moment. It was time. The envelope containing the affidavit was in her hand.

'Geoffrey, I have something for you.'

She lifted the envelope and held it out towards him.

His hand rose instinctively to take it.

'What's this?' he said, envelope in hand.

'I think you'll find it's of interest,' she said, walking into court before he had time to reply.

She had done it. She had played her part. Now it was up to Porter.

The public seats were filling up. Sinéad was already there, sitting with three people Lena thought were probably members of the Reid family. As Lena took her seat at the table below the judges' bench, Sinéad's smile signalled no deterioration in Maguire's condition.

Hamilton sat down at the opposite end of the same table, diagonally across from her, looking puzzled as he saw the packed press gallery. Lena watched as he opened the envelope she had given him and start to read its contents. He then whispered to his junior counsel and both of them turned and scowled at her. In walked Sir Basil Simpson and two other judges. They, too, raised their eyebrows at the unexpected multitude of reporters. Hamilton began speaking with his customary hauteur.

'Your Lordships, I appear on behalf of the Crown Solicitor's Office.'

It was Porter's turn now. He drew himself up to his imposing height, adjusted his wig and spoke resolutely.

'Your Lordships, I appear on behalf of Sinéad and Luke Maguire, instructed by William Gordon & Company.'

Lena's nerves were stretched to breaking point. This was it.

'May I thank the court for graciously allowing me to appear at such short notice,' Porter said, the epitome of relaxed confidence, prompting simpering smiles from the bench and anguish in Lena's heart. Go, Porter, go, she thought, before Hamilton stands up again.

'I beg the court's indulgence in bringing to Your Lordship's attention,' Porter went on – it seemed to Lena far too languidly – 'some recently uncovered but incontrovertible evidence that the RUC shot Danny Maguire dead when he posed no conceivable threat.'

Like two synchronised swimmers, Hamilton and his junior stood up shouting, 'Objection, objection.'

But Porter pressed on.

'This evidence,' he shouted above the din, not at all slowly now, 'was discovered four days ago at an RUC secure storage depot in Carrickfergus. I have a diagram to that effect here with me.'

Porter had a copy of Lena's diagram in his hand and waved the paper over his head. Hamilton, his mouth opening and then closing like a fish, finally managed to be heard.

'I protest most vehemently, Your Lordships. This new information has not been disclosed to the Crown. My learned friend knows perfectly well that if he wishes to refer to affidavit evidence, the Crown should be put on notice and be provided with a copy well in advance.'

'My understanding,' said Porter lightly, still on his feet, 'is that Their Lordships have already been provided with a date-stamped copy and, indeed, Crown counsel also has a copy of said affidavit. I think I see it there,' he pointed, 'in your own hands, Mr Hamilton. Maybe you'd like to read it aloud to the court?'

The judges' faces darkened. Hamilton was now so angry he could barely speak.

'This is completely out of order,' he spluttered.

Porter, his work done, sat down.

'As a matter of urgency,' said Hamilton, 'I ask for an immediate adjournment to consider this unexpected and unwarranted development …'

He continued standing, leaning forward, awaiting word from the judges who conferred with each other. Lena stared modestly down. Porter had managed even more than thirty words. Glancing at Sullivan in the front row of the public gallery, she could see his jaw dropping while, in the press gallery, journalists were madly scribbling. Sinéad just looked bemused. Sir Basil then spoke.

'We agree with Crown counsel. We adjourn these proceedings. Defence and Crown counsel, be good enough to come to our chambers immediately.'

Porter stood up again. 'I think you will find, my lord,' he said, 'that amongst your papers, perhaps in your offices, is the relevant affidavit I spoke of, carrying the official stamp of the Courts Office, clearly dated and timed yesterday morning.'

'All rise,' said the court clerk.

As the judges left the courtroom, reporters also began scampering out. Lena felt Hamilton's eyes burning into her back as she rose and walked out too, alongside Porter and Casey. Passing the public benches, she grabbed Sinéad's hand, pulling her along beside her. Sullivan had the wit to tag along. With reporters in their wake shouting questions, the five of them walked swiftly to the booked consulting room. As the door swung closed, Lena's impassive face melted.

'You did it,' she told Porter, hugging him.

'Elementary,' Porter replied. 'Although I suspect Simpson is about to give me a severe ticking off.'

'Will someone explain what the hell just happened?' asked an exasperated Sullivan.

'Lena has evidence that Sinéad's husband was murdered,' said Casey. 'It's early days yet – but that's how it looks.'

Lena turned to Sinéad.

'I couldn't tell you any earlier,' she said. 'That's why I was at Luke's house on Saturday. When things calm down a bit, I'll explain.'

The lawyers were all high on adrenaline, but Sinéad's eyes began to fill with tears and she pulled a tissue from her coat pocket. That silenced them for a few seconds before Casey turned to Lena.

'You'll have to talk to the press now if you want this on the lunchtime news. I'll see you all in half an hour at the café where we met this morning.'

Porter left for his dressing down with Simpson, closely followed by Casey to the Law Library, leaving Lena, Sinéad and Sullivan alone in the small consulting room.

'I'm still clueless,' said a puzzled Sullivan.

'Here, both of you, take a minute to read this,' Lena said.

Sullivan and Sinéad scanned the press release and diagrams, occasionally looking up at Lena, astounded.

'We have to go,' she said. 'If they ask you questions, just follow my lead.'

The three of them walked through the marble lobby and out into the plaza where the cameras were waiting. A few months earlier, Lena would have eaten her eyeballs rather than speak to the press, but she forced herself now to be calm and clear. After everything she had been through, she only had to hold her nerve a while longer. Clamping her jaw shut to stop it trembling, with one arm around Sinéad's shoulders and Sullivan by her side, she held out copies of the press release. Eager hands snatched them away. Lena took a deep breath and plunged into a short explanation, hooking her finger around the handle of her briefcase to demonstrate the impossibility of the police version of events.

'As solicitors for the Maguire family, we need to know who first concocted, and then hid, these untruths from the court, the public and the families. Only a judge-led, independent, public inquiry can do that.'

The reporters first focused on Sinéad.

'Mrs Maguire, what's your response to this morning's events?'

Sinéad had fought a lonely battle for years before Luke's release and this was the moment she had feared would never arrive.

'The police killed Danny in cold blood and were lying

from the start,' she said with steely conviction. 'What we heard in court today proves it.'

Lena looked across at Sullivan, her eyes appealing for him to join in.

'My name is Stephen Sullivan and I practise law in New York City,' he said boldly. 'I have been following this case on behalf of American Lawyers for Justice in Ireland and I'll be presenting a full report on today's events to the United States Congress. I can assure you, ladies and gentlemen, there will be consequences.'

As the impromptu press conference ended, Lena, Sinéad and Sullivan walked away. Across the road, Casey was waiting at a corner table in the coffee bar. Unbelievable, as it seemed to Lena, the entire drama had taken less than an hour from start to finish. Before long, Porter joined them.

'I got off lightly,' he said. 'Simpson has read Lena's affidavit and it's pretty clear cut. Not even Sir Basil could avoid the rather obvious conclusions.'

The lawyers began congratulating each other for their differing roles in the morning's business while Sinéad, her usually pale cheeks flushed, waited patiently for a gap in the conversation.

'Mr Porter, I've never met you before,' she said, 'but my family and the Reids are forever in your debt. Without you and Brendan and Lena, we would have known none of this.'

Her simple words silenced the jubilant lawyers. For them, the court drama had amounted to a tense professional challenge. For Sinéad, Lena thought, it must have been excruciatingly painful.

'You must be exhausted, Sinéad,' she said.

'I'm tired but very happy, Lena,' she replied. 'I've arranged for one of the twins to take me home but first I'm going to the graveyard in Lurgan to tell Danny about all this.'

As Sinéad left, the sense of anticlimax intensified as everyone's adrenaline levels began returning to normal and they realised it was time for each of them to go their separate ways. Lena was the first to break the awkward silence.

'So, what happens now?' she asked the other three. 'I'm presuming the police officer who killed Danny Maguire will be suspended, but what about all the others who perjured themselves?'

No one seemed to have answers.

'Lena thinks only a public inquiry can resolve this mess,' Casey said. 'She's absolutely right but I'm not holding my breath. Going on past form, they may enlist another police force to investigate, allegedly independently.'

'That would certainly be their way,' said Porter. 'While there's any kind of investigation, however weak, the government can play for time, claiming they "don't want to prejudice the outcome". Anyhow, Lena, sorry for the inconvenience but I need to get back to London.'

The small group split up outside the café. Sullivan for his hotel to get over jet lag, Casey for the Law Library and Lena for the airport with Porter.

'Are you prepared for the fall-out from all this?' he asked her on the way. 'I'm not the only one facing some fairly dire consequences.'

'If Gordon sacks me, Braithwaite will take me back in London.'

Porter decided to get to the point.

'Your relationship with Edward Gordon,' he said. 'Georgie has been filling me in. Wedding bells seem to have been on the cards.'

'I'm hoping he'll understand,' she said, 'but I have no idea what ludicrous story his father will give him.' At the airport, Porter promised to fill Georgie in and muttered a few kind words about 'how courageous' she was. Lena said nothing but wished she was going with him – back to sanity and London, but there was more work to be done here first – the fight was now on for a full, independent inquiry.

As she drove home, she lamented on how her life had changed since the trip to Donegal. She had been a little stressed but full of hope and plans for the future. Five days ago, all that had changed. Since Seapark, she had crashed from one crisis to the next, living on a diet of coffee, gin and adrenaline. The excitement and stress had kept her going. Now, all that energy draining from her body, she felt hollowed out, emptied, as if she had driven over the edge of a cliff into a bottomless chasm. The future was a blank. She pulled into a lay-by on the road to Ballynahinch, where no one could see her, slumped her head onto the steering wheel and sobbed. Gordon would be incandescent. She had effectively cut him out of decision-making, enlisted Porter's services without approval and ignored office rules on press coverage. A few months back, at a dinner in Gordon Hall, she recalled John Graham using a term she had not heard before – 'fellow traveller'. She had asked for an explanation. Around the table, there were nervous smiles before Hamilton had explained.

'A fellow traveller is an apologist for the Provisional IRA, Lena. Pestilence. Vermin,' he had said. 'Someone who moves amongst us but is not of us.'

Would the Gordons, all of them, decide she was now 'vermin' and 'a pestilence'? She rather feared they would. Pulling herself together, she arrived home in time for the early evening news and was sitting upright, gripping the kitchen table for the local 5 p.m. headlines. The story was second in the running order – just a straight news report. The BBC national six o'clock TV news barely mentioned it. Then the phone rang, and she had to endure fifteen minutes of her father fretting over William Gordon's feelings.

'What were you thinking of, going to that man Maguire's house?' he asked. 'He should have known better and forbidden you to come anywhere near him.'

When he passed the phone to her mother, Charlotte's main concern was that Lena had failed to brush her hair before the press conference. 'You looked like you'd been pulled through a hedge backwards,' she said. Lena found this strangely reassuring. Some things never changed.

Casey then rang with good news that the SDLP had tabled questions in the House of Commons but went on to be brutally honest about the likely outcome.

'They can demand a public inquiry all they like, but there's not a snowflake's hope in hell.'

'What about Dublin?' Lena asked. 'Danny Maguire carried an Irish passport. Can't they step in?'

'They'll fire off a stiff letter or two to the secretary of state and mention it at the next summit, but that will be the extent of it,' Casey said. 'My thinking is London will invite some poor sod from over the water to lead an investigation.

If he gets anywhere near the truth, they have an arsenal of ways to undermine him.'

The nine o'clock TV bulletin was an improvement. It ran clips of Sinéad and Sullivan and then a cautious analysis from a legal affairs correspondent concluding the Crown immunity issue had yet to run its course. Still no mention of any public inquiry. Later in the evening, her mood sinking, she tuned in to *Today in Parliament*.

At first, it seemed encouraging. Labour's shadow spokesman on Northern Ireland asked for a response 'to claims in a Belfast court today that members of the RUC Headquarters Mobile Support Unit were involved in ambushing and killing two unarmed members of the public'.

Tom Cadogan, the conservative secretary of state for Northern Ireland's reply was a classic non-answer: 'The honourable member is fully aware of the long-established convention that this house does not comment on legal actions before the courts.'

Lena's hopes were raised when Fearghal McNally, the SDLP MP for Newry/Armagh, announced his party would refuse to take part in political talks at Stormont unless the government agreed to a public inquiry – but they were dashed again when Cadogan wound up by saying, 'This government fully intends to comply with its international obligations on human rights.' This, Lena suspected, meant entirely the opposite. It seemed Casey and Porter were correct. She could feel the tectonic plates on which her life was built moving under her feet. Her very identity was being stolen. All the millions of moist-eyed Brits on successive Remembrance Sundays, how would they feel if they knew the country's political elite tolerated such epic law-breaking, up to and including murder?

Despairing, she crawled into bed and tried to sleep. In the morning, despair gave way to anger. There was nothing on the news to suggest the chief constable would suspend the police officers who had murdered Danny Maguire or those who had conspired to cover it up. It was as if nothing at all had happened. She drove into Belfast for lunch with Sullivan.

'I can't believe the secretary of state hasn't already announced a public inquiry,' she blurted out as soon as they were alone.

'Don't be so bloody naïve, Lena,' he said.

'I'm "naïve" to expect an inquiry?'

'Of course. They were bound to fight back. Anger is politically immature. I'm not surprised and neither should you be. We're not entirely helpless, though. We'll embarrass the shit out of them in the States. I'm flying home today to hit the phones and organise a speaking tour. Watch the Brits sweat once Uncle Sam gets involved. If they don't concede – which they won't – we'll set up our own independent tribunal of inquiry, over here in Ireland, maybe next spring.'

Lena tried to look interested. What could a US speaking tour possibly achieve? A community inquiry seemed just another futile response. Having seen Sullivan to the bus station, she decided on her own plan of action. No more prevarication. She would confront Gordon.

'You've really done it now,' Geraldine said as she arrived in High Street. 'Mr Gordon has left for Fermanagh and given me strict instruction not to give you any new cases and I've to open all your mail. What are you going to do?'

'I don't know yet but ask William to let me know when he'll be returning to Belfast so we can talk it over.'

She walked along the lough shore that evening where a summer storm was whipping up black waves. Even the geese were cowering behind rocks. For the first time since leaving London for New York she felt powerless, drifting, helpless.

10

With no other casework and a head buzzing with indecision, Lena decided a legal visit with Darren Barrett in Crumlin Road would at least be a temporary distraction. Gordon had not yet relieved her from working on his bail application.

'I'm getting dog's abuse in here,' he told her in the legal block. 'They're asking why I stick with "that Provo bitch" as my lawyer.'

Lena decided she had put up long enough with Barrett's foul mouth.

'I'm still working hard on getting you bail, Darren – no easy task as the courts will consider there's every likelihood of you both re-offending and absconding. The least you could do is show some respect.'

'Keep your hair on. I was only telling you what they're saying.'

'Very well, I'll be in touch when I have news.'

Barrett, she suspected, would certainly not be the only one who thought her a 'Provo bitch'. It was, at least, a change from 'Lena the Dreamer' but all the old insecurities that she thought were consigned to the past were beginning to raise their heads once again. As the days rolled past, she knew she was drifting aimlessly. Aside from Maguire, her continued employment in Belfast depended entirely on the unlikely event of Gordon changing his mind – and getting bail for The Shankill Stinger. Hoping for good counsel, she phoned Martin Porter.

'Sullivan's talking about some kind of speaking tour in the States,' she said. 'He's also proposing what he calls "an independent tribunal of inquiry" in the spring.'

'So I've heard,' Porter said. 'A tribunal of any kind, even unofficial, is at least an attempt to hold their feet to the fire.'

'But what can a "community inquiry" possibly achieve?'

'It keeps up the momentum. Our opponents only have four tactics: deceit, deny, delay and death. You have any better ideas?'

'I guess not. Do you know, the last time I felt this helpless was fully twenty years ago, stuck at school on my own for failing a Maths exam as everyone else trooped off to see *Doctor Zhivago*.'

'Yeah, Georgie told me about that. A little more consequential now, though.'

'Gordon is skulking down in Fermanagh after leaving instructions I'm not to get any new cases. I'm thinking of asking Braithwaite if I can return to London next month.'

'If there's a problem, let me know. Georgie and I will make sure they take you back. Don't dismiss Sullivan's plans, though. I might even get involved myself.'

Lena visited London the following week, where Braithwaite, to her relief, said she could return in October.

'Your old office has been reallocated,' he said, 'but I'm sure we'll find you another one.'

There were no plaudits, she noted, for her achievements in Belfast, although they had received copious press coverage. Braithwaite's resigned tone spoke volumes. She was a liability. That evening, when her father picked her up from Andover railway station, he also appeared to view her as an embarrassment.

'Well, this is a pickle. What does William have to say about it?'

He worries more about William's opinion than mine, she thought.

'I haven't heard from him. How's Mother?'

'She's as worried as I am. I wonder if you ever consider how your impetuous behaviour and rash decisions affect her?'

'Her worries are over then, I'm returning to Braithwaite's in October.'

'Finally, a sensible decision,' he said.

They were uneasily silent for the rest of the journey but the countryside, yellow waves of swollen wheat ripening in the fields, lifted her mood a little. At home, her mother began needling her.

'So, you're home to lick your wounds,' Charlotte began. 'People whisper and think we don't hear. They come to church just to stare at me, the mother of someone who's working for a grubby little Irish terrorist.'

'I've done nothing wrong, Mum. You could always stand up for me,' Lena replied. Charlotte just sniffed dismissively and returned to her magazine.

When she stopped for petrol at Matt's, even he seemed quieter than usual. 'I'm sure you have your reasons, Miss Dawson,' he said.

After lunch on Sunday, she went into the study to talk to her father.

'You say you found proof the police shot them in cold blood,' he said. 'They must have had a reason.'

'Can there be any legal reason for summary execution? Then lying about it? They were murdered, pure and simple.'

'If the boot had been on the other foot, they wouldn't have thought twice about murdering the police officers.'

'In that case,' she said, 'I would be happy to prosecute Danny Maguire.'

'There are always bad apples in any police force. It doesn't mean the whole barrel is rotten.'

'The "rotten apple" argument? You're better than that, Dad, surely. How can Jerusalem be built "in England's green and pleasant land" if state forces execute unarmed people with impunity?'

'I'm worried you're ruining your career and so is William.'

An arrow of white-hot anger ran through her. William Gordon had not responded to the message she had left with Geraldine, but he and her father had already been discussing her future.

'What's he got to say?'

'He thinks you're right to return to London. He only wants the best for you.'

Like hell, she thought. William wants me out of his office and a million miles away from his precious son.

Hoping for consolation, she walked over to St Michael's and sat on a bench in the graveyard but all it did was remind her of the evening she and Edward had listened to the bells ringing out across the fields. How happy she had been but that innocence was lost forever. She now carried a burden of knowledge that could never be lain down.

In the car returning to the airport, she decided it was time to confront her father about his role in Kenya.

'Throughout my childhood, I clearly remember you telling me you had spoken out intentionally because those four

Kenyans were murdered at Nakuru. Then it all changed and you said it was accidental.'

Her father sighed. 'I spoke out deliberately, Lena, but it changed my life and your mother's. I couldn't stay in the army afterwards. I was trying to prevent you making the same mistake.'

'But was it a mistake? You did the right thing.'

'The right thing for me, perhaps, but not for Charlotte. There's always a heavy price to pay for challenging authority.'

At Glenbarry, she found a message from Sinéad. Maguire had recovered sufficiently to be visited. At the Royal Victoria Hospital, they were shown into a side room – never a good sign. Five minutes later, the consultant arrived.

'There's still a bullet fragment near his spine. On balance, we think it's too risky to operate. We think he will walk again if he maintains an exercise regime. You only have thirty minutes. He's still weak.'

Two stony-faced police officers stood guard outside Maguire's room, the irony not lost on Lena or, very probably, on them. Maguire was clean-shaven and looked paler than ever. Sinéad slid an arm under his neck on the pillow and kissed his forehead. Lena held back, standing awkwardly at the end of the bed.

'I'm sorry you were hurt,' Maguire began. 'I knew I was in the firing line and should never have allowed you to visit.'

'You warned me and I ignored you. In any case, I was a complete coward,' she said, 'hiding in the bathroom.'

'You were far more important to me alive than dead.'

'You had no time to make that decision,' she said, 'not as the door was being smashed down.'

'You'd be surprised what I have time for,' Maguire replied. 'I've time to thank you, Casey and Porter for preventing the RUC destroying the evidence.'

'I'll pass that on when I speak to them,' she said.

Maguire then turned to Sinéad. 'I have to get out of here,' he said, 'it's too dangerous.'

'Don't worry,' Lena said. 'There are two RUC men on duty outside your door.'

Luke smiled, painfully. 'Oh Lena,' he said, 'you're still not thinking of them as the enemy.'

'But they're not. They're here to protect you. Surely you're safe in a hospital?'

'We killed two Brits at Musgrave Park Hospital not so long ago.'

'I can't believe there's no talk yet of a public inquiry.'

'Entirely predictable,' he replied, 'but we're not beat yet. Steve Sullivan sent a message in last week, proposing a community tribunal. I think we'll go with that. It'll keep the pressure on the RUC and the Northern Ireland Office.'

'Steve Sullivan's written to you?' Lena asked, hiding her surprise. How, she wondered, did Sullivan even know Maguire, other than listening to him at meetings in the US?

'We worked out a long time ago,' Maguire said, 'that the shortest distance between Belfast and London is through Washington. The Brits' Achilles' heel is their obsession with the "special relationship". Sullivan has been quietly using his influence for years.'

Something else she hadn't known, Lena thought. Unaware of her discomfort, Maguire turned to Sinéad. 'If you tell the doctors that you're a nurse, they might let me out early. Would you look after me for a while in Clonard?'

'Of course. We'll get a bed put in downstairs.'

As they began discussing ways of getting Luke out of the hospital, Lena slipped quietly away. They were all making plans and none of them involved her. She was returning to London before long. Feeling very small, she drove home, opened the cupboard in the spare room and buried her face in the blue silk lining of one of Edward's waistcoats. If she breathed in deeply, she caught the faintest, maddening smell of his aftershave. The next morning, she wrote to him.

'Dearest Edward, although I believe I acted both professionally and honourably, I know you disagree. I wish you understood but I realise that may not be possible. I am not hard to find if you want to talk it over, although I am planning to return to London in October. Whatever you decide, I will always value our time together as infinitely precious. I wish you nothing but the best, now and in the future. Lena.'

Before she could change her mind, she drove to the village and tapped the envelope into the post-box, listening as it hit the bottom. Two days later, when Sinéad rang saying Maguire was back in Kashmir Road and wanted to see her, she agreed, if only to tell him she was leaving. When she arrived, he was tucked into a hospital bed in the tiny living room that still bore the scars of the RUC forensic search, drill-holes in the walls and floorboards.

'Gordon has ordered I get no more work,' she said. 'I was in London last week. My job there is still open and I'll be returning in a couple of months.'

'There's no need for that, Lena. There are dozens of families here who could do with your help,' he said.

'I've split up with his son, the man I had been seeing before all this.'

'The UDR man? If you loved him, I'm sorry but did you really expect anything else? As I said in this very room just before the attack, you're going to have to change sides. I know you disagree and I respect that – but others won't. They'll decide for you. If he's broken with you because you did the right thing, I'm afraid that's your proof.'

Lena was in no mood for a fight. 'I'm no different now than I was, Luke. There's nothing for me here but bad memories.'

Sullivan, when she rang him, was also disappointed she was leaving Belfast.

'What about the tribunal?'

'What on earth will a half-assed inquiry held in some draughty community hall achieve?' she asked him. 'Other than giving London the satisfaction of ignoring it?'

'We've already enlisted UN support and got funding. Martin Porter has agreed to be a panellist, although it means missing out on some lucrative cases in London.'

Lena was taken aback.

'You know what the Buddha said?' Sullivan went on. 'There are two mistakes one can make on the road to truth; not going all the way, and not starting.'

'I'm a realist, Steve, not a Buddhist,' she replied.

When she rang Georgie Porter, even she seemed to think there was merit in the tribunal proposal.

'If you feel excluded, darling, maybe you should reconsider. Martin and Sullivan are all for it. At least show some interest.'

Lena's mood lifted a little when Geraldine rang to say the police and Public Prosecution Service had decided not to oppose her bail application for Darren Barrett. It was a small victory, she had nothing else on, so she arranged for a legal meeting at Crumlin Road. As Barrett sauntered into the visiting block, he looked fit and healthy. Jail, she thought, was the best thing that could happen to some people.

'I've good news for you, Darren,' she said. 'You're going to have to report to the police station at Tennent Street every day; give up your passport and accept a nine o'clock curfew – but they've agreed to bail.'

'Shit, that's heavy-duty,' he said.

'Your call, Darren. If a judge agrees, the police won't object. But, hey, you can always stay here.'

'Let me think about it.'

'Nonsense, Darren. You'll accept those conditions and be grateful.'

'I suppose so.'

'Good. That's settled then. I'll be off to arrange it.'

But Darren seemed reluctant to let her go.

'Your friend Maguire is lucky we didn't get him that night. Is he out of hospital yet?'

'He's a client, not a friend, Darren, and I can't divulge anything about him in exactly the same way my professional ethics bar me from telling him anything about you.'

'Wind your neck in. I was only asking.'

'Your UDA friends,' she said, 'could have killed me

along with Maguire that night and you'd have been short of a solicitor.'

'I'd have found another soon enough.'

Lena, annoyed that she had allowed him to provoke her, chose to let that one go and rose to leave. Their business was concluded and this was just irritating.

'Okay, Darren, that's your lot. I'll be writing shortly with a court date to fix bail.'

Barrett now had a knowing and rather repellent grin on his face.

'Sit down,' he said. 'I've a bit of news for you. One good turn deserves another.'

'Oh, yes?' she said, still standing.

'You'll never guess what I heard.'

He was playing with her like a cat with a wounded mouse.

'I haven't a clue, Darren,' she said, continuing to pack her briefcase.

Barrett seemed determined to extract maximum enjoyment from his moment. 'You're going to thank me for this.'

'I doubt anything overheard in Crumlin Road stands up to much scrutiny. Jail gossip is notoriously unreliable.'

'Well, this isn't unreliable. I got it straight from the horse's mouth.'

'Okay, let's have your precious bit of gossip. Better out than in, Darren.'

'It's about the attack on Maguire.'

'I think we know quite enough about that already.'

'It wasn't an attack on him, you know. You were the target. He was just a bonus.'

Glacial chills raced down Lena's spine but she somehow managed not to visibly react.

'The Branch thought you were a bloody nuisance and needed rid of,' he went on.

'Little old me, Darren? Surely not.'

'No, it was definitely you,' Barrett said. 'One of the lads in here has a brother who was on the squad. The Branch showed him a photograph. It was you all right, at a farmhouse with a brick chimney, somewhere in County Down. There was a red Mini in the driveway.'

Lena's alarm leapt to near panic, realising Barrett was speaking about Glenbarry. The police must have photographed her coming out of the cottage.

'The Peelers knew you were at Maguire's house that evening. They tipped off our people who came across the peaceline to the Falls in a stolen van.'

Lena struggled to remain composed.

'Well, Darren, if there was any supporting evidence,' she said, 'then I'd be worried. But as there's not, I shan't waste any time on it.'

'I'm only telling you as a favour,' finished Darren, crestfallen. He had expected his nugget of gossip to scare her half to death.

Determined not to give him that satisfaction, Lena rose and briskly shook his hand.

'Thanks, Darren, I'll file that away as one of the fairy tales of Ireland, shall I? I'll send your regards to Sharon.'

'Tell her to come and visit me, will you?'

'I'll ask her. See you soon and behave yourself.'

Outside she stumbled through the potholes in the prison car park which seemed to go on forever but, once inside her Mini reassured herself Darren's gossip was invented. The UDA had been after Maguire, everyone knew that. No harm, though, in talking it over with Casey. She hoped he wouldn't think she was over-reacting but she'd be passing his house on the way home anyway. Seeing her on his front doorstep, Casey's face fell.

'What's up?' he said. 'It's not like you to drop by unannounced.'

'Can we talk in the garden for a minute?' she asked. 'I've just come from a visit with Darren Barrett.'

'Into each life some rain must fall,' said Casey. 'What's that idiot said that has you worried?'

Sitting on a stone bench in Brendan's back garden, Lena ran through what Barrett had just told her.

'What do you think?' she asked. 'Prison gossip?'

'Who knew you were at Seapark that Friday afternoon?' Casey asked.

'No one except the policeman at the security hut who escorted me to the car.'

'And after you left? Who exactly did you tell about the door handle?'

'I drove to Fermanagh and told William Gordon. But he didn't want me killed. I'm pretty sure that, at the time, I was his son's intended.'

'Agreed. Not even I think he would have tried to engineer your murder – not at that stage anyhow. You then went to meet Maguire. How was that arranged?'

'I used a public phone in a roadhouse outside Dungannon – but I said nothing about Seapark, just a cock-and-bull story that I had some Elgar recording Maguire wanted.'

Casey paused, the cogs and wheels rotating inside his head.

'In the Law Library,' he eventually concluded, 'we have a pretty reliable saying: *Cui bono*? Who stood to gain from your elimination?'

'Well, obviously RUC Special Branch,' Lena said, 'but how would they have known – either about the car or my visit to Maguire?'

She began to breathe more easily as Casey reassured her.

'Listen Lena, it's just UDA jail talk. They're probably using Barrett to put the fear of God into you. Go home, watch some TV, eat and get some sleep.'

Back in the cottage, Lena followed Casey's advice, poured a glass of wine and retreated to the sofa with Peanut, reminding herself of the Sherlock Holmes dictum that, once you have eliminated the impossible, whatever remains, however improbable, is the truth. Casey's deduction was the only rational explanation – the UDA was boasting, trying to scare her. Considering what else it was involved in, that was small beer.

When Geraldine phoned the next day with an invitation to speak to William Gordon, it was a relief. At least it would clear the air. He was frowning behind his desk as she walked into his office.

'Well, Lena, I was talking to Heather Collins last week. Her maternity leave is nearly over. She'll be returning to work soon.'

Lena decided to put him out of his misery.

'Relax, William. After all that's happened, I hardly expect to stay. I've already arranged to return home in

October. I'll clear my desk today and wind down any remaining casework from home so you and Edward can avoid bumping into me.'

William was too embarrassed to answer. He looked out of the window, adopting a glassy stare, waiting for her to leave the room. What a miserable little coward, she thought.

For the rest of the day, she boxed up her notes on the Maguire case for the tribunal and asked Geraldine to courier them back to Glenbarry. Then she drove home and began planning her exit. There was nothing to keep her in Belfast. If the US speaking tour materialised, she could fly from London. The tribunal would take months of preparatory work but, as a key witness, she was barred from professional involvement.

On the bright side, she had always assumed that, someday, there would be a wedding in Little Woldham, children, a home in the country. All that was back on her agenda now – not shoot-to-kill, police lies and loyalist murderers. As if to validate her decision, news began filtering in during the afternoon of an IRA bombing in Coleraine. Pictures of paramedics stretchering injured civilians through smoke and rubble made her even more determined to get away. But there was one person she had yet to tell. Sinéad, back home in Tyrone from nursing Maguire, was at least due an explanation.

There was no answer at the white bungalow's front door, so she walked round the back and found Sinéad fighting a gale, retrieving sheets from a washing line. They got the flapping laundry into a basket and walked inside where Sinéad put on the kettle.

Sitting at the same fireside where she had first begun to understand the Maguires, Lena said she would be leaving shortly.

'Luke wants me to stay on to help with other cases,' she said, 'but I'm going home. I'm sorry to disappoint you.'

'At least you have a choice.'

'And you, Sinéad? You're only in your forties, still a young woman. Surely, you're not going to spend the rest of your life fighting the system as well as recovering from heart failure.'

'The heart thing doesn't really scare me, to be honest Lena. Nothing will ever be as bad as watching Danny die.'

Lena would once have hurriedly changed the subject. Now she listened respectfully as Sinéad reminisced.

'I held his hand, stroked his forehead, leaned over and whispered that I would love him forever,' she said. 'Then a few words I remembered from school came into my head: "Goodnight, sweet prince, and flights of angels sing thee to thy rest". It's from *Hamlet*.'

Lena had the wit to remain silent.

'I know people will say he was just a wee Fenian from the wrong side of the tracks. But he was my sweet prince. People tell me grief is a burden and it will gradually lift but it still feels like a monster on my back, hunched over my shoulders, its arms around my neck, its nails digging deep between my ribs, clawing at my heart.'

Lena could think of no appropriate response. Gripping the steering wheel hard on the road back to Glenbarry, she cursed the politicians who had failed to resolve Northern Ireland's conflict and had instead created conditions where decent people engaged in violence. And what contribution had she made towards ending it? Nothing at all. Luke Maguire would spend the rest of his life thinking of her as cowardly, selfish and disappointing. Edward was clearly glad to see the back of her. Gordon could not even look her in the eye. She should be ashamed of herself. And she was.

Back in the cottage, she poured a glass of wine and turned on the radio. Bonnie Tyler was belting out 'Total Eclipse of the Heart' – a self-pitying dirge Lena had always cordially disliked. As she reached to turn the radio off, however, she realised the words echoed her own thoughts.

'Once upon a time I was falling in love. But now I'm only falling apart. There's nothing I can do. A total eclipse of the heart.'

Oh God, she thought, now I've really reached rock bottom. Slumping into the nearest chair, she lay her forehead on crossed arms at the kitchen table and sobbed. She had come to Belfast to exploit its tragedy as a career stepping stone. Instead, it had chewed her up and spat her out. As she deserved. When a loud knock came from the front door, she ignored it but it persisted. She wiped her eyes and, exasperated, got up to see who was disturbing her so late.

As she pulled the door open, she was pushed backwards. A tall male figure slammed her against a wall, his hand over her mouth, kicking the door shut behind him. Her eyes widened seeing a revolver held low in his right hand. He reeked of stale tobacco.

'Not so much as a fucking squeak or I'll shoot. Understand?'

The voice was English, London. She nodded.

He lifted his hand from her face and poked the gun at the coats hanging in the hall.

'Put one of those on.'

She pulled a coat on. He jabbed the gun into the small of her back.

'Go into the garden. Through the back door. I'm right behind you.'

Outside on the paving, he took the gun from her back and told her to turn around. She obeyed, clamping her lips tight to stop them shaking. The moon was behind him so his face remained in shadow, a scarf wrapped around his mouth and nose, leaving just his eyes visible.

'Who the hell are you?' she asked.

'I work for the government you hate so much,' he said.

'How do I know who you are?'

'You can call me Ronnie. Let's just say I serve Her Majesty.'

'Anyone could say that.'

He sighed. 'Don't waste time. Your family lives in Hampshire. You have a friend called Olivia who you meet in Salisbury and until recently you had a boyfriend, Edward Gordon.'

'So you're some kind of spook – MI5 or whatever you call yourselves.'

'Now you listen. Special Branch has been keeping tabs on you for a while, snooping around the Danny Maguire case. Any fall-out from that godawful debacle was their problem not ours but one of them, we'll call him Norman, is making trouble for everyone.'

He was talking too fast. She could hardly keep up.

'Your visit to Seapark got Norman all het up. One of

the oiks there phoned RUC HQ to say you were making drawings. Norman decided to find out why but you were AWOL that Friday. They checked the ferries and airports. No Eleanor Dawson visiting London. The only place you could be was Gordon's place in Fermanagh. Norman has a pal working down there, Paul something-or-other, who knows the family, so he was told to drop by that Friday night to scout around.'

'Are you talking about Paul Donaldson?'

'Possibly. He did what he was told and reported back that you'd just left having dropped news that had rattled Gordon senior about evidence of some kind. Nothing was easier than tailing you to your office the next day and then to Maguire's place. From the Branch's standpoint, it was perfect. If you and Maguire were dispatched together, all the loose ends would be nicely tidied up. Maguire being suspect number one for the Armagh bombing, no one would ever think you were the target.'

'Surely it wasn't police officers who attacked Maguire's house?'

'Are you mad? That's not how it works. Norman, or one of the other Branch boneheads, took a run up the Shankill and told the lads that the roads around Clonard would be unusually quiet that Saturday evening, particularly around Maguire's house in Kashmir. They didn't need much encouragement. I heard they were queuing up for the job.'

Lena was struggling to keep up.

'My father's a veteran, he would have been screaming from the rooftops if I'd been killed.'

'You're dead in the home of a notorious terrorist that

you're probably screwing. Just the ravings of a grief-stricken old man.'

'I have an influential lawyer friend in New York. He would also have kicked up a stink.'

'Steve Sullivan? Just another IRA patsy,' he spat the words out.

'So, I was the target?'

'Two birds with one stone. That was what the Branch intended. Bloody UDA. Bunch of useless twats.'

'Edward, Gordon's son, does he have a role in this?'

'Don't ask me.'

'And Paul Donaldson? Did he know what was being planned?'

'He must have had a fair idea.'

'But the plan failed. I'm still here, alive and kicking.'

'For the time being.'

'What does that mean?'

'We know all about Sullivan's plans to parade you around the States – and that he's raising funds for some kind of circus over here. We'll take the hit – we have friends in DC. But Norman and the other morons in Special Branch don't like the idea of you telling stories in public. As far as they're concerned, you're unfinished business. They won't screw up a second time. If I were you – and thank God I am not – I would make myself scarce around here for the foreseeable.'

Lena was thinking as fast as she could but Ronnie was looking around the garden, about to leave.

'Why are you telling me all this? Why not just go ahead?'

'You've got it all wrong, dearie.' He spoke as if she were

a child. '*We're* not responsible for this cock-up. It wasn't *us* who shot Danny Maguire while he was unarmed and it wasn't *us* who tried to kill you. If it had been, you would be tucked neatly under a gravestone in Hampshire by now. Blame those numbskulls in Special Branch with their heads up their arses. We don't care whether you live or die but certain parties in London could do without a murdered solicitor right now, risking the back-channel and giving grandstanders like Fearghal McNally an excuse to pull out of talks.'

'What "back-channel"?' Lena asked but his eyes were sliding over her shoulder and around the garden. He was planning his exit.

'I'm leaving now. Stay exactly where you are until you hear my bike slowing down at the junction on the Killyleagh Road,' he said. 'There are plenty of flights out of Aldergrove. I suggest you get on one sharpish, unless you want to become a footnote in the history of this godforsaken dump. Take care now.'

Turning, he crossed the lawn and disappeared into the dark. Lena heard the roar of his motorbike accelerating and walked back into the cottage, going yet again through the routine of locking all the doors and windows and pulling all the curtains. Her hands were freezing, her body stiff and aching. She ditched her wine into the sink and poured a large brandy in its place before sitting at the kitchen table and thinking, very hard.

She remembered with a jolt seeing Paul Donaldson's blue BMW turning into the gateway as she was leaving on the night she had visited the Hall after Seapark. At the time she had presumed for one of his late-night powwows with Edward – but he could have been snooping. After their row, Edward would have been miserable and would have welcomed Paul's arrival, drawing him into the library. The two of them would have sat with their whiskeys, as usual, at the fireside. What had then passed between them? How would she ever know? The outcome was the same. The irony was that she had already decided to leave; Ronnie's visit just meant sooner. She listened to the midnight news, searched out Casey's final sleeping tablet, gulped it down with a brandy to make sure it worked and got into bed. Too frightened and exhausted to cry, she lay rigid and trembling on her back and prayed more intensely than she had for years. 'Please God, dear God, get me out of here, just let me go home.' Peanut jumped onto the bed and curled up beside her. She could kid herself she was not alone. Finally, the tablet and the brandy did the trick.

She woke reasonably clear-headed and began to think about packing but returned repeatedly to what Ronnie had claimed. What if he was just another liar? If what he said was true, then Darren Barrett was right for once in his miserable life. Was that likely? Only Paul, William and Edward knew for sure what was said that night in Fermanagh. If she wanted the truth, she would have to confront them. The thought of not knowing for the rest of her life was intolerable. She showered, put on make-up, stared at her white but resolute face in the mirror and forced down a slice of toast in the kitchen.

First, she phoned Edward's office at the Gordon Hotel headquarters in Belfast. His PA said he was in meetings all day at Ballycastle, way up north in County Antrim, so she drove from Belfast along the twisting road that hugged the coastline. Even this stressed, she managed to take pleasure in driving past the sprinkling of old-fashioned seaside towns, ice-cream parlours and shopfronts bedecked with brightly coloured buckets and spades. Approaching Ballycastle, she began to map out how she should approach the encounter when a solution occurred. She would treat it as any detective would. She had sat in on a thousand police interviews, listening as interrogating officers claimed to know more than they did while watching for small discrepancies, contradictions and reactions across the interviewing table. She'd catch him that way.

Arriving at the hotel just after eleven, she asked the receptionist to tell Mr Gordon that Lena Dawson had arrived to see him. After a tense fifteen minutes' wait, a bellboy escorted her up in the lift, leaving her in an over-decorated anteroom. When Edward appeared at his office door, he silently held it open. She walked past him and sat in a chair, facing his desk and the window behind. He gave her a wide berth as he walked around the desk and sat down facing her. How was it possible, she thought, that she had once been in a warm bed with this rock, this monolith? As he sat down, she looked over his shoulder to the Mull of Kintyre on the Scottish coast in the distance.

'To what do I owe this very unwelcome visit?' he began.

'I've come to say I'm sorry,' she said.

'Not nearly as sorry as I am,' he said.

'You misunderstand me, Edward. I'm sorry for what *you* have done.'

First round to me, she thought, seeing his surprise.

'Me?' Edward said. 'You've some nerve. You broke your

word and gave confidential legal information to a terrorist. My only error was ever trusting you.'

'Let's talk about trust then, Edward,' Lena said, 'trust between solicitor and client. You're right, I did give Luke Maguire news of important new evidence. He certainly had as much, if not more right to it than your father.'

'So your loyalty to a terrorist took priority over your promise to my father. I actually defended you that night at the Hall. I told Dad you had a "reliable moral compass". But your decision to bypass him, to go behind his back – that I could never defend. You allowed the situation to spiral out of control.'

'Out of control? Do you mean that if I had delayed taking action, your father and his police cronies could have controlled events more to their liking?'

'Of course not. You had given your word to consult my father first, so he could deal with the situation professionally.'

'Professionally? Is that what he's told you? That I acted "unprofessionally" in giving our clients – to whom we owe our primary allegiance – information that the RUC had illegally hidden from them?'

'You went behind his back and took unilateral action with that reckless fool Casey.'

'Brendan Casey knows more about the law than you and your father will ever comprehend.'

'Geoff Hamilton would say different.'

'I bet he would. Tell me, after I left Gordon Hall that Friday night, did Paul Donaldson drop by?'

'He's welcome any time. So what?'

'I imagine you two had one of your cosy fireside chats.'

'I'm entitled to talk to anyone I want to.'

She could so easily imagine how it had gone – Paul faking concern about her driving home so late, Edward explaining she had turned up out of the blue for a late-night meeting on the Maguire case.

'I'll tell you, Edward, what I really think,' Lena said. 'I think your father told you that night at the Hall that I had driven down to see him because I had come across something important.'

'He said there was trouble over the Maguire case and you'd be meeting Geoff Hamilton on Monday to discuss a significant development but that was all.'

'And of course, when Paul asked why I had left so late at night, you gave him the same explanation?'

'My private conversations with friends are none of your business.'

'I've no complaint if you'd told him that we'd argued. Paul is your closest friend. What you're not entitled to do is tell a serving police officer that I had driven 160 miles late at night for an unscheduled meeting with your father because of a significant development in the Maguire case.'

She waited for his reaction. Edward seemed to be struggling. He stretched an arm behind his neck as if to support his head and looked up at the ceiling. His expression turned from anger to consternation. It was enough. She had him.

'I think that is exactly what happened,' she said, pressing home her advantage. 'What you don't know is that your great friend Paul was snooping on behalf of police headquarters in Belfast and reporting back to them on my meeting with your father – whereupon they followed me to Maguire's house and set the UDA on us, intending to kill us both. And if they had succeeded, you would have been partly responsible.'

The concerned look on Edward's face changed back to rage, his hands gripping the arms of his chair. He first leaned forward, staring at her, and then slammed back into his chair.

'You're talking complete and utter nonsense.'

'Are you denying you told Paul I was at the Hall to see your father over the Maguire case?'

Her voice accusing him was calm but intense. Her eyes were fixed on him, unblinking.

'So what if I did mention it?'

'Did it not occur to you that Paul might just possibly tell the people he works with?'

She was implacable, relentless.

'Paul's friends in Belfast tried to murder me, Edward. They very nearly succeeded. They put Luke Maguire in a wheelchair.'

'Get out of here,' he said. 'I never want to see your scheming face again.'

'I think I'm entitled to the truth, Edward, about why I was nearly killed.'

'How dare you accuse Paul? Get out.'

'Don't worry. I'll be leaving this revolting place before they try to kill me again and wound another innocent victim.'

'Luke Maguire, innocent victim? Don't make me laugh.'

'No one's laughing, Edward.'

Anger then got the better of her. This was her only chance to hurt him.

'I wonder what made you decide I was the right girl for you?' she said. 'Did you want a perfect, pink English rose? You didn't want a woman, Edward. You wanted a red, white and blue tribal trophy to dangle on your arm. You're pathetic.'

With that, she stood up and left. Edward's face had told her everything she needed to know.

On the ninety-minute drive back to Belfast, she had time to bitterly conclude that, when the chips were down, Edward was his father's son, not the talented, perceptive man with whom she had fallen in love.

At Gordon's office in High Street, she marched past a wide-eyed Geraldine, straight in to see William. He was red-faced, flustered, putting on his coat to scurry home. Clearly, Edward had phoned ahead. She shut the door firmly to stop him.

'Don't you start on me,' he said. 'All I did was give my son the smallest of details. I never even saw Donaldson that night.'

How repellent he was, trying to blame his own son.

'So, Edward phoned you. How much did he say?'

'He told me you're making some wild claim that we were to blame for the UDA attack at Maguire's place.'

'Blame is probably the wrong word, but yes, you were wrong to say anything to Edward, and he was wrong to tell Paul Donaldson. Your professional duty was to our client. You're lucky you don't have the deaths of two people on your conscience.'

'What are you going to do?' he spluttered.

'Nothing – for now. I'm getting out of Belfast tomorrow and I won't be back. But I'll be telling my father about this so it's probably best if you don't ring him. Of course, you may be called as a witness if anyone is ever arrested for the attack in Kashmir Road. You'll have a chance then to tell the truth – if you choose to.'

William's face fell. He had not thought of that. For the second time in a day, Lena had skewered a Gordon. It might be a Pyrrhic victory, but she had, at least, done that. Bidding goodbye to a speechless Geraldine, she walked down the stairs.

Now, there was just one more person to tell. She drove up the Falls Road, parked outside the Sinn Féin office and handed over a written message inside a sealed envelope with 'CONFIDENTIAL' writ large on the outside. She had no intention of using the phone again until she had left Northern Ireland. The note asked Maguire to meet her at three o'clock in the car park at Divis Mountain, high above West Belfast.

Maguire arrived, struggling on his crutches, and they walked to a picnic table where they could talk privately, surrounded only by bog cotton and heather. It was an open secret that the army had listening equipment on the mountain, but it was trained down into West Belfast, not at a picnic table in the wilderness.

'The bad news,' Lena said, 'is that I'm leaving for London in the next twenty-four hours instead of October. I've made my mind up, so spare yourself trying to persuade me otherwise. I'll go through with the US tour and I'll give evidence at the tribunal. But that's all.'

'Is there any good news?'

'Yes. It seems the UDA were not trying to kill you. They were trying to kill me.'

'And the source for that fascinating information?'

'I had a visitor yesterday at Glenbarry. A Londoner, judging by his accent, who says he works for British intelligence, if that's not a paradox. He told me what went on behind the scenes the night before the shooting. He calls himself Ronnie.'

'They always call themselves Ronnie. And you know he works for military intelligence how?'

'He knew all about my parents, my friends in England, the place where I live in County Down. He despises Special Branch, by the way, calls them "numbskulls".'

'He's not alone in that. So tell me what had "gone on behind the scenes", as you put it.'

'You already know that, having left Seapark, I drove to Fermanagh almost immediately and told William Gordon about the door handle. He promised to say nothing until we met at the office on Monday. What I didn't know, until yesterday, is that one of his son's friends, an RUC man called Paul Donaldson, was sent by his headquarters to snoop around Gordon Hall later that night. You saw Paul once – he was the guy at the airport who spotted you when we landed after Strasbourg.'

'Shit, Lena. You didn't tell me before that the RUC were there.'

'I thought he had arrived for an innocent chat with Edward Gordon but it seems Special Branch knew I'd made sketches at Seapark and sent Donaldson to the Hall to find out what he could. Edward made some reference to it, innocently enough – he didn't know that Donaldson was spying. In any case, RUC headquarters knew something was up and let loose the dogs of war.'

From a sceptical start, Maguire was now listening very closely. 'So, that Saturday, the Branch followed you to Kashmir Road, tipped off the UDA and they came looking for you – or more accurately both of us.'

'That's about the height of it, Luke. You told me not to come to your door and I should have listened.'

'The UDA must have been delighted.'

'They've tried to kill me once, and they'll try again. That was the point of Ronnie's visit. I have to get out.'

'Must I remind you, Lena, they are plotting and planning to kill me every day of the week? Do you see me running away?'

'This is your battle, Luke, not mine.'

'It's your government telling the world they uphold the rule of law.'

'What can I do about that?'

'You've already done plenty. They wouldn't be trying to kill you otherwise. Regard it as a back-handed compliment.'

'Well, hooray for that. I now believe the RUC and MI5, or whoever Ronnie works for, are capable of anything, anything at all – and no one would ever know.'

'Ronnie was sent to persuade you to leave and he seems to have succeeded.'

'He told me something he called "the back-channel" would be at risk if I was killed.'

Maguire didn't sound surprised at the mention of a 'back-channel'.

'Don't flatter yourself. If the Coleraine bomb didn't kill off the back-channel, I hardly think your demise would make any difference. No, they want rid of any lawyer with the brains and courage to fight them.'

A cold wind whistled through the wire fencing around them. It was starting to get dark. Lena was emotionally exhausted. Maguire was irritated and angry.

'Okay,' he said. '*Sin é*. We'll leave it for the time being. I'm tired out.'

As they walked slowly back to the car park, Maguire lifted a crutch and pointed south.

'From up here,' he said, 'you can see the Cooley Mountains across the border. Lough Neagh's over there. On a clear day, you can see Scotland and the Sugarloaf mountain in County Wicklow. These islands will be at peace someday. But one thing I know for certain, the kind of crap we're dealing with now has to end – the RUC and UDR are going to have to go.'

'And the IRA? They'll have to go, too.'

He did not dissent.

They shook hands awkwardly at the car park, his minder drove him away and, after a short wait, Lena drove down herself, bypassing the city into County Down. Edward and William, Maguire and Barrett, Donaldson and Ronnie all have their battles, she thought. I'm out of it. From the cottage in Glenbarry, she rang her landlord in Canada to give notice and then her flat-sitter in London who agreed to move out after Christmas. It all felt very final. After a few hours of packing, the cottage looked bare. Soon she would be queuing for the ferry at Belfast docks. The nightmare would be over.

In the morning, she went for a last walk along Strangford Lough to say goodbye to the geese who had returned from Canada to overwinter along the shore as they had done for centuries, their lonely honking muffled by the fog. She would be in London while they rested up and ate eelgrass all winter. Passing a hawthorn bush, its tortured branches bent nearly double by the prevailing wind, she remembered the day she had pointed it out to Edward. 'That's my favourite tree. No matter what the weather throws at it, it survives. I wish I had half its endurance,' she had said.

Edward had pulled her towards him, telling her she was the most resilient person he had ever met, framing her face with his hands and kissing her long and deeply. In that moment, she had felt entirely content.

Parking back at the cottage, her daydreaming was shattered. A Range Rover was already sitting in the driveway but she decided gunmen were unlikely to turn up in broad daylight. Walking around to the back of the cottage to try and see who was inside, she heard the piano – the first notes of 'Singing Bird', one of Edward's favourites. He must have assumed, she thought, that she had already left and come to pick up his blasted clothes. Damn. She was going to have to confront him again. Leaning against an outside wall, she listened to the music for a few moments, reluctant to interrupt. A wave of misery swept over her but she wiped her eyes, steadied herself, walked to the front door and let herself in. Through the open living room door, she saw Edward lifting his head. The best form of defence was attack, she told herself, opening hostilities.

'What on earth are you doing here?'

Edward stood up and began speaking, as if reading from a script.

'I've come to apologise for some of what I said in Ballycastle.'

Lena could not believe what she was hearing.

'Some of it?' she said. 'It was all disgraceful. What was it you called me? A "schemer"?'

'At the time, I thought you were. Are you really leaving?'

'I'm about to drive to the Liverpool ferry.'

She allowed the silence to hang.

'There are things I need to say before you go,' he said, his voice lowering a decibel.

'I think you've already said quite enough. You and your father both. I really don't have the time for any more of your crap.'

'For once in your life, Lena, shut up and listen. This is hard enough for me as it is,' he said, clearing his throat. 'I don't know how to start except by saying I believe you were right about Paul.'

Lena was silenced.

'After you left Ballycastle, I met him for a drink and told him what you'd said. I called it nonsense, ridiculous. He agreed with me, of course, but something wasn't quite right. I've known Paul for years. We've soldiered together, got drunk together. We're brothers-in-arms. But he could not look me in the eye. He's a bad liar, I'll give him that. But he was lying. I'm sure of it.'

'Lying is the least of his sins,' she said. 'Does Paul know about this Damascene conversion?'

'I doubt it, but he'll soon guess when I don't return his calls. What's frustrating is there's nothing I can do about it. No one is going to arrest Paul for merely looking guilty. I'm sorry beyond words, Lena.' He sank onto the sofa. 'You could have been killed.'

Lena sat beside him and repeated that she had to leave to catch the ferry.

'You can't leave now,' he said. 'You can't imagine how bloody awful I feel. We'll work something out.'

'Edward, I have no choice. A man came here two days ago, warning me. When I saw your car outside, I thought it might be him, or his friends, coming back.'

'What are you talking about?'

'When I travelled up to see you in Ballycastle, I didn't do so on a whim. A man, saying he was with the security services, MI5 or whatever, was here telling me about Paul snooping at the Hall. He also said the Branch will try again. I've already stayed too long.'

'But the evidence you discovered is all over the papers. Why would they want to kill you now?'

'It's Special Branch that want me dead not MI5. They are more concerned about safeguarding what they call "back-channel" talks with Sinn Féin. They seem to be falling out amongst themselves.'

'Jesus Christ. What a mess. I'll drive to Belfast with you. I have my personal protection weapon in the car in case they try between now and the ferry.'

Lena refused his offer. 'The Branch don't yet know I've been alerted. I'll be out of Northern Ireland before they find out. We could still drive to Belfast together, though, after I've finished packing.'

She stood to go upstairs and sensed him also standing, just behind her, then felt his hand on her right shoulder, gently holding her back. For a second, she leaned back against him, her back against his chest, his breath warm on her hair. The temptation to turn around was almost irresistible but she stepped forward and his hand fell. From upstairs, she heard him playing Chopin, telling herself that, at this crisis in his life, his true nature was reasserting itself. She rinsed their coffee cups, locked the patio doors and they made their way together through the front door to the driveway, staring back at the cottage in the late afternoon sun.

'Could you look after Peanut in Fermanagh?' she asked, breaking the silence. 'I was going to leave him with Mother in Little Woldham but I'd rather he stayed here. He's a lovely wee thing.'

'Sure, leave your cat with me. I think I can just about be trusted with that.'

They switched the cat carrier from her Mini to his Range Rover and took one final look at the cottage.

'I'm an entirely different person from the girl you brought here in April,' she said.

'We've both changed,' he replied.

Lena walked to the Mini, lowering herself into the driver's seat. It was impossible to believe she was leaving him behind.

'I'll stop when I reach the docks,' she told him through the open window. 'We can say our goodbyes there.'

He nodded and, as so often before, their two cars drove in convoy slowly down the drive and turned right for Belfast. On the half-hour journey, Lena realised her days of searching for 'Mr Darcy' were over. She no longer needed Edward to validate or protect her. She could do that for herself. He had revealed his true self in his heartfelt apology. At the quayside, their planned farewell never materialised – the dockhands waved her straight onto the ship. She could only quickly glance over at his car as she drove up the ramp. Later, staring out over the black water at the fading lights of Belfast and Carrickfergus, she allowed herself a rueful smile. In spite of everything, Edward had wanted her to stay.

Eight months later, back in London, Lena finally accepted she was in the doldrums with little hope of a favourable wind. No closer to a partnership at Braithwaite's, she was keeping an ear open for vacancies in one of the big London-based human rights firms where her notoriety might be an advantage instead of a liability. She suspected her colleagues still called her 'Lena the Dreamer' behind her back, but now, instead of cringing, she reminded herself what she had achieved and tried to dismiss it.

The remarkable lack of interest any of them expressed about her time in Belfast, she decided, with Georgie's honourable exception, sprang from a mixture of ignorance and embarrassment. How would anyone living in Watford or Woking even begin a conversation about UDA gunmen or MI5 enforcers? The US speaking tour over St Patrick's Day in March had made her feel an imposter, as she had predicted, but it had at least given her time with Sullivan to talk over Ronnie's claims.

'It dovetails with what we reckon is happening backstage,' he said. 'There's a push to use the back-channel between Whitehall and the republican leadership. You may think Luke Maguire charmless but he would certainly have treated your unfortunate demise as an act of extremely bad faith.'

'But, if killing me would have caused political problems, why were Special Branch so set on it?' she asked.

'Well, firstly your evidence to the tribunal, of collusion between the Branch and the UDA, would have been embarrassing and might even led to heads rolling,' he said. 'Secondly, people often wrongly assume a consistency between state agencies. The government may want peace but there are plenty in the upper echelons of the RUC who fear a "sell-out" – some sort of deal with the IRA. For them, peace would be hugely destabilising. First item on Sinn Féin's agenda would be police reform, changing the name of the RUC and God knows what else.'

'So much for upholding the rule of law.'

'As far as the RUC and London goes, you and I, the Maguire and Reid families – all of us,' Sullivan said, 'are just straws in the winds of state. Wasn't it Lord Palmerston who said, "London has no friends and no enemies – just interests"? Your death would have complicated the government's plans, so they decided to let you live.'

Lena's shattered innocence allowed her to concede that Sullivan's premise, one she would once have dismissed as a crazy conspiracy theory, had the ring of authenticity. After the US tour, she had returned to London, viewing the upcoming tribunal with piqued curiosity, to the extent of taking annual leave in June to attend its opening day at Derry's Guildhall. It was rather grandiosely titled: 'An Independent Inquiry into the 1984 Shooting of Daniel Maguire and Seán Reid and Related Incidents'. When it was first announced, she had run into Georgie Porter's office.

'It seems I'm a "related incident",' she said. 'That's shorthand for bloody RUC Special Branch doing their best to get me and Luke Maguire shot dead.'

She had to admit that, even before it began its hearings, the tribunal had begun to prove its worth. Who would otherwise be demanding answers on the shooting at Drumfad? When news broke that Trevor Gibson was retiring early as assistant chief constable 'on health grounds', she was unsurprised. Questions about his possible involvement in the attack on Kashmir Road would inevitably have arisen from her testimony. Retirement meant he could legally refuse to give evidence. In mid-June, before the tribunal's opening session, Lena phoned Sinéad to say she'd be flying over. Sinéad's latest echocardiogram was encouraging and she was also going to attend.

'Luke's decided to come in a wheelchair rather than crutches because he doesn't want to fall over in front of the press. We have a new solicitor, Ciaran Summers. He's great, but he's not you, Lena.'

Twenty camera crews had gathered as Lena arrived at Guildhall Square. They were filming a dark-haired man in a wheelchair who spoke without notes, his voice carrying on the wind across the plaza. Lena stood listening, wearing the same black suit she had bought on the day of the city centre bombing. Casey, in his barrister's wig, stood twitchy beside her, anticipating the moment he would begin his opening address for the Maguires. Lena continued watching as Sinéad pushed her brother-in-law up the ramp and into the Guildhall before she and Casey followed them inside.

'What does it feel like, Lena?' Casey whispered, once they were through security. 'Seeing your work come to fruition?'

'It feels peculiar to be just an onlooker,' she replied, 'and this is most definitely not the official public inquiry we deserved.'

'Well, it's a damn sight better than nothing,' said Casey.

What Lena really felt was overwhelming pity for Luke in his wheelchair and sympathy for Sinéad and the Maguire and Reid families, for whom this was just one step in a long battle that was surely destined to last for decades. She took a seat in the third row of the packed public gallery, no longer with any legal status – just an ordinary member of the public, barred from professional involvement in order to be able to give evidence herself when the tribunal began daily sittings in the autumn.

Maguire was in a spot reserved for wheelchair users at front of the room, close to the witness box and the lawyers. Martin Porter, lending a little glamour to proceedings, sat on a dais beside the other two panellists, an academic from Colombia and a Norwegian UN human rights official. Lena was already guessing how it would end. Best case, two dozen files on the DPP's desk citing murder and conspiracy to pervert the course of justice – but she was closely managing her expectations. The inquiry, being unofficial, could not compel witnesses to give evidence. The lawyers would have to be careful about defamation and contempt of court, although they would sail as close to the wind as they could.

The tension Lena always enjoyed began to build as the protagonists took their seats – sadly though with the absence of defendants. Still, she told herself, the guilty parties would be sweating as they watched the TV and newspaper reports, fearing that, sooner or later, their collars would be felt. When Casey began speaking, he used all the right touchstone words: 'conspiracy', 'murder', 'cover-up', 'execution' and 'shoot-to-kill'.

Lena listened intently, contrasting it with the tedious proceedings she endured daily in the London courts. In the afternoon, she began drifting in and out of the hearing, shaking hands with various well-wishers and hoping for a private word with Maguire. As the tribunal wrapped up for the day, she lingered in the Guildhall entrance lobby to intercept him as he left.

'A word with you please, Mr Maguire,' she said as he drew near, pushed by an unfamiliar minder. It felt awkward speaking down to him in his wheelchair.

'That went well,' they said together. Then Maguire, as usual, dispensed with the niceties.

'How can you walk away from all this, Lena?'

Lena's heart sank. Nothing had changed.

'I had no choice, as you well know. Don't make it worse.'

'As ever, Lena, making yourself the victim. Surely you can't just settle back in London?'

'I told you before. This isn't my battle.'

'But this isn't about you. It's about resolving a conflict that – as you once said – "should never have started". Please reconsider.'

'I hear there are shedloads of young solicitors coming through Queen's who are going to astound us all with their ingenuity,' she said. 'I'm hardly irreplaceable.'

'There's a group of families in Tyrone I'd like you to meet. There's evidence that UDR men in the local barracks are in league with the UVF at Moygashel and slaughtering all around them.'

'You'll have to find someone else to take that on, Luke. I'm booked on a flight home in two days.'

She was grateful when Maguire's minder, hovering nearby, returned, saying the press were waiting for him before following him out onto the plaza and watching from the back of the crowd. He was then pushed to a waiting vehicle and quickly gone. Rumours abounded that supporters in the US had paid for its armour plating. Sullivan's supporters had also contributed to the tribunal's expenses. Without them, it could hardly have reached first base.

The following morning, Lena took the train from Derry to Belfast. She had written the previous month from London to let Edward know she would be in Northern Ireland for the tribunal's opening, suggesting they might meet for dinner 'if you have time'. When a secretary had rung her back with a time and date, she had called Geraldine for news.

'He doesn't come into the office as much as he used to,' she had said. 'The Gordons are building a new hotel up in Derry. What about you, Lena, do you miss us?'

'Of course. London is pretty boring after Belfast.'

'You used to say Belfast was boring.'

'Well, it was, at the beginning, but it certainly warmed up.'

Edward was sitting at the best table in the new rooftop restaurant of the Gordon Hotel when she joined him. She noticed his hair was longer, curling slightly over the top of his shirt collar. They air-kissed politely.

'It's lovely to see you.'

'And you, Lena.'

They sat down.

'Before we order, can I ask something?' she said.

'Direct as always,' he said, flapping open his napkin.

'What terms are you on with Paul?'

'Give me some credit, Lena. He conspired to kill you. After you left, I confronted him at the barracks in Fermanagh and said I believed he had some role in the attack. He didn't put up much of a fight and put in for a transfer shortly afterwards. I believe he's now working out of an RUC station near Larne.'

They ordered dinner and wine.

'You'll be called to give evidence at the Drumfad inquiry when it begins work in September,' she said.

'I've no interest in it,' he replied.

'I was very discreet in my written statement about events at Gordon Hall, but it will all come out under cross-examination. You and your father will be asked to testify.'

'Geoff Hamilton says your inquiry has no right to compel witnesses and, if you identify anyone, they can sue for defamation,' he said.

So, Lena thought, he's interested enough to find that out.

'People will draw inferences, possibly wrongful inferences,' she said, 'if you do not appear to answer questions, or at least provide a written statement.'

'None of this has anything to do with me. I am highly unlikely to agree to go within 500 miles of your wretched inquiry.'

'Your new hairstyle suits you well,' she said. 'You look positively Byronic.'

'Well, I resigned from the UDR after what happened

so I'm spared regimental discipline. My membership of the Ulster Unionists lapsed too. My heart wasn't in it.'

'I'm sorry, Edward. That was such a large part of your life. William must be disappointed.'

'I don't see him so often these days. The new hotel in Londonderry keeps me busy. I've grown to like the place. There's a choral society there and I'm their accompanist.'

Disturbed by visions of Edward surrounded by adoring sopranos, Lena changed the subject.

'Derry's doing well, isn't it? Are you involved in lobbying for a university up there?'

Edward gave a cheerless smile.

'Don't assume I'm a nationalist, Lena, just because I've left the UDR.'

They sat silent for a few seconds as a waiter refilled their glasses.

'Both of us seem to be distancing ourselves from our fathers,' Lena said once they were alone again.

'How is George?' he asked. 'I don't think he speaks to my father much.'

'I think we can safely say that ship has sailed,' she said.

They both smiled weakly.

As the evening wore on and the wine took effect, all Lena's good intentions of remaining distant evaporated and she began hoping he would ask her to stay. But no suggestion came. On the footpath outside, they hugged as a taxi drew up to take her to Casey's home where she was staying overnight. Once again, she felt the roughness of the skin on his neck, the strength in his shoulders. Please let him ask me to stay, she thought, as they drew apart. She was sure he wanted to. The thought of leaving him was suddenly unbearable. She had to say something.

'I could stay if you wanted.'

He held her at arm's length and smiled.

'What you really want, Lena, is to get on the plane to London tomorrow, knowing you've left me behind broken-hearted. I'm not going to let that happen.'

'So, I'm still capable of breaking your heart, Edward?'

'Get out of here,' he growled, opening the taxi door.

At the airport next morning, the nationalist-leaning *Irish Tribune* front page headline read, 'RUC Elite Squad Set Up Deadly Ambush' while the unionist-led *Belfast Monitor* said, 'Government Slams "Biased" Inquiry'. As the plane flew over Belfast and the County Down coast, she thought of what was happening down there – the hatred and hypocrisy. But also an almost superhuman grace, good humour and stoicism. She thought back to the day she had first driven off the Liverpool ferry. Would she have turned back then, if she had known what was ahead? Possibly. Within an hour, London lay below. No one, she thought, except perhaps Martin Porter, understood how dull she found life there now. In Belfast, every day held the potential for high drama. In London, every day was the same as the one before.

A month later, after a long morning spent with an aggrieved husband in a divorce case, Lena leaned out of her office window above High Holborn to get some air. Two floors down, cars were honking, buses were belching out fumes, and people with deep frowns on their faces were rushing about self-importantly. The thought of enduring it for the next thirty years was unbearable. Luke had accused her of wasting her life away in London and she was beginning to believe he was onto something.

On impulse, she called Niall Harrison, Edward's mate and her old landlord – still working in Canada. She didn't really expect him to answer but he picked up. No, no one was living at Glenbarry. A friend had left a month ago, and it was lying empty. He was even thinking of selling it.

Lena said she would be in touch again and did some quick calculations. The inquiry in Derry had opened and was due to begin daily hearings in September. As a material witness, she couldn't be paid but she knew the story inside out and Brendan Casey could use her behind the scenes. Luke had already asked her to meet a group of families in Tyrone on collusion. 'The Stinger' would also pass cases her way. There wouldn't be much money at the start, but she could survive for a few months on her savings. It would be scary knowing there were powerful people who wanted her silenced but the tribunal would eventually expose the collusion between Special Branch and the UDA in the attack at Kashmir Road – and they wouldn't try again, would they?

It would be enthralling to drive into Belfast every day for legal battles with people like Geoffrey Hamilton – and show William Gordon what a fool he had been to lose her services. Maguire was confident she would make a difference and, to be honest, beating the system had given her a taste for it. What did she have to lose? A small flat in London and a dead-end job.

What if she packed as much into her car as she could this evening and left London tomorrow for the Liverpool ferry? She could be in Glenbarry for breakfast on Sunday. She rang Niall Harrison back in Toronto, agreed to rent the cottage, lifted her briefcase and strode through the general office towards the lift. Georgie could explain to Braithwaite and he'd probably be relieved to be rid of her. She'd face her parents once she had settled in at Glenbarry.

Epilogue

The next day, with the sun rising over Belfast Lough, Lena stood on the prow of the ferry watching the derelict chimneys of the city's northern suburbs poking their way through the dawn mist. She was anticipating, with some relish, the apoplectic fits William Gordon and Geoffrey Hamilton would have on news of her return. Edward's response was less certain. She had been gone nearly a year and he was no hermit. As Casey had pointed out at the time, she had been perfectly aware of the likely outcome of acting on the Seapark diagram and notes without consulting his father. But she had no regrets. If Edward couldn't see why she had done it, then so be it. He would have to visit Glenbarry at least once to give Peanut back.

There were more cheerful things to look forward to. The Mourne Mountains would be in her backyard. She would be swapping exhaust fumes for the fresh air blowing over the County Down coast. Later that morning, once she'd let herself into the cottage at Glenbarry, she would drive into town and join the families ambling along the Newcastle waterfront. She might take the Strangford ferry over the whirlpools and currents to Portaferry or drive up the Antrim coast and have lunch beside the waterfalls in the great glen of Glenariff. She was no romantic, though. In Belfast, it would be business as usual. Bombings and shootings. Hopes raised at talk of peace. Hopes dashed. But still, hope. She would find an office near the courthouse on Crumlin Road and inveigle

Geraldine away from Gordon's to join her. She might still be 'Lena the Dreamer' but her dreams were realistic, honourable and based on sound principles.

When the message came over the PA system for drivers to return to their cars, she stepped confidently down to the car deck to meet whatever lay ahead.

ACKNOWLEDGEMENTS

I would firstly like to thank my late husband, Gerry O'Hare, for challenging me to write a credible murder scene and for graciously accepting, much later, that I had managed to do so. Thanks to my family for their patience over the years; Jane, Sue (RIP), Ana, David, Felix, Georgie, Tessie and Helena. Heartfelt thanks to Darragh Mackin (Phoenix Law) who gave patient, accurate and prompt advice during this book's long gestation and to Patricia Coyle (Harte Coyle Collins) who examined the newborn for legal issues. Special thanks to Stephen Sansome who sorted out many technical problems at short notice with great patience. Particular thanks to Richard Harvey, legal counsel at Greenpeace, who with the late South African lawyer and politician, Kader Asmal, conducted an independent inquiry into shoot-to-kill and produced a report (*International Lawyers' Inquiry into the Lethal Use of Firearms by the Security Forces in Northern Ireland*, 1985) that should have led, but didn't, to charges or prosecutions. The example of lawyers Pat Finucane (RIP 1989) and Rosemary Nelson (RIP 1999), both killed by loyalists in collusion with state forces, also helped inspire this book.

I would also like to thank my friends TL Thousand, Steve McCabe, Danny Morrison, Leslie Van Slyke, Mary Savage, Jude Whyte, Sinead Burns, Rosie Cowan, Adrienne Reilly, Stan Nikolov, Louanne Martin, Benjamin Marx, Margaret and Mark Urwin, Eoghan

Corry, the staff of the Pat Finucane Centre, Sara Duddy, Dessie Roddy, Anne Sheehan and Mairead McCann of Fruithill Nursing Home, Claire Armstrong, Donna and James Cushnan, Bridget Carr, Roisin Gibbons, Anne, Aidan (RIP), Jack and Stephen Langan, John and Sadie Friel, Sean and Cathy McKenzie, Nuala and John Connolly, Séamus McGettigan, Liz and Tony Finlay, Francis Diver and John McAteer of the *Tirconaill Tribune*, Margaret and Mark Urwin, Geraldine Breslin, Matt and Helen Peoples, Susan McKay, John and Mary Rainey, Frank Sweeney, John and Neil Sheils, Liz Rigby and Fiona Senior, Cathy Kelly, Owen Bowcott, Lorna Donlon, Joyce and Damien Greene, Rachel Hooper and Lena Ferguson.

I had periods of illness while writing this book and would like to thank the staff of Grosvenor Road Health Centre, particularly Dr Linda Kelly, and the Cardiac Departments at the Royal Victoria and Musgrave Park Hospitals.

Many thanks to Mary Feehan of Mercier Press for her faith in me and to Dee Collins, Head of Books at Mercier, for her thoughtful, patient and expert editing.

A word about the genesis of this story. It dates back to 1982 when, for the first time, I was working the graveyard shift at BBC Belfast. In the early hours, an RUC press officer rang to say the force had shot three men dead after a car crashed through a police checkpoint. I duly wrote up this version of events for the morning news bulletins. Much later, of course, I discovered it was untrue. Somewhat incredibly, inquests into the deaths of Gervaise McKerr, Eugene Toman and Sean Burns, all killed at a supposed

RUC checkpoint on 11 November 1982 in County Armagh, have yet to commence. Likewise, inquests into the shootings of Seamus Grew and Roddy Carroll at another supposed checkpoint on 12 December 1982 have yet to begin while questions also remain over the killing on 24 November 1982 of Michael Tighe and the wounding of Martin McCauley near Lurgan. The history of British investigators called in to assist with such investigations is hardly more positive. John Stalker, the former Deputy Chief Constable of Greater Manchester, was maligned and removed from his post after attempting to inquire into the above shoot-to-kill deaths (for more, read Paddy Hillyard's *Decades of Deceit: The Stalker Affair and its Legacy*, Beyond the Pale Books). As for the murder of Pat Finucane, the findings of former London police chief, Sir John Stevens, have yet to be made public although we know that, of the 210 loyalist suspects arrested by his team, only seven were *not* working for a branch of the 'security forces'. Questions also remain over the killing of solicitor, Rosemary Nelson.

There are two legal inaccuracies in the book, retained for plot purposes: in the 1980s, legal aid was not available for advocacy purposes in inquest proceedings and police files/post-mortem reports were not available to defence solicitors.

ANNE CADWALLADER